电子信息与通信专业英语

（第 2 版）

主　编　赵淑清

哈尔滨工业大学出版社

内 容 提 要

本书以培养学生专业英语阅读能力为主要目标。内容包括：数字电路及接收机、信号处理和数据处理信息与通信基本理论及应用、信号处理专题以及一些电子仪器、设备及部件的说明书。

本书可作为大学电子信息工程和通信工程专业三、四年级本科生的专业英语教材，也可供广大工程技术人员使用。

图书在版编目(CIP)数据

电子信息与通信专业英语/赵淑清主编.—2版.
—哈尔滨：哈尔滨工业大学出版社,2007.8
ISBN 978-7-5603-1450-1

Ⅰ.电…　Ⅱ.赵…　Ⅲ.①电子技术-英语-高等学校-
教材②通信工程-英语-高等学校-教材　Ⅳ.H31

中国版本图书馆 CIP 数据核字(2007)第 131208 号

出版发行　哈尔滨工业大学出版社
社　　址　哈尔滨市南岗区复华四道街 10 号　邮编 150006
传　　真　0451-86414749
网　　址　http://hitpress.hit.edu.cn
印　　刷　肇东粮食印刷厂
开　　本　880mm×1230mm　1/32　印张 10.5　字数 313 千字
版　　次　2007 年 8 月第 2 版　2007 年 8 月第 7 次印刷
书　　号　ISBN 978-7-5603-1450-1
定　　价　18.00 元

前 言

本书的目的是为本科生打下良好的专业英语基础。本书从基本电子线路到计算机应用,基本覆盖了电子信息工程和通信工程专业技术基础课所学的内容。考虑到学生将来可能从事的科学研究和电子及通信设备的应用、研制和开发,还选择了一些热门研究领域的课题和一些电器设备以及 DSP 芯片或部件的说明书。

本书共有五章,第一章是数字电路和模拟电路;第二章是信号处理和数据处理,包括数字信号、数字滤波器和图像处理的内容,此外还包括数据库及一个实用软件包;第三章是信息、通信的基本理论及应用,包括语音通信、PCM、GPS 及软件无线电的内容;第四章信号处理专题包括了近年来信号处理领域中的一些热门课题;第五章收集了一些电子仪器、设备以及 DSP 芯片或部件的说明书和手册。每节后面列出一些单词,并对一些句子进行了注释。单词和注释以专业词汇和专业性较强的句子为主,主要是使读者能够正确理解书中所叙述的原理和阐述的观点。

本次修订更换了一些内容,增加了三个附录,对较长的篇幅进行了压缩,同时还对发现的错误进行了更正。为了更好帮助选择学习内容,在附录中增加了内容提要,给出了每节的主要内容及应用背景。

本书可作为电子信息工程和通信工程专业大学三、四年级学生的专业英语阅读材料。

　　参加本书编写的还有王大明、王若楠、张永钋、梁冰霜。在编写的过程中得到了哈尔滨工业大学电子与通信工程系的一些博士、硕士研究生的大力帮助,在此表示诚挚的感谢。由于编者水平有限,书中难免还存在一些缺点和错误,殷切希望广大读者批评指正。

编　者

2007 年 9 月于哈工大

CONTENTS

1

Digital Circuits and Analog Circuits

1.1 DIGITAL CIRCUITS

Digital design can be divided into two general areas. The first is the creation and production of direct hardware from available building blocks. The second is the computer software or programming aspects, which may or may not involve the design of hardware items.

The second area employs techniques that are quite different from those of conventional hardware design and also require a substantial investment in special test equipment for efficient development and debugging. The quantity of information needed is worthy of a separate book and is not covered here.

Many aspects of computer technology, however, are very important in conventional hardware design. Among these are the programmable read-only memories referred to as PROMs and the read-write memories called RAMs (random-access memories). The word "firmware" is commonly used for these applications.

The design of digital circuits differs greatly from the design of analog circuits, being more like a systems design on a small scale. For the large part it consists of connecting standard building blocks without the use of modifying passive components. Many circuits do, of course, contain both analog and digital parts, and the construction of these systems is a mixture of the two techniques.

1.1.1　Basic Circuits

Digital design is based on the simple concept of yes or no, true or false, high or low, and so on. Electronically the basic circuit is the NAND gate.[1] A simple version is shown in Fig.1.1.

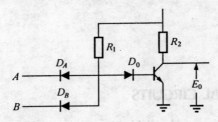

Fig.1.1　Simple NAND gate

If both A and B are open or tied to a (+) voltage, a current flows from R_1 through the base-emitter junction of the transistor, which is turned "hard-on" or put into the so-called saturation mode.[2] E_0 is then near ground potential, and its output is called a "0" or "low." If either A or B or both are grounded, the current through R_1 is diverted to that ground. This provides a voltage drop of one diode at the anode of D_0. However, a voltage equal to two diode drops, that of D_0 and the transistor, is required to turn the transistor on. With the transistor off, E_0 approaches the $V +$ level and is called a "1" or "high."

It will be noticed that an inversion is involved in this circuit. That is, if the inputs are low, the output is high, and vice versa. To make the circuit noninverting would require an extra stage. This is why digital circuitry is based on inverting logic. The word NAND is a contraction of the phrase "INVERTING AND."

With each logic element there is a "truth table" that explains how the unit works. These tables are generally in positive logic. This means that the function is described for input signals that are 1's. Negative logic is when the function is described in terms of input zeros. The use of negative logic is often confusing and is not used in this text. The truth table for the two-input NAND gate is shown in Fig. 1.2.

A	B	Out
0	0	1
0	1	1
1	0	1
1	1	0

Fig. 1.2   Truth table for a NAND gate

This table states that if both A and B are 1 (High or Hi), the output is a 0 (Low or Lo). It is sometimes easier for the beginner to think in terms of an AND gate followed by an inverter. The logic of an AND gate states that if both A and B are Hi, the output is Hi. An AND gate is really a NAND gate followed by an inverter.

If we look again at the truth table, it also says if A or B is a 0 the output is a 1. In other words, the NAND circuit does a NAND function with respect to 1's at the input and a NOR function with respect to 0's at the input. If the two inputs are tied together, the NAND circuit becomes an inverter. Fig. 1.3 shows three common symbols. The small circle at the output means inverting, so that if the circles are removed the three symbols become AND, OR, and EXCLUSIVE OR respectively.

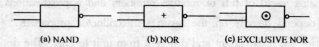

(a) NAND   (b) NOR   (c) EXCLUSIVE NOR

Fig. 1.3   Some standard gates

The truth tables for the NOR and EXCLUSIVE NOR are shown in Fig. 1.4. The NOR truth tables states that if A or B are a 1, the output

is a 0. The EXCLUSIVE NOR is the same thing except the condition that
both *A* and *B* are 1's.

A	B	Out		A	B	Out
0	0	1		0	0	1
0	1	0		0	1	0
1	0	0		1	0	0
1	1	0		1	1	1
(a) NOR				(b) EX-NOR		

Fig.1.4   Truth tables

From the truth table of the NAND gate we know that if one or more
of the inputs to the NAND gate is a 0, the output is a 1. Inverting the 1
produces a 0, and we have a NOR gate. This is a very poor way to make
a NOR gate, and not the manner in which they are made. The purpose of
the example was to demonstrate a simple use of the NAND gate and the
process by which more complex building blocks can be evolved.

An important difference should be noted at this time between digital
and analog components. There is very little need for the circuit designer
to know how a digital function is accomplished. If the job is well done,
the important properties such as propagation delay, power consumption,
number of leads, and the need for supporting modules will be favorable.
If the performance specifications of the device are adequate, attempting to
study the technique is generally a waste of time. The reason for this is
that a digital device is exact. It is yes or no. This does not mean that it
necessarily produces a correct result, but it does produce a defined one.
The analog world of full of relative numbers and approximations, all of
which depend heavily on the basic semiconductor properties.[3] These
properties are both variant and different from unit to unit. The designer of
the digital blocks faces the same problems, but once the digital unit has
been properly designed and built, the circuit designer is largely relieved
of these considerations.

When digital circuits are operated near their maximum speeds they approach a failure mode that is largely analog in nature and all the troubles and uncertainties of the analog circuit are back.[4] High-frequency performance is specified in different ways. One common expression is "maximum toggle frequency." This means that the output is going between the logic Hi and Lo states at its fastest possible rate but without the duty cycle or rise and fall times defined. It does not mean that the device can operate properly at that speed. Just how fast the device can operate depends on an analog type of analysis of the system.

The speed limitations of a digital circuit show up in four different forms: propagation delay, setup time, rise time, and fall time.[5] Propagation delay is basically the time between a signal edge's entering a device and leaving the device. When a number of digital devices are connected in series, their propagation delays add up. When a similar set of digital devices are operating in parallel, their propagation delays, because of the tolerances, is not necessarily the same.[6] This problem is sometimes referred to as "skew." It is, of course, essential in digital circuits that signal edges occur in a known order. It is a further absolute requirement that this order preserve a minimum time between signal edges of concern. This is called setup time. But simply, a signal must remain at an input for a certain minimum amount of time or it will not be recognized.

The rise and fall times limit the response by not reaching the next logic level in time to be recognized. The rise and fall times can be somewhat controlled through good layout to reduce capacitance and inductance, by limiting the number of stages that are driven, and by the occasional use of a pull-up resistor in the output circuits.[7]

To summarize, the problems with digital circuits increase rapidly as the toggle frequencies are approached. Much difficulty is avoided if the operating frequencies are limited to one half of the minimum value and if the setup times are increased by a factor of 2 or 3 over the manufacturer's stated minimum values.

1.1.2 Family Groups

A number of different classes of digital circuits are in current use. The most popular are TTL, MOS, and ECL.[8]

1. *TTL*

TTL, which means transistor transistor logic, is most commonly used for small and medium-scale integration (MSI). There are two basic forms of TTL. The first and original group has a low-power/low-speed version and the standard line. The later designs are Schottky clamped, which come in quite a few versions and are still growing. The Schottky diodes are used to prevent the transistors from going into saturation, with a resulting increase in speed for a given power dissipation.

The older families, including the 54H/74H are obsolete and used only for replacement. The low-power Schottky, 54LS/74LS, and the standard Schottky, 54S/74S, have been around for a long time. The newer versions include the family 54F/74F called FAST and two Texas Instruments versions, 54AS/74AS and 54ALS/74ALS. There are designated Advanced Schottky and Advanced Low Power Schottky, respectively. All of the TTL families represent different tradeoffs between power consumption and speed.

If speed is not required, the Low Power class is a good choice, not only because of low power consumption, but because its low speed makes it insensitive to many high-frequency spikes and glitches.[9]

Although open inputs to TTL logic act as a high, it is not a good practice to leave them disconnected in final circuitry. This is because the maximum speed is lowered and the noise susceptibility is increased. It is also not a safe practice to tie these inputs to the 5 V line because the breakdown voltage of the input lines are only 5.5 V compared to 7 V for the supply pin. Unused open inputs can be connected to the output of a spare gate that is held at a high or a 1 kΩ resistor can be inserted between the gate lead and the + 5 V supply. One resistor can be used for up to 25 gates in some logic families. A better way, however, is to use two resistors and a couple of microfarads of capacitance to form a stable Hi of about 3.5 V.

One exception to this is the LS series where most of the devices have diode inputs, which can be directly connected to the + 5 V supply. Some of them have emitter inputs, however, which must be connected through the 1 kΩ resistor.

The families are almost completely pin compatible, but for some strange reason there are a few exceptions. The power pin for dual-in-line sockets is usually # 16 (or # 14) and the ground pin # 8 (or # 7) depending on whether it is a 16-pin or 14-pin package.[10] But, again, not always.

2. MOS

Mos logic comes in two forms. The first is called CMOS, where C stands for complementary, which means that both *N* channel and *P* channel transistors are used in a complementary fashion. These are mediumspeed devices that can be operated at 3 to 15 V. For example, a 54C73 flip-flop has a typical toggle frequency of 4 MHz at 5 V and 11 MHz at 10 V. If the speed limitations are acceptable, these devices are, on an all-around basis, clearly superior to the other families of logic. They have the lowest power consumption, high noise immunity (at 10 V), symmetrical drive capability at a good current level, and a very high input impedance. They are competitive with TTL in cost and are approaching TTL in the availability of logic functions, which are increasing rapidly. As contrasted to the other forms of logic, all inputs must be tied to a high or a low because they are open-gate leads of the MOSFETs and the devices simply do not know where they are if the gate lead is left open. One good feature is that the inputs can be safety connected to *B* + for a high. Particular attention should be given to power consumption, which depends strongly on the operating frequency and load.

The second form of MOS logic is not really a family of logic elements but a collection of MSI and LSI (large-scale integration) that takes advantage of the small size and the low-power consumption of the MOS transistor to fabricate very large arrays. Typical of these devices are random-access memories (RAMs), read-only memories (ROMs), and microprocessors. These devices can be made by either N channel or P channel processes. They are generally constructed so that their drive levels are TTL compatible and can be mixed with TTL circuits. Many MSI and LSI devices are available in both MOS and TTL. In these cases the TTL is used only if its superior speed is required.

3. *ECL*

The last of the logic families to be discussed is called emitter-coupled logic, or ECL for short. This differs from the other forms of logic in that the transistors are operated in a linear mode and not allowed to go into saturation. ECL is therefore the fastest of all logic forms. It also consumes the most power. ECL devices operate from a -5.2 V power supply, a logic low is -1.8 V, and a logic high is -0.9 V. The output stages are open-ended emitter followers, which are externally terminated with a 51 resistor to a -2 V supply. This clutters up the circuit a bit, and the -2 V supply because of its low voltage must have a low efficiency. The basic ECL gate is the OR/NOR as contrasted to the NAND gate for TTL.

1.1.3　Building Blocks

There is really not much difference between "basic circuits" and "building blocks," except that the term "building blocks" implies that the function is contained in one package and is generally more complex. The tabulations that follow represent a very coarse selection of some of the more common classifications. A suitable knowledge of the available products must come from the manufacturer's data sheets and not from a textbook.

1. *Function Generators and Clock Drivers*

"Function generator" is a broad term that includes clock generators. Clock drivers are included in this section because often the clocks drive many devices and the drive requirements can be quite severe.

The SN74LS124 is a useful dual voltage-controlled square-wave generator. It has a range of 0.12 Hz to 50 MHz, tunable by a voltage and selectable capacitor. A crystal can also be used in place of the capacitor if desired.

The Signetics 555 is very popular basic timer that makes a good square-wave generator up to about 100 kHz. It is low in cost, has excellent stability, and can use 10 MΩ resistors to reduce the size of the required capacitor.

2. *Flip-Flops*

In the early days of digital electronics flip-flops were the basic building block. They were used in great quantities to make counters, memories, and much miscellaneous logic. The design of synchronous counters from flip-flops can be tricky, but now counters of all kinds are available and the average circuit designer seldom needs to design them. The two kinds of flip-flops used the most are the *J-K* and the *D*.

The *J-K* flip-flop has two control lines, *J* and *K*, which allow four logical operations. The block diagram and the truth table are shown in Fig.1.5 *J-K* flip-flops are actuated by a clock edge to do the function defined by the *J* and *K* inputs. The figure shows a negative edge transition such as that used on the SN7473. Others, for example, the SN74109, operate on the positive edge. This device has two principal applications. The first is as part of some overall logic operation. The results of this logic operation are placed on the *J* and *K* lines, and the clock then makes Q a high or a low in accordance with the truth tables. This mode of operation is used widely in the construction of synchronous counters and various types of memories. The second and more common application is as a divide-by-2 counter. The f-f is often used following counters to produce a square wave. For example, if a counter is used to divide a given frequency by 100, the output has a duty cycle of 1 to 99 (or sometimes less). Aside from being hard to see on an oscilloscope, this may not be a satisfactory waveform. The usual way is to program the counter to divide by 50 and then use the f-f to divide by 2, which produces an exactly symmetrical wave. Most oscillators do not produce a symmetrical waveform. Again, this problem is easily solved by designing the oscillator for twice the frequency and following it with an f-f.

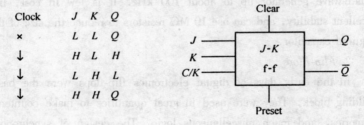

Clock	J	K	Q
×	L	L	Q
↓	H	L	H
↓	L	H	L
↓	H	H	Q

Fig.1.5　Truth table of a *J-K* f-f

Two *J-K* f-f's can be connected as shown in Fig. 1. 6 to get a synchronous divider by 4, and since f-f's often come two to a package, this is commonly done. To divide by more than 4 requires additional logic and a counter is generally more suitable. The *J-K* f-f is available with many modifications for logical flexibility. There are asynchronous clear and preset inputs, which set Q to a low or high. These inputs override the clock. Then the J and K

Fig.1.6　*J-K* divided by 4 counter

inputs are combined with various other gates to provide different logical combinations. On these devices the individual truth tables must be studied to determine their usefulness.

The D f-f is sometimes referred to as a latch or memory element. It has one input called D, and when the device is clocked, whatever is at D goes to Q.[11] It is also a one-stage shift register.

If there is a high on the input D it is clocked to Q on the rising edge of the clock. However, because of the delay time the input signal does not get to D of the second stage in time to be clocked. The signal must wait for the next rising edge and consequently is advanced one stage per clock pulse. This is a very useful device and is widely used.

3. *Counters and Dividers*

Counters are a very important part of digital circuits and come in many varieties. Unfortunately, because of different notations, operating techniques, and generally poor application literature they are often confusing to use and understand. A divider is a special form or use of counter, as is explained in the section that follows. Table 1.1 lists some types.

Table 1.1 Counter variations

9310	Programmable decade counter
9316	Programmable binary counter
CD4029A	CMOS up/down programmable counter
SN74192/93	Up/down programmable counter
DM8520	Modulo N divider
MC 14526	Programmable divider

Fig. 1.7 illustrates a typical counter. This is a 4-bit device, with the count appearing on the Q lines. A count of 16 is possible over the range of 0000 = 0 to 1111 = 15. As the clock continues, the count cycles over this range. When the count reaches its maximum value (1111) a pulse appears on the EOC (end of conversion) line. This is the divider

output. If all that is required is a division of the clock frequency, the Q inputs are not required. The EOC pulse is also used in the counting operation. One application is to enable the counters to be used in multistage operations for large counts. A second use is the connection of the EOC pulse to the P. E. (parallel enable) pin to allow programmed counts of less than the maximum. The programming is done by setting the P inputs to the appropriate 1's and 0's. For example, if $P_0 = 0$, $P_1 = 0$, $P_2 = 1$, $P_3 = 1$. We have the digital number $1100 = 12$ (remember that P_0 is LSB and P_3 is MSB). This would then produce a division of $16 - 12 = 4$.

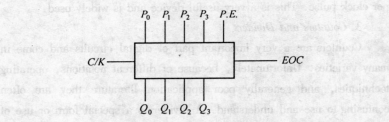

Fig.1.7 Typical counter

An up/down counter used in the down counter mode makes a very convenient programmable counter. It turns out that the programmed input and the count are the same. There are, however, some complications with this connection. The 9316, for example, needs an inverter between the T.C. (same as EOC) output and the P.E. input. There is a more subtle reason, however, that must be checked in all counters. When the terminal count is applied to the parallel enable, the output count is returned to the preset value. This, however, is not necessarily a simultaneous process. As soon as one bit is changed, the terminal count is in the process of disappearing. If it disappears before the proper count change has been completed, the counter operates incorrectly. The solution to the problem is to put sufficient delay between the terminal count and the parallel enable.

4. *Shift Registers*

Shift registers are, for the most part, easy to understand and use. They usually consist of a string of D f-f's. Accordingly, the entire contents of the S-R is moved one position to the right on each clock pulse. There are normally five classifications:

(1) Parallel in/parallel out(bi-directional).

(2) Parallel in/parallel out.

(3) Serial in/parallel out.

(4) Parallel in/serial out.

(5) Serial in/serial out.

These are descriptive titles and need little explaining, except perhaps for one point. All shift registers have a serial output because this is the last bit of a parallel output.

The bi-directional device is, of course, the most flexible. It is available in TTL as the SN54194 and in CMOS as the MC14194B. It can move to the left as well as to the right.

At times the input logic is different from that of the D f-f. For example the SN74195 has a J-$\overline{K}$ input. This has the truth table shown in Table 1.2.

Table 1.2　Truth table of the SN74195 **shift register**

J	K	Function
0	0	Shift and set first stage to a low
0	1	Shift and retain first stage
1	0	Shift and invert first stage
1	1	Shift and set first stage to a high

The CMOS MC14557B is a 1-bit to 64-bit variable length S/R, that can be programmed by six control lines to the desired length.

5. *Decoders*

A decoder could be called a line selector. This is shown by Fig.

1.8. The two control lines have four states and therefore any one of four output lines can be seleted. Decoders include the following products:

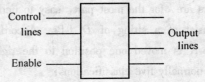

Control lines ─────

Enable ─────

Output lines

Fig.1.8   Decoder

The 9321 a dual 4 line out/2 line control.

The 9311 a 10 line out/line BCD control.

The 9311 a 16 line out/4 line binary control.

In CMOS the 14555B is a dual 4 line out with a high on the selected line, and the 14556B is the same with a low on the selected line.

6. *The Comparator*

The digital comparator compares one set of data lines with another set. If the data are the same, an output is developed. In the case of the SN7485 there are two additional outputs that state which of the two words is larger. These units can be directly cascaded without external gates but, as with the counters, the maximum clock rate is slower.

A very handy dual 4-bit digital comparator is the Motorola device MC4022.

7. *The Monostable*

The normal monostable has an output with a definite time duration. The digital monostable puts out a pulse that is equal to the time required to count a given number of clock pulses and starts and finishes in synchronism with the clock. The 9602 monostable is a good all-around device. It can be made to trigger on either rising or falling edges and has complementary outputs. It is retriggerable and has an asynchronous reset control. An important feature is that it can also be made nonretriggerable, as shown in Fig.1.9.

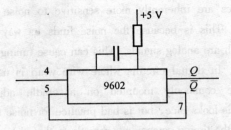

Fig.1.9 Nonretriggerable monostable

From the truth table on the data sheets it is seen that the monostable triggers on a L to H if pin 5 is high. However, once the device is fired, $\overline{Q}$ changes to a low and any additional pulses do not affect the duration of the pulse. The 9602 has a minimum pulse width of about 90 ns. When shorter pulses are required, the circuits shown in Fig.1.10 can be used. Here we see that when the input is low, there is a low and a high at the input of the output gate and the output is high. When the input goes high, there are two highs at the input to the output gate and the output drops to a low for the propagation time of the three gates. This is 25 to 55 ns for an SN7400.

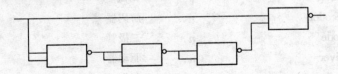

Fig.1.10 Delay monostable

If longer pulse widths are desired, for a given capacitor size, the 96L02(which can use a 200 K timing resistor) or the CMOS MC14528 (used at 5 V for compatibility) can be employed. These devices are pin compatible. The MC14528, however, has its timing capacitor connected from the resistor to ground. A monostable that can solve some unique problems is the NSC DM7853, which will trigger on both raising and falling edges.

Monostables are inherently more sensitive to noise than standard digital circuits. This is because the noise finds its way to the timing waveforms which are analog signals. This can cause timing variations and false triggering. In digital circuits where wire wrap is used the timing components are commonly mounted on a cradle adjacent to the monostable. This looks nice, but is bad practice for noise rejection. It is better to solder the timing components directly to the wire-wrap pins. The noise can also enter the power pin, so that extra filtering may be needed at that point. Noisy lines should be routed away from the monostable. To summarize, monostables are handy devices but should be used only when necessary and then with care.

New Words and Phrases

anode	*n.*	正极
capacitance	*n.*	电容
cascade	*v. n.*	级联
clamp	*v. n.*	箝位(电路)
cradle	*n.*	托架
debug	*v.*	调试
decoder	*n.*	解码器
diode	*n.*	二极管
driver	*n.*	驱动器
fabricate	*v.*	制作,构成
firmware	*n.*	固化软件
glitch	*n.*	短时脉冲
impedance	*n.*	阻抗
inductance	*n.*	电感
layout	*n.*	布线
leads	*n.*	引线
latch	*n.*	锁存器

microfarad	*n.*	微法
miscellaneous	*a.*	各种各样的
monostable	*a.*	单稳态的
MOSFET	*abbr.*	金属氧化物半导体场效应管
obsolete	*a.*	陈旧的
oscilloscope	*n.*	示波器
package	*n.*	封装
passive	*a.*	无源的
pin	*n.*	管脚
PROM	*abbr.*	可编程只读存储器
propagation	*n.*	传播
RAM	*abbr.*	随机存储器
saturation	*n.*	饱和
Schottky	*n.*	肖特基(半导体器件)
skew	*v. n.*	时滞
specification	*n.*	指标,规格
spike	*n.*	尖脉冲
susceptibility	*n.*	敏感性
toggle	*n.*	触发(器)
transistor	*n.*	三极管
trigger	*v.*	触发
pull-up resister		负载电阻
base-emitter junction		基极－发射极结
competitive with		与……不相上下
driving capability		驱动能力
duty cycle		脉冲持续期
flip-flop		触发器
negative logic		负逻辑
noise immunity		抗干扰性
positive logic		正逻辑

power consumption	功耗
shift register	移位寄存器
truth table	真值表

Notes

1. NAND gate，与非门，下文出现的 AND，OR 和 NOR 分别是与门、或门、或非门，EXCLUSIVE OR 和 EXCLUSIVE NOR 分别为异或门和异或非门。

2. If both A and B are open or tied to a (+) voltage, a current flows from R_1 through the base-emitter junction of the transistor, which is turned "hard-on" or put into the so-called saturation mode. 如果 A 和 B 都是开路的或连正电压，电流从 R_1 通过三极管的基极发射极结，调整三极管(工作点)接近或进入饱和状态。

3. The analog world of full of relative numbers, tradeoffs, and approximations, all of which depend heavily on the basic semiconductor properties. 模拟领域充满了相对数、折衷和近似，所有这些都很大程度地取决于半导体的基本特性。

4. When digital circuits are operated near their maximum speeds they approach a failure mode that is largely analog in nature and all the troubles and uncertainites of the analog circuit are back. 当数字电路以接近它们最大的速度工作时，它们也接近了一个失效的模式，这个模式在本质上很大程度是模拟的，并且所有的模拟电路的麻烦和不确定性又随之而来。

5. The speed limitations of a digital circuit show up in four different forms: propagation delay, setup time, rise time, and fall time. 数字电路速度的限制以四种不同的形式表现出来：传播延迟、建立时间、上升时间和下降时间。

6. When a similar set of digital devices are operating in parallel, their propagation delays, because of the tolerances, is not necessarily the same. 当一组相近的数字器件并行工作时，由于器件的公差，传播延迟可以不必相同。

7. The rise and fall times can be somewhat controlled through good layout to reduce capacitance and inductance, by limiting the number of stages that are driven, and by the occasional use of a pull-up resistor in the output circuits. 通过优化布线减少电容和电感、限制驱动的级数、必要时在输出电路中应用负载电阻的方法,可以控制上升和下降时间。

8. TTL,MOS 和 ECL 分别为晶体管 – 晶体管逻辑、金属氧化物半导体逻辑和射极耦合逻辑。

9. If speed is not required, the Low Power class is a good choice, not only because of low power consumption, but because its low speed makes it insensitive to many high-frequency spikes and glitches. 如果不要求速度,低功率类是一个好的选择,不仅因为低功耗,而且由于低速使得它对很多高频尖脉冲和短时脉冲都不敏感。

10. The power pin for dual-in-line sockets is usually # 16 (or # 14) and the ground pin # 8 (or # 7) depending on whether it is a 16-pin or 14-pin package. 双列直插式的电源管脚通常是 # 16(或 # 14),接地管脚是 # 8(或 # 7),这取决于它是 16 脚还是 14 脚的封装。

11. It has one input called D, and when the device is clocked, whatever is at D goes to Q. 它有一个输入端称为 D,当设备被选通时,无论 D 是什么都会转到 Q。

1.2　RECEIVER

The purpose of a receiver is to select a desired group of frequencies from one transmitter, get rid of all unwanted signals and noise, and then demodulate the signal to obtain the modulating information. The better the receiver does its job, the closer the demodulated signal will resemble the original signal from the transmitter. Regardless of the type of demodulation required, the main functions performed by a receiver are filtering and amplifying. The superheterodyne receiver is the logical choice for the job.

1.2.1 Superheterodyne Receiver

Since it is easier to design narrow-band, steep-skirt filters and obtain high gains at lower frequencies, the "superhet" receiver is an efficient design. All incoming signals are mixed with the output of a local oscillator and the difference frequency is selected and amplified by the intermediate frequency amplifiers. The big benefit is that these amplifiers remain at a fixed frequency and only the RF amplifier and local oscillator need be tunable. Fig. 1.11 is a block diagram of a typical superhet receiver. One further benefit is the fact that the gain is concentrated at two or sometimes three different frequencies. This reduces the gain required at any one frequency and leads to more stable amplifiers. When over 120 dB of RF gain is involved, every little bit helps. [1]

The function of each item in Fig. 1.11 can be explained as follows:

1. *RF amplifier*

It should have just enough gain, usually about 10 dB, to establish the overall noise figure of the receiver. The tuned circuits at the input and output need only be selective enough to reject image signals and other spurious signals that could intermodulate and appear at the intermediate frequency. Some AGC may be needed to prevent overloading on strong signals. The RF amplifier may also be called on to suppress any tendency for the local oscillator to radiate out to the antenna and interfere with other

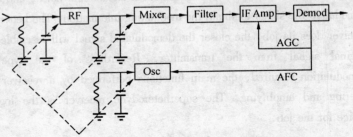

Fig. 1.11   Block diagram of a superheterodyne receiver

listeners.

2. *Mixer and local oscillator*

The mixer has two inputs, one from the RF amplifier and one from the local oscillator. The nonlinearities of the mixer will create numerous intermodulation products, and one of these, the sum or difference frequency, will occur at the IF frequency. Usually, there will be a second frequency, the image, that can also mix with the oscillator frequency and produce an output at the IF. Depending on the type of mixer used, conversion gains from − 10 dB to + 30 dB are common. The local oscillator must be tunable, yet have a low drift rate and relatively low sideband noise, since this could increase the noise level of the receiver.

3. *IF filters and amplifiers*

This section establishes the overall bandwidth and adjacent channel selectivity of the receiver. The bulk of the receiver's gain will be concentrated here and some type of automatic gain control will be included to adjust for variations in received signal strength. The IF is usually at a lower frequency than the RF, but, in some special cases, the IF may be higher to reduce spurious intermodulation and image problems.

4. *Demodulators*

For each type of modulation used (i.e., AM, FM, SSB, PM), a number of different circuits exist. Some will have gain, others a loss.[2] Some will require a reference input(i.e., SSB and phase modulation), others won't. The demodulation may also be required to produce outputs to AGC or AFC circuits. The recovered audio level (or video, etc.) will determine the amount of gain required in the following audio or video amplifiers.

1.2.2 Specifications

Before beginning the design of a receiver, it is necessary to consider the specifications required of the final result. In most cases this ends up as a compromise between what the designer would like and what is possible. The determining factor will usually be financial limitations. The following should then be considered before proceeding:

1. *Tuning range*

What range of frequencies must be tuned and will it be tuned continuously or in discrete channels? A short-wave receiver, for example, must continuously tune from 3 to 30 MHz and will usually require some band switching. The local oscillator will be a continuously tunable type. Demodulators will be needed for AM, SSB, and CW, and IF bandwidths should correspond. For CB, a narrow range of frequencies from 26.965 to 27.405 are needed and will be tuned as 40 discrete channels. The local oscillator will therefore likely be a phase-locked loop synthesizer. Demodulation could be either AM or SSB.

2. *Sensitivity*

Often, too much emphasis is put on sensitivity without attention to other details. For example, a 100-kHz navigation receiver will pick up so much atmospheric noise that a 100-μV desired signal from the antenna could be obscured at times. On the other hand, a 0.1-μV signal at 150 MHz will often be readily distinguishable from background noise.

3. *Bandwidth*

When the modulation type and channel spacing are known, it is possible to determine the IF bandwidth and its skirt characteristics. For FM-stereo broadcasting, a bandwidth of 350 kHz is required. For AM aircraft communications, a bandwidth of 30 kHz is common—not to provide wide bandwidth for high audio-frequency response but to accommodate frequency tolerances in the transmitters and receivers. The filter-skirt characteristics will be set to reject adjacent channel signals as required.

4. *Spurious signals*

If unwanted signal can sneak into the receiver at the IFfrequency, various spurious frequencies are generated through intermodulation and cross-modulation, any good design can be useless.[3]

Typical specifications for several good receivers are as follows:

(1) *FM stereo tuner*: frequency range 88 ~ 108 MHz

Sensitivity:	1.8 μV across 300-Ω input for 20 dB of quieting
Selectivity:	100 dB for channels 400 kHz either side of center frequency
Bandwidth:	350 kHz at -6-dB points
Image rejection:	90 dB
Spurious rejection:	90 dB
IF rejection:	90 dB
AM suppression:	65 dB
Capture ratio:	1.5 dB[4]

(2) *Shortwave receiver*: frequency range 3.0 ~ 30 MHz

Sensitivity:	0.5 μV for 10 dB S + N/N ratio[5]
Bandwidth:	2.3 kHz at -6 dB, 5.5 kHz at -60 dB (SSB mode)
Image rejection:	60 dB
IF rejection:	75 dB

(3) *CB receiver*: frequency range 26.965 ~ 27.405 MHz

Sensitivity:	0.5 μV for 10 dB S + N/N ratio
Bandwidth:	6 kHz at -6 dB 20 kHz at -60 dB
Image rejection:	60 dB

Once the specifications are carefully determined, it is time to start the design. But what is the best starting point? Generally, the most sensitive points will be the two nonlinear circuits, the mixer and the detector. The IF amplifier takes up the slack between the two, and the

RF amplifier picks up the deficiencies of the mixer.

1.2.3   Mixers

The mixer section of the receiver should ideally produce an IF output only at the difference (or sum, for up-conversion) of the two input frequencies. One of these inputs will be the local oscillator signal and the other will be the desired RF signal. Again, ideally, no other combination of input signals should produce an IF output. If such frequencies do exist, filters must be provided to remove them before they reach the mixer.

The closest thing to an ideal mixer is any circuit with a perfect square-law transfer characteristic. In addition to the input signals and their second harmonics appearing at the output, the sum and the difference will also appear. The difference is usually the one signal desired and so is selected by IF filtering. The amplitude of the difference signals will be proportional to the product of the original RF signal level and the local oscillator level. Any other two signals at the input could also produce an output at the IF if they are separated by an amount equal to the difference frequency. However, the output level they produce will be proportional to their signal levels.

Some discrimination against unwanted mixing products can therefore be had if all RF input levels to the mixer are kept as low as possible and the local oscillator signal kept as high as possible.[6] The one desired signal will therefore be stronger than all the undesired ones. This is described in Fig. 1.12. The mixer circuit has four signals at its input, all of the same level. The local oscillator signal level is included for reference and is much higher than the other four. The IF filters only pass signals between 0.4 and 0.6 MHz. RF frequencies C and D can mix with the oscillator and produce outputs at 0.45 and 0.55 MHz, respectively, well within the IF passband. One will be the desired signal and the other is the image, which should be removed by filtering before reaching the mixer. Two other signals, *A* and *B*, happen to be separated by 0.5 MHz, so they will also produce a mixing product (which contains the combined modulation of each) within the IF passband. However, the amplitude of this signal will be much lower than the desired IF signal. Therefore, best results are obtained by:

(1) Selecting a square-law mixer.

(2) Using high local oscillator levels.

(3) Maintaining low RF signal levels.

(4) Providing proper filtering ahead of the mixer.

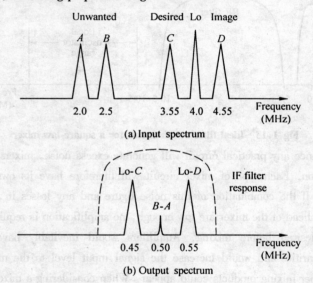

Fig. 1.12　Spectrum of input signal for

a square-law mixer and the outputs within the IF passband

If the ideal square-law mixer can be built, what is the minimum filter that is required ahead of it? We have already seen that the image has to be removed and also any group of frequencies that could themselves mix and produce an IF output.[7] The limiting case is shown in

Fig.1.13. The IF filters are placed at 5.0 MHz and have nearly vertical skirts. The RF filters ahead of the mixer also have nearly vertical skirts and cover the range 5.5 ~ 10.0 MHz, nearly a 1-octave range. The RF bandwidth is just narrow enough (4.5 MHz) that no two signals can exist within the passband to cause mixing. The image frequencies would lie in the range 15.5 ~ 20.0 MHz and are also outside the filter range. In a practical design, the filters would have wider skirts, so the useful range of the mixer would be an even smaller portion of the theoretical 1-octave bandwidth.

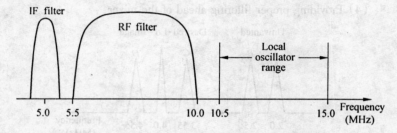

Fig.1.13   Ideal filter requirements for a square-law mixer

Since any practical circuit will generate excess noise, mixers are no exception. Each type of mixer circuit will therefore have its own noise figure. If the combination of this noise figure and any losses in the RF filters ahead of the mixer are low enough, no amplification is required nor even desired before mixing. Amplifiers would inevitably have some nonlinearities and would increase the signal input level to the mixer so that other mixing products could appear. When considering a mixer noise figure, it should be remembered that two frequencies could contribute to noise output at the IF frequency, the desired frequency and its image. Removal of the image by placing a filter between the antenna and the mixer is not always sufficient. If the mixer "sees" a resistive impedance at the image frequency, thermal noise will be added. The filter should therefore appear as a short circuit at the image frequency.

If the noise figure is too high, an RF amplifier will be necessary. Its gain must be just adequate to set the overall noise figure to the desired level and no more. In fact, a little negative feedback in this stage will improve the linearity and the resulting loss of gain will actually be welcome.

1.2.4 RF Amplifiers

Once the desired range of input signal levels to the mixer has been chosen, the RF amplifier can be designed (or eliminated) as required. Its gain should be just sufficient to bring the weakest signal from the antenna up to whatever level is needed to override noise generated in the RF amplifier and mixer. The total noise factor of the receiver will be given by

$$F = F_1 + \frac{F_2 - 1}{G_1}$$

where, F_1—noise factor of the first stage

F_2—noise factor of the second stage

G_1—power gain from input to second stage

For the arrangement shown in Fig. 1.14, the RF amplifier has a gain of 12 dB ($8:1$) and the mixer has a loss of 4 dB ($0.398:1$). The noise figure of the RF stage is 2.0 dB(1.585) and of the IF amplifier is 2.5 dB (1.778). The overall noise figure would then be

$$F = F_1 + \frac{F_2 - 1}{G_1} = 1.585 + \frac{1.778 - 1}{8 \times 0.398} =$$

$$1.829 \text{ (or } 2.62 \text{ dB)}$$

```
        Gain=12 dB              Loss=4 dB
   ┌──────────┐           ┌──────────┐           ┌──────────────┐
──▶│    RF    │──────────▶│  Mixer   │──────────▶│ IF Amplifier │──▶
   └──────────┘           └──────────┘           └──────────────┘
    NF=2.0 dB                                       NF=2.5 dB
     (1.585)                                         (1.778)
```

Fig.1.14 Noise figures, gains, and losses of a receiver

The RF amplifier has therefore provided enough gain so that the overall noise figure of 2.62 dB is only 0.62 dB higher than that of the RF amplifier itself. Higher gain would provide little overall improvement and would simply cause more problems with the mixer.

After the gain and noise figure are set, the next requirement is the filtering associated with the RF amplifiers. Part of this will depend on the mixer and part on the amplifier itself. If the mixer also has a significant third-order component, several new frequencies could end up in the IF passband. These would be:

(1) IF = RF ± 2OSC, RF = 16 or 26 MHz

(2) IF = 2RF ± OSC, RF = 2.75 or 7.75 MHz

(3) IF = 3RF,　　　RF = 1.667 MHz

The examples shown alongside assume an IF of 5.0 MHz and the local oscillator at 10.5 MHz, a situation taken from Fig.1.13. The first new frequencies (1) at 16 MHz and 26 MHz would be outside the passband of the minimum 1-octave filters (5.5 ~ 10 MHz) and, also, if balanced mixers are used, the mixer would not function at even harmonics of the oscillator. This frequency then does not present any problem. The second pair (2) represents signals at 2.75 or 7.75 MHz. The latter lies right in the middle of the 1-octave filter range, so that if the mixer has significant third-order distortion, added filtering would be needed. The one choice is half-octave filters, the other is narrow-band, continuously tunable filters (with their tracking problems). Other spurious signals can be created by harmonics produced within the RF amplifier itself; such is the case with frequency (3) where a third harmonic created by amplifier nonlinearities could pass straight through the mixer. The 1.667 MHz input can easily be eliminated with filters ahead of the RF amplifier.

The total spurious frequency problem therefore depends to a great extent on the linearity of the RF stage, on filters before and after this stage, and on the mixer itself. The big problem involves gain control. To maintain low-level signals at the mixer input, the gain of the RF stage may need to be reduced at some time. For automatic gain control, the amplifier must have a nonlinear transfer characteristic so that a change of bias produces a change in gain. The resulting second-order nonlinearities could then produce spurious signals, which would cause mixing products to appear within the IF passband, particularly since the filters ahead of the RF stage are usually minimal. If AGC is used, good RF filtering is required.

A better approach is to make the amplifiers very linear, even by going to the extremes of balanced amplifiers with negative feedback. Gain control can then be manual—either turning a potentiometer or switching in resistive pads, or automatic if linear devices are used.

The idea of a linear, two-terminal device that will not distort a signal yet can change its resistance with a voltage change may seem strange. A small incandescent lamp is one example. If a DC voltage is applied across the lamp and slowly changed, the current flowing into the bulb will not change linearly with the applied voltage. As the filament heats up, its resistance will increase. Any rapid voltage changes, however, will cause linear current changes, since the thermal time constant of the filament will be long enough to hold the resistance constant for a while.[8] Such an idea has been used for automatic level control of good-quality audio oscillators for years. The modern equivalent of the lamp is the PIN diode. At low frequencies the device acts like a diode, but at higher frequencies it acts like a variable resistor, since the lifetime of its charge carriers is quite long (up to 500 ns). Above about 10 MHz (depending on the particular diode), a linear attenuator can be made that can be varied with a DC control voltage.

1.2.5   IF Amplifiers

The intermediate frequency section of a receiver is placed between the first mixer and the final detector circuits. It must:

(1) Provide a high amount of gain, 60 ~ 100 dB, and reduce this when strong signals are present.

(2) Filter out all unwanted signals outside the passband.

(3) Limit amplitude variations in the case of FM signals, thereby determining the FM capture ratio.

(4) Limit the amplitude of noise pulses in the case of AM and SSB signals.

These tasks must be performed without destroying the noise figure set by the receiver's front end and without introducing distortion products within the desired passband.

For the majority of receivers, a total gain of at least 20 dB will exist in the RF and mixer stages, so the IF noise figure is usually not significant. For the few cases where no RF stage is used and the mixer operates with a conversion loss, the IF noise figure will be very important. Any losses in the IF filters ahead of the amplifying stages must be considered; for if an RF gain of 15 dB, a mixer loss of 6 dB, and an IF filter loss of 9 dB occur, the IF signal level will be right back to where it was at the antenna terminals. The IF noise figure would then be very important.

Attention to noise figure itself is not sufficient, as the total noise bandwidth must also be considered. One part of this has already been pointed out; the image frequency from the mixer will add thermal noise in addition to the possibility of interfering signals. The total noise bandwidth could then be twice as wide as the IF filter bandwidth. The other noise problem can occur whenever separate filters and amplifiers are used.

As shown in Fig. 1.15, there is no filtering after the integrated circuit used for the gain. The total noise output to the detector would then be the narrow-band noise through the IF filter from the RF amplifier and mixer plus the broadband 10 or 20 MHz generated within the IC. Some addi-tional noise bandwidth filtering should therefore be provided between the IC and the detector.

Fig.1.15   IF amplifier

Distortion must also be considered. Since the IF amplifiers must be capable of automatic gain control, they must have a square-law or second-order transfer characteristic (V_{out}/V_{in}). Gain can then be changed by varying the amplifier's bias. As long as the second-order characteristic is maintained, no distortion will occur, assuming that the IF filters are relatively narrow band, less than 1 octave. All harmonics and intermodulation products will then fall outside the passband, so the amplifier will appear linear. But if any odd-order distortion is present, undesirable in-band mixing products and compression will appear. This type of distortion can obviously occur in the bipolar transistors normally used for the IF amplifiers, and the amount can be controlled through careful biasing and selection of the transistors used. It can also occur in some not-so-obvious components. Any quartz, ceramic, or mechanical filters involve physical movement of their internal elements and there will be symmetrical limits to this linear motion. The filters themselves can therefore be a source of distortion, particularly if the applied signal level is too high. Ferrite materials commonly used in filters can also be a source of nonlinearities. For very demanding applications, then, each component of the receiver must be carefully analyzed for its contribution to the final performance of the receiver.

New Words and Phrases

bias	n.	偏置
bulb	n.	灯泡
bulk	n.	大多数
ceramic	n.	陶瓷
deficiency	n.	不足
demodulate	v.	解调，检波
distinguishable	a.	可分辨的
distortion	n.	失真
drift	n.	漂移
ferrite	n.	铁酸盐
filament	n.	灯丝
filter	n.	滤波器
frequency	n.	频率
harmonic	n.	谐波
inevitably	adv.	不可避免
intermodulate	v.	互调
mixer	n.	混频器
nonlinearity	n.	非线性
obscured	a.	模糊的
octave	n.	倍频程
overloading	v.	过载
pad	n.	板，垫
passband	n.	通带
phase	n.	相位
potentiometer	n.	电位计
quartz	n.	石英
radiate	v.	辐射
resemble	v.	像，类似

RF	*abbr.*	射频
sensitivity	*n.*	灵敏度
skirt	*n.*	边缘
spurious	*a.*	寄生的,虚假的
superheterodyne	*a.*	超外差的
tendency	*n.*	趋向
transmitter	*n.*	发射机
AGC	*abbr.*	自动增益控制
AFC	*abbr.*	自动频率控制
CW	*abbr.*	连续波
CB	*abbr.*	民用波段
thermal noise		热噪声
atmospheric noise		大气噪声
balanced mixer		平衡式混频器
FM-stereo broadcasting		调频立体声广播
image signals		镜像信号
incandescnet lamp		白炽灯
intermediate frequency		中频
local oscillator		本地振荡器
negative feedback		负反馈
noise figure		噪声系数
phase-locked loop		锁相环
tuned circuits		调谐回路
two-terminal device		双端口器件

Notes

1. When over 120 dB of RF gain is involved, every little bit helps. 当涉及的射频增益超过120分贝,每一点都有用。
2. For each type of modulation used (i.e., AM, FM, SSB, PM), a number of different circuits exist. Some will have gain, others a loss. 对于所应用的各种调制方式(如调幅、调频、单边带和脉冲调制),都有一

些不同的电路。一些可获得增益,另一些则插入损耗。

3. If unwanted signal can sneak into the receiver at the IF frequency, various spurious frequencies are generated through intermodulation and cross-modulation, any good design can be useless. 如果不期望信号不知不觉地在中频进入接收机,通过交调和互调产生会很多寄生频率,那么,再好的设计也没用。

4. Capture ratio: 1.5 dB. 捕获率为 1.5 dB,即 FM 信号大于其它信号至少 1.5 dB,才能听到。

5. Sensitivity: 0.5 μV for 10 dB S + N/N ratio. 灵敏度:对于信号加噪声功率与噪声功率比为 10 dB 时,灵敏度为 0.5 μV。

6. Some discrimination against unwanted mixing products can therefore be had if all RF input levels to the mixer are kept as low as possible and the local oscillator signal kept as high as possible. 如果到混频器的所有射频输入电平都保持尽可能地低,并且本振信号尽可能地高,就能对一些不期望的混频分量抑制。

7. We have already seen that image has to be removed and also any group of frequencies that could themselves mix and produce an IF output. 我们已经看到,必须移去(滤除)镜像频率以及任何一组可以互相混频并产生中频输出的频率。

8. Any rapid voltage changes, however, will cause linear current changes, since the thermal time constant of the filament will be long enough to hold the resistance constant for a while. 然而任何快速的电压变化都能导致电流线性变化,因为灯丝的热时间常数将足够长可以暂时保持电阻为常数。

2

Signal Processing and Data Processing

2.1 DIGITAL SIGNAL AND DISCRETE-TIME SYSTEMS

2.1.1 Signals and Systems

Signals are scalar-valued functions of one or more independent variables. Often for convenience, when the signals are one-dimensional, the independent variable is referred to as "time." The independent variable may be continuous or discrete. Signals that are continuous in both amplitude and time (often referred to as continuous-time or analog signals) are the most commonly encountered in signal processing contexts. Discrete-time signals are typically associated with sampling of continuous-time signals. In a digital implementation of a signal processing system, quantization of signal amplitude is also required. Although not precisely correct in every context, discrete-time signal processing is often referred to as digital signal processing.

Discrete-time signals, also referred to as sequences, are denoted by functions whose arguments are integers. For example, $x(n)$ represents a sequence that is defined for all integer values of n and undefined for noninteger values of n. The notation $x(n)$ refers to the discrete-time function x or to the value of the function x at a specific value of n. The distinction between these two will be obvious from the context.

Some sequences and classes of sequences play a particularly important role in discrete-time signal processing. These are summarized below.

The unit sample sequence, denoted by $\delta(n)$, is defined as

$$\delta(n) = \begin{cases} 1, & n = 0 \\ 0, & \text{otherwise} \end{cases} \qquad (1)$$

The sequence $\delta(n)$ plays a role similar to an impulse function in analog system analysis.

The unit step sequence, denoted by $u(n)$, is defined as

$$u(n) = \begin{cases} 1, & n \geqslant 0 \\ 0, & \text{otherwise} \end{cases} \qquad (2)$$

Exponential sequences of the form

$$x(n) = A\alpha^n \qquad (3)$$

play a role in discrete-time signal processing similar to the role played by exponential functions in continuous-time signal processing. Specifically, they are eigenfunctions of discrete-time linear systems and for that reason form the basis for transform analysis techniques. When $|\alpha| = 1$, $x(n)$ takes the form of a complex exponential sequence typically expressed in the form

$$x(n) = Ae^{j\omega n} \qquad (4)$$

Because the variable n is an integer, complex exponential sequences separated by integer multiples of 2π in ω (frequency) are identical sequences, i.e.,

$$e^{j(\omega + k2\pi)n} = e^{j\omega n} \qquad (5)$$

This fact forms the core of many of the important differences between the representation of discrete-time signals and systems and that of continuous-time signals and systems.

A general sinusoidal sequence can be expressed as

$$x(n) = A\cos(\omega_0 n + \Phi) \tag{6}$$

where A is the amplitude, ω the frequency, and Φ the phase. In contrast with continuous-time sinusoids, a discrete-time sinusoidal signal is not necessarily periodic and if it is, the period is $2\pi/\omega_0$ only when $2\pi/\omega_0$ is an integer. In both continuous time and discrete time, the importance of sinusoidal signals lies in the facts that a broad class of signals can be represented as a linear combination of sinusoidal signals and that the response of linear time-invariant systems to a sinusoidal signal is sinusoidal with the same frequency and with a change in only the amplitude and phase.

In general, a system maps an input signal $x(n)$ to an output signal $y(n)$ through a system transformation $T\{\cdot\}$. This definition of a system is very broad. Without some restrictions, the characterization of a system requires a complete input-output relationship—knowing the output of a system to a certain set of inputs does not allow us to determine the output of the system to other sets of inputs. Two types of restrictions that greatly simplify the characterization and analysis of a system are linearity and time invariance, alternatively referred to as shift invariance.[1] Fortunately, many systems can often be approximated in practice by a linear and time-invariant system.

The linearity of a system is defined through the principle of superposition:

Linearity $\quad T\{ax_1(n) + bx_2(n)\} = ay_1(n) + by_2(n) \tag{7}$

where $T\{x_1(n)\} = y_1(n)$, $T\{x_2(n)\} = y_2(n)$, and a and b are any scalar constants.

Time invariance of a system is defined as

Time invariance $\quad T\{x(n - n_0)\} = y(n - n_0) \tag{8}$

where $y(n) = T\{x(n)\}$ and n_0 is any integer. Linearity and time invariance are independent properties, i.e., a system may have one but not the other property, both or neither.

For a linear and time-invariant (LTI) system, [2] the system response $y(n)$ is given by

$$y(n) = \sum_{k=-\infty}^{+\infty} x(k)h(n-k) = x(n) * h(n) \qquad (9)$$

where $x(n)$ is the input and $h(n)$ is the response of the system when the input is $\delta(n)$. Eq.(9) is the convolution sum.

As with continuous-time convolution, the convolution operator in Eq.(9) is commutative and associative and distributes over addition:

Commutative:

$$x(n) * y(n) = y(n) * x(n) \qquad (10)$$

Associative:

$$[x(n) * y(n)] * w(n) = x(n) * [y(n) * w(n)] \qquad (11)$$

Distributive:

$$x(n) * [y(n) + w(n)] = [x(n) * y(n) + x(n) * w(n)] \qquad (12)$$

In continuous-time systems, convolution is primarily an analytical tool. For discrete-time systems, the convolution sum, in addition to being important in the analysis of LTI systems, is important as an explicit mechanism for implementing a specific class of LTI systems, namely those for which the impulse response is of finite length (FIR systems). [3]

Two additional system properties that are referred to frequently are the properties of stability and causality. A system is considered stable in the bounded input-bounded output(BIBO) sense if and only if a bounded input always leads to a bounded output. [4] A necessary and sufficient condition for an LTI system to be stable is that its unit sample response $h(n)$ be absolutely summable.

For an LTI system,

Stability $$\sum_{n=-\infty}^{\infty} | h(n) | < \infty \qquad (13)$$

Because of Eq. (13), an absolutely summable sequence is often referred to as a stable sequence.

A system is referred to as causal if and only if, for each value of n, say n_0, $y(n)$ does not depend on values of the input for $n > n_0$. A necessary and sufficient condition for an LTI system to be causal is that its unit sample response $h(n)$ be zero for $n < 0$. For an LTI system.

Causality $$h(n) = 0 \text{ for } n < 0 \qquad (14)$$

Because of Eq. (14), a sequence that is zero for $n < 0$ is often referred to as a causal sequence.

2.1.2 Frequency-Domain Representation of Signals and Systems

In this section, we summarize the representation of sequences as linear combinations of complex exponentials, first for periodic sequences using the discrete-time Fourier series, next for stable sequences using the discrete-time Fourier transform, then through a generalization of discrete-time Fourier transform, namely, the z-transform, and finally for finite-extent sequences using the discrete Fourier transform, and finally we review the use of these representations in characterizing LTI systems.

1. *Discrete-Time Fourier Series* [5]

Any periodic sequence $\tilde{x}(n)$ with period N can be represented through the discrete-time Fourier series (DFS) pair in Eqs. (15) and (16).

$$\tilde{x}(n) = \frac{1}{N} \sum_{k=0}^{N-1} \tilde{X}(k) e^{j(2\pi/N)nk} \qquad (15)$$

$$\tilde{X}(k) = \frac{1}{N} \sum_{n=0}^{N-1} \tilde{x}(n) e^{-j(2\pi/N)nk} \qquad (16)$$

The synthesis equation expresses the periodic sequence as a linear combination of harmonically related complex exponentials. The choice of interpreting the DFS coefficients $\tilde{X}(k)$ either as zero outside the range $0 \leqslant k \leqslant (N-1)$ or as periodically repeated does not in any way affect Eq.(15). It is a commonly accepted convention, however, to interpret $\tilde{X}(k)$ as periodic to maintain a duality between the analysis and synthesis equations.

2. Discrete-Time Fourier Transform[6]

Any stable sequence $x(n)$ (i.e., one that is absolutely summable) can be represented as a linear combination of complex exponentials. For a periodic stable sequences, the synthesis equation takes the form of Eq. (17), and the analysis equation takes the form of Eq.(18).

$$x(n) = \frac{1}{2\pi} \int_{-\pi}^{\pi} X(\omega) e^{j\omega n} d\omega \qquad (17)$$

$$X(\omega) = \sum_{r=-\infty}^{+\infty} x(n) e^{-j\omega n} \qquad (18)$$

To relate the discrete-time Fourier transform and the discrete-time Fourier series, consider a stable sequence $x(n)$ and the periodic signal $\tilde{x}_1(n)$ formed by time-aliasing $x(n)$, i.e.,

$$\tilde{x}_1(n) = \sum_{r=-\infty}^{+\infty} x(n + rN) \qquad (19)$$

Then the DFS coefficients of $\tilde{x}_1(n)$ are proportional to samples spaced by $2\pi/N$ of the Fourier transform $x(n)$. Specifically,

$$\tilde{X}_1(k) = \frac{1}{N} X(\omega) \Big|_{\omega = (2\pi k/N)} \qquad (20)$$

Among other things, this implies that the DFS coefficients of a periodic signal are proportional to the discrete-time Fourier transform of one period.

3. z-Transform

A generalization of the Fourier transform, the z-transform, permits the representation of a broader class of signals as a linear combination of complex exponentials, for which the magnitudes may or may not be unity.[7]

The z-transform analysis and synthesis equations are as follows:

$$x(n) = \frac{1}{2\pi j} \oint_c X(z) z^{n-1} dz \qquad (21)$$

$$X(z) = \sum_{n=-\infty}^{+\infty} x(n) z^{-n} \qquad (22)$$

From Eqs. (18) and (22), $X(\omega)$ is related to $X(z)$ by $X(\omega) = X(z)|_{z=e^{j\omega}}$, i.e., for a stable sequence, the Fourier transform $X(\omega)$ is the z-transform evaluated on the contour $|z| = 1$, referred to as the unit circle.

Eq. (22) converges only for some values of z and not others. The range of values of z for which $X(z)$ converges, i.e., the region of convergence (ROC), corresponds to the values of z for which $x(n)z^{-n}$ is absolutely summable.[8] We summarize the properties of the ROC in more detail later. Complete specification of the z-transform requires specification not only of the algebraic expression for the z-transform but also of the ROC. For example, the two sequences $a^n u(n)$ and $-a^n u(-n-1)$ have z-transforms that are identical algebraically and that differ only in the ROC.

The synthesis equation as expressed in Eq. (21) is a contour integral with the contour encircling the origin and contained within the region of convergence. While this equation provides a formal means for obtaining $x(n)$ from $X(z)$, its evaluation requires contour integration. Such an integral can be evaluated using complex residues, but the procedure is often tedious and usually unnecessary. When $X(z)$ is a rational function of z, a more typical approach is to expand $X(z)$ using a partial fraction equation. The inverse z-transform of the individual simpler terms can usually then be recognized by inspection.

There are a number of important properties of the ROC that, together with properties of the time-domain sequence, permit implicit specification of the ROC. These properties are summarized as follows:

Property 1.   The ROC is a connected region.

Property 2.   For a rational z-transform, the ROC does not contain any poles and is bounded by poles.

Property 3.   If $x(n)$ is a right-sided sequence and if the circle $|z| = r_0$ is in the ROC, then all finite values of z for which $|z| > r_0$ will also be in the ROC.

Property 4.   If $x(n)$ is a left-sided sequence and if the circle $|z| = r_0$ is in the ROC, then all values of z for which $0 < |z| < r_0$ will also be in the ROC.

Property 5.   If $x(n)$ is a stable and causal sequence with a rational z-transform, then all the poles of $X(z)$ are inside the unit circle.

4. Discrete Fourier Transform

In the previous segment, we discussed the representation of periodic sequences in terms of the discrete Fourier series. With the correct interpretation, the same representation can be applied to finite-duration sequences. The resulting Fourier representation for finite-duration sequences is referred to as the Discrete Fourier transform (DFT). [9]

The DFT analysis and synthesis equations are

$$X(k) = \sum_{n=0}^{N-1} x(n)e^{-j(2\pi/N)kn}, \ 0 \leqslant k \leqslant N - 1 \qquad (23)$$

$$x(n) = \frac{1}{N}\sum_{k=0}^{N-1} X(k)e^{-j(2\pi/N)kn}, \ 0 \leqslant n \leqslant N - 1 \qquad (24)$$

The fact that $X(k) = 0$ for k outside the interval $0 \leqslant k \leqslant N - 1$ and that $x(n) = 0$ for k outside the interval $0 \leqslant k \leqslant N - 1$ is implied but not always stated explicitly.

The DFT is used in a variety of signal processing applications, so it is of considerable interest to efficiently compute the DFT and inverse DFT. A straight-forward computation of the N-point DFT or inverse DFT requires on the order of N^2 arithmetic operations (multiplications and additions). The number of arithmetic operations required is significantly reduced through the set of Fast Fourier transform (FFT)[10] algorithms. Most FFT algorithms are based on the simple principle that an N-point DFT can be computed by computing two ($N/2$)-point DFTs, or three ($N/3$)-point DFTs, etc. Computation of the N-point DFT or inverse DFT using FFT algorithms requires on the order of $N \log N$ arithmetic operations.

In the previous segment we reviewed the representation of signals as a linear combination of complex exponentials of the form $e^{j\omega n}$ or, more generally, z^n. For linear systems, the response is then the same linear combination of the responses to the individual complex exponentials. If in addition the system is time-invariant, the complex exponentials are eigenfunctions. Consequently, the system can be characterized by the spectrum of eigenvalues, corresponding to the frequency response if the signal decomposition is in terms of complex exponentials with unity magnitude or, more generally, to the system function in the context of the more general complex exponentials z^n.

The eigenfunction property follows directly from the convolution sum and states that with $x(n) = z^n$, the output $y(n)$ has the form

$$y(n) = H(z)z^n \qquad (25)$$

where

$$H(z) = \sum_{k=-\infty}^{+\infty} h(k)z^{-n} \qquad (26)$$

The system function $H(z)$ is the eigenvalue associated with the eigenfunction z^n. Also, from Eq.(26), $H(z)$ is the z-transform of the system unit sample response. When $z = e^{jw}$, it corresponds to the Fourier transform of the unit sample response.

Since Eq. (17) or (21) corresponds to a decomposition of $x(n)$ as a linear combination of complex exponentials, we can obtain the response $y(n)$, using linearity and the eigenfunction property, by multiplying the amplitudes of the eigenfunctions z^n in Eq. (22) by the eigenvalues $H(z)$, i.e.,

$$y(n) = \frac{1}{2\pi j} \int_c H(z) X(z) z^{n-1} dz \qquad (27)$$

Eq. (27) then becomes the synthesis equation for the output, i.e.,

$$Y(z) = H(z) X(z) \qquad (28)$$

Eq. (28) corresponds to the z-transform convolution property.

2.1.3 Systems Characterized by Linear Constant-Coefficient Difference Equations

A particularly important class of discrete-time systems are those characterized by linear constant-coefficient difference equations (LCCDE) of the form

$$\sum_{k=0}^{N} a_k y(n-k) = \sum_{k=0}^{M} b_k x(n-k) \qquad (29)$$

where the a_k's and the b_k's are constants. Eq. (29) is typically referred to as an Nth-order difference equation.

A system characterized by an Nth-order difference equation of the form in Eq. (29) represents a linear time-invariant system only under an appropriate choice of the homogeneous solution, i.e., linearity and time invariance are additional constraints to the equation itself. Even under these additional constraints, the system is not restricted to be causal.

Assuming the system is linear, time-invariant, and causal, the response of a system characterized by Eq. (29) can be obtained recursively. Specifically, we can rewrite Eq. (29) as

$$a_0 y(n) = \sum_{k=0}^{M} b_k x(n-k) + \sum_{k=1}^{N} a_k y(n-k) \qquad (30)$$

Since we are assuming that the system is linear and causal, if $x(n) = 0$ for $n < n_0$ then $y(n) = 0$ for $n < n_0$. With this assumed zero state, $y(n)$ can be generated recursively from Eq. (30). This recursion is illustrated in a linear signal flow graph form in Fig. 2.1, where z^{-1} represents a unit delay. While the recursion in Eq. (30) will generate the

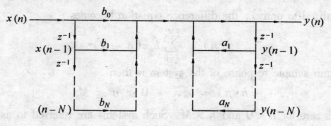

Fig. 2.1 Direct form I realization of an Nth-order difference equation

correct output sequence and, in fact, represents a specific algorithm for computing the output, the result will not be in an analytically convenient form.[11] A convenient procedure to obtain the solution analytically is through the use of the z-transform. Specifically, applying the z-transform to both sides of Eq. (30) and using the linearity and time-shifting properties, and after appropriate algebraic manipulation, we obtain

$$H(z) = \frac{Y(z)}{X(z)} = \frac{\sum_{k=0}^{M} b_k z^{-k}}{a_0 - \sum_{k=1}^{N} a_k z^{-k}} \qquad (31)$$

Eq. (31) specifies the algebraic expression for the system function, which we note is a rational function of z. It does not, however, explicitly specify the ROC. If we assume that the system is causal, then the ROC associated with Eq. (31) will be the region outside a circle passing through the outermost pole of $H(z)$. If we do not impose causality, then in general there are many choices for the ROC and correspondingly for the system impulse response.

1. Finite Impulse Response[11] and Infinite Impulse Response Systems

When N in Eq. (30) or (31) is greater than zero, the system impulse response is a linear combination of exponentials and consequently is of infinite length. In this case, the system is referred to as an infinite impulse response[12] (IIR) system. When $N = 0$ (assuming a_0 is normalized to unity), the difference equation becomes

$$y(n) = \sum_{k=0}^{M} b_k x(n - k) \qquad (32)$$

The unit sample response of the system is then

$$h(n) = b_n, \qquad 0 \leqslant n \leqslant M \qquad (33)$$

and is zero for $n < 0$ and $n > M$. Such systems are referred to as finite impulse response[13] (FIR) systems.

Generally in designing a discrete-time filter to meet certain prescribed specifications, a design utilizing both poles and zeros, i.e., an IIR design, results in far fewer overall delays and coefficients than an FIR design. On the other hand, there are certain situations in which FIR filters are preferable to IIR filters. One major advantage of FIR filters is that they can be designed such that the impulse response is symmetric, i. e., so that $h(n) = h(M - 1 - n)$ where M is the filter length, in which case the frequency response is real to within a linear phase factor $e^{-j[2\pi(M-1)/2]\omega}$. Causal IIR filters cannot be designed to have a symmetric impulse response. Also, since one realization of FIR filters is directly through Eq. (32) as the sum of weighted taps on a delay line, implementation of FIR filters is well matched to certain technologies, in particular the use of CCDs and other charge transfer devices and surface acoustic wave devices. [14]

2. Linear Signal Flow Graph Representation of Linear Constant-Coefficient Difference Equations

The flow graph in Fig. 2.1 is generally referred to as direct form I realization of the Nth-order difference equation. This realization can be viewed as a cascade of two systems, one implementing the zeroes of $H(z)$ and the other the poles. Since each of these is an LTI system, the order in which they are cascaded can be reversed. After doing so, and combining the two chains of delays into a single chain of delays, the linear signal flow graph in Fig. 2. 2 results. This representation is typically referred to as the direct form II realization of the difference equation.

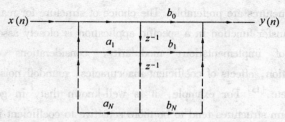

Fig.2.2 Direct form Ⅱ realization of an Nth-order difference equation

The rational function $H(z)$ in Eq. (31) can also be rearranged in a number of other ways leading to other realizations of the Nth-order difference equation. For example, $H(z)$ can be expressed as a product of second-order factors in the form where we have assumed that $N = M$ and N is even. If this is not the case, we can simply include terms with zero coefficients. The signal flow graph structure suggested by Eq. (34) is the cascade structure. The parallel form structure is obtained by expanding $H(z)$

$$H(z) = \frac{b_0}{a_0} \prod_{k=1}^{N/2} \frac{1 + \beta_{1k}z^{-1} + \beta_{2k}z^{-2}}{1 + \alpha_{1k}z^{-1} + \alpha_{2k}z^{-2}} \tag{34}$$

in a partial fraction expansion. For example, if we expand $H(z)$ in second-order terms, again assuming N is even, we can write $H(z)$ as

$$H(z) = \frac{b_N}{a_N} \sum_{k=1}^{N/2} \frac{1 + \gamma_{0k} + \gamma_{1k}z^{-1}}{1 + \alpha_{1k}z^{-1} + \alpha_{2k}z^{-2}} \tag{35}$$

Eq. (35) then corresponds to the parallel form realization where each section is implemented in direct II form.

There are, of course, many variations on the cascade and parallel forms, such as the use of both first- and second-order sections, different ordering of sections, the specific form used for each of the sections, etc. There are also many forms in addition to the basic ones that we have summarized here.

The direct form II, cascade, and parallel structures are perhaps the most commonly encountered, although in specialized situations certain other structures are preferable. The choice of structure for realization of a given transfer function in a specific application is closely associated with issues of implementation: modularity, considerations of parallel computation, effects of coefficient inaccuracies, roundoff noise, dynamic range, etc. [15] For example, it is well-known that, in general, the direct-form structures tend to be more sensitive to coefficient inaccuracies than either the cascade or parallel structures since in the direct-form structures, pole and zero locations are controlled through the coefficients of high-order polynomials, whereas in the cascade and parallel forms they are controlled through the coefficients of first- and second-order polynomials.

The basic structures just described were discussed in the context of a general difference equation with both poles and zeros, i.e., IIR filters. For FIR filters, both the direct form I and II structures reduce to the tapped delay line structure in Fig. 2.3. As indicated earlier, one of the potential advantages of FIR filters lies in the fact that they can be designed and implemented to have exactly linear phase. Since linear phase FIR filters have a symmetric impulse response, i.e., $h(n) = h(N-1-n)$, the direct-form structure in Fig. 2.3 can be rearranged in this case to reduce the number of multipliers by first adding terms with identical coefficients and then carrying out the multiplication.

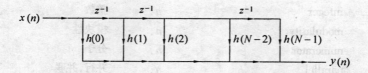

Fig.2.3   Direct form realization of an FIR system

FIR filters can also be implemented as a cascade of first-and/or second-order zeros. Generally, however, the most typical implementation of FIR filters is in direct form since technologies such as charge transfer devices are best suited to implementing a direct tapped delay line structure.

New Words and Phrases

argument	*n*.	自变量
associative	*a*.	结合的
cascade	*n*.	级联
causality	*n*.	因果性
CCD	*abbr*.	电耦合器件
commutative	*a*.	交换的
context	*n*.	上下文
convolution	*n*.	卷积
decomposition	*n*.	分解
denominator	*n*.	分母
distinction	*n*.	区别
distributive	*a*.	分配的
eigenfunction	*n*.	特征函数
eigenvalue	*n*.	特征值
encircle	*v*.	环绕,包围
even	*a*.	偶数的
exponential	*n*.	指数
inaccuracy	*n*.	不准确

integer	*n.*	整数
modularity	*n.*	模块性
numerator	*n.*	分子
parallel	*n.*	并行,并联
quantization	*n.*	量化
recursion	*n.*	递归
sequence	*n.*	序列
stability	*n.*	稳定性
tap	*n.*	抽头
tedious	*a.*	冗长的
trigonometric	*a.*	三角的
weight	*n.*	加权
absolutely summable		绝对可和的
analysis equation		分解方程
arithmetic operation		算术运算
contour integral		围线积分
dynamic range		动态范围
finite-extent sequence		有限长度序列
homogeneous solution		齐次解
inverse z-transform		逆 Z 变换
linear combination		线性组合
order of N^2		N^2 数量级
pole-zero plot		零极点图
principle of superposition		叠加原理
region of convergence (ROC)		收敛域
roundoff noise		舍入噪声
scalar-valued		标量
shift invariance		移不变
synthesis equation		综合方程
tapped delay line		抽头延迟线
time-aliasing		时间折叠

Notes

1. Two types of restriction that greatly simplify the characterization and analysis of a system are linearity and time invariance, alternatively referred to as shift invariance. 两种类型的限制大大地简化了对系统的描述和分析,它们是线性和时不变性,时不变性也称为移不变性。

2. Linear and time-invariant (LTI) system 线性时不变系统

3. For discrete-time systems, the convolution sum, in addition to being important in the analysis of LTI system, is important as an explicit mechanism for implementing a specific class of LTI systems, namely those for which the impulse response is of finite length (FIR systems). 对于离散时间系统,卷积和除了在分析线性和时不变系统时很重要,在实现一种特殊的线性和时不变系统即有限冲激响应系统时,也因其清晰的概念显得很重要。

4. A system is considered stable in the bounded input—bounded output (BIBO) sense if and only if a bounded input always leads to a bounded output. 一个系统当且仅当一个有限的输入导致一个有限的输出时,才被认为在有限输入——有限输出意义下是稳定的。

5. Discrete-time Fourier Series (DFS) 离散时间傅立叶级数

6. Discrete-time Fourier Transform 离散时间傅立叶变换

7. A generalization of the Fourier transform, the z-transform, permits the representation of a broader class of signals as a linear combination of complex exponentials, for which the magnitudes may or may not be unity. z-变换是广义的傅立叶变换,它可以把很多信号表示成幅度不同的复指数的线性组合。

8. The range of value of z for which $X(z)$ converges. i.e., the region of convergence (ROC), corresponds to the values of z for which $x(n)z^{-n}$ is absolutely summable. $X(z)$收敛时 z 值的范围,即收敛域,对应 $x(n)z^{-n}$绝对可和的 z 值。

9. Discrete Fourier Transform (DFT) 离散傅立叶变换

10. Fast Fourier Transform (FFT) 快速傅立叶变换

11. While the recursion in Eq. (30) will generate the correct output sequence and, in fact, represents a specific algorithm for computing the output, the result will not be in an analytically convenient form. 而式(30)表示的递推公式将产生正确的输出序列,事实上,它还描述了一个计算输出的明确算法,但其结果并不是一个简便的解析形式。

12. Infinite Impulse Response (IIR)无限冲激响应

13. Finite Impulse Response (FIR)有限冲激响应

14. Also, since one realization of FIR filters is directly through Eq.(32) as the sum of weighted taps on a delay line, implementation of FIR filters is well matched to certain technologies, in particular the use of CCDs and other charge transfer devices and surface acoustic wave devices. 并且由于 FIR 滤波器的实现是直接通过式(32)对延迟线上的加权抽头取和,FIR 滤波器的实现与(应用)某些技术相似,特别是用电耦合器件和其他电荷传输器件及声表面波器件。

15. The choice of structure for realization of a given transfer function in a specific application is closely associated with issues of implementation: modularity, consideration of parallel computation, effects of coefficient inaccuracies, roundoff noise, dynamic range, etc. 选择一个在特定应用场合实现给定传输函数的结构与实施问题密切相关:模块化、并行计算的考虑、系数不准确的影响、舍入噪声、动态范围等等。

2.2   DIGITAL FILTER

The design of digital filters can be thought of as involving two stages:(1) the specification of the desired properties of the filter and (2) the approximation of the specifications using a discrete-time system. Although these two steps are not independent, it is usually convenient to treat them separately.

A typical form for the specification is depicted in Fig. 2.4 for a lowpass filter in which δ_1 and δ_2 represent the allowable passband and stopband tolerance and ω_p and ω_s, respectively, denote the passband and stopband edge frequencies.

Many filters used in practice are specified by such a tolerance scheme, with no constraints on the phase response other than those imposed by stability and causality requirement; i. e., the poles of the system function must lie inside the unit circle.[1] In designing FIR digital filters, we more often impose the constraint that the phase be linear, thereby again removing phase from consideration in the design process.

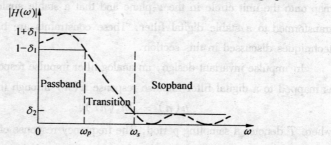

Fig.2.4　A typical form for digital lowpass filter specification

Given a set of specifications, the filter design problem becomes a problem in functional approximation to obtain a discrete-time linear system whose frequency response falls within the prescribed tolerances.[2] IIR systems imply approximation by a rational function of z, while FIR systems imply polynomial approximation. There are a variety of design techniques for both types of filters, ranging from closed-form procedures, which involve only substitution of design specifications into design formulas, to algorithmic techniques, where, for example, a solution may be obtained by an iterative procedure.

2.2.1　Design of IIR Digital Filters from Analog Filters

The classical approach to the design of IIR digital filters involves the transformation of an analog filter into a digital filter meeting prescribed specifications. This approach is motivated principally by the fact that the art of analog IIR filter design is highly advanced and, since useful results can be achieved, it is advantageous to utilize the design procedures already developed for analog filters.

In transforming an analog system to a digital system, we generally require that the essential properties of the analog frequency response be preserved in the frequency response of the resulting digital filter. Loosely speaking, this implies that we want the imaginary axis of the s-plane to map onto the unit circle in the z-plane and that a stable analog filter be transformed to a stable digital filter. These constraints are basic to the techniques discussed in this section.

In impulse invariant design, an analog filter impulse response $h_a(t)$ is mapped to a digital filter impulse response $h(n)$ through the relation

$$h(n) = Th_a(nT) \tag{1}$$

where T denotes a sampling period. The frequency response of the digital filter $H(w)$ is related to the frequency response of the analog filter $H_a(\Omega)$ as

$$H(\omega) = \sum_{k=-\infty}^{+\infty} H_a\left(\frac{\omega}{T} + \frac{2\pi k}{T}\right) \tag{2}$$

Any practical analog filter will not be bandlimited, and consequently there is interference between successive terms in Eq. (2) (i. e., aliasing). However, if the analog filter approaches zero at high frequencies sufficiently rapidly, the aliasing may be negligibly small and a useful digital filter can result from the sampling of the impulse response of an analog filter.

In structuring the design problem, we begin with discrete-time specifications that are then mapped to corresponding analog specifications, and the resulting analog filter is then mapped back to discrete time. From this point of view, the parameter T in the impulse invariant design procedure has no effect and often for convenience is chosen as unity.

The basis for impulse invariance as just described is to choose an impulse response for the digital filter that is similar in some sense to the impulse response of the analog filter. The use of this often is motivated not so much by a desire to maintain the impulse response shape but by the knowledge that if the analog filter is bandlimited, then the digital filter frequency response will closely approximate the analog frequency response. However, in some filter design problems, a primary objective may be to control some aspect of the time response such as the impulse response or the step response. [3] In such cases a natural approach would be to design the digital filter by impulse invariance or a step invariance procedure.

Impulse invariance as a procedure for mapping analog filter designs to digital filter designs has the limitation that the analog filter must (at least approximately) have a bandlimited frequency response. [4] As an alternative, the bilinear transformation for mapping analog to digital designs maps the entire $j\Omega$-axis in the s-plane to one around the unit circle in the z-plane, and consequently there is no aliasing. By necessity, however, the mapping from analog to digital frequency is nonlinear. Consequently, in contrast to impulse invariance, the bilinear transformation is useful only for mapping analog filter designs that have piecewise-constant frequency characteristics.

The bilinear transformation is given by

$$s = \frac{2}{T}\left(\frac{1 - z^{-1}}{1 + z^{-1}}\right) \tag{3}$$

The parameter T has again been included in the mapping since this commonly appears in some texts. However, just as with impulse invariance, and with the point of view that we begin the process with specifications in terms of discrete-time frequency, the parameter T will cancel.

With the use of the bilinear transformation, discrete-time frequency ω *is related to continuous-time frequency* Ω by

$$\omega = 2\tan^{-1}(\Omega T/2) \qquad (4)$$

Although the bilinear transformation can be used effectively in mapping a piecewise-constant magnitude characteristic from the s-plane to the z-plane, the distortion in the frequency axis will manifest itself in terms of distortion in the phase characteristic associated with the filter. If, for example, we were interested in a digital lowpass filter with a linear phase characteristic, we could not obtain such a filter by applying the bilinear transformation to an analog lowpass filter with a linear phase characteristic.

2.2.2 Computer-Aided Design of IIR Digital Filters

In the previous section we have seen that digital filters can be designed by transforming an appropriate analog filter design into a digital filter design. This approach is reasonable when we can take advantage of analog designs that are given in terms of formulas or extensive design tables, e. g., frequency-selective filters such as Butter-worth, Chebyshev, or elliptic filters.[5] In general, however, analytic formulas do not exist for the design of either analog or digital filters to match arbitrary frequency response specifications or other types of specifications. In these more general cases, design procedures have been developed that are algorithmic, generally relying on the use of a computer to solve sets of linear or nonlinear equations. In most cases the computer-aided design techniques apply equally well to the design of either analog or digital filters with only minor modification. Therefore, nothing is gained by first obtaining an analog design and then transforming this design to a digital filter.

Most algorithmic design procedures for IIR filters take the following form:

(1) $H(z)$ is assumed to be a rational function. It can be represented as a ratio of polynomials in z (or z^{-1}), as a product of numerator and denominator factors (zeros and poles), or as a product of second-order factors.

(2) The orders of the numerator and denominator of $H(z)$ are fixed.

(3) An ideal desired frequency response and a corresponding approximation error criterion is chosen.

(4) By a suitable optimization algorithm, the free parameters (numerator and denominator coefficients, zeros and poles, etc.) are varied in a systematic way to minimize the approximation error according to the assumed error criterion.

(5) The set of parameters that minimize the approximation error is the desired result.

2.2.3 Design of FIR Filters

In contrast to IIR filters, there is not available a set of continuous-time FIR design techniques that can be exploited in the design of discrete-time FIR filters. Consequently, FIR design is most typically carried out directly in the discrete-time domain.

The most straightforward approach to FIR filter design is to obtain a finite-length impulse response by truncating an infinite-duration impulse response sequence.[6] If we suppose that $H_d(\omega)$ is an ideal desired frequency response, then

$$H_d(\omega) = \sum_{n=-\infty}^{\infty} h_d(n)e^{-j\omega n} \qquad (5)$$

where $h_d(n)$ is the corresponding impulse response sequence, i.e.,

$$h_d(n) = \frac{1}{2\pi}\int_{-\pi}^{\pi} H_d(\omega)e^{-j\omega n}d\omega \qquad (6)$$

In general, $H_d(\omega)$ for a frequency-selective filter may be piecewise constant with discontinuities at the boundaries between bands. In such cases the sequence $h_d(n)$ is of infinite duration and it must be truncated to obtain a finite-duration impulse response $h(n)$. The truncation corresponds to representing $h(n)$ as the product of the desired impulse response and a finite-duration "window" $w(n)$, i.e.,

$$h(n) = h_d(n)w(n) \qquad (7)$$

Correspondingly, in the frequency domain.

$$H(\omega) = \frac{1}{2\pi}\int_{-\pi}^{\pi} H_d(\theta) W(\theta - \omega)\mathrm{d}\theta \qquad (8)$$

That is, $H(\omega)$ is the periodic convolution of the desired frequency response with the Fourier transform of the window. Thus the frequency response $H(\omega)$ will be a "smeared" version of the desired response $H_d(\omega)$.[7] The choice of the window is governed by the desire to have $w(n)$ as short as possible in duration so as to minimize computation in the implementation of the filter, while having $W(\omega)$ highly concentrated in the frequency domain so as to faithfully reproduce the desired frequency response. These are, of course, conflicting requirements. Examples of some commonly used windows are Hanning, Hamming, Blackman and Kaiser windows.

While FIR filters obtained by windowing are relatively easy to design, they are not optimum, i.e., do not have the minimum passband or stopband ripple for a given filter order and transition bandwidth. The Parks-McClellan algorithm provides a procedure for designing linear phase FIR filters that are optimal in the sense of minimizing the maximum weighted error over a specified set of frequency bands. The algorithm is based on expressing the frequency response of a linear phase FIR filter as a linear phase factor times a weighted trigonometric polynomial. For example, for a causal linear phase FIR filter of length $N = 2M + 1$, the impulse response has the symmetry property

$$h(n + M) = h(-n + M) \qquad (9)$$

and $H(\omega)$ is of the form

$$H(\omega) = e^{-j\omega M}\left[h(0) + \sum_{k=1}^{M} 2h(n)\cos(\omega n)\right] =$$

$$e^{-j\omega M}\left[\sum_{k=0}^{M} a_k(\cos\omega)^k\right] \tag{10}$$

Given the desired specifications for $|H(\omega)|$, determination of the coefficients a_k and equivalently the impulse response values $h(n)$ becomes a problem in polynomial approximation. An efficient algorithm to solve this polynomial approximation problem exists and is widely used to design optimal FIR filters.

2.2.4 Applications of filter

One of the most common problems in signal processing is to extract a desired signal from a noisy measured signal

$$x(n) = s(n) + v(n) \tag{11}$$

where $v(n)$ is the undesired noise component.

The noise signal $v(n)$ depends on the application. For example, it could be a white noise signal or a periodic interference signal.

The common method of extracting $s(n)$ from $x(n)$ is to design an appropriate filter $H(z)$ which removes the noise component $v(n)$ and lets the desired signal $s(n)$ go through unchanged.[8] According to linearity, we can express output signal due to the input of Eq . (11) in the form

$$y(n) = y_s(n) + y_v(n) \tag{12}$$

where $y_s(n)$ is the output due to $s(n)$ and $y_v(n)$ is the output due to $v(n)$.

The two design conditions for the filter are that $y_v(n)$ be as small as possible and $y_s(n)$ be as similar to $s(n)$ as possible. In general, these conditions cannot be satisfied simultaneously. To determine when they can be satisfied, we express them in the frequency domain in terms of the corresponding frequency spectra as follows: $Y_s(\omega) = S(\omega)$ and $Y_v(\omega) = 0$.

Applying the filtering equation $Y_s(\omega) = H(\omega)X(\omega)$ separately to the signal and noise components, we have the conditions

$$Y_s(\omega) = H(\omega)S(\omega) = S(\omega)$$
$$Y_v(\omega) = H(\omega)V(\omega) = 0 \tag{13}$$

The first requires that $H(\omega) = 1$ at all ω for which the signal spectrum is nonzero, $S(\omega) \neq 0$. The second requires that $H(\omega) = 0$ at all for which the noise spectrum is nonzero, $V(\omega) \neq 0$.

These two conditions can be met simultaneously only if the signal spectra do not overlap. In such cases, the filter $H(\omega)$ must have passband that coincides with the signal band, and stopband that coincides with the noise band.[9] The filter removes the noise spectrum and leaves the signal spectrum unchanged.

If the signal and noise spectra overlap, as is the typical case in practice, the above conditions cannot be satisfied simultaneously. In such cases, we must compromise between the two design conditions and trade off one for the other. Depending on the application, we may decide to design the filter to remove as much noise as possible, but at the expense of distorting the desired signal. Alternatively, we may decide to leave the desired signal as undistorted as possible, but at the expense of having some noise in the output.

The filter $H(\omega)$ is chosen to be an ideal lowpass filter with passband covering the signal bandwidth, say $0 \leqslant \omega \leqslant \omega_c$. The noise energy in the filter's stopband $\omega_c \leqslant \omega \leqslant \pi$ is removed completely by the filter, thus reducing the strength of the noise. The spectrum of the desired signal is not affected by the filter, but neither is the portion of the noise spectrum that falls within the signal band. Thus, some noise will survive the filtering process.

The amount of noise reduction achieved by this filter can be calculated using the noise reduction ratio (NRR). Denoting the input and output mean-square noise values by

$$\sigma_v^2 = E[v(n)^2]$$

and

$$\sigma_{y_v}^2 = E[y_v(n)^2]$$

we have $\text{NRR} = \dfrac{\sigma_{y_v}^2}{\sigma_v^2} = \displaystyle\int_{-\pi}^{\pi} |H(\omega)|^2 \dfrac{d\omega}{2\pi} = \sum_n h_n^2$ (14)

Because $H(\omega)$ is an ideal lowpass filter, the integration range collapses to the filter's passband, that is, $-\omega_c \leqslant \omega \leqslant \omega_c$. Over this range, the value of $H(\omega)$ is unity, giving

$$\text{NRR} = \frac{\sigma_{y_v}^2}{\sigma_v^2} = \int_{-\omega_c}^{\omega_c} \frac{1}{2\pi} d\omega = \frac{\omega_c}{\pi} \tag{15}$$

Next, we calculate the corresponding noise reduction ratios, discuss the tradeoff between transient response times and noise reduction and present some examples.

It is desired for first-order IIR smoother filter to extract a constant signal $s(n) = s$ from the noisy measured signal

$$x(n) = s(n) + v(n) = s + v(n) \tag{16}$$

where $v(n)$ is zero-mean white Gaussian noise of variance σ_v^2. Consider the following IIR lowpass filter

$$H(z) = \frac{b}{1 - az^{-1}}$$

$$|H(\omega)|^2 = \frac{b^2}{1 - 2a\cos\omega + a^2}$$

where the parameter a is restricted to the range $0 < a < 1$. Because the desired signal $s(n)$ is constant in time, the signal band will only be the DC frequency $\omega = 0$. We require, therefore, that the filter have unity response at $\omega = 0$ or equivalently at $z = 1$. This condition fixes the overall gain b of the filter

$$H(1) = \frac{b}{1-a} = 1 \Rightarrow b = 1 - a$$

The NRR of this filter can be calculated from Eq. (14) by summing the impulse response squared. Here, $h_n = ba^n u(n)$; therefore, using the geometric series, we find

$$\text{NRR} = \frac{\sigma_{y_v}^2}{\sigma_v^2} = \sum_n h_n^2 = b^2 \sum_{n=0}^{\infty} a^{2n} = \frac{b^2}{1-a^2} = \frac{1-a}{1+a} \quad (17)$$

This ratio is always less than one because a is restricted to $0 < a < 1$. To achieve high noise reduction, a must be chosen near one.

To understand how this filter works in the time domain and manages to reduce the noise, we rewrite the difference equation in its convolutional form

$$y(n) = b \sum_{m=0}^{n} a^m x(n - m) =$$
$$b[x(n) + ax(n-1) + a^2 x(n-2) + \cdots + a^n x(0)]$$

This sum corresponds to the accumulation or averaging of all the past samples up to the present time instant. As a result, the rapid fluctuations of the noise component $v(n)$ are averaged out. The closer is a to 1, the more equal weighting the terms get, resulting in more effective averaging of the noise. [10]

The problem of extracting a low-frequency signal $s(n)$ from the noisy signal $x(n) = s(n) + v(n)$ can also be approached with FIR filters. Consider the third-order filter

$$H(z) = h_0 + h_1 z^{-1} + h_2 z^{-2} + h_3 z^{-3} \quad (18)$$

The condition that the constant signal $s(n)$ go through the filter unchanged requires that the filter have unity gain at DC, which gives the constraint among the filter weights

$$H(1) = h_0 + h_1 + h_2 + h_3 = 1 \quad (19)$$

The NRR of this filter will be

$$\text{NRR} = \sum_n h_n^2 = h_0^2 + h_1^2 + h_2^2 + h_3^2 \tag{20}$$

The best third-order FIR filter will be the one that minimizes this NRR, subject to the lowpass constraint expressed in Eq. (19).[11] To solve this minimization problem, we use the constraint

$$h_3 = 1 - h_0 - h_1 - h_2$$

Substituting for h_3 in Eq. (20), we find

$$\text{NRR} = h_0^2 + h_1^2 + h_2^2 + (h_0 + h_1 + h_2 - 1)^2 \tag{21}$$

The minimization of this expression can be carried out easily by setting the partial derivatives of NRR to zero.[12] It follows that all four h's will be equal to each other, $h_0 = h_1 = h_2 = h_3$. But, because they must sum up to 1, we must have the optimum solution

$$h_0 = h_1 = h_2 = h_3 = \frac{1}{4}$$

and the minimized NRR becomes

$$\text{NRR}_{min} = 4 \cdot (\frac{1}{4})^2 = \frac{1}{4}$$

The I/O equation for this optimum smoothing filter becomes

$$y(n) = \frac{1}{4}[x(n) + x(n-1) + x(n-2) + x(n-3)]$$

More generally, the optimum length-N FIR filter with unity DC gain and minimum NRR is the filter with equal weights

$$h_n = \frac{1}{N}, n = 0, 1, \cdots, N-1 \tag{22}$$

and I/O equation

$$y(n) = \frac{1}{N}[x(n) + x(n-1) + x(n-2) + \cdots + x(n-N+1)] \tag{23}$$

Its NRR is

$$\text{NRR} = h_0^2 + h_1^2 + \cdots + h_{N-1}^2 = \frac{1}{N} \tag{24}$$

Thus, if N is large enough, the NRR can be made as small as desired.

Again, as the NRR decrease, the filter's time constant increase.

We note that the IIR smoother is very simple computationally, whereas the FIR smoother performs better in terms of both the NRR and the transient response. In the sense that for the same NRR value, the FIR smoother has shorter time constant, and for the same time constant, it has smaller NRR.

New Words and Phrases

depict	*v.*	描述
denote	*v.*	表示
stopband	*n.*	阻带
impose	*v.*	强加
stability	*n.*	稳定性
causality	*n.*	因果关系
prescribe	*v.*	指定
polynomial	*n.*	多项式
algorithm	*n.*	算法
iterative	*a.*	迭代的
classical	*a.*	经典的
approach	*n.*	方法
motivate	*v.*	激发
loosely	*adv.*	宽松地
map	*v.*	映射
bandlimit	*v.*	限带
aliasing	*n.*	混迭
negligibly	*adv.*	可忽略地
manifest	*v.*	出现,表明
analytic	*a.*	解析的
minor	*a.*	较小的
criterion	*n.*	准则

systematic	*a*.	系统的
straightforward	*a*.	直截了当的
truncate	*v*.	截断
window	*n*.	窗函数
smeared	*a*.	被模糊的
convolutional	*a*.	卷积的
trigonometric	*a*.	三角的
polynomial	*n*.	多项式
transient response		瞬态响应
geometric series		几何级数
edge frequency		截止频率
imaginary axis		虚轴
impulse invariant		冲激不变法
step response		阶跃响应
bilinear transformation		双线型变换
piecewise-constant magnitude		分段恒定幅度
computer-aided design		计算机辅助设计
rational function		有理函数
stopband ripple		阻带波纹
transition bandwidth		过渡带宽

Notes

1. Many filters used in practice are specified by such a tolerance scheme, with no constraints on phase response other than those imposed by stability and causality requirements; i. e., the poles of the system function must lie inside unit circle. 实际应用的很多滤波器都是指定一个容许的方案,不是约束相位响应而是要满足稳定性和因果性的要求,即系统函数的所有极点必须在单位圆内。

2. Given a set of specifications, the filter design problem becomes a problem in functional approximation to obtain a discrete-time linear system whose frequency response falls within the prescribed

tolerances. 给定一组规定参数,滤波器设计问题便成为获得一个频率响应落在指定容限内的离散时间线性系统的逼近问题。

3. However, in some filter design problems, a primary objective may be to control some aspect of the time response such as the impulse response or the step response. 然而,在一些滤波器设计问题中,主要的目的是控制时间响应的某个方面,如脉冲响应或阶跃响应。

4. Impulse invariant as a procedure for mapping analog filter designs to digital filter designs has the limitation that the analog filter must (at least approximately) have a bandlimited frequency response. 冲激不变法作为将模拟滤波器设计映射到数字滤波器设计的过程有着一定的限制,因为模拟滤波器必须(至少接近)具有有限的频率响应。

5. This approach is reasonable when we can take advantage of analog designs that are given in terms of formulas or extensive design table, e.g., frequency-selective filters such as Butterworth, Chebyshev, or elliptic filters. 当我们能利用根据公式或设计表格给定模拟设计方法时,如巴特沃斯、切比雪夫、椭圆滤波器等选频滤波器,这个方法是有道理的。

6. The most straightforward approach to FIR filter design is to obtain a finite-length impulse response by truncating an infinite-duration impulse response sequence. FIR 滤波器最直截了当的方法是截断无限长脉冲响应序列以获得有限长脉冲响应。

7. Thus the frequency response $H(\omega)$ will be a "smeared" version of the desired response $H_d(\omega)$. 这样频率响应 $H(\omega)$ 将是理想频率响应的一个被模糊了的形式 $H_d(\omega)$。

8. The common method of extracting $s(n)$ from $x(n)$ is to design an appropriate filter $H(z)$ which removes the noise component $v(n)$ and lets the desired signal $s(n)$ go through unchanged. 从 $x(n)$ 里面提取 $s(n)$ 的通常方法是设计一个适当的滤波器 $H(z)$,它能够移除噪声分量 $v(n)$,同时使需要的信号 $s(n)$ 无改变的通过。

9. In such cases, the filter $H(\omega)$ must have passband that coincides with the signal band, and stopband that coincides with the noise band. 在这种情况下,滤波器 $H(\omega)$ 的通带必须与信号频带相一致,其阻

带必须与噪声频带相一致。

10. The closer *a* is to 1, the more equal weighting the terms get, resulting in more effective averaging of the noise. *a* 越接近于 1,各项的加权就越平均,导致对噪声的平均更有效。

11. The best third-order FIR filter will be the one that minimizes this NRR, subject to the lowpass constraint expressed in Eq .(19). 最佳的三阶滤波器就是能够使这个 NRR 最小,同时满足式(19)的低通约束条件。

12. The minimization of this expression can be carried out easily by setting the partial derivatives of NRR to zero. 这个表达式的最小值可以通过令 NRR 的偏导数等于 0 而很容易的计算出来。

2.3 IMAGE ENHANCEMENT

2.3.1 Introduction

Image enhancement and restoration techniques are designed to improve the quality of an image as perceived by a human. In recent years enhancement has come to describe those techniques that work well as judged by human observers even though the mathematical criteria are not completely understood. For example, rectification of a geometrically distorted image produces an obvious improvement in quality to a human observer. No objective measure of this quality improvement has yet been discovered. Image restoration is applied to the restoration of a known distortion for which an objective criterion can be applied.[1]

Contrast enhancement techniques are described in this section. Very effective techniques require only simple piecewise linear or nonlinear transformations. A novel technique, which is based upon a mapping of the gray levels to achieve a uniform distribution, is next considered. The generalization of this method to permit the specification of the enhanced image histogram is also considered.

Contrast generally refers to a difference in luminance or gray level values in some particular region of an image function. If we assume that the values of $f(x,y)$ correspond to luminance values at the point (x, y), then we imply that it is a real-valued, nonnegative function, since light intensity cannot be negative. The range of $f(x,y)$ will be assumed to be finite, i.e., $[m,M]$, and large values of $f(x,y)$ will correspond to bright points.

A reversed situation arises when considering photographic transparencies, if the image function values are directly related to optical density. Recall that the film intensity transmittance function $t(x,y)$ was defined as the local average of the ratio of light intensity transmitted to the intensity incident, and clearly, $0 \leqslant t(x,y) \leqslant 1$. In the development of a photographic transparency, the areas exposed to light turn into silver metal and thus are opaque. Since the optical density was defined as the negative logarithm of the transmittance, i.e.,

$$D(x,y) = -\lg t(x,y) \tag{1}$$

then

$$0 \leqslant D(x,y) \leqslant \infty$$

Thus, density values near zero correspond to clear areas and large density values correspond to dark regions on the transparency. Since neither photographic films, the human visual system, nor image displays have perfectly symmetrical responses, the reversal of dark and light areas or negative process may be used for enhancing information.

For any given imaging system, only a finite luminance or optical density range will be available. An image function, $f(x,y)$, describing either situation would thus have a finite maximum and minimum. The difference between the maximum and minimum values of $f(x,y)$ is called the contrast range and is an important parameter for any imaging system. The ratio of the maximum to the minimum values is called the contrast ratio and is also a commonly used parameter. For example, film with an optical density contrast range between 0.1 and 1.0 is transparent in normal light, but one with a density range between 10 and 100 is almost totally opaque. Each has a contrast ratio of 10.

In optical systems, contrast is defined for spatial frequency gratings as

$$C = (M - m)/(M + m) \qquad (2)$$

We may alter the gray level values and thus change the contrast of the information in an image by effecting a linear or nonlinear transformation, i.e., by forming a new image function, $g(x, y) = T[f(x, y)]$ for each (x, y), where T is some mapping. We will first consider position invariant transformations that may be characterized by a transfer function. Furthermore, we will assume an ideal, unity transfer function scanning and display system, except when otherwise noted, for compensation transformations.[2]

2.3.2 Scaling Transformation—Linear

A simple but useful model is the scaling transform. Suppose we have a digital image for which the contrast values do not fill the available contrast range. That is, suppose our data cover a range (m, M), but that the available range is (n, N). Then the linear transformation

$$g(x, y) = \{[f(x, y) - m]/(M - m)\}[N - n] + n$$

expands the values over the available range.

This transformation is often necessary when an image has been scanned, since the image scanner may not have been adjusted to use its full dynamic range.

Let us now assume that the input image function f and the output image function g are continuous random variables with probability distribution $p_f(x)$ and $p_g(y)$, respectively. Then, if the input probability distribution is known and zero outside the range $[m, M]$ and the system is linear, it is easy to determine the output probability distribution. Since the output distribution is of exactly the same form as in the input distribution.

$$F_g(y) = \text{Prob}(g \leqslant y) =$$
$$\text{Prob}\{f \leqslant [(y - n)/(N - n)](M - m) + m\} =$$
$$\begin{cases} 0, & x < m, \\ F_f(x), & m < x < M, \\ 1, & x > M. \end{cases} \quad (3)$$

Now suppose that the transfer function is linear over the range (m, M), but that the input distribution is not restricted to this range, and a clipping procedure as shown in Fig.2.5 is used.

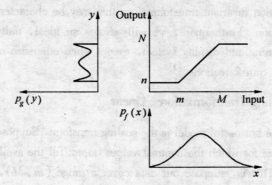

Fig.2.5 Clipping procedure

For this situation, the output distribution is

$$F_g(y) = \begin{cases} \int_{-\infty}^{m} p_f(x)\,dx & \text{if} \quad y = n, \\ F_f(x) & \text{if} \quad n < y < N, \\ \int_{M}^{\infty} p_f(x)\,dx & \text{if} \quad y = N. \end{cases} \quad (4)$$

Thus the output distribution is not identical to the input distribution but has "spikes" at the extreme values. Since the clipping procedure is used on most image scanners, it is important to recognize the results of this procedure.

As a final example, let us consider the underuse of the dynamic range. For this situation, the same scaling transformation is used, but we assume that the maximum output used N is less than that available A. Again, the probability distribution of the output is of exactly the same form as the input. However, if the output function is now quantized with the number of quantization levels set for the range (n, A), an extremely coarse quantization and subsequent false contouring may result.

Let us now consider the mapping of output image values g into digital image values $\hat{g}$ for three cases of exact over- and underuse of the input dynamic range. The quantization process for case 1 produces an ideal di-gital approximation to the continuous probability function. For case 2, the spikes on the continuous probability function are also mapped into spikes in the discrete probability function, while for case 3, a coarse quantization occurs. Since we have noted that the quantization noise for a linear quantization is approximately uniformly distributed, the underuse of the available dynamic range also produces a much larger level of quantization noise than is necessary.

At this point, we may say that case 1 is one ideal or preferred situation. Case 2 is undesirable because a distortion of the image information is produced. Although case 3 produces a coarser quantization and larger quantization noise than necessary, it is preferable to case 2. This analysis is based on the assumption that the input is useful information.

2.3.3 Piecewise-Linear Transformations for Contrast Enhancement

A piecewise-linear transformation is often useful for contrast enhancement.[3] For example, a three-step piecewise-linear transfer function between the input and the output is shown in Fig.2.6.

As a practical example of the usefulness of this transformation, let us assume that the input image contains scratches and black emulsion blobs in addition to the useful image information. For this situation, the piecewise linear clipping transformation may be preferable to the linear transformation, since it localizes the noise information to the extreme values and provides a linear mapping of the useful information. A nonlinear digital smoothing

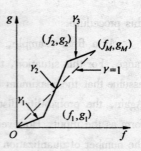

Fig.2.6 **Three-step piecewise linear transfer**

operation that maps the extreme values into the local average of the neighboring points would now eliminate the effects of the scratches and emulsion blobs.

This function is defined by

$$
g = \begin{cases} \gamma_1 f + b_1; & 0 \leq f < f_1; \quad \gamma_1 = g_1/f_1, \ b_1 = 0, \\[2mm] \gamma_2 f + b_2; & f_1 \leq f < f_2; \quad \gamma_2 = \dfrac{g_2 - g_1}{f_2 - f_1}, b_2 = g_1 - f_1\gamma_2, \\[2mm] \gamma_3 f + b_3; & f_2 \leq f \leq f_M; \quad \gamma_3 = \dfrac{g_M - g_2}{f_M - f_2}, b_3 = g_2 - f_2\gamma_3. \end{cases}
$$

$$(5)$$

Note that this mapping may also be used to compress the values below f_1 and linearly map the values between f_2 and f_M. Thus the range of values between f_1 and f_2 is expanded.

If a segment slope is less than unity, the image contrast information in that range is compressed; if the slope is greater than unity, the image contrast information is enhanced. The input density break points b_1 and b_2 and the segment slopes γ_1, γ_2, and γ_3 may often be selected in a reasonable manner from observation of the gray level histogram.[4] If the histogram is of a Gaussian nature with low-level noise and perhaps a dark peak due to an undesirable image edge, then the break points may be determined by selecting a probability threshold T.[5] This threshold may be based on an estimate of the amount of low-level noise. If the information contained in the very low-and high-density regions is completely noise, the slopes γ_1 and γ_3 should be set equal to zero. This procedure will expand the contrast range of the information. If it is likely that some useful information may be visible in these extreme regions, then small nonzero values of γ_1 and γ_3 may be used; however, the image contrast range will not be changed. There is another desirable histogram situation. If the image information is made of a mixture of three components each of which has a Gaussian distribution, then the break points may be selected at the maximum likelihood thresholds between the distributions.[6] If the density functions are not known, then the minimum values between the modes are reasonable breakpoints. The slopes γ_1 and γ_3 may be chosen proportional to the probability of useful information being contained in the region.

Another method for selecting the breakpoints is from consideration of the effects on low-and high-contrast edge information. With γ_2 greater than unity, the most likely low contrast edges are greatly enhanced while the most likely high contrast edges are only partially compressed.[7] Finally, a practical situation for which this transformation is useful arises when a scratched transparency is scanned. The useful information may have a Gaussian distribution, but the scratch, because of its 100% transmittance, will produce a peak in the histogram on the dark side. A suitable choice of the breakpoint b_2 and a slope γ_3 equal to zero will move the peak to the position of b_2. Alternative solutions are to set these values equal to the average input value or to use a smoothing procedure.

2.3.4 Logarithmic Transformation

A very useful nonlinear mapping is represented by $g(x, y) = \lg f(x, y)$, $f(x, y) > 0$. A graph of this relationship is shown in Fig. 2.7.

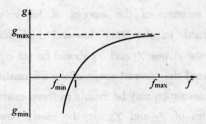

Fig.2.7　Logarithmic transformation

This transformation expands the contrast of the small values of f and compresses the large values. Also note that the shape of this curve can be changed considerably by changing the values of f_{min} and f_{max}.

The log transformation has several desirable effects.

(1) It makes the gray levels relate linearly to optical density rather than film transmittance or intensity. Suppose the film transmittance function is $t(x,y)$. Then the density function is

$$D(x,y) = -\lg t(x,y)$$

If the transparency is illuminated by a unit amplitude, uniform plane wave, the transmitted luminance $l(x,y)$ is

$$l(x,y) = t(x,y)$$

If this luminance signal is linearly converted into an electronic signal $e(x,y)$, then

$$e(x,y) = kt(x,y)$$

If this electronic signal is linearly converted to a displayed luminance $d(x,y)$, then

$$d(x,y) = Ct(x,y) = C\varepsilon^{-D(x,y)}$$

Thus, displayed luminance is related exponentially to film density. If one inserts a log amplifier circuit, an electronic signal $E(x,y)$, where

$$E(x,y) = \ln e(x,y)$$

will be produced. However, the displayed luminance

$$d(x,y) = C\ln(x,y) = CD(x,y)$$

is linearly related to film density and the displayed strips will have equal widths.

(2) It makes the low-contrast detail more visible by enhancing low-contrast edges.

(3) It provides a constant signal-to-noise ratio for quantization noise.

(4) It somewhat matches the response of the human visual system (HVS).

(5) It usually provides a more equal distribution of gray levels.

(6) It transforms multiplicative noise into additive noise.

Because of these considerations, the log operations have become a standard option on most scanning equipment. They are also easily implemented in hardware with an operational amplifier with a transistor in the feedback loop.

2.3.5 Exponential Transformation

Another nonlinear transformation that has been used mainly in conjunction with the logarithmic transformation in multiplicative filtering operations is the exponential transformation. To obtain a unity transfer function system in which a log transformation is used in the input, an exponential operation must be used in the output.

The effect of the exponential transfer function on edges in an image is to compress low-contrast edges while expanding high-contrast edges. This generally produces an image with less visible detail than the original and this is not a desirable image enhancement transformation.[8] However, an important feature of the exponential transformation is that the result is always nonnegative.

2.3.6 Histogram Equalization

We have seen that the logarithmic transformation generally expands a peaky input probability distribution into a broader output distribution. For example, the log normal distribution is transformed into a normal distribution. The broader output distribution results mainly from the expansion of low-contrast information, and thus the log image has enhanced low-contrast detail.

We may expand the concept of transforming the image probability function in a systematic manner by reviewing a basic theorem from probability theory.

1. Theorem

Let X be an absolutely continuous random variable with range ($a \leqslant X \leqslant b$), and distribution function $F(x) = \text{Prob}(X \leqslant x)$. Then the random variable defined by

$$Y = F_X(X)$$

has a uniform $(0,1)$ distribution, i.e.,

$$F_Y(y) = \begin{cases} 1, & 1 \leqslant y, \\ y, & 0 \leqslant y < 1, \\ 0, & y < 0. \end{cases} \tag{6}$$

The proof is direct: since F_X is continuous,

$$F_Y(y) = \text{Prob}[F_X(X) \leqslant y],$$

$$F_Y(y) = y, \quad \text{for } 0 \leqslant y \leqslant 1.$$

If $F_X(y)$ is not absolutely continuous, it may contain jumps. Then Prob $[F_X(X) \leqslant y]$ may have many values and the theorem does not hold.

The theorem states that any absolutely continuous random variable may be transformed into a uniformly distributed random variable.[9] Since the theorem does not hold if X is not absolutely continuous, the use of this transformation for digital image functions is based on the approximation of an absolutely continuous function by a finely quantized function.[10] We may clarify this approximation by the following extension.

2. *Lemma*

Let X be a discrete random variable with values

$$x_i = (b - a)i/N + a, \quad i = 0, \ldots, N,$$

i.e., $a \leqslant x_i \leqslant b$ and distribution function $F_X(x) = \text{Prob}(X \leqslant x)$, which is a jump function with maximum jump equal to ε. That is,

$$\max_i [F(x_{i+1}) - F(x_i)] = \varepsilon, \quad i = 1, 2, \ldots, N.$$

Then the discrete random variable Y, defined by $Y = F_X(X)$, has an approximately uniform distribution in the sense that

$$F_Y(y) = 1, \quad 1 \leqslant y,$$
$$F_Y(y) = 0, \quad y \leqslant 0,$$

and

$$y - F_Y(y) \leqslant \varepsilon, \quad 0 < y < 1.$$

The proof is again direct. Since X is discrete, Y is also a discrete random variable with values $y_i = F_X(x_i), i = 0, 1, \ldots, N$, e.g., $y_0 = F_X(x_0) = F(a)$ and $y_N = F_X(x_N) = F(b) = 1$. $F_X(a) \leqslant y_i \leqslant 1$. Since the mapping is one to one, the probability function of Y is equal to the probability function of X, which is equal to the jump at x_i, i.e.,

$$g_Y(y_i) = g_X(x_i) = y_i - y_{i-1}, \quad i = 0, 1, \ldots, N - 1,$$

where for convenience we define $y_{-1} = 0$.

Now the distribution function of Y at any jump point of y_i is simply

$$F_Y(y_i) = \sum_{j=0}^{i} g_Y(y_j) = \sum_{j=0}^{i} (y_j - y_{j-1}), \tag{7}$$

which is a telescoping sum and reduces to

$$F_Y(y_i) = y_i - y_{i-1} + y_{i-1} - y_{i-2} + \cdots + y_0 = y_i.$$

For any value $y_i \leqslant y \leqslant y_{i+1}$, we have

$$F_Y(y) = \sum_{j=0}^{y_i \leqslant y} (y_j - y_{j-1}) \leqslant y_i \leqslant y \leqslant y_{i+1}, \tag{8}$$

so

$$y_i - F_Y(y) \leqslant y - F_Y(y) \leqslant y_{i+1} - F_Y(y).$$

The smallest value of $y_i - F_Y(y)$ occurs when $y = y_i$, and the largest value of $y_{i+1} - F_Y(y)$ occurs when $y = y_i$. Thus,

$$0 \leqslant y - F(y) \leqslant y_{i+1} - y_1 \leqslant \varepsilon$$

since the jumps are bounded by ε.

Since this inequality holds for any subinterval $[y_i, y_{i+1}]$ in the interval $[0, 1]$, we have $y - f(y) \leqslant \varepsilon$. [11]

This theorem simply states that if we approximate a continuous distribution so that the largest jump is ε, then the distribution transformation produces a distribution which differs from a uniform distribution by at most ε. Clearly, as ε is made smaller, the distribution more closely approximates the uniform distribution.

For many classes of images, the "ideal" distribution of gray levels is a uniform distribution, and the above theorem shows us how to obtain a uniform distribution with a gray level transformation. In general, a uniform distribution of gray levels makes equal use of each quantization level and tends to enhance low-contrast information. To use this transformation, we may

(1) compute the histogram of the image gray level values,

(2) add up the histogram values to obtain a distribution curve, and

(3) use this distribution curve for the gray level transformation $g = D(f)$.

Several other points about the computer implementation of the distribution transform should be noted. First, note that although the input random variable X took on equispaced values on the interval $[a, b]$, the random variable Y does not in general take on equispaced values on the interval $[0, 1]$. That is, a scaling transformation must be performed to obtain the same contrast range $[a, b]$. Also, if the X values are coarsely quantized before scaling, then a large reduction in the number of distinct gray levels may occur because the transformed values are closely spaced. [12] We have found the approximation to work very well if the input image has from 512 to 1 024 distinct gray level values. Also, since the human visual system can distinguish less than 64 distinct gray level values, some reduction in the number of distinct gray level values is permissible. The effect of the transformation may be increased by reducing the number of distinct levels in the distribution curve.

Finally, although this transformation is very effective for enhancing low-contrast detail, it does not discriminate between low-contrast information and noise.

A numerical example will now be given to illustrate the computational procedure for histogram equalization. Consider the simple 8×8, eight gray level image. The first step is to compute the histogram of the image. The number of occurrences may then be divided by the total number of pixels to produce relative frequency values. The gray level value, number of occurrences and relative frequencies are shown in the first three columns of Table 2.1. The next step is to compute the empirical distribution function by accumulating the relative frequency values. The distribution function is computed by

$$y_I = F_x(x_I) = \sum_{i=0}^{I} p(x_i). \qquad (9)$$

The values of this function are also shown in Table 2.1. This is the desired mapping function except for scaling. Since the original gray level values are integers and the distribution function varies between 0 and 1, some method of scaling must be used. Also, for display the output gray levels should be integers. One solution to the scaling is to first convert the input gray levels to normalized values that range between 0 and 1. This may be accomplished by simply dividing by the maximum gray level value since the minimum is 0.

$$x_I = \frac{1}{7} I. \qquad (10)$$

These values, which are also shown in Table 2.1, may then be mapped directly using the distribution mapping. For example, $x_I = 0.143$ maps into $y_I = 0.125$, etc. The resulting y_I values must now be scaled to the integer range of the input. This is accomplished by the *scaling operation*

$$J = \text{Int}[7(y_J - 0.125)/0.875 + 0.5], \qquad (11)$$

where Int is the integer truncation function and 0.5 has been added to provide symmetrical rounding. The scaled output values are shown in Table 2.1.

Table 2.1　Histogram equalization procedure

I^a	$x_I = I/7^b$	n_i^c	$p(x_I) = P(I)^d$	$y_I = F_x(x_I)^e$	J^f	$P(J)^g$
0	0.000	8	0.125	0.125	0	0.125
1	0.143	0	0.0	0.125	0	0.0
2	0.286	0	0.0	0.125	0	0.0
3	0.429	0	0.0	0.125	0	0.0
4	0.571	31	0.484	0.609	4	0.484
5	0.714	16	0.250	0.859	6	0.250
6	0.857	8	0.125	0.984	7	0.141
7	1.000	1	0.016	1.000	7	–

[a] Original gray level values.

[b] Scaled values.

[c] Number of occurrences.

[d] Relative frequencies.

[e] Distribution function.

[f] Scaled output gray levels.

[g] Relative frequencies of equalized gray levels.

New Words and Phrases

accomplish	$v.$	完成
clipping	$n.$	剪切
coarse	$a.$	粗糙的
deviation	$n.$	背离

discriminate	v.	区别
distinguish	v.	分辨
eliminate	v.	消除
empirical	a.	经验的
emulsion	n.	感光乳剂
enhancement	n.	增强
equispaced	a.	平均分布的
expose	v.	使曝光
extreme	a.	尽头的
grating	n.	光栅
histogram	n.	直方图
inequality	n.	不等式
judge	v.	鉴定,判断
jump	n.	阶跃
localize	v.	使局部化
luminance	n.	亮度
occurrence	n.	出现
opaque	a.	不透明的
perceive	v.	感知
photographic	a.	照相的
pixel	n.	象素
profile	n.	轮廓
rectification	n.	矫正
restoration	n.	恢复
reversal	n.	颠倒,反转
reversed	a.	相反的
scratch	n.	刮痕
slope	n.	斜坡
smooth	n. v.	平滑
spatial	a.	空间的

symmetrical	*a.*	对称的
threshold	*n.*	门限
transmittance	*n.*	透明性,传递函数
transparency	*n.*	幻灯片,透明度
truncation	*n.*	截断
underuse	*n.*	使用不足
contrast ratio		对比度
dynamic range		动态范围
empirical distribution function		经验分布函数
exponential transformation		指数转换
false contour		伪轮廓
feedback loop		反馈环
human visual system		人的视觉系统
intensity modulation		亮度调制
log normal distribution		对数正态分布
logarithmic transformation		对数转换
maximum likelihood threshold		最大似然门限
objective criterion		客观准则
operational amplifier		运算放大器
probability distribution		概率分布
quantization noise		量化噪声
random variable		随机变量
uniform $(0,1)$ distribution		0 到 1 上的均匀分布

Notes

1. Image restoration is applied to the restoration of a known distortion for which an objective criterion can applied. 图像恢复是应用客观准则恢复一个已知失真的图像。

2. Furthermore, we will assume an ideal, unity transfer function scanning and display system, except when otherwise noted, for compensation transformations. 进一步,除非特别指出,我们还假定作补偿变换的是一

个具有理想的、单位的传输函数的浏览和显示系统。

3. A piecewise-linear transformation is often useful for contrast enhancement. 分段线性变换常用于对比度变换。

4. The input density break points b_1 and b_2 and the segment slopes $\gamma_1^{'}$, γ_2 and γ_3 may often be selected in a reasonable manner from observation of the gray level histogram. 输入密度函数的断点 b_1, b_2 和斜率 γ_1, γ_2 和 γ_3 通常用观察灰度直方图的方法来合理地选择。

5. If the histogram is of a Gaussian nature with low-level noise and perhaps a dark peak due to an undesirable image edge, then the break points may be determined by selecting a probability threshold T. 如果直方图具有高斯特性、带有低噪声并且在不理想的图像边缘有较暗的峰值,这时将选择一个概率门限 T 来确定断点。

6. If the image information is made of mixture of three components each of which has a Gaussian distribution, then the break points may be selected at the maximum likelihood thresholds between the distributions. 如果图像信息是由三个部分混合而成,而每部分都具有高斯分布,那么将在各个分布之间用最大似然门限确定断点。

7. With γ_2 greater than unity, the most likely low contrast edges are greatly enhanced while the most likely high contrast edges are only partially compressed. 当 γ_2 大于单位值,最有可能的是低端对比度大大增强,而高端对比度仅有部分压缩。

8. This generally produces an image with less visible detail than the original and thus is not a desirable image enhancement transformation. 一般来讲这样产生的图像的细节要比原始图像差,因此不是一个理想的图像增强变换。

9. The theorem states that any absolutely continuous random variable may be transformed into a uniformly distributed random variable. 这个定理说明任何绝对连续的随机变量都可能转换成均匀分布的随机变量。

10. Since the theorem does not hold if X is not absolutely continuous, the use of this transformation for digital image functions is based on

the approximation of an absolutely continuous function by a finely quantized function. 由于当 X 不是绝对连续时该定理并不成立,对数字图像函数做这个变换是基于用非常小间隔的量化函数对绝对连续函数的逼近。

11. Since this inequality holds for any subinterval $[y_i, y_{I+1}]$ in the interval $[0,1]$, we have $y = f(y) \leqslant \varepsilon$. 由于这个不等式对区间$[0,1]$上的任意子区间$[y_i, y_{I+1}]$都成立,得到 $y = f(y) \leqslant \varepsilon$。

12. Also, if the X values are coarsely quantized before scaling, then a large reduction in the number of distinct gray level occur because the transformed values are closely spaced. 同样,如果 X 值在变换比例之前粗量化,由于被变换的值分布在很近的区段,那么灰度值的数量将大大减少。

2.4　DATA BASE

2.4.1　DATA

The overall objective of the Data Base Management System is to control and use data effectively. Therefore, an important purpose of this introduction is to review what data is and how it may be used.

Data is a representation of the real world. We can't expect it to represent the entire world. Only the portion of particular interest to one or more applications is represented. One portion of the real world containing individuals of a like type is called a population. The population consists of individuals. An individual may be one of a group of people, as in a personnel application where the individuals of the population consist of employees.

Individuals may be entities or objects rather than people. Thus, for an accounts receivable application, individuals are companies, the account, the client. For an inventory application, the individuals are parts for which we wish to assure that there is a minimum number in stock.

Each individual has properties, some of which are of interest to us and some of which are not. A personnel file might record an employee's height, weight, sex, hair color and so forth, but not his car type nor his bank account number.

Then data is a representation in the computer of a portion of the real world called the population and describes certain properties of the individual members of this population.

Let us review terms which describe units of data. For this introduction, the discussion is oversimplified to the situation which prevailed before the advent of data bases but is put into perspective shortly. The units of data are presented in Fig. 2.8, where we see an individual in his population. The individual has characteristics called attributes. An example is an attribute named HEIGHT. An attribute name is the name of an attribute which is described in the data base, or file— in this case, HEIGHT. In the figure the individual has a height described as 5'10". We say that 5'10" is the attribute value.

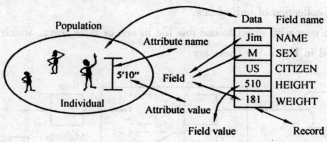

Fig. 2.8   Data quanta and their relation to the population

Corresponding to each attribute of interest there is a quantity of data called the field. For this field, there is a field name and a field value. The field name, often the same as the attribute name (but it need not be), helps us refer to this field. The field value is some representation, appearing in the field, which might be binary, decimal, hexadecimal, etc., of the original attribute value for this individual.

Fig. 2. 8 shows a collection of all applicable fields for one individual, called a record. The record, therefore, is a collection of field values for a single individual. Field names are not usually contained in the record; we use them to identify and refer to fields.

Before the advent of data bases each user or user group "owned" and was responsible for his own data and for keeping it up to date.[1] The important thing to recognize about a population is that it changes in several ways which we shall examine. There is hardly a population of importance which does not change in some way; one which does not change at all is called an archive.[2] If we use an obsolete representation of today's population, processing this data will produce erroneous results. Therefore, it is important that the representation be as current as possible.

We have called a collection of individuals a population. For each individual there is a record and there should be as many records as individuals. This collection of records is called the file to distinguish it from the collection of individuals.

The user may select to use this file in one of three ways, which are illustrated in Fig.2.9. These are:

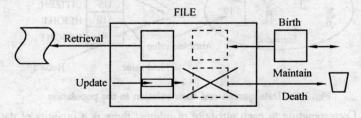

Fig.2.9 Functions performed on the file

• **Retrieve**—examine one or more records to extract information but not otherwise affect the record of the file;

- **Post**—alter a *record* because the individual has changed and the record should now reflect the altered attributes of the individual;

- **Maintain**—not only do individuals change but so does the population, by the addition and deletion of individuals—so maintenance alters the *file* to reflect the alteration in the population.

For retrieval a user needs information about one or more records. For instance, an account holder may wish to know the current balance in his account. This access to the account holder's record does not alter the record in any way. Information is copied from the record, formated and printed or displayed to the user.

To post or modify a file, the system is informed of which individuals have incurred a change, which attributes have changed and what the new values are for these attributes. Posting then consists of finding a record for an individual for which a change has occurred in one of his attribute values and replacing old field values with new field values, representations of the new attribute values. This is shown in Fig.2.9 in the center. Posting, according to this definition, changes records, not files.

Maintenance means adding or deleting records from the file rather than simply altering some of the records which comprise the file. Consider the employees on our staff. These employees come and go as they are hired and fired. We need new records for hired employees; we can (sometimes) dispose of records for employees that have departed. Maintenance consists of adding (birth) or deleting (death) these records to or from our file to perceive an altered population.

File design depends not only on the kind of activities needed but also upon the point in time when each needs to be done. When a number of requests for access to a file are saved and grouped together to be handled at one time, this is called batch processing.[3] The file is processed at certain times only, and may be unavailable at other times.

In contrast there is real time processing. When a savings account holder requests his balance, we give him an immediate answer—the file is always available. Some activities may use batch processing while others use real time processing; whenever a request appears it is immediately scheduled to be acted upon—it is not saved.

Thus for a banking application, retrieval may use real time processing, while updating and maintaining may be done daily on a batch basis.

A second feature of importance is the frequency of use. This is applicable in batch processing where a file need be available only when it is in use.

Finally, there is the activity ratio or turnover which describes the percentage of the file involved in batch processing each time the file is put into use.

2.4.2 APPLICATIONS

1. *The Application*

An application is some instance when one or more than one file is used. The use may be retrieval, posting, maintenance or creation. An application requires the presence of a program which controls the computer; it provides instructions for whatever actions place the data in the new required state. This program is generally written by a programmer in a procedure oriented language (POL), sometimes called a compiler language. Before the program can run, it must be translated into machine language and debugged.

When a data base management system (DBMS) is in use, again, there is a need to access files. However, many DBMS's have a built-in facility so that unsophisticated users can "talk" directly to them without writing a program. This facility is called a query processing facility. Here DBMS accepts the user's request directly and provides answers directly to him.

Hereafter, when we refer to an application, and we will do that often, we refer to the use of one or more files which require the writing of a program. This program is called the application program.

A terminal application program accesses, posts, modifies or creates files through the database and has the additional properties that it can communicate with an on-line user by means of one or more terminals. Thus the data retrieved by the terminal application program may be sent to a viewer via the terminal. The operator may also enter data directly at the terminal. The terminal program is written by an application programmer. It is separate and apart from any query processing facility that the DBMS may provide. This facility is discussed later.

We now continue to examine files, discussing the file group and the file family initially in the nonDBMS environment. In this way we clarify the structures before viewing them in the DBMS environment.

2. *File Group*

Most application programs, other than those designed for simple retrieval, require several files. Each file represents a population of a different sort. For instance, a program to control inventory generally contains three files:

• the stock file represents the stock currently on hand—one record describes each item and indicates the number of parts that can be found and on which shelf;

• the vendor file describes the vendor population—each record describes a vendor which sells one or more of the inventory items;

• the purchase order file describes purchase orders issued to vendors for stock which is in low supply.

The application program activates a file directly. The physical manifestation of the file is its occurrence upon a volume mounted upon a device.[4] The application program activates the computer, causing the device to position the volume and thus gain access to the file. Whenever access is needed, a large number of contingencies arise requiring the writing of a major piece of code. This code can be replaced by a single module usually supplied by the computer manufacturer which we refer to as the Access Method. Hereafter we see the application program as activating the Access Method, which is responsible for managing the file.

Fig. 2. 10 displays this schematically. The application program is connected to three Access Method modules. Each module is in charge of a single file. The files shown as rectangles in the figure are encircled to indicate that they form a file group. A line joins each file to a circle which stands for the population that the file represents. These three circles are also encircled to indicate that they form a population group. In our inventory example, the populations are the stock reports, the vendor information and the purchase orders.

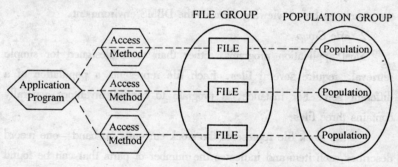

Fig. 2. 10   The application program

We shall see later how the DBMS gives the application program a unified view of all the pictured files. This view is called the subschema or external model. The program works with this single representation of the data instead of three or more files as formerly.

3. *Application Family*

It is rare that a commercial data processing problem can be handled completely and properly by a single application program. Most commercial applications have many files, representing many populations, and several application programs are provided to do the whole job.

Fig. 2. 11 illustrates this. A tangible example is forthcoming subsequently. In the figure we see three application programs, as conveyed by the hexagons. These programs comprise the application family.

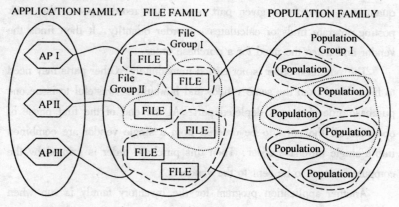

Fig. 2. 11   File family and population family

Each application program has a set of files that it works with its file group. These file groups may overlap, as shown in the figure; one file may be associated with two or more application groups.

The collection of these files is called the file family. The file family is then defined as containing a set of files where each file is used by some application program in the application family.

Each file corresponds to and represents a population. Then, clearly, there is a group of populations called the population family which corresponds to the file family.

Consider the inventory example. We have examined earlier the stock posting application program. This is only one of the activities required of the inventory family.

For the stock posting activity, one input is a stock change file. It contains a description of how many items of each kind were physically removed from stock during the posting period. Deliveries were also made to the plant during this period. They are recorded and entered into the system. The stock posting program posts each part record according to the number of parts withdrawn from stock or put on the shelf. When the quantity on hand for a given part reaches the reorder point, the stock posting program finds or calculates a reorder quantity. It then finds the vendor and notes the need for a purchase order.

The purchase order is not issued immediately. Other parts may need to be ordered from the same vendor and it would be wasteful to issue one purchase order for each depleted part. At the end of the first phase of operation all the parts to be ordered from a single vendor are combined into a single purchase order. Then this purchase order is printed by the computer system to be sent to the vendor.

Another application program for the inventory family is run when shipments are received. The items are put into stock and the stock receivable application program goes to work. It correlates the shipping invoice with the purchase order and the report from the stock clerk who has placed the item on the shelf.

Eventually the company is billed for the stock received. During this third phase the bill is correlated with the invoice for the merchandise received and the purchase order originally sent to the vendor. It should be remembered that we don't always get what we order. Some of the merchandise is back-ordered; some merchandise is shipped in quantities less than or greater than that in the original order. As an example of the latter, if we order 100 units, we may be delivered a gross of the item because they are packed in one gross containers.

Finally, shown at the bottom of the figure, is a reconciliation program which matches up the checks issued against the bank statement, to make sure that the company's bank balance has been correctly figured.

4. *Relations*

The application family deals with many populations. Individuals in different populations or, sometimes, within the same population relate to each other with respect to one or more of these applications. What is a "relation"?

A relation is a quality which binds together two or more individuals. Let us itemize a few of the relations which prevail among individuals in the inventory example:

(1) A bin holds parts for storage.

(2) A vendor sells parts to us.

(3) A purchase order requests sale and shipment of several different parts.

(4) An invoice heralds the arrival of a shipment and perhaps a nonshipment (back order).

(5) A bill requests payment for one or more shipments.

(6) A check provides payment for one or more bills.

(7) A statement confirms payment of one or more checks.

The *relation* should be clear in each of these statements for it binds together: *bin* and *part* for(1); *vendor* and *part* for(2); etc.

2.4.3 Need for the Data Base System

1. *Coordination within an Application Family*

First consider the problem of file handling. For the files of the application family where no DBMS is present, each application program is separate and distinct. There is no coordination between application programs in the same family. Usually, though not always, application programs are run at different times. Even when two applications are running concurrently under multiprogramming, no coordination is possible.

We have seen how two application programs may have recourse to the same file. In the inventory example of the last section, the purchase order file is needed by three different programs:

- The purchase order is first created by the stock posting program and a record describing it is placed in the purchase order file.

- The stock receivable program is informed when some or all of the merchandise ordered is received and notes this on the purchase order file.

- The accounts receivable program determines that merchandise ordered and received has been paid for and is thus on the purchase order file.

Not only may a single file have multiple users, but each user may have different needs with respect to a file record. That is, different attributes of the same individual are needed for different application program.

One solution to the problem that a single file has multiple users is to provide a physically different file for each application program. The difficulty is that they not be identical: one may be updated by its application program while the other is not. In some situations this is viable. Consider a personnel file and a payroll file. Both describe individuals employed by our firm. Each contains a record for the individual. However, the characteristics of the individual of interest to personnel are for the most part different from those needed in the payroll application. Some characteristics are necessary for both, such as the employee's salary. When his salary changes, both files must be altered to reflect this. Other characteristics are also duplicated, such as number of dependents, state of residence, etc., but these change infrequently. Since the area of overlap is small, it is possible to keep separate files without interfering with either application.

2. One File for All

The duplicate file solution provides the advantage that each application program gets only the data it requires and doesn't have to review extraneous material. A disadvantage may rule out a duplicate file solution entirely; common information which changes has to be changed in both files. That is, if one application program makes a change in a field; this is recorded in its copy of the file. However, if another application program needs current data contained in that field, it must have the current value in its copy of the file. A duplicate file solution would never work well with the inventory application.

As an alternate solution, only one copy of a file is provided for the entire application family. Then, when one application program changes common data, the new value is available to all. There are two disadvantages to this solution:

• Each record for a file which has multiple application program users must contain all the data required by any user.

• Changes in file design require application program redesign for all users.

It is clear that if a record provides data to several users, it must be large enough to include all the data that any user might need. This means that a particular user has to provide a work area of full record size, even though he may need only a small portion of that data. His application program is built to examine only those fields which he references. Hence it must be designed to skip over intervening fields of any interest to that application program. This is not a serious problem, but it is time consuming and makes application programs longer.

Suppose that the data requirement for one application program changes. This is a common occurrence. It is rare that an application program remains stable for more than a few months. State, local and federal governments change their tax requirements constantly, requiring that new data fields be inserted in each individual's record. When the application program's needs require changes in the data, then the file design should reflect these changes. The record is reorganized, and the file copied, so that each record is now larger than in the old version. This is not difficult.

A great obstacle arises when we realize that other application programs use this same file. If the record size has grown, work areas in *every* application program must be enlarged, even if the new fields are put at the end of the record.

When the placement of fields is altered, each application program must be rewritten to accommodate the new placement of fields. One small change may thus require that all application programs in the family be altered to accommodate it.

3. DBMS Solution

One of the most important properties of the DBMS is that it isolates users from each other. The DBMS carries internally a unified record containing all the information which might be needed by any user. When a particular application program addresses the DBMS, the response is to take the composite record, break it apart, reassemble it and provide only the data required by this application in the user's work area. This overcomes the first restriction noted above.

Consider now how the DBMS reacts to a change in one user's needs. The DBMS will create a new composite record, modified to include the data required by this one user. Of course this user's program must be altered to accommodate the new data. A record containing this new data field will be supplied to the user's application program upon request by the DBMS.

Suppose that the other users' needs have not altered. The DBMS will pass the computer record through filters to produce a record suited to each of their needs. Naturally none contains the added data. Hence the other application programs will not have to be altered in any respect.

4. *Integrated Record View*

Before DBMS the application program had several sources of data which were separate files. For an inventory posting problem it has to deal with these separate sources of data:

- The transaction file lists additions and withdrawals from stock.
- The inventory file lists storage on hand.
- The parts file describes each part.
- The vendor file describes the supplies.
- The purchase order file describes pending deliveries.

The program manipulates, coordinates and correlates records in various files.

After DBMS, all internal files are integrated without the intervention of the application program. Only the transaction file is external, because transaction data comes in from outside the system. Consequently, in both systems the application program activates this file. The stored data under the DBMS is integrated into a single composite record called the subschema record, to which we devote much space later.

The subschema record integrates all data related to an individual into a single package. Consider an inventoried part for which activity is in progress. For that part the application program needs to have:

(1) its description,

(2) the stock on hand and its location,

(3) its vendor,

(4) outstanding purchase orders.

The application program finds all this combined into a single convenient record, the subschema record. Whenever the application program requests a record, it gets all this data.

The data is aggregated from separate sources. Previously we have called an individual source a "record." A better term is segment. A segment is data about a single individual in one population. A record is now defined as a set of related segments. We shall still talk about files which may now consist of segments or records, the former under a DBMS.

New Words and Phrases

access	*n.* *v.*	存取
advent	*n.*	出现
aggregate	*v.*	汇集
attribute	*n.*	属性
client	*n.*	客户
composite	*a.*	合成的
contingency	*n.*	可能性
coordination	*n.*	协调
dispose	*v.*	除去
duplicate	*v.*	复制
entry	*n.*	记录项
erroneous	*a.*	错误的
extraneous	*a.*	无关的
family	*n.*	系列
field	*n.*	域,字段
hexagon	*n.*	六边形
hexadecimal	*a.*	十六进制的
individual	*n.*	个体
intervene	*v.*	干涉
inventory	*n.*	报表
invoice	*n.*	发票,装货清单
isolate	*v.*	隔离
itemize	*v.*	详细说明
manifestation	*n.*	表示
merchandise	*n.*	商品

obsolete	*a.*	陈旧的
obstacle	*n.*	障碍
occurrence	*n.*	(数据库中)具体值
oversimplify	*v.*	过分简单化
perceive	*v.*	察觉
perspective	*n.*	远景
population	*n.*	总体
post	*v.*	登记,记录
prevail	*v.*	流行
purchase	*v.*	购买
quanta	*n.*	量,总数
reassemble	*n.*	重新装配
recourse	*n.*	求助
retrieve	*v.*	检索
stock	*n.*	库存
subschema	*n.*	子模式
tangible	*a.*	现实的
terminal	*n.*	终端
turnover	*n.*	流通量,营业额
update	*v.*	更新
vendor	*n.*	卖主
viable	*a.*	可行的
activity ratio		活动率
procedure oriented language		面向过程语言
query processing facility		查寻处理功能
real time processing		实时处理
rule out		消除

Notes

1. Before the advent of data bases each user or user group "owned" and

was responsible for his own data and for keeping it up to date. 在数据库出现之前,每个用户或用户组拥有并对自己的数据负责更新。

2. There is hardly a population of importance which does not change in some way; one which does not change at all is called an archive. 不以某种方式变化,就几乎没有总体的重要性,根本就不变化的总体称为档案(文件)。

3. When a number of requests for access to a file are saved and grouped together to be handled at one time, this is called batch processing. 许多存取文件的需求被存储起来,并在一个时间上成批被处理,这种情况称为批处理。

4. The application program activities a file directly. The physical manifestation of the file is its occurrence upon a volume mounted upon a device. 应用程序直接组织文件。文件实际表现是根据计划安装好尺寸的数据库的具体值。

2.5　SKYvec SOFTWARE TOOLKIT

2.5.1　Advanced Software Development Environment

The SKYvec Software Development Environment speeds application development and porting for the entire SKYbolt family of VME accelerators, SKYstation desktop accelerators, and complete SKYsystem VME solutions. SKYvec includes compilers, libraries, development tools, a run-time executive, and host computer support. Each component is designed to provide a familiar and congenial development environment for users of UNIX-based workstations. They provide a high degree of source-code transparency allowing straight-forward porting of applications to SKY's products. [1]

1. *SKYvec Software Components*

• SKYvec C and FORTRAN compilers—automatically optimize, vectorize, and parallelize.

• Standard Math and Vector Library—couple the power of SKY's vectorizer with over 600 industry-standard calls and low-level routines.

• SKY Parallel Compute Cluster Toolkit—enables the four-processor Shamrock to be programmed transparently as a single processor, increasing performance up to 4x.[2]

• SKYmpx Run-time Executive—provides fully-prioritized preemptive multi-tasking

• Complete set of i860 development tools—includes assembler, linker, source-level debugger, instruction-level debugger, instruction-level simulator, object management utilities, and execution profiler.

2. *Software Development and Open Systems Standards*

The SKYvec Development Environment has been developed to ensure ease-of-use and to minimize development time. Through the use of standard UNIX, ANSI C and Fortran 77, SKY has provided an environment for developers that is both portable and maintainable.

SKYvec runs applications on SKY's accelerators at the highest levels of performance. It builds upon familiar workstation-based tools and extends these open-systems standards:

• SKYvec C and F77 accept all code constructs compatible with the ANSI Standards.[3]

• SKYvec C and F77 are command-line superset compatible compilers.

• Vectorization, parallelization and optimization directives are contained in source code comments or the compiler command line.

• SKYvec assembler, linker, librarian, symbolic debugger, simulator, and object management utilities are adaptations of Intel tools.

• SKYvec *libc. a* is symbol name and argument list compatible with a subset of UNIX System V, SunOS and Ultrix.

• SKYvec system services include the X Window system, named pipes, sockets, signals, shared memory, semaphores, and messages.

• SKYvec source-level debugger and profiler are adaptations of the GNU tools.

• SKYvec's Standard Math Library calls are fully compatible with library calls from Floating Point Systems and Quantitative Technologies. Many existing programs can be ported without modification.

• SKYvec's Parallel Compute Cluster Toolkit is compatible with SKY's Standard Math Library. Compilers link cluster versions at the user's request to provide transparent parallel processing.

2.5.2   SKYvec Programming Models

The fastest accelerator board in the world is only as good as the software that supports it. That's why the SKYbolt family is supported by SKYvec, a full suite of development tools, libraries, and operating software all designed to get your application up and running fast.

SKYvec software supports two distinct programming models for the SKYbolt family. In the multi-computer model, each processor in a SKYbolts is programmed independently. Multiple SKYbolts can be used together on a single application through IPC connections at the system level. On *Shamrock* platforms, users can program the four processors as a single unit or "compute cluster." A compute cluster will automatically process the application in parallel without user intervention or code modification.

1. *Multi-Computer Programming*

This programming model treats each i860 as a separate processor target for executing a separate program or program thread. In a system with multiple processor, each i860 is uniquely identified by board, daughtercard and processor number. At start-up, each processor is assigned a fixed memory partition. The i960 can also allocate shared memory for sue during IPC. At load time, a separate kernel is written to each of the individual memory regions for execution by the processors.

2. *Parallel Compute Cluster Programming*

This program model treats an entire four-processor *Shamrock* daughtercard as a single computational unit. From a user's perspective, the compute cluster is a single processor. One of the i860 processors, the master, runs the application. The other three act as slave processors. The auto-parallelization compiler option is used to generate an executable that runs on the entire cluster rather than on just a single processor. The compiler will then link in routines from the Parallel Compute Cluster Toolkit instead of the Standard Math Library.

At start up, the master begins the application while the slaves wait on the Barrier Register, a synchronization and communication facility built into the Shamrock hardware.[4] When a *Shamrock* cluster routine is executed, all four processors operate on independent threads of the code with different sections of data. When the cluster routine completes, the master resumes execution. Communication between the threads occurs through shared memory and the Barrier Registers.

3. *Standard Math and Vector Libraries*

SKYvec subroutine libraries are available from C, FORTRAN, or assembly language programs. All of them take advantage of automatic SKYvec optimizations and vectorizations and the i860's internal cache. The subroutine libraries include:

- Standard Math Library containing hundreds of single- and double-precision routines.[5] An industry-standard calling interface for ease of use and source code compatibility with older applications that use QTC or FPS library calls.

- The Parallel Compute Cluster Toolkit lets you issue a single library call that is executed across four processors.

- Scalar arithmetic functions defined by the ANSI C and FORTRAN 77 specifications.

- Standard SKY vector library of over 600 functions of real, double, and complex data types.

- Most of the *libc. a* functions are available on the workstation host.

- Berkeley named pipes, sockets, and signals for interprocess communication.

- System V shared memory, messages, and semaphores to support multitasking interprocess communication.

- X11R4 window system client to support partitioning of applications into graphic and computational components.

4. *Parallel Compute Cluster Toolkit*

All SKYvec Standard Math Library routines are available in the cluster model via automatic loop parallelization. In addition, the *Shamrock* Parallel Compute Cluster Toolkit includes essential routines such as:

- FIR Filters and Convolutions.
- 2D FFTs and Long 1D FFTs.
- Matrix multiply.
- Vector intrinsics (exp, log, sin, cos, atan, sqrt., div).
- Mean, min, and max.

The calling sequence for each of these routines is identical to its uniprocessor counterpart from the SKYvec Standard Math library. This allows you to develop and test your application on a uniprocessor board and then execute it on a *shamrock* without changing any of the code. Simply recompile it with the compute cluster command line option and link in the *Shamrock* Parallel Compute Cluster Toolkit.

5. *List I/O Processing*

The System Processor manages all the I/O traffic on and off the motherboard and between daughtercards. Since the System Processor is a programmable device, rather than simple DMA hardware, it can manage a list of I/O operations.[6] This list can include multiple long, short or variable size blocks. Conditional branches can be added to the list to provide different transfers based on data recevied. The list is created in the i860 application and downloaded back to the i960 at runtime. To the user, only the i860 is being programmed, but variable, asynchronous and overlapped I/O is occurring while the i860 is processing.

2.5.3 SKY's Vectorizing and Parallelizing Compliers

SKYvec automatic optimizing, vectorizing, and parallelizing compilers translate ANSI-standard C or FORTRAN programs into binary code suitbale for SKY's application accelerator products. The compilers share a common intermediate language form; a vectorizer, an optimizer, an instruction scheduler, and a code generator. Both C and FORTRAN programs benefit from the same internal optimization and vectorization strategies.[7] C and FORTRAN modules can be linked into a single executable.

The vectorizer recognizes opportunities to substitute optimized subroutines for vectorizable code constructs. The optimizer eliminates needless computation and conserves registers. The instruction scheduler saves CPU cycles at run time through dense packing of primitive scalar operations into the i860's multi-operation instructions. The code generator and assembler translate the SKYvec intermediate form into an executable module.

1. *Automatic Vectorization*
- Global data flow analysis and dependency testing.
- Statement reordering to allow vectorization.
- Induction variable recognition and simplification.
- Loop fusion and fission to conserve registers and permit more effective vectorization.[8]
- Recognition of vector idioms, including sum and min/max reductions, dot products, product reductions, first/last condition, and scatter/gather opportunities.

- Interchanging loops to allow or improve vectorization.
- Scalar and array expansion to allow vectorization.
- Renaming of scalars to break vector dependencies.
- Recognition of diagonal array accesses.
- Management of the i860's internal cache as a vector register file, including "strip mining."
- Vectorization of INTEGER data type expressions as well as REAL (float) and DOUBLE PRECISION (double). Also, vectorization of intrinsic functions that have vector versions (e.g., SIN and COS)

2. *Automatic Optimizations*

- Common sub-expression elimination, both globally and within basic blocks.
- Constant folding and propagation.
- Subroutine and function in-line expansion.
- Compile-time evaluation of constant arithmetic and logical expression.
- Removal of loop-invariant instructions.
- Recognition of scalar idioms and strength reductions [e.g., square_root($X * X$)$\Rightarrow$abs(X)]
- Automatic assignment of register variable.
- Register renaming across loops to conserve registers.
- Register coloring, an assignment algorithm designed to minimize register spills to memory.
- Load/store elimination for loops.
- Live/dead statement analysis to conserve registers and provide diagnostic information.
- Cross-jumping to reduce executable size.
- Local optimizations specific to the i860.

3. *Automatic Parallelization*

- Dependency analysis to determine feasibility.
- Automatic software cache management across processors.

• Generation of all start-up, shut-down and synchronization code to program four processors as one.

• Performance analysis to select fastest processing mode-single threaded or multi-threaded.

• Parallel Compute Cluster routines used as appropriate.

4. *SKYvec C*

Language-specific SKYvec C features include:

• Integer types of 8, 16, and 32 bits.

• Iterator construct, for data abstraction and for driving loops.

• Nested functions complete with up-level references.

• Nested functions as parameters to other functions.

• Intrinsic functions for runtime efficiency (e.g., _abs, _min).

• Extensive pragma set for detailed compilation control.

• Optional *lint*-like diagnostics.

• Compatible with the ANSI standard adopted in 1989 and with the AT & T Portable C Compiler.

• Many compilation controls and options.

5. *SKYvec F77*

Language-specific SKYvec F77 features include:

• Analysis of parameters and vectorization of statements that refer to them.

• Recognition of hand-rolled loops based on GO TOs.

• Vector load before store and preservation of store order.

• Vectorization of:

-COMPLEX data type expressions.

-Loops containing not-logical IF (e.g., computed GO TOs)

-Indirect addressing as scatter/gather.

-Statements referring to FORTRAN statement functions.

• User-callable system subroutines.

• Extended data type set, including:

CHARACTER	LOGICAL * 1 and * 4
DOUBLE PRECISION	REAL * 4 and * 8
COMPLEX * 8 AND 16	octal ('xxxx' o)
INTEGER * 2 AND 4	hexadecimal ('xxxx'X)。

* Expanded statement types, including:

  RECORD, NAMELIST, DO WHILE, ENCODE & DECODE.

* Support for direct and indirect recursive subroutine calls, and POINTER and STRUCTURE declarations.

* ANSI-standard, IBM VS, and DEC VAX intrinsic function.

* Choice of standard or free-form source formats.

* Enhanced internal file I/O (including unformatted binary) for frequently used files.

* Support for application-specific libraries via user-definable intrinsic function replacement.

* Many compilation controls and options.

6. *i*860 *Assembler*

The SKYvec adaptation of Intel's asm860 provides explicit control of processor resources. Features include:

* Common Object File Format (COFF) output files.
* Long identifiers—up to 80 characters.
* Conditional assembly.
* Macro language.
* Enforcement of i860-unique coding rules.
* Optional source and code listings.
* Symbolic debugger support.
* Detection of logic error.

7. *i*860 *Linker*

The *lnk*860 accepts COFF (Common Object File Format) object files and generates a SKY executable. The linker accepts object files from all of the other tools, allowing you to link output from both compilers and the assembler. Command line options allow you to specify the location in memory of the text, data, and BSS sections, specify symbols; produce a load map; rename the output file; and display additional information during processing.

2.5.4 Development Support Tools

1. *Object Management Tools*

SKYvec object code management tools include:

- *nm*860, which presents symbol table information in ASCII[9] form.

- *ran*860, which extracts entry point information form an archive format library and puts it into a directory module in the archive.

2. *SKYvec Debuggers and i860 Simulator*

SKYvec sim860 provides instruction-level simulation with an easy to use debugger-style interface. This allows you to verify program operation without an installed SKYbolt. Features include:

- Refer to memory/registers with symbolic names.

- Examine and modify user-accessible registers and memory sections.

- Display i860 pipeline stages.

- Set code and data breakpoint.

- Disassemble i860 instructions symbolically.

- Display stack frames.

- Execute programs in single-step mode.

- Estimate internal cache hit ratios.

- Track all i860 interrupt mechanisms.

- Handle memory management properly.

*gdb*860, the SKYvec source-level debugger, is an adaptation of GNU gdb, distributed with most UNIX systems. It can be run with a standard command line interface or under X Windows. *gdb*860 incorporates all of the features you need in a high-level debugger, including:

- Automatic display modes so that you can trace expression value changes.
- Value history that retains values displayed by the print command.
- Ability to change to a different file during a gdb session.
- Breakpoints that can be set at function entry points, line numbers, or conditionally.
- Ability to execute a command sequence when you encounter a breakpoint.
- Ability to examine/modify data in memory.
- Format options that determine how information is displayed.

3. *Execution Profiler*

The gprof860 profiler summarizes the runtime activity of an application program at both the subroutine level and the basic block level. It shows the time spent in each routine within a program as well as the calling/called-by relationships among routines. This information can suggest opportunities for performance tuning and provide diagnostic assistance to the programmer. SKYvec *gprof860* is an adaptation of GNU *gprof*, a compatible superset of the profiler generally supplied with UNIX systems.

The Standard Math Library provides an extensive list of vector routines for use with the SKYbolt and *Shamrock* product families. The Standard Math Library lets you add powerful, direct vector calls to your source code. All lower level details, like cache management and strip mining, are handled by the compiler. And, because these issues are handled during compilation, your source code remains portable. You automatically reap the benefit of any compiler enhancements. The Standard Math Library uses the industry standard call syntax originally standardized by Floating Point Systems (FPS) and Quantitative

Technologies (QTC). Source code that uses this standard runs on SKYbolt without changing a single line of code.

4. *Features & Benefits*

• Includes hundreds of single- and double-precision routines. There is no need to hand code algorithms—the right routine, at the right precision, is ready for your use.

• Uses the industry standard FPS/QTC calling sequence. Many existing programs can be compiled and run without modification.

• Callable from both FORTRAN and C; there are no language constraints.

• Reduce your load module size by linking with just the single-precision or just the double-precision portion of the library.

• Mark temporary vectors for additional performance improvement.

• Group vector calls share a common iteration count to reduce overhead.

• Runs on all SKYbolt products including Shamrock.

• Incorporates automatic strip-mining and cache management to make direct vector calls effortless.

5. *Extensive Function List*

The Standard Math Library not only gives you most of the standard FPS routines, it also incorporates functionality from the SKYvec Vector Library and Quantitative Technologies' popular Math Advantage library. Most functions are available in both single- and double-precision.

Functions are available in all these categories:

• Basic real and complex vector operations.

• Basic integer and logical vector operations.

• Basic math and trigonometric functions.

• Signal and image processing.

• Maximum/minimum functions.

• Dot product (sum) functions.

- Coordinate conversions.
- Data conversion and manipulations.
- BLAS routines.

2.5.5　The Standard Math Library

Not only does the Standard Math Library give you a standard easy-to-use interface and access to an extensive list of vector operations, it also gives you room for improvement. Here are three small steps that will bring you dramatic performance improvements.[10]

Step 1: Use Standard Math Library calls directly:

vadd (a,1,b,1,temp, 1, length);

/* temp [ ] = a [ ] + b [ ] */

vadd (temp, 1, c, 1, d, 1, length);

/* d [ ] = temp [ ] + c [ ] */

Step 2: Collect and bracket library calls to reduce overhead:

start_vector (length);

vadd(a,1,b,1,temp,1,length);

* temp [ ] = a [ ] + b [ ] */

vadd \ (temp, 1, *c, 1, d, 1, length);

/* d [ ] = temp [ ] + c [ ] */

end_vector ( );

Standard Math Library calls, like all library calls, incur some overhead. If you are counting instructions even a small amount of overhead is too much. Reduce the overhead by bracketing sequences of library calls with start_vector and end_vector statements. As long as all of the bracketed calls use the same iteration count (operate on the same number of data points), you can dramatically reduce your overhead. This lets the compiler perform additional optimizations, such as removing redundant operations, grouping operations and replacing multiple operations with their triadic equivalents.

Step 3: Mark intermediate results for storage in temporary vectors:

```
start_vector (length);
mark_temp(temp);
vadd(a,1,b,1,temp,1,length);
    /* temp [] = a [] + b [] */
vadd (temp, 1, c, 1, d, 1, length);
    /* d [] = temp [] + c [] */
end_vector ();
```

Moving data in and out of cache takes precious cycle and sometimes it's just not necessary. If you've bracketed a sequence of vector calls, chances are that some of the calls generate intermediate results. The results from one call serve as input to load it back in to serve as input later, wastes precious cycles. [11] Just use a mark_temp statement to signal that a value is to be reused. The compiler will leave it in cache in a special temporary vector saving you costly load and store operations.

2.5.6 SKYmpx Runtime Executive

The SKYvec runtime executive, SKYmpx, provides the execution environment for your application. It consists of host-based software and an i860 kernel and i960 monitor that execute on the SKYbolt board. The i960, acting as a system processor, fields all local system service requests for the executing task. This includes local interprocess communication and multitasking management. Requests that require host intervention, such as I/O, are passed back to the host and are rounted appropriately by the host-based software.

Since the SKYbolt is a real memory architecture, each process on the i860 requires a separate memory partition. These partitions, up to seven, are defined by the user through the creation of a configuration file and can be reconfigured every time the SKYbolt is started up. The host-based software handles all initialization and the first partitioning SKYbolt memory, using a configuration file or defaulting to a single partition.

The System Processor provides central control in support of symmetric multitasking. On board, the i960 manages the task list, starting and stopping tasks on a priority time-sliced basis.[12] The i960 executes a complete context call, updating the task list, halting, redirecting, and restarting the i860. Reliance on the host and the i960 frees the i860, marking it practical to multitask even on uniprocessor SKYbolts.

New Words and Phrases

adaptation	*n.*	自适应
ANSI	*abbr.*	美国国家标准
asynchronous	*a.*	异步的
barrier	*n.*	屏蔽
cache	*n.*	高速缓存
cluster	*n.*	组,集合
daughtercard	*n.*	子卡
diagonal	*a.*	对角的
DMA	*abbr.*	直接存储器存取
dramatically	*adv.*	引人注目地
frame	*n.*	结构,框架
I/O	*abbr.*	输入输出
idiom	*n.*	习惯用语
interrupt	*v.*	中断
intrinsic	*a.*	本质的
iterator	*n.*	迭代器
maintainable	*a.*	可维护的
motherboard	*n.*	母板
nested	*a.*	嵌套的
optimize	*v.*	优化

overhead	*n.*	开销
overlapped	*a.*	重叠的
parallelize	*v.*	并行化
platform	*n.*	平台
preemptive	*a.*	优先的
primitive	*a.*	原始的
prioritize	*v.*	优先
quantitative	*a.*	定量的
recursive	*a.*	递归的
redundant	*a.*	多余的
retain	*v.*	保持
scheduler	*n.*	调度表
semaphore	*n.*	信号,标志
simulation	*n.*	仿真
socket	*n.*	插槽
spill	*v.*	溢出
superset	*n.*	超集
toolkit	*n.*	工具箱
transparency	*n.*	透明度
triadic	*a.*	三个一组的
vectorize	*v.*	向量化
workstation	*n.*	计算机工作站
conditional branch		条件分支
dot products		点积
long identifiers		长标识符
macro language		宏语言
shut-down		关机
strip mining		露天采矿
subroutine libraries		子程序库
time-sliced		时间片

Notes

1. They provide a high degree of source-code transparency allowing straight-forward porting of applications to SKY'S products. 它们提供高度的源码透明度，允许与 SKY 产品直接的输入输出操作。

2. Enable the four-processor Shamrock to be programmed transparently as a single processor, increasing performance up to 4x. 可以使四处理器的 Shamrock（一种 DSP 板的名字）作为一个处理器编程，并使其性能等于一个处理器的四倍。

3. SKYvec C and F77 are command-line superset compatible compilers. SKYvec C 和 F77 是命令行扩展集兼容的编译器。其中 SKYvec C 和 F77 是 SKY 开发的 C 和 Fortran 语言编译器。

4. At start up, the master begins the application while the slaves wait on the Barrier Registers, a synchronization and communication facility built into the Shamrock hardware. 启动时，主处理器开始执行应用程序，而从处理器等待屏蔽寄存器。屏蔽寄存器是建在 Shamrock 硬件上的一个同步和通信的设备。

5. Standard Math Library containing hundreds of single and double-precision routines. 标准数学库包括几百个单精度和双精度子程序。

6. Since the System Processor is a programmable device, rather than simple DMA hardware, it can manage a list of I/O operations. 由于系统处理器是一个可编程器件，它可以管理一系列输入和输出操作，要比简单的 DMA 硬件好。

7. Both C and FORTRAN programs benefit from the same internal optimization and vectorization strategies. C 和 Fortran 程序都从同样的内部优化和向量化对策中得到好处。

8. Loop fusion and fission to conserve registers and permit more effective vectorization. 循环汇合和分裂到保存寄存器，允许更有效的向量化。

9. ASCII, American standard code for information interchange. 美国信息交换标准码

10. Not only does the Standard Math Library give you a standard easy-to-

use interface and access to an extensive list of vector operations, it also gives you room for improvement. 不仅标准数学库给你一个容易地使用接口和存取大范围的向量操作表的规范,还给你改进的余地。

11. Moving an intermediate result out of cache only to load it back in to serve as input later, wastes precious cycle. 将中间结果移出高速缓存,仅仅在稍后作为输入时才把它装回高速缓存,这将浪费宝贵的时间。

12. On board, the i960 manages the task list, starting and stopping tasks on a priority time-sliced basis. 在板上,i960 管理任务列表,以时间片(一般在毫秒量级)为单位根据优先级开始和停止作业。

Communications

3.1 SPEECH COMMUNICATIONS

The word telecommunications is used to describe communications at a distance which involve some form of equipment. Thus, a conversation over a telephone system is certainly a telecommunication whereas two people shouting at each other is not. For a telephone conversation the telecommunication equipment is both mechanical and electrical. Although this is true of most of the systems which we will consider, it is certainly not a prerequisite for a telecommunications system. For instance a conversation using a voice tube, i.e., an acoustic system, would also be classed as a telecommunication. For most of the section we will concentrate on electrical systems.

Fig.3.1 shows a simple telecommunications system. Note that this particular system only permits simplex communications, i.e., messages can only be sent in one direction. Furthermore, the input source and output destination are not shown. In general we will not include either the input source or output destination in our diagrams. We shall always assume that the input source is a human voice and that the input is speech. Similarly we shall assume that the output is always speech and its destination is another human. (The reader should be aware that considerable research is being done into systems for which, instead of speech, the output is a printed version of the message. This topic, called speech recognition, is extremely interesting but we will not discuss it here.)

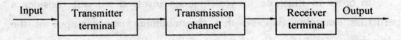

Fig.3.1 Simple telecommunications system

In a typical system the transmitter terminal will contain an input transducer which converts the speech pressure waves in the air into an electrical signal. This input transducer is commonly called a microphone. Similarly, within the receiver terminal is a loudspeaker, i.e., an output transducer which converts the received electrical signal back into sound. The transmission channel is the medium by which the electrical signal is conveyed from the transmitter terminal to the receiver terminal. The people who provide the input sound by speaking into the microphone and receive the sound after transmission by listening to the loudspeaker are called the communicators. In practice the transmitter or receiver terminal will probably contain an amplifier. This then guarantees that even a small sound at the input to the transmitter microphone will produce a sound at the output of the receiver loudspeaker. In order to discuss examples and illustrate their properties we must introduce some extra terminology and make some definitions. We begin by looking at the electrical signals which will be conveyed through our telecommunications system.

3.1.1 Signal-to-noise Ratio and Bandwidth

Before we can talk about the system we need to know the capabilities of the microphone and the loudspeaker. First of all we need to know the sensitivity of the microphone, i.e., the electrical power output from the microphone for the minimum required speech input signal level. Then, for the loudspeaker, we must be able to specify the electrical input power it requires to produce an adequately audible output for the minimum required output signal load.[1] Finally, we need to know the power loss due to the transmission channel.

In order to illustrate the calculations involved we will consider a particular example. Suppose that the minimum power output of the microphone is 0.015 mW and that the power which must be delivered to the loudspeaker for minimum signal level is 15 mW. Then, in order to produce a sound at the loudspeaker which corresponds to that at the microphone, we must provide an amplifier which "recovers" the loss in the cable and "implements" the gain of 15:0.015 which represents the power ratio of loudspeaker to microphone. If there is a power loss of 3 dB in the cable, we must provide an amplifier with a gain of (10 lg (15/0.015) + 3) dB = 33 dB.

Now that we know the capacity needed for our amplifier the next question to consider might be where we should place it. One possibility is in the transmitter terminal, a second is in the receiver terminal and we might even wish to consider placing one in each of them. This is not a particularly easy decision and is likely to be influenced by many factors. The amplifier itself will need to be powered and it may be considerably easier to provide the necessary power at one of the terminals rather than at the other. If there is one amplifier and it is placed in the transmitter then, essentially, only the microphone signals will be amplified. But if, on the other hand, it is placed in the receiver then the received signal will be amplified. This received signal is likely to contain unwanted noise which may be acquired by the signal during its transmission and, of course, the noise will also be amplified.[2] Noise may take many forms and, in order to illustrate some of them, we discuss what happens to the signal as it passes through the channel.

The first problem is that some of the signal power may be lost during transmission. As the signal passes through a telecommunications system it suffers attenuation in the passive parts of the system, e. g. , lines and radio paths. In addition a certain amount of noise and interference is likely to affect the signal. Although the attenuation can be compensated for by subsequent amplification, in practice the amplifier itself will add further random noise to the signal. Thus each time the signal is boosted it is more heavily contaminated by noise. Clearly, if we are to assess a system, we must have some meaningful way of measuring the noise in a channel and of comparing the levels of noise at different points in the system. In order to do this it is common practice to refer to the signal-to-noise ratio, normally abbreviated to S/N, at each point. By convention this is a power ratio and is equal to the signal power divided by the noise power.

When a signal enters the transmission channel it already contains a certain amount of contaminating noise. Then during transmission, whether down a line or over a radio path, both the signal and noise are attenuated. However while this attenuation is taking place extra noise is also being added to the signal. (In the case of a cable system this addition might be "thermal" noise from its resistive parts while for a radio path it might be "sky noise.") Thus the signal-to-noise ratio at the output of the transmission channel is likely to be considerably lower than at the input. Similarly when an amplifier is used, although the signal and noise which are present at its input are amplified by the same factor, the signal-to-noise ratio is lowered still further because the amplifier adds extra noise from both the passive and active components within it. In fact just about every part of a telecommunications system will contribute to the deterioration of the signal-to-noise ratio of the signal passing through it.

Let us now return to the simple telecommunications system of Fig.3.1. Another important factor to be considered is the ratio of the acoustic power produced by the loudest and quietest inputs to the input terminal. This is normally referred to as the dynamic range of the message source. A reasonable quality system should, typically, be able to cope with a dynamic range of about 70 dB. But to achieve this we must ensure that the entire system is able to handle such a range of signals. If any part of the system cannot cope with the highest input then this will probably cause considerable distortion of the signal.

Another consideration for a telecommunications system is the bandwidth it can manage. In order to have a meaningful discussion of this we must first review some of the fundamental properties of linear circuits.

Suppose we have a circuit with a set of input signals $X = \{x_1, x_2, \ldots\}$ which produces outputs $Y = \{y_1, y_2, \ldots\}$, where, for each i, y_i is the output corresponding to the input x_i. The circuit is said to satisfy the principle of homogeneity, if, whenever any x_i is multiplied by a constant and input to the circuit, the output signal is y_i multiplied by the same constant (see Fig. 3. 2a). The circuit satisfies the principle of superposition if when the input signal is the superposition (or sum) of x_i and x_j (for any two input signals x_i and x_j) the output signal is the sum of y_i and y_j (see Fig.3. 2b). Any circuit which satisfies both principles is called a linear circuit.

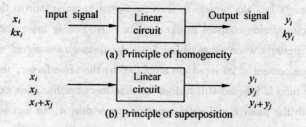

(a) Principle of homogeneity

(b) Principle of superposition

Fig.3.2   Linear circuit

Many of the components and circuits of telecommunications systems are either linear or, when restricted to a limited range of values for the input and output, may be considered as such. This range is also usually referred to as the dynamic range of the appropriate component or circuit. If our telecommunications system includes components which are not actually linear but we wish it to act as a linear circuit for all messages, then we must ensure that the dynamic range of the entire system is at least as large as that of the message source. Failure to do this will, as we have already seen, probably lead to distortion of the signal output from the receiver. This causes a particular problem for circuits involving scramblers. It means we must make sure that the scrambling technique does not lead to transmitted signals whose dynamic range goes beyond that of the channel, the receiver terminal or, indeed, any part of the transmitter terminal through which it must pass.

So far we have given no justification for our implicit assumption that linear circuits are desirable. We will now see how advantageous linear circuits can be. We know that any circuit modifies the electrical signal at its input to produce an electrical signal at its output. Clearly we would like to be able to analyse the circuit's response to every possible input signal. (We call the set of all possible input signals the input space.) However it is almost certainly not practicable or desirable to generate every possible input signal in order to determine the corresponding output. But if the circuit under consideration is linear, then knowledge of the output corresponding to two input signals gives the response to all input signals which are obtained from the original two by either superposition or multiplying by constants. Thus, by determining the actual outputs corresponding to a few input signals, one can use the principles of homogeneity and superposition to deduce the outputs from a much larger number of inputs. A subset of the input space is called a generating set if every possible input signal can be obtained by multiplying its elements by suitable constants and/or adding together appropriate combinations of them. Thus if we have a linear circuit and can find a generating set for our input space then, as soon as we know the output corresponding to each of the generating signals, we can use the principles of homogeneity and superposition to deduce the output of any possible input signal.

As we have already observed most telecommunications channels may be regarded as linear circuits, at least for signals within their dynamic range. It is also possible to find a generating set for the input signals and the most popular one is probably the set of sinusoids.

If a signal, or waveform, is written as a sum of sinusoids then the sinusoids which actually occur in this sum are called the frequency components of the signal. The bandwidth of a signal is then the range of frequencies occupied by the frequency components of the signal and the bandwidth of a telecommunications system is the range of frequencies which the system can handle. Thus, as an example, the bandwidth of a typical hi-fi amplifier might be specified as 15kHz, which would mean that it could handle signals whose frequency components take any value from 0 to 15 kHz.

If a signal is to be transmitted through a system, then, in order to avoid any distortion, it is clearly necessary to ensure that the range of frequencies which the system can handle includes all the frequency components of the signal. In other words the system bandwidth must be at least as large as that of the signal. It is perhaps not so obvious that it is also desirable that the bandwidth of the system should be no larger than that of the signal. If the system's bandwidth is too large then the system may accept more noise than is necessary and this, of course, will result in a decrease in the signal-to-noise ratio. Obviously noise and interference should be kept to a minimum. Thus, in all telecommunications systems where noise may be significant, it is common practice to ensure that the frequency characteristics of the channel, transmitter terminal and receiver terminal (including amplifiers, etc.) are the same as those of the signal. In particular the bandwidth should be the same for both the system and the message.

As an illustration of this we will consider the tuning of a radio. At any given instant there are numerous signals arriving at the radio's antenna but, nevertheless, it is usually possible to tune the radio so that it only emits the signals of a chosen programme. This is achieved by including, as part of the receiver, an electrical circuit which will only pass frequencies which lie within a small bandwidth, typically about 8 kHz. Such a circuit is called a bandpass filter. When the radio is tuned, the central frequency of the band passed by this circuit is adjusted so that it corresponds to that of the signal of the chosen programme (see Fig.3.3).

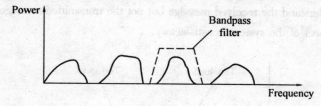

Fig.3.3 Tuneable receiver

The bandpass filter is designed so that all signals outside its selected band are attenuated to a negligible level. This careful matching of the bandwidths of the telecommunications system and the message source improves the audio quality of the system. However it causes great problems for the scrambler designer. Most scramblers are retrofitted to existing telecommunications systems which are likely to operate in narrow bandwidths. But, as we shall see later, most sophisticated forms of scrambling increase the signal bandwidth and so, since the existing bandwidth is likely to be narrow, the user may end up with a system in which the scrambled speech occupies a larger bandwidth than that supported by the rest of the system. This is one of the major reasons for losses in speech quality. The extent of the degradation will, of course, vary from system to system. The degradation may also appear to vary from listener to listener and, for all telecommunications systems, the assessment of the acceptability of the received signal is very subjective.

In any telecommunications system, whether it employs scramblers or not, the listener's perception characteristics are important. When scramblers are included in the system then it is necessary to test the intelligibi-lity of both the received speech and the transmitted speech. Obviously we want the received speech to be understandable while the transmitted speech should have little or no intelligibility to any listener. The "measure" of the intelligibility in each case is usually nothing more than the reaction of a number of listeners. If a sufficient number of users can understand the received message but not the transmitted message then that aspect of the system is satisfactory.

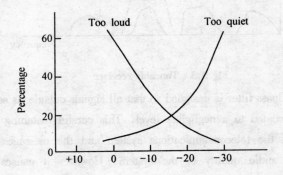

Fig.3.4　Relative acoustic power level (dB)
Typical results from user tests for "loudness"

Although user trials are the ultimate test for a system, we must never forget that, no matter how good the system may be, it will almost certainly be impossible to please all users. As an illustration consider the graph of Fig.3.4 which illustrates a number of users' assessment of how loud a system should be. The volume commenced at a particular level, 0 on the horizontal axis, ar ð then the acoustic power was varied. From the graph we can see that, at 5 dB below the original reference level, 10% of the users thought the resulting speech was too quiet while about 40% thought it was too loud. If users can disagree so dramatically in such a simple test then there is clearly no hope of unanimous agreement about levels of intelligibility, etc. The designer can do nothing more than perform sufficient tests to convince himself that he is pleasing most of the people most of the time. At least this is the situation for the received signal. If, during his tests, he finds one solitary listener who can understand his scrambled message he will probably conclude that the system is not secure enough.

3.1.2   Transmission Channels

For convenience we shall loosely classify transmission channels under two general headings: bounded and radio. Bounded channels will include electrical conduction in wires, cables etc. and optical fibres while radio channels include all forms of electromagnetic radiation in space e. g. microwave, satellite, etc..

There is, of course, no reason why a particular telecommunications system should not include both bounded and radio communications. One obvious example of such a system is provided when a telephone conversation takes place between one user in a car while the other is in an office. This is likely to entail a radio link from the car to the local exchange of the second user and then a line from this exchange to the office. However, for the moment, we will consider each of the two categories separately.

  1. *Bounded media*

Wire pairs are widely used for telephone communications. They used to be carried overhead on poles but, since this is both unsightly and inconvenient, the normal modern practice is to use buried cables which each carry a large number of twisted wire pairs. [3] The twisting of the pairs is important since it reduces crosstalk, i.e., the effect of stray electric and magnetic fields from one pair affecting another.

Although the twisting of the pairs reduces crosstalk, the use of wire pairs is limited. One reason is that crosstalk increases as the frequency increases. Another, even more important, reason is that increasing the frequency also increases the loss (attenuation) of the pair. In fact, the loss will also depend on the metal used as the conductor.

The difficulty of having a frequency-dependent line loss can be overcome, to some extent, by using devices called equalisers and repeaters. An equaliser is a device which has the inverse response to that of the line i.e., the attenuation introduced by an equaliser decreases as the frequency increases. Thus the idea is to design an equaliser whose response compensates for that of the line. The overall response will then be constant. Once the loss is constant a repeater, which is essentially an amplifier to compensate for the losses, can be added to the line. Thus, by placing equalisers and repeaters at fixed intervals along the cable, it appears that it might be possible to produce a flat response. This spacing of the repeaters and equalisers will clearly depend on the highest frequency to be used; the higher the frequency required the shorter the allowable distance between repeaters and equalisers. Unfortunately, in practice, the attenuation at the higher frequencies is likely to be so bad that too many repeaters and equalisers will be needed, and thus this type of approach can only be used for a very limited frequency range.

There are a number of ways of trying to achieve higher frequency transmissions. One is to use a coaxial cable which consists of a pair of concentric cylindrical conductors that are held in position by insulators. The outer conductor is there to act as an electrical shield and, as such, is likely to be less effective at frequencies below 60 kHz. Just as we saw for the twisted wire pair, the usable bandwidth and the repeater spacing are closely connected. For instance, in order to obtain an upper frequency of 61.6 MHz a coaxial cable with inner and outer diameters of 2.9 and 9.5 mm, respectively, requires a repeater spacing of 1.5 km.

When we discussed bandwidths we pointed out that speech occupies about 3 kHz. In the last few paragraphs we have been discussing channels with frequencies up to 61.6MHz. In view of the limited range of the human voice, the reader may be wondering why we are so concerned about these very high frequencies. To illustrate the reason we will look at an example. Suppose that, we are laying a submarine cable to act as the transmission channel for transatlantic telephone calls. Clearly the cost of such an operation is enormous. To use it for one call at a time would make each call very expensive. So the submarine cable is designed so that it can carry thousands of calls simultaneously and this is achieved by sending the various calls within different frequency bands. Clearly the higher the maximum frequency which the cable can carry the larger the number of calls it can carry. Thus our reason for wanting to use high frequencies is to reduce the cost of each transmission. This argument applies not only to submarine cables but to many other types of transmission links including, for example, trunk lines and satellite channels.

It is, of course, not sufficient to say that we transmit the various calls within different frequency bands. We must say how this is achieved. The technique of achieving this multiplicity of calls over a single channel involves the general idea of multiplexing and one particular method is frequency division multiplexing (FDM).

The electrical signal generated when speech is directed into a microphone is called the base-band signal and normally has a frequency range extending from 300 Hz to 3.3 kHz. In most telecommunications systems the shape and frequency components of this base-band signal are normally modified in some way in order to obtain a form which is more suitable for transmission. This process is called modulation and the process of recovering the base-band signal from the modulated signal is called demodulation. As we have already observed there are two main reasons for modulation. One is to change the signal into a form and a band where more efficient transmission is possible and the other is to make possible the simultaneous transmission of a number of signals over the same channel. We will return to modulation later and look at the various techniques which are available. For the moment we will merely mention that in frequency division multiplexing many base-band signals are moved to a number of different frequency ranges and that, by combining (multiplexing) them to produce a single signal, this then enables the simultaneous transmission of a number of signals.[4] In any given situation the choice of modulation technique will depend on many factors including, for instance, the environment and the particular telecommunications systems. It may also be influenced by the type of scrambling scheme to be employed.

In practice a coaxial cable with the dimensions described above is capable of simultaneously transmitting nearly 11 000 different telephone calls. The signals are multiplexed at the transmitter and demultiplexed at the receiver.

It is possible to achieve even wider bandwidths on certain other bounded transmission channels. For instance hollow conducting pipes, known as waveguides, can be used for the propagation of radiowaves. Waveguides are used for frequencies in the range of 2 to 11 GHz or, equivalently, for wavelengths in the range 15 to 2.7 cm. Radio waves of such high frequencies are called microwaves.

Telephone channels, in common with many other transmission media, exhibit certain amounts of time delay which are likely to vary with the frequency components of the voice signal. This delay range from 3 to

30 ms.

No discussion of bounded media would be complete without mentioning optical fibres. This medium uses optical waveguides in the form of glass fibres which carry modulated light signals. Schemes of this type permit vast bandwidths and, as they become more common, are likely to have an important effect on speech security. Among other possible advantages, their use will certainly make the actual interception of the signals considerably harder.

2. Radio

Radio transmission channels use radio wave propagation between antennae at the transmitter and receiver. The radio transmitter uses a modulation process to produce a radio frequency (RF) signal, i.e., to convert the message signal into a form which is suitable for transmission. Normally the transmitter will also need to contain an amplifier to ensure that the transmitted signal will be strong enough when it reaches the receiver.

Radio waves are unbounded in the sense that they are propagated into the atmosphere. However in practice they will almost certainly be bounded by the earth's surface and ionosphere. (The ionosphere is the region, about 50 ~ 400 km above the earth's surface, where various conducting layers of ionised gases exist. The different layers tend to reflect different frequency bands.)

When discussing radio it is common practice to assign well-known names to various specific frequency ranges. In Table 3.2 we give a list of these names.

Very-low-frequency waves are used principally for navigational and military purposes. They are bounded by the earth's surface and the ionosphere and are guided by effects which include diffraction at the earth's surface and refraction at the ionosphere.[5]

Table 3.2   The various frequency bands

Frequency range	Name
0 Hz ~ 3 kHz	Extra low frequency (elf)
3 kHz ~ 30 kHz	Very low frequency (vlf)
30 kHz ~ 300 kHz	Low frequency (lf) or long wave
300 kHz ~ 30 MHz	Medium frequency (mf) or medium wave
3 MHz ~ 30MHz	High frequency (hf) or short wave
30 MHz ~ 300 MHz	Very high frequency (vhf)
300 MHz ~ 3GHz	Ultra high frequency (uhf)
3 GHz ~ 30 GHz	Super high frequency (shf)
30 GHz ~ 300 GHz	Extremely high frequency (ehf)

The ef and mf waves are used mainly for radio broadcasting and rely on propagation over the curvature of the earth's surface. In the mf waveband propagation also takes place by sky waves and this presents a number of problems. For example, sky waves exhibit both regular (i.e., daily and seasonal) and irregular fluctuations with ionospheric conditions. They allow communications over longer distances but this advantage is countered by the fact that they are subject to multipath propagation and selective fading. Multipath propagation occurs when the transmitted signal reaches its destination by more than one route. If, for instance, the receiver gets two reflected waves, of which one has been reflected once and the other twice, then the fact that they have travelled paths of different lengths means that the two waves will arrive at the receiver with a relative delay.

The hf band is extremely popular and is usually very heavily overcrowded. Its uses include long distance broadcasting plus maritime and aeronautical communications. Unfortunately a consequence of its popularity is that there tends to be considerable interference caused by different stations operating on the same frequency. This tendency for users to concentrate on a few of the frequencies arises from their need to avoid the fading which, as we saw when we discussed the mf waves, results from the sky wave propagation. In this particular band it is common practice to avoid fading by changing frequency to certain "good" frequencies which are determined by the forecasts of ionospheric conditions and are, as a consequence, known to most users. For short distances hf ground wave propagation also occurs and this tends to be used for land mobile and ship-to-shore communications.

Both vhf and uhf are mainly used over short distances and rely on direct waves. These waves are often a combination of direct and ground reflected waves over distances which, typically, vary from a few kilometers to a few hundred kilometers, depending on both the terrain over which the waves must propagate and the height of the antennae.[6] There is one definite advantage to this type of short range communication and that is the virtual lack of interference from other stations. Both vhf and uhf are used for television broadcasts and, in addition, vhf is also used for high-quality radio.

Most microwave communications are restricted to point-to-point communications. They tend to be transmitted over broad bands and use direct wave propagation. A particular example of this is provided by the so-called line-of-sight radio relay systems[7] used in telephone networks. In these systems the stations are mounted on hills or towers in order to achieve a direct, or line-of-sight, path from station to station. Each station consists of a transmitter and receiver for each direction and, by building an appropriate number of stations, links can be established to "cover" an entire country. There are two advantages to this type of system. The first is the need for only a relatively small transmission power (typically of the order of 10 W) and the second is that highly directional antennae can be employed. This latter remark, of course, applies to all point-to-point systems.

Our discussion of the transmission channel led us, quite naturally, into considering various components of the receiver's and transmitter's terminals.

The two most familiar terminals are probably the telephone and the radio receiver. Each of these has characteristics which we have come to accept and, possibly, assume are fundamental properties. For instance, most people take it for granted that a telephone system is always full-duplex and that a broadcast radio is merely simplex. These are merely characteristics of these two terminals when used in their most common environment. When the environment changes then the other properties of the channel may change as well. For instance a mobile radio, as used by police forces, is often a half-duplex device. A more relevant, and in many ways unfortunate, example is that a full-duplex system like the telephone will often be reduced to half-duplex when scrambling is introduced. The reasons for this are complicated and we will not discuss them now. For the moment we will accept it as a fact and look at the consequences. It is important to realise that the fact that a system is half-duplex does not, necessarily, say anything about the channel. Two possibilities are:

(1) the channel allows transmission in either direction, but only one way at a time, and.

(2) the channel allows full-duplex communications but the terminals are constructed in such a way that transmission is only possible in one direction at any given moment.

When scrambling is added to a telephone system it is usually relatively easy to preserve half-duplex operation. However it is likely to be extremely expensive, and in some cases virtually impossible, to maintain the terminals as full-duplex devices. Once again there are many reasons and some of them are complicated. The fundamental reason is simply that it is difficult to combine or reconcile the properties and characteristics of the scrambler with those of the telephone system. As a simple illustration we will consider the effect of echoes on the system.

An echo is a delayed version of the message which is produced by reflections in the system. Not surprisingly if these echoes reach the earphone of the message originator they are likely to be very distracting. Furthermore, the degree of distraction will probably increase as the delays get larger. A normal telephone network is designed to ensure that only acceptable delays occur. But if scramblers are introduced to the system they are likely to introduce extra delays which may result in an unacceptable system. Furthermore if the echoes become scrambled the user will be faced with the extra distraction of having unintelligible signals in his earphone.

We can summarize our discussion of voice transmission by saying that we shall, broadly speaking, identify the transmission channel between the terminals by its bandwidth and the impairments which might occur to the signals which it carries. We shall be particularly concerned about the following five principal causes of impairments:

(1) attenuation and its variation with frequency,

(2) noise,

(3) non-linearity of the channel,

(4) changes in propagation time with frequency,

(5) echoes.

Now that we have completed our brief overview of voice message transmission. Our aim is to establish some of the techniques necessary to examine the properties of speech signals and to tackle the problem of converting the analogue signals to digital ones.

New Words and Phrases

acoustic	a.	声学的
active	a.	有源的
aeronautical	a.	航空的
attenuate	v.	衰减

contaminate	*v.*	污染
convey	*v.*	传输
crosstalk	*n.*	串话
decibel	*n.*	分贝
deterioration	*n.*	变坏，劣化
diffraction	*n.*	衍射
distortion	*n.*	失真
distract	*v.*	使混乱
equaliser	*n.*	均衡器
homogeneity	*n.*	均匀性
intelligibility	*n.*	可理解性
interference	*n.*	干扰
ionosphere	*n.*	电离层
jamming	*n.*	干扰
loudspeaker	*n.*	扩音器
maritime	*a.*	海上的
microwave	*n.*	微波
passive	*a.*	无源的
prerequisite	*n.*	先决条件
refraction	*n.*	折射
relay	*n.*	中继
retrofit	*n.*	改型
scrambler	*n.*	扰码器
sinusoid	*n.*	正弦
sophisticate	*v.*	弄复杂
tackle	*v.*	处理
telecommunications	*n.*	电信
terminology	*n.*	术语
terrain	*n.*	地形
transducer	*n.*	传感器

waveguide	*n*.	波导
coaxial cable		同轴电缆
full-duplex		全双工
instantaneous power		瞬时功率
line-of-sight		视线
multipath propagation		多径传播
optical fibre		光纤
out-of-phase		不同相
principle of superposition		叠加原理
signal-to-noise ratio		信噪比
sky noise		大气噪声
speech recognition		语音识别

Notes

1. Then, for the loudspeaker, we must be able to specify the electrical input power it requires to produce an adequately audible output for the minimum required output signal load. 再就是扩音器,我们必须能规定输入的功率,它要求对于最低需求的输出负载产生一个听得见的输出的声音。

2. This received signal is likely contain unwanted noise which may be acquired by the signal during its transmission and, of course, the noise will also be amplified. 这个接收的信号很可能包含不期望的噪声,而这个噪声可能是在信号传输的过程中获得的,当然这个噪声也将被放大。

3. Wire pairs are widely used for telephone communications. They used to be carried overhead on poles but, since this is both unsightly and inconvenient, the normal modern practice is to use buried cables which each carry a large number of twisted wire pairs. 双绞线广泛用于电话通信。过去常常把它们架在电杆上,但由于这样既难看又不方便,现在通常的做法是用地下电缆,每条电缆包括大量双绞线。

4. For the moment we will merely mention that in frequency division

multiplexing many base-band signals are moved to a number of different frequency ranges and that, by combining (multiplexing) them to produce a single signal, this then enables the simultaneous transmission of a number of signals. 现在我们只提一下频分多路复用技术,很多基带信号搬移到一些不同的频率范围,把它们合成后产生一个单一的信号,这样可以同时发射多个信号。

5. They are bounded by the earth's surface and the ionosphere and are guided by effects which include diffraction at the earth's surface and refraction at the ionosphere. 它们受地球表面和电离层所束缚,又由地球表面衍射和电离层折射引导向前。

6. These waves are often a combination of direct and ground reflected waves over distances which, typically, vary from a few kilometers to a few hundred kilometers, depending on both the terrain over which the waves must propagate and the height of the antenna. 这些波通常是通过一定距离传播的直达波和地面反射波的合成,典型地从几公里至几百公里,取决于波传播时通过的地形和天线的高度。

7. line-of-sight radio relay system 视距无线电中继系统

3.2 PCM AND DIGITAL TRANSMISSION

3.2.1 Introduction

This process of converting an analogue wave form such as that of telephone speech to a digital form inevitably involves an increase in bandwidth or in the frequency spectrum occupied in the medium being used and would appear at first to be a rather pointless complication of the process of conveying voice signals. The technical and economic advantages will be explained in following sections but a brief initial outline may help to put things in perspective.

For many years there have been attempts to realise the economic potentialities of time division multiplexing (TDM).[1] It is by no means a new concept and was used in telegraphy before telephony came on the scene. The devices used were simply synchronised commutators where one at the sending end "sampled" each of a number of individual channels in sequence and transmitted the samples in sequence. [2] The other device at the receiving end received the samples and distributed them in the correct sequence to the corresponding individual channels. Obviously there was a problem of maintaining the commutators in synchronism. This problem remains but modern electronic methods have provided cheap and reliable ways of achieving the required result.

Where, as in telegraphy, the information is digital, i.e. comprises a succession of units of information limited to a very few discrete values, e.g. the binary mark and space of telegraphy, TDM is extremely simple and cheap.

It has long been known that an analogue wave form of limited bandwidth restricted to an upper frequency limit of f_1 may be accurately con-veyed by transmitting instantaneous samples at a sampling rate slightly in excess of $2f_1$. If these samples are transmitted as narrow pulses then the pulses corresponding to several channels may be sent consecutively in a regular cycle and it thus becomes feasible to apply TDM to analogue information. [3]

This form of TDM has been used for transmission purposes and also for switching, and various modulation techniques have been employed: for instance pulse amplitude, pulse width and pulse position. In switching, where the samples can be transmitted over wide band highways, reasonable control of signal impairments can be achieved but on junction and trunk routes the inevitable distortion of the pulses in amplitude and phase make it very difficult to control inter-channel interference or crosstalk without prohibitively costly equalising.

It was partly in this quest for a more satisfactory answer to the TDM problem and partly to counter the high noise levels of earlier radio links that the late Alec Reeves over 30 years ago conceived the idea of PCM in which an analogue wave form is sampled at regular intervals by narrow pulses and a numerical "description" of the amplitude of each sample is transmitted in place of the analogue wave form.

Although originally conceived against the background of noisy radio links the first large scale commercial use of PCM has been on cable pairs. The economic importance of increasing the capacity of the vast quantities of copper pairs now installed on short- and medium-haul routes has long been recognised. The relatively poor crosstalk and noise characteristics of these pairs has proved a major obstacle to the introduction of multiplexing by traditional FDM methods. With PCM it has proved practicable as will be explained in the following sections, to use two regular cable pairs to handle from 24 to 32 conversations.

The conversion of analogue information to a binary digital form of coding introduces a new range of opportunities and problems. The key to the attractions of digital transmission resides in the concept of regeneration. In classical analogue communication systems the limiting factor in the establishing of a satisfactory connection between two remote users is the signal/noise ratio. Modern methods have established very satisfactory standards in regard to the limiting of attenuations of the signal, but no analogue amplifier can prevent the inevitable accumulation of noise. Each time the signal is amplified so also is the noise which has been added to it within the pass band involved.

The characteristic of digital transmission is that since the signal has a restricted number of states (typically for binary data only two) then provided the acquired noise on any section does not exceed the level at which ambiguities (errors) will occur in recognising which state was transmitted, the signal may be regenerated without error and noise is not accumulated.[4] This is true in regard to all essential characteristics of the signal except for a residual form of noise known as phase or timing jitter, i.e. the varying displacement in time of the pulses from their ideal isochronous positions.

This ability of regeneration to avoid almost all noise accumulation results in the signal/noise ratio required on each section to reduce regeneration interpretation errors to a negligible quantity being much lower than an analogue system could tolerate on a complete connection.[5] This means that the wider frequency spectrum requirements of the digital mode are more than counterbalanced (certainly on enclosed media) by the vastly improved noise and interference tolerance. This is an example of exchanging bandwidth for signal/noise ratio.

3.2.2   Theoretical Considerations of PCM

Any practical communication system must be a compromise between the requirements for high quality and low cost. The frequency spectrum will be limited by the bandwidth which can be made available and there must be varying degrees of cumulative distortion and noise. PCM cannot eliminate the transmission degradations but it does reduce and simplify them by confining them essentially to considerations of digital error rate and timing or phase jitter. This state of affairs is attained by acceptance of certain impairments introduced at the terminal analogue/digital and digital/analogue conversion processes. It is necessary to start by an examination of these impairments and the steps which have to be taken to hold them to a subjectively satisfactory level. It must be emphasised that the subjective aspects are very important and vary from one type of information to another, for instance as between speech and television. This section examines the problem mainly in relation to speech.

It is impossible in one short section to treat the theory in any depth. What will be attempted here is to indicate the nature of the issues involved and the ways in which an acceptable code of practice is being established.

The essential elements involved in the terminal processes are: sampling, quantising, companding and coding. The last is inescapably involved with the desired characteristics of digital transmission which will be dealt with further in subsequent sections. Some reference is needed here, however, because it is also involved with the practical implementation of quantising and companding.

Most of that which follows is relevant to the basic process of digitising a single voice channel and the need for this will probably arise. It should be remembered, however, that nearly all systems in use to date are multiplex systems and these processes of sampling, quantising and coding and their receiving counterparts are conducted sequentially by a common unit serving a number of voice channels. This sequential operation by a common unit is then the essential basis of the multiplexing process.

1. Sampling

PCM represents in many ways the culmination of a long search for effective methods of employing time division multiplexing in the handling of analogue information. The basis of all such approaches is the idea of periodic sampling and PCM shares with all the earlier attempts the inherent limitations.

The first limitation is the relationship of the bandwidth or more accurately the upper limit of the spectrum to the sampling rate. The theory that a wave form limited to an upper frequency f may be completely con-veyed by sampling at a rate of $2f$ is obviously as it stands theoretical idealism. It pre-supposes infinitely short sampling periods, a signal of infinite duration and perfect filters. The first of these issues is relatively unimportant and the distortion due to a sampling period of finite but practically feasible duration, for example 2% or 3% of the sampling rate, is quite negligible.

The other considerations are of practical importance. A signal such as speech is in its essential nature a succession of short duration periods of transmitted power with little or no sustained repetition, and filters are necessarily imperfect, especially if they are to be simple and cheap.

Determination of a practical compromise for a sampling rate to handle voice signals over the 300 ~ 3 400 Hz spectrum now firmly established for telephony involves, therefore, some examination of the limitations of practicable methods of sampling and the counterpart of demodulating and filtering, together with some consideration of subjective issues concerning the tolerance of voice communication to particular classes of distortion.

A value of 8 000 samples per second has received world-wide agreement and is now one of the solidly established parameters.

In PCM the subsequent operations of quantising and coding occupy a finite time and it is normal to use a sample-and-hold arrangement to retain a record of the short duration sample for the period in which it is necessary to operate upon it.

With direct coupling to relatively long lines, in other words with interoffice junctions or trunks, any analogue modulation of pulses such as in pulse amplitude modulation (p. a. m.) must present acute crosstalk pro-blems demanding wide bandwidth or sophisticated equalising or both. This has been one of the main obstacles to the use of the p. a. m. on any scale in transmission. Within the restricted physical dimensions of a PCM terminal the problems are manageable. Careful design and engineering is still needed but very high standards of accuracy in the transfer of a sample magnitude have been achieved.

Ideal sampling and sampling switches would operated in + and − directions on an AC wave form. There are considerable complexities in this ideal approach, including the imperfect linearity of any semiconductor devices at very low voltage levels. In practice it is usual therefore to work in one sense only by superimposing on the AC wave form a standing DC component of a magnitude equal to or greater than the peak AC voltage that is desired to handle. This is referred to as a pedestal.

In earlier experimental systems this DC pedestal corresponded directly to an equivalent pedestal in the coder. General practice now is still to employ a pedestal or DC bias to enable unidirectional gates to be used, but otherwise to employ AC coupling and derive the centre point value by relatively long term integration.

In the demodulation or recovery stage, the handling of narrow samples is a rather more involved problem than that of initial sampling. Theory declares that the recovered pulses are passed through a low pass filter. However, if sufficient power is to be delivered to avoid the need for considerable subsequent amplification of the analogue signal it is desirable, in order to avoid very high instantaneous power levels, to stretch the duration of the pulse. This results in a $\sin x / x$ reduction in the received level where x is the length of the stretched pulse expressed in radians as a fraction of one cycle of half the analogue frequency. Thus, if each pulse is stretched to the start of the subsequent pulse then at the Nyquist limit $x = \pi/2$. This degree of pulse stretching produces a theoretical 4 dB loss at the Nyquist limit. This higher frequency attenuation characteristic can be corrected by the filter characteristic if extreme linearity is not of great importance.

There are many alternatives available. One popular procedure is to deliver the output pulse into a capacitor so that a particular voltage pulse transfers a corresponding amount of energy and this can be made high enough to limit subsequent amplification to a reasonable value. This is a satisfactory method but it requires careful engineering, since the reservoir capacitor is now in effect part of the filter and the frequency relationships must be appropriately chosen to ensure substantially complete transfer of the energy of each pulse.

2. *Quantising*

The next problem to be examined is that of the distortion arising from the fundamental requirement of PCM that samples transmitted cannot be continuously variable but must be chosen from a finite set, the number of which is a function of the length of the binary number we are prepared to assign for the transmission of each sample.

Fig.3.5 shows a section of wave form being sampled. The permitted sampling approximations are indicated by the horizontal lines. It is assumed that the value selected is the nearest one + or − (in practice for reasons of convenience, the next lowest one is taken and at the recovery

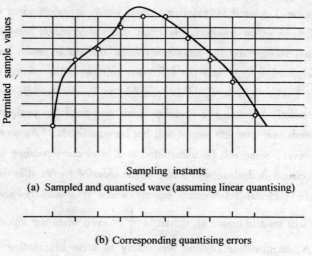

Sampling instants

(a) Sampled and quantised wave (assuming linear quantising)

(b) Corresponding quantising errors

Fig.3.5 Sampling of a wave form

stage half a step value is added, which has identically the same result.) The quantising errors are shown below. It will be seen that the mean value is $\pm \frac{1}{4} S$ where S is the magnitude of one step. Except where there is a fortuitous correlation between sampling rate and transmitted frequency, and this occurs infrequently in speech, the mean power is represented by:

$$\int_{-\frac{1}{2}S}^{+\frac{1}{2}S} (x^2 dx)/S = \frac{1}{12}S^2$$

The random nature of this distortion results in a frequency content which is substantially flat over the pass band of the channel.

This is generally called "quantising noise" but since it is dependent on the existence of a signal it is a form of distortion as distinct from a constant background noise.

There does exist a form of noise (generally referred to as "idle channel noise") related to quantising noise which is independent of the signal. If there exists an absolutely exact and stable match between the idle channel voltage and the reference voltage and stable match between the idle channel voltage and the reference voltage at the centre of the quantising ladder then it would be possible to locate the idle channel condition exactly between two decision levels and until the peak-to-peak noise exceeds one quantum step it will not be quantised.[6] As soon as it does, however, noise will be transmitted at a level corresponding to S^2. Since the circuit is dealing with a step of the order of 1 mV, it is difficult to hold the pedestal relationship exactly where it should be and any deviation will tend to create an output of $\frac{1}{4}S^2$ even when the input noise is less. A manifestation of this very likely to arise in practice is the difficulty of guaranteeing that there will be no residual mains hum at this level. If such hum causes the apparent pedestal to move to and fro over a decision level apart from the direct quantisation of the hum, at a frequency of the 100 cycle order periods of extreme sensitivity to higher frequency noise will occur. There is thus a tendency to create a low level high frequency noise chopped at the hum frequency. This is subjectively more intrusive than steady noise. However, the self-centering arrangements and minor variations in gate behaviour can cause fluctuations and resultant chopping at even lower and more noticeable frequencies.

Optimal design is therefore a matter for rather careful compromise. In any case in systems now in use and planned, the idle channel noise at a level between − 60 dB and − 70 dB is quite unnoticeable except in extremely quiet listening situations.

3. *Companding*

One of the major problems of practical PCM is the very wide range of power levels to be handled. The range within the speech of one speaker is some 25 dB. Due to the differences between loud and quiet talkers and the attenuation of established connections before a PCM link is encountered, we are faced with a need to handle a range of some 60dB. If the lowest level to be handled just exceeds one step and peak clipping is reasonably limited then this 60 dB on a uniform step basis would involve about ± 1 000 levels.

This would not be catastrophic in regard to digital transmission rate (11 digits instead of the currently accepted eight digits). It would, however, reduce the economic attractions as far as pure transmission is concerned and it would greatly increase the cost and complexity of the terminal conversion processes.

To counter this difficulty we may take advantage of a practice which has become well established in many areas of conventional transmission, namely companding. In instantaneous companding the voltage of the wave form being transmitted is compressed in accordance with an appropriate law and at the receiving end the inverse expansion occurs. Companding is used in the main in a somewhat complementary manner to lift the level on line of the low level signals while maintaining the peaks of the high level signals within a predetermined power limit. This improves the low level signal/noise ratio but at the expense of changing a constant level noise into one related to signal level in accordance with the companding law.

It must be recognised at the outset that voice signals are particularly amenable to this treatment because the probability distribution of voice energy levels tends to separate the high frequency low level fricatives from the relatively low frequency but high level vowels. Partly as a consequence of this and partly as a consequence of the subjective responses of the human ear and brain, speech communication is highly tolerant of noise levels directly related to the signal level. Much subjective testing by D. L. Richards and others has established that the vast majority of listeners are unable in the environment of telephony to detect signal dependent noise more than 25 dB below signal level, and even 20 dB is noticed by relatively few.

To secure a linear relationship between quantising noise and signal level involves a logarithmic relationship between the number of steps and the signal level. A truly logarithmic curve would not pass through the origin (number of steps 0 and level 0) and there have been many curves examined which offer a reasonable compromise. Two have been the subject of much debate by the CCITT.[7] These may be expressed as follows:

$$A \text{ law} \begin{cases} F(x) = \dfrac{1 + \lg Ax}{1 + \lg A} & \dfrac{1}{A} \leqslant x \leqslant 1 \\[2mm] F(x) = \dfrac{1 + Ax}{1 + \lg A} & \dfrac{0}{A} \leqslant x \leqslant \dfrac{1}{A} \end{cases}$$

$$\mu \text{ law} \quad F(x) = \dfrac{\lg(1 + \mu x)}{\lg(1 + \mu)}$$

The A law is in effect truly logarithmic for higher levels with a linear bottom section comprising the tangent through the origin.

The μ law has a comparable overall form but is nowhere truly logarithmic and nowhere truly linear, though it approximates to these characteristics at the extremes.

It was established fairly early in studies that a seven- or eight-digit binary number giving a total of ± 64 or ± 128 levels was likely to be adequate and would not result in undue complexity or cost of implementation. The problem is one of compromise to hold in balance the following requirements:

(1) To handle high level voice signals with acceptable peak clipping. This means the onset of clipping should be in the region of + 2 or + 3 dB for a sinusoid at a point of zero equivalent.

(2) To maintain the signal/noise ratio over the upper levels at a figure in the 20 ~ 25 dB region or better.

(3) To have the smallest quantum steps small enough to maintain transmission of low lever fricatives to the lowest practicable level. This means coverage of 60 dB or more.

(4) To maintain idle channel noise in the region of 1 000 W or less.

The use of the A law with A about 100 enables these requirements to be met with some margin assuming eight digits, i.e. ± 128 levels.

The process of companding may be executed by a compression operation on the speech wave form followed by linear quantising and the inverse operation at the receiver. Suitable compressors can be constructed by employing the non-linear characteristics of diodes and arranging a suitable diode/resistor network. This was done on many of the earlier systems. However, the specification and control of the diode characteristics is difficult, particularly in regard to the essential matching of complementary pairs. This becomes increasingly important when PCM switching enters the picture and any coder may be connected to any of a number of different decoders.

Later systems have therefore tended to use linear sampling and non-linear quantising and as a further aid to simple implementation to replace the smooth curve of the A or μ law by a series of straight line segments. With a reasonable number of segments the increase in quantising noise due to the departure from the smooth curve is negligible and this procedure does result in the cheapest implementation of high reproducible compression and expansion and the resultant satisfactory matching of any transmitter with any receiver.

4. *Coding*

Coding, that is the expression of a quantised sample magnitude in terms of a binary number for transmission over the channel, may be executed in many ways. The main categories may be described as:

Parallel coding

Sequential coding

Counting.

The basis of counting methods is to count the successive levels on a simple binary counter at an accurately controlled rate of count and simultaneously to develop a steadily rising potential (sawtooth wave form). If, when this potential matches that of the sample, the counting is arrested the desired coding has been achieved.

An interesting version of this method comprises the replacement of the linear (sawtooth) wave form by an exponential decay of the sample, the count being arrested when a predetermined limit is reached. This gives effectively logarithmic compression.

Counting methods such as these have the merit of being monotonic and although there may be inaccuracies due to deviations in the slope of the sawtooth, these will be consistent from sample to sample. The sequential methods to be described next introduce greater risks of irregularities and discontinuities in the shape of the companding curve.

The main objection to counting methods is that unless very high speed counters are used the time involved in step-by-step counting of samples involving a large number of levels is excessive.

The procedure which is most convenient for the handling of PCM voice is the sequential method or the development of the code digit by digit. Fig.3.6 indicates the essential nature of this method. The sample is compared digit by digit with a potential derived from a weighting network representing the cumulative total as the number is built up. Each decision is final and requires no subsequent modification, so that digits may be transmitted to line as the coding proceeds. Further, it is relatively simple to make the weight assigned to say the last three digits a function of the preceding interim total, which leads to easy implementation of the segmented approximation to the companding law. This is particularly simple if the ratio of the slopes of consecutive segments is an integral number.

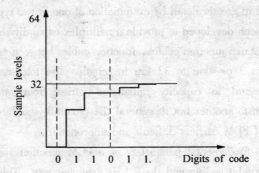

Fig.3.6 Principle of sequential encoding (linear)

This method of coding and the use of a segmented curve leads to the adoption of symmetrical binary as the code structure. In thus, one digit defines the sign of the sample in regard to a selected centre point and the remaining digits define in a straight binary manner the magnitude of the sample + *ve* or − *ve* regardless of sign.

In current specifications the aim has been to achieve performance standards which are satisfactory not only for one link but for a number of consecutive links with interconnection at audio level. This process must share with f.d.m. the inevitable degradation of the frequecy/loss curve due to consecutive filters but it also means that the quantising and idle channel noise will be additive. The effect in regard to quantising noise is substantially that of r.m.s. addition. Idle channel noise is rather more complicated to deal with. It must inescapably be responsive to the presence or absence of loss in the audio interconnection and to the pedestal relationship prevailing at each stage. In general the build-up is rather less than straight r.m.s. addition and low frequency modulation by hum tends to become less prominent.

3.2.3　PCM Junction Systems

The application of the principles outlined in the previous section may be illustrated in greater detail by examination of one or two typical systems which have been developed to provide a multiplex capability over standard 0.63 and 0.9 mm junction cables. Junction cables between exchanges are typically from 3 or 4km to 32 km in length. The tolerances on these cables in regard to capacity unbalance varies from one telephone administration to another but in general the crosstalk standards make the application of FDM carriers difficult and uneconomic.

The two fundamental parameters of a PCM junction system are the seven- or eight-bit coding and the 8 kHz sampling rate. This establishes the bit rate of 56 000 or 64 000 bits per second (56 or 64 kb/s) as the channel bit rate. Both seven- and eight-bit coding are used but the seven-bit systems use the eighth bit for signalling. The eight-bit systems accommodate signalling in a different way. Eight bits at 8 kHz sampling or 64 kb/s has therefore become a CCITT established standard. The system bit rate is therefore $64N$ kb/s where N is the number of time slots. This may be the same as the number of voice channels but in some systems one or more slots are used for control functions.

The next controlling factor is that as the pairs used for PCM must be deloaded it is convenient to place regenerators at the loading coil spacings in effect as replacements for the loading coils. This establishes a section length of about 1 828 m, varying slightly with different administration practices.

The controlling factor in system capacity tends, therefore, to be crosstalk, in that the cumulative crosstalk from other systems, in general mainly NEXT (near-end crosstalk) from RETURN channels, must be below the minimum received signal level by a sufficient margin to ensure effectively error-free signal detection at each regenerator.

1. *Line Transmission Methods*

The line transmission methods of practical systems are a function of the nature of the process of regeneration.

This process makes several demands on the detail of the transmission technique. Transmission must be balanced and although this can be done without transformer coupling it is expensive and complex to organise and substantially impossible.[8] In practice, therefore, transformer coupling is used and power is fed over the phantom circuit. The use of transformer coupling requires that there should be no long term DC content in the bit stream and that the low frequency end of the spectrum should attenuate rapidly to simplify equalising.

These requirements cannot be met by simple binary modulation. There have been several proposals for special forms of low disparity binary coding, inescapably employing some measure of redundancy, but the practice adopted in the ATT T1 system has gained widespread acceptance. This is to employ a modified ternary modulation where a space or "0" is no current and a mark or "1" is either $+ve$ or $-ve$, the two senses alternating. This ensures no DC but it does not, ensure clock content. On T1 this clock content is ensured by a slight restriction of the codes used (all "0"s are omitted) so that a minimum appearance of "1"s is provided.

This quasi-ternary transmission, referred to as bipolar or in this particular form as a.m.i. (alternate mark inversion), admittedly imposes a 6 dB improvement requirement on the signal/noise ratio.

2. *The Basis of Regeneration*

Consideration of pseudo-ternary line modulation, which has become widely accepted practice, shows that the wave form in the line has no discrete component at the system bit rate. If, however, it is reasonably equalised and then rectified the required frequency becomes available. In most systems the transmitted wave is a half width pulse. On an isolated system it might be practicable to equalise up to the frequency corresponding to the full bit rate and this would give very uniform drive. This, however, uses twice the bandwidth necessary to convey the information and very significantly increases the crosstalk. To convert a large number of pairs in a cable to digital working, it is therefore necessary to hold the upper end of the pass band to as low a frequency as possible above the frequency of the essential half bit rate. This means that some measure of what in data transmission is called inter-symbol interference must arise. To secure reasonable stability in the phase of the extracted wave form, which will be used to drive the regenerator clock circuit, it is necessary to maintain a stable amplitude and to slice the wave form at the correct level. Clock is generated by using this extracted wave form to drive a resonant circuit with a suitably chosen " Q." Inevitably there are irregularities in this operation and there will be some resultant phase jitter.

3. *Framing and Signalling*

Before outlining typical systems it is necessary to refer to two other system requirements. First, any TDM system of transmission must include some redundant bits (i.e. bits not used for the PCM voice information) to define the frame of the system and enable the constituent channels to be identified. Second, some capacity must be provided for transmitting control signals, in particular "seize" and "clear" signals. Later such signalling may use common channel methods as in CCITT No. 6 Signalling.

New Words and Phrases

acute	*a.*	剧烈的
albeit	*conj.*	虽然

a.m.i.	*abbr*.	交替极性码
ATT (= AT&T)	*abbr*.	美国电话电报公司
bipolar	*a*.	双极性的
burst	*n*.	脉冲
catastrophic	*a*.	灾难的
chop	*v*.	断续
commutator	*n*.	转接器
companding	*n*.	压缩
complementary	*a*.	互补的
culmination	*n*.	顶点
damaging	*a*.	有破坏性的
debate	*n*.	讨论,争论
decay	*v*. *n*.	衰减
disparity	*v*.	不均衡
equalize	*v*.	均衡
facsimile	*n*.	传真
fortuitous	*a*.	偶然的
frame	*n*.	帧
fricative	*n*.	摩擦音
hum	*n*.	嗡嗡声
idle	*a*.	空载的
impairment	*n*.	损伤
inevitable	*a*.	不可避免的
interconnection	*n*.	互联网络
intrusive	*a*.	打扰的
isochronous	*a*.	同步的
jitter	*v*.	抖动
junction	*n*.	中继
manifest	*a*.	显然的
manifestation	*n*.	显示

mariner	*n.*	水手
monotonic	*a.*	单调的
Nyquist	*n.*	奈奎斯特
obstacle	*n.*	障碍
outset	*n.*	开端
PCM	*abbr.*	脉冲编码调制
peculiar	*a.*	特殊的
pedestal	*n.*	基准电平
phantom	*n.*	仿真
predominance	*n.*	优势
preliminary	*a.*	初步的
pseudo	*a.*	伪的,假的
quantise	*n.*	量化
recur	*v.*	重现
redundant	*a.*	冗余的
regeneration	*n.*	再生
reorganisation	*n.*	重新组织
representative	*a.*	典型的
residual	*a.*	剩余的
sacrifice	*v.n.*	牺牲
signalling	*n.*	信令
statistical	*a.*	统计的
stream	*n.*	流
stretch	*v.*	伸展
sustain	*v.*	持续
tangent	*n.*	正切
telegraphy	*n.*	电信技术
telephony	*n.*	电话学
ternary	*a.*	三进制的
unnoticeable	*a.*	不显著的

vowel	*n*.	元音
quanta ambiguity		量化模糊
quantising ladder		量化阶梯
quantum step		量化步长
reservoir capacitor		储存电容器
sample-and-hold		采样保持
sawtooth wave		锯齿波
tolerate on		不允许在……方面
weighting network		加权网络

Notes

1. Time division multiplexing (TDM) 时分多路复用

2. The devices used were simply synchronised commutators where one at the sending end "sampled" each of a number of individual channels in sequence and transmitted the samples in sequence. 所应用的设备只是同步交换机,在发送端顺序地对每个通道采样,并顺序地将这些采样值发送出去。

3. If these samples are transmitted as narrow pulses then the pulses corresponding to several channels may be sent consecutively in a regular cycle and it thus becomes feasible to apply TDM to analogue information. 如果这些采样值作为窄脉冲传输,那么对应几个不同信道的脉冲可以在一个整周期内连续地送出去,这样将使时分多路复用技术用于模拟信息成为可能。

4. The characteristic of digital transmission is that since the signal has a restricted number of states (typically for binary data only two) then provided the acquired noise on any section does not exceed the level at which ambiguities (errors) will occur in recognising which state was transmitted, the signal may be regenerated without error and noise is not accumulated. 数字传输的特点是信号只有有限个状态数(典型地,二进制数据只有两个),那么假定任何一个状态所含的噪声不超过这个状态传输后识别时发生模糊(错误)的电平,信号可以无误差地重建,而噪声则

不会积累。

5. This ability of regeneration to avoid almost all noise accumulation results in the signal/noise ratio required on each section to reduce regeneration interpretation errors to a negligible quantity being much lower than an analogue system could tolerate on a complete connection. 信号重建时要避免所有噪声的积累,这种能力将使每部分所需信噪比降低,即降低重建判读误差到一个可忽略的量,这个量远远低于模拟系统在一个完善的线路中容许的量。

6. If there exists an absolutely exact and stable match between the idle channel voltage and the reference voltage at the centre of the quantising ladder then it would be possible to locate the idle channel condition exactly between two decision levels and until the peak-to peak noise exceeds one quantum step it will not be quantised. 如果在空载信道电压和量化阶梯中心的参考电压之间存在一个绝对精确和稳定的匹配,那么就可能在两个判决电平之间精确地定位空载信道状态,直到峰-峰噪声超过一个量化步长,它才被量化的。

7. CCITT, International Telephone and Telegraph Consultative Committee. 国际电话与电报顾问委员会。

8. Transmission must be balanced and although this can be done without transformer coupling it is expensive and complex to organise and substantially impossible. 传输必须是平衡的,尽管没有变压器耦合还是可以做到的,但造价高且构造复杂,实质上是不可能的。

9. On T1 this clock content is ensured by a slight restriction of the codes used (all "0"s are omitted) so that a minimum appearance of "1"s is provided. 在 T1 中,通过对使用的码字有略微的限制来保证时钟分量,都是"0"时忽略,这样就预防了较小出现"1"的情况。

10. To secure reasonable stability in the phase of the extracted wave form, it is necessary to maintain a stable amplitude and to slice the wave form at the correct level. 为了保证从波形提取的相位适当稳定,必需维持稳定的幅度并在适当的电平削波(限幅)。

3.3 GLOBAL POSITIONING SYSTME

3.3.1 Introduction

Global Positioning System (GPS) is space-based radio positioning system that provides time and three-dimensional position and velocity information to suitably equipped users anywhere on or near the surface of the earth.[1]

The GPS system is composed of three parts. These parts are the space, control, and user components. The space component constitutes the satellite portion of the GPS system.

The control component of the GPS system consists of a master control station, five monitoring stations, and three ground antennas. The master control station is located in Colorado Springs, while the other stations and antennas are distributed around the world. The stations monitor the satellites' functionality and their orbits. Any changes that the master control station deems necessary are transmitted to the satellites.

The user component consists of the individual users of the GPS system who use their receivers to calculate precisely their geographical location, velocity, and time.

Users calculate their positions by measuring their distance from the GPS satellites which are within view. The satellites act as reference points in space. At least four satellites are needed for the calculations. The user's receiver measures the apparent range of each satellite by calculating the delay of each satellite's position and time that the signal needs in order to travel to the user.[2] The receiver then calculates the user's position, velocity and time.

The GPS offers two levels of accuracy: the Standard Positioning Service (SPS) and the Precise Positioning Service (PPS). The SPS is used by civilians while the PPS is used in the United States military.

3.3.2 Principles of GPS

The GPS satellites broadcast signals, which contain information enough to compute the distance x of the location from the satellite. Once the distance is known, the point in question can be anywhere on a circle of radius x in 2-D and a sphere in 3-D with the satellite as the center.[3] By knowing the distance from another satellite, the possible positions of the location are narrowed down to two points. Two intersecting circles have two points in common. To distinguish between the two locations, distance from another satellite can be computed or the ridiculous answer can be eliminated. This assumes a precise clock at the GPS receiver. Inaccuracies in the clock can lead to erroneous results if using two satellites or inconsistent equations if using three. To overcome this limitation, the distance from three satellites is computed and algebraic laws are applied to achieve the correct position.

Accurate 3-D measurements require four satellites. To achieve 3-D real time measurements, the receivers need at least four channels. Receivers equipped with only one channel have to measure the distance sequentially from multiple satellites and can take 2 to 30 seconds.

The NAVSTAR (Navigation Satellite Timing and Ranging) system, operated by the US Department of Defense, is the first such system widely available to civilian users.

NAVSTAR is a constellation of 24 satellites and a planned life-span of 7.5 years. There are 24 operational satellites in six circular orbits 20 200 km above the earth at an inclination angle of 55 degrees with a 12 hour period.[4] The satellites are positioned so that at least six of them are in view at any time and at any point in the world. The satellites continually broadcast location and time information. In any event, the constellation will provide a minimum of four satellites in good geometric positions. Up to 10 GPS satellites are normally seen assuming a 10 degree elevation. The satellites are equipped with several cesium clocks, which provide high timing accuracies. The satellites are in synch with each other. Positional accuracy of 100 meters, timing accuracy of 300 nanoseconds and frequency accuracies of a few parts in 10 can be obtained.

Each satellite transmits on two L band frequencies, L1 1575.42 MHz and L2 1227.6 MHz.[5] L1 carries a precise P code and a coarse acquisition CA code. L2 carries the P code. The P code is normally encrypted so that only the CA code is available to civilian users, however, some information can be derived from the P code. Incidentally, when P code is encrypted, it is known as Y code. A navigation data message is superimposed on these codes. The same navigation data message is carried on both frequencies.

There have been three distinct groups of NAVSTAR satellites so far. The groups are designated as blocks. The block I satellites were intended for system testing. The block II satellites were the first fully functional satellites, including cesium atomic clocks for timing as well as the ability to implement selective availability. The latest satellites, the block III versions, include autonomous navigation.

Satellite operating parameters such as navigation data errors, signal availability failures, and certain types of satellite clock failures are monitored internally within the satellite. If such internal failures are detected, users are noticed within six seconds. Other failures may take from 15 minutes to several hours.

Each satellite has some identifying numbers. First is the NAVSTAR number which identifies the specific satellite hardware. Second is the space vehicle SV number. This number is assigned in order of launch. The third is the pseudo-random noise code number PRN. This is a unique integer number which is used to code the signal from that satellite. Some receivers identify the satellites that they are listening to by SV, others by

PRN. The NAVSTAR system provides two sets of services SPS and PPS.

1. *Standard Positioning Service SPS*

SPS provides standard level of positioning and timing accuracy that is available, without qualification or restrictions, to any user continuously on a world wide basis.[6] Most receivers are capable of receiving and using the SPS signal. The SPS accuracy is intentionally degraded by the DOD by the use of Selective Availability based on US security interests. This service provides 100 meters horizontal accuracy, 156 meters vertical accuracy and 167 nanoseconds time accuracy. The signals providing standard positioning service are inherently capable of greater accuracy than this.

2. *Precise Positioning Service PPS*

PPS is the most accurate positioning, velocity, and timing information continuously available, worldwide, from the basic GPS. PPS signals can only be accessed by authorized users with cryptographic equipment and keys and specially equipped receivers. US and Allied military, certain US Government agencies, and selected civil users specifically approved by the US Government, can use PPS. The accuracies achievable using PPS are 17.8 meters horizontal accuracy, 27.7 meters vertical accuracy and 100 nanoseconds time accuracy.

3. *Selective Availability SA*

SA is the intentional degradation of the SPS signals by a time varying bias by the DOD to limit accuracy for non-US military and government users. The potential accuracy of the CA code is around 30 meters, but it is reduced to 100 meters. The SA bias on each satellite signal is different, and so the resulting position solution is a function of the SA bias.

3.3.3 Differential GPS

Differential GPS (DGPS) is simply the normal GPS system with an additional correction signal beamed from a stationary point on the ground. This corrective signal is broadcast over any authorized communication channel and improves the accuracy of SPS GPS.

A fixed position on land is chosen to be used as another reference point in addition to the GPS satellites. This land-based reference point, whose correct geographical location is known, receives the GPS signals, determines its position as indicated by the GPS satellites, and then calculates the SA distortion by comparing the GPS-determined position against its known position.[7] The land-based reference point then broadcasts the difference caused by the SA distortion. Users then use the broadcast difference to improve the calculations of their positions.

DGPS is a method of eliminating errors in a GPS receiver to make the output more accurate. This process is based on the principle that most of the errors seen by GPS receivers in a local area will be common errors. These common errors are caused by factors such as clock deviation, selective availability, drift from predicted orbits, multi-path error, internal receiver noise and changing radio propagation conditions in the ionosphere.[8] If a GPS receiver is placed at location for which the coordinates are known and accepted, the difference between the known coordinates and the GPS calculated coordinates is the error. This receiver is often called a base station.

The error, which the base station has determined, can be applied to other GPS receivers called rovers. Since the sources of the error are continuously changing, it is necessary to match the error correction data from the base station very closely in time to the rover data. One way of doing this is to record the data at the base station and at the rover. The data sets can be processed together at a later time. This is called post processing and is very common for surveying applications. The other way is to transmit the data from the base station to the rover. The error calculation is made in the rover in real time. This process is called real-time DGPS.

Differential GPS offers accuracies of a few meters better than the military's precise positioning service. It also facilitates detection of erroneous signals from the satellites.

3.3.4   Other Radio Navigation Systems

1. *GLONASS*

The Russian system, GLONASS, is similar in operation and may prove complementary to the NAVSTAR system. The GLONASS constellation is composed of 24 satellites, eight in each of three-orbital planes.[9] The satellites operate in circular 19 100 km orbits at an inclination angle of 64.8 degrees and with a 11-hour, 15 minute period. Each satellite transmits on two L frequency groups. The L1 group is centered on 1 609 MHz while the L2 group is centered on 1 251 MHz. Each satellite transmits on a unique pair of frequencies. The GLONASS signals carry both a precise P code and a coarse acquisition CA code. The P code is encrypted for military use while the CA code is available for civilian use.

2. *Long-Range Navigation LORAN-C*

LORAN was one of the earliest and the most successful systems for ground-based radio navigation. Two versions are currently in operation: LORAN-C, which serves civilian users and LORAN-D, which serves the military. These are medium to long range, low frequency time-difference measurement systems. A master and usually up to four secondary transmitting stations put out a set of radio pulses centered on 100 kHz, in a precisely timed sequence. The receiver measures the difference in arrival time between these transmissions from different stations and estimates the position. LORAN-C transmissions can be worked out to ranges over 1 500 kilometers from master stations, providing accuracies of 100 to 500 meters. Shorter range accuracies of better than 30 meters are also available.

3. *TRANSIT*

TRANSIT was the first operational satellite navigation system. Developed by Johns Hopkins Applied Physics Laboratory, the system was intended as an aid to submarine navigation.

The TRANSIT system allows users to determine position by measuring the Doppler shift of a radio signal transmitted by the satellite. Users are able to calculate position within a few hundred meters as long as they knew their altitudes and the satellite ephemeris.

The system has several drawbacks. First, the system is inherently two dimensional. Second, the velocity of the user must be taken into account. Third, mutual interference between the satellites restrict the total number of satellites to five. Thus, satellites would only be visible for limited periods of time. These drawbacks pretty much eliminate aviation applications and severely limit land-based applications.

4. *Timation*

Developed in 1972 by the Naval Research Laboratory (NRL), Timation satellites were intended to provide time and frequency information. The original satellite flew with stable quartz crystal oscillators. Later models flew with the first space-borne atomic clocks. The third satellite acted as a GPS technology demonstrator.

3.3.5 Applications of GPS

1. *Accurate Time*

Internally in the NAVSTAR system, time is kept as GPS time. GPS time is a composite time composed of the times of all available satellite and monitor station clocks. It is monitored by the GPS Operational Control System and by the US Naval Observatory and is steered to keep it within 1 microsecond of UTC. GPS can be used to determine accurate time globally. GPS belongs to the dynamic system achieved by the atomic time scales.

Inexpensive GPS receivers operating at known positions provide a timing accuracy of about 0.1 microsecond with only one satellite in view. With more sophisticated techniques, one can globally synchronize clocks precisely. Presently achievable accuracy of time via GPS is some tens of nanoseconds, however one nanosecond is considered possible.

Ultra precise time transfer is possible few nanoseconds but requires advanced preparation, coordination of the two sites and tracking of specific satellites during specific time periods.[10]

2. *Frequency Counters*

GPS receivers can be optimized for frequency and time applications. Accurate frequency counters, time interval counters, frequency calibrators and phase comparators can be built using the GPS technology. Accurate frequency and timing offset measurements can be made. The GPS clock module is a GPS receiver optimized for frequency and time applications.

3. *Geographic Information Systems*

GPS technology is used extensively in geographic information systems (GIS). These systems combine cellular data networks for communication, GPS for vehicle location, and geographic information system tools for mapping display.

4. *Recorded Position Information*

The GPS position information can be used in a variety of ways. Some of the uses are to track executives, to determine charges in highway toll, to search for stolen cars, to study the migratory patterns animals, etc. Animals are equipped with GPS receivers and with wireless transmitters. The GPS determined position is transmitted to the control station. This information is used to track animals and for studying their nomadic patterns.

5. *Aviation*

GPS technology is being applied in aircraft safety systems, air traffic control system, and zero visibility landing. GPS technology can be used to plot aircraft altitude to a pitch of one-tenth of one degree. In future, pilots will do more monitoring, while computers will issue air traffic instructions.

6. *Emergency Systems*

GPS technology is being used to develop emergency messaging products. With the aid of a wireless communication link, the emergency system communicates the GPS derived position information and the specifics of the situation to the base station.

7. *Intelligent Highway Systems*

Intelligent Highway Systems will combine GPS technology with communications, controls, navigation and information systems to improve highway safety, ease traffic congestion. Car Navigation System uses a specialized computer that uses the signals from GPS satellites to track the driver's progress on a digital map. It may provide services like the shortest route.

New Words and Phrases

functionality	*n.*	功能性
geographical	*a.*	地理的
broadcast	*v.*	播放
ridiculous	*a.*	荒谬的
inaccuracy	*n.*	错误
erroneous	*a.*	错误的
inconsistent	*a.*	不一致的
constellation	*n.*	星座
elevation	*n.*	仰角
cesium	*n.*	铯
encrypt	*v.*	加密
autonomous	*a.*	自主的
authorized	*a.*	经授权的

cryptographic	a.	用密码写的
intentional	a.	故意的
degradation	n.	劣化
bias	n.	偏置
ionosphere	n.	电离层
surveying	n.	测量
complementary	n.	互补
sophisticated	a.	成熟的
migratory	a.	迁徙的
nanosecond	n.	纳秒
apparent range		视在距离
multi-path		多径
mutual interference		相互冲突
quartz crystal oscillator		石英晶体振荡器
DOD(Department of Defense)		国防部(美国)
UTC(Universal Time Coordinated)		协调世界时

Notes

1. Global Positioning System (GPS) is space-based radio positioning system that provides time and three-dimensional position and velocity information to suitably equipped users anywhere on or near the surface of the earth. 全球定位系统 (GPS) 是空基的无线定位系统,它可以为地球表面及附近的任何地方装备有适当接收机的用户提供时间、三维空间地理位置和运动速度的信息。

2. The user's receiver measures the apparent range of each satellite by calculating the delay each satellite's position and time that signal needs in order to travel to the user. 用户端接收机通过计算每颗卫星位置的延迟和信号传送到用户所需的时间来测量每颗卫星的视在距离。

3. Once the distance is known, the point in question can be anywhere on a circle of radius x in 2-D and a sphere in 3-D with the satellite as the center. 一旦知道这个距离,所考虑的点可以是在二维空间以 x 为半

径的圆上的任何地方或是在以卫星为中心的三维球体上的任何地方。

4. There are 24 operational satellites in six circular orbits 20 200 km above the earth at an inclination angle of 55 degrees with a 12 hour period. 在距离地球 20 200 公里的六个圆轨道上运行着以 55 度的倾角和 12 小时为周期的 24 颗卫星。

5. Each satellite transmits on two L band frequencies, L1 1575.42 MHz and L2 1227.6 MHz. 每颗卫星发射两个 L 波段频率的信号,其中 L1 的频率是 1575.42 MHz 和 L2 的频率是 1227.6 MHz。

6. SPS provides standard level of positioning and timing accuracy that is available, without qualification or restrictions, to any user continuously on a world wide basis. 不需要资格认证和限制,SPS 对在全球范围内的用户提供标准级别的有效精度的定位和定时。

7. This land-based reference point, whose correct geographical location is known, receives the GPS signals, determines its position as indicated by the GPS satellites, and then calculates the SA distortion by comparing the GPS-determined position against its known position. 如果这个陆基参考点的准确地理位置已知,在这个点上接收 GPS 信号,根据 GPS 卫星确定它的位置,然后通过比较 GPS 确定的位置和已知位置来计算 SA 的失真。

8. These common errors are caused by factors such as clock deviation, selective availability, drift from predicted orbits, multi-path error, internal receiver noise and changing radio propagation conditions in the ionosphere. 这些公共误差是由像时钟偏离、选择的有效性、轨道的漂移、多路径误差、内部接收机噪声以及电离层无线电波传输条件的改变等因素引起的。

9. The GLONASS constellation is composed of 24 satellites, eight in each of three-orbital planes. GLONASS 星座由 24 颗卫星组成,在三个轨道平面内分别有八颗卫星。

10. Ultra precise time transfer is possible few nanoseconds but requires advanced preparation, coordination of the two sites and tracking of specific satellites during specific time periods. 更高的时间准确度可

以到达亿分之一秒,但是这需要提前准备,在特定周期内协调两点并跟踪指定卫星。

3.4 SOFTWARE RADIO

As communications technology continues its rapid transition from analog to digital, more functions of contemporary radio systems are implemented in software, leading toward the software radio.

Throughout last thirty years, radio systems migrated from analog to digital in almost every respect from system control to source and channel coding to hardware technology. And now the software radio revolution extends these horizons by liberating radio-based services from chronic dependency band, channel bandwidth, and channel coding.[1] This liberation is accomplished through a combination of techniques that includes multi-band antennas and RF conversion, wideband Analog to Digital conversion and Digital to Analog conversion, and the implementation of IF, baseband, and bitstream processing functions in general-purpose programmable processors.[2]

3.4.1 Software Radio

1. *Hardware-based Radio Designs*

In wireless communications, information is encoded into radio waves. These are collected (or transmitted) from (to) the air by the antenna. The received signal is then passed to a series of components that extract the useful information and convert it into the output of the radio. The basic design is the same whether the radio signal is destined for a cell phone, microwave repeater, or AM/FM car radio.

Traditional radios are based on the super heterodyne (superhet) receiver circuit. In the superhet receiver, the incoming signal (at the radio frequency, RF) is first down-converted to a lower intermediate frequency (IF).

The IF is then filtered for noise and amplified before being demodulated to produce the baseband signal that represents the desired information. This analog baseband signal may be passed directly to further downstage processing, or may first be digitized and subjected to additional signal processing. There are several important reasons for down-converting to a lower and standardized IF. First, it is easier, and hence less expensive, to build filters and amplifiers   especially linear amplifiers

for a lower frequency signal. Second, the use of a common IF enables standardization and hence the realization of scale and scope economies in the design of radio components.

Traditional designs for implementing the superhet receiver architecture were optimized for specific frequencies and applications and each of the stages were implemented in hardware that was closely coupled. This was due largely to the difficulties inherent in and limitations in the state of the art in the design of analog signal processing components. [3] Analog processing is much more complicated than digital processing, which is one of the key reasons why the transition to digital signals is so important.

2. *Software Radio Designs*

Software radio alters traditional radio designs in three distinct and complementary ways: it moves analog/digital (A/D) conversion as close to the receiving antenna as possible, substitutes software for hardware processing, and facilitates a transition from specialized to general-purpose hardware. [4] The difference between traditional radio and software radio is shown in Fig.3.7.

First, moving the A/D conversion closer to the antenna makes it possible to apply the advances of digital computing and communication technology sooner in the radio. This is beneficial directly because digital components are less complex and lower cost than analog components. Additionally, this makes it easier to take advantage of advances in digital signal processing. These include advanced techniques for encoding information and separating signal from noise.

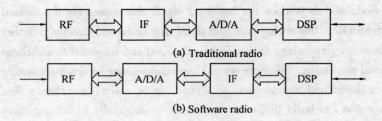

(a) Traditional radio

(b) Software radio

Fig.3.7   The difference between traditional radio and software radio

Second, substituting software for hardware increases flexibility. This flexibility makes customization easier and helps deliver a degree of future-proofing. That is, replacing software especially if this can be done remotely is faster and lower-cost than replacing hardware. New features and capabilities can be implemented when available (upgrade ability) or when desired (customize ability). This can allow services to be changed more rapidly, or equivalently, time to market is reduced. Additionally, the reliance on software processing can eliminate redundant hardware chains, as found in dual-mode phones, for example.

Third, software radio facilitates the transition from specialized to general-purpose hardware. Initially, dedicated hardware embodied in Application Specific Integrated Circuits (ASICs) may be replaced by Field Programmable Gate Arrays (FPGAs) and Digital Signal Processors (DSPs). Prospectively, there is a hope that general-purpose computing platform will be able to support software radios. At any given point in time, a specialized chipset will typically achieve higher performance than a general-purpose processor. However, once Moore's Law drives the general-purpose processor past a performance threshold such that it can perform the necessary radio functions well enough, the advantages of general-purpose hardware come to the forefront.

The transition to general-purpose hardware also makes it more likely that there will be open interfaces.[5] That is, general-purpose hardware derives its value from its ability to be combined into systems for many different purposes. This requires the ability to "mix and match" the hardware with diverse complementary hardware and software.

3.4.2 The software Radio Architecture

1. *Recevier*

In order to shift as much functionality as possible from the analog to the digital domain of a software radio receiver, the analog-to-digital interface has to be shifted from baseband to IF or even to RF. This leads to a "generic" software radio terminal architecture comprising an analog section, a band-pass analog-to-digital converter and a digital signal processing unit.

The analog section provides the band-pass signal either at IF or even RF. Since channel selection by means of an analog filter bank is not really an approach to a software programmable terminal, we suggest a fixed wide-band analog section with a wide-band channel filter having a bandwidth equal to the digitization bandwidth. [6] There are two approaches to the AD conversion or digitization.

(1) Full Band Digitization

The whole bandwidth of the software radio service is digitized, i. e. all channels of all services to be supported. This bandwidth can easily extend to some 100 MHz. Taking into account the interferer characteristics, the dynamic range of the A/D has to be larger than 100 dB (while digitizing a bandwidth of some 100 MHz). Being the most elegant one, this solution cannot be realized power and cost effectively with today's technologies.

(2) Partial Band Digitization

Employing the superhet receiver principle to the software radio receiver, this approach uses a digitization bandwidth equal to the widest channel bandwidth of all supported services.

Since our intention is to present architecture of a software radio receiver that is realizable today, we have to refrain from full band digitization. Thus the digitization bandwidth, and hence the bandwidth of the fixed analog channel filter, is at least equal to the widest channel bandwidth of all supported services.

In order to accommodate for wide-band and narrow-band signals the A/D has to sample the signal at a relatively high sample rate. Hence, the first stages of the digital signal processing unit have to perform the digital down-conversion, sample-rate adaptation and channel selection at high sample rates, requiring very efficient implementations of these 'critical functionalities'. Thus the prepared signal can be then standard-specifically processed on a digital signal processor at symbol rate.

2. *Smart Antenna*

The antenna of the software radio spans multiple bands, up to multiple octaves per band with uniform shape and low losses to provide access to available service bands. In military applications, for example, a mobile terminal may need to employ VHF/UHF line of sight frequencies, UHF satellite communications, and HF as a backup mode. Switched access to such multiple bands requires octave per band an agile frequency reference in the RF segment.[7] In addition, multiple antenna elements may be part of a beam forming network for interference reduction or space division multiple access (SDMA).

The relationship between interference cancellation capacity and the number of antenna elements varies. A single auxiliary element, for example, can reduce interference of a large number of interferences. Algorithms that reduce interference through non-spatial techniques can also reduce a large number of interferers with one or with no auxiliary antenna elements.[8] Beam forming of N antenna elements can place N-1 adaptive nulls on interferers sufficiently separated in azimuth. But coherent multipath may require a distinct null for each distinct multipath direction, reducing the number of interferers accordingly. Polarization scrambling form nearby reflecting surfaces may require 2N + 1 elements for N paths. The structure of the antenna array(s) determines the number of distinct physical and logical signal processing paths in the RF conversion and IF demands for directional selectivity. Multipath compensation and interference suppression versus wideband low-loss antennas versus afford ability define the tradeoffs of the antenna segment.

3. *The RF Conversion*

RF conversion includes preamplification, and conversion of RF signals to and from standard intermediate frequencies suitable for wideband A/D/A conversion. In most radio bands, RF conversion will be analog. Certain critical RF problems are exacerbated in the software radio. These include the need for amplifier linearity and efficiency across the access band. RF shielding of processors may also be necessary to avoid the introduction of processor clock harmonics into the analog RF/IF circuits.

4. *A/D/A Converters*

W_a, the bandwidth of the IF to be digitized, determines what kinds of A/D techniques are feasible. According to the Nyquist criterion for band limited signals f_s, the sampling rate of the A/D converter, must be at least twice W_a. Practical systems typically require modest oversampling

$$f_s > 2.5 W_a$$

Wideband A/D/A converters access broad instantaneous segments of spectrum, typically 10 to 50 MHz. Such wide access may also be achieved in parallel sub-bands of more modest 1 to 10 MHz bandwidth each. The dynamic range of each parallel sub-band depends on the dynamic range of A/D/A converters. Since the product of dynamic range times sampling rate is approximately constant for a given A/D/A technology, narrower sub-bands generally increase the useful dynamic range, albeit at the cost of increased system complexity.

The placement of wideband A/D/A conversion before the final IF and channel isolation filters enables digital signal processing before detection and demodulation, and reduces the cost of mixed channel access modes.

5. *Channel Selection and Interferer Cancellation*

In a software driven communications receiver, the task of channel selection and interferer cancellation has to be performed by means of digital filters. Basically this could be done using band-pass filters at IF (or RF) or using low-pass filters at baseband after digital down-conversion. For reasons of reducing the complexity and power consumption we suggest this task to be performed at the lowest possible sample rate at baseband. Since the tasks of decimation, sample rate adaptation, channel selection and interferer cancellation, basically are filter operations, they can be performed highly intermeshed using the same filters. [9]

3.4.3 The goal for software radio

The ultimate goal for software radio is to perform the A/D conversion directly at the antenna so that all signal processing could be done in software. However, that is not practical today. The question of where one does the A/D conversion determines what radio functions can be moved into software and what types of hardware are required. [10] What is feasible is a moving target, as radio and its complementary technologies continue to improve. Disagreements about what will be feasible when and at what cost have led to disagreements about the proper definition for software radio.

At one extreme, one might consider calling it software radio if software is used at any stage within the radio. By this definition, a multi-mode cell phone that uses software to control which hardware chain is operational during a call may be construed as a software radio, or perhaps, software defined radio. [11] At the other extreme, one might choose to reserve the term software radio for only the narrowest of cases A/D conversion at the antenna with all radio functionality implemented in software running on general-purpose hardware.[12] Therefore, we consider it software radio if it involves A/D conversion at the IF stage with the capability to support software processing thereafter.

Whether subsequent stages are implemented in dedicated or general-purpose hardware is not critical to the definition of software radio, but certainly, the earlier A/D conversion and software implementation make it more feasible to shift to general-purpose hardware.

Two key technical limitations make it infeasible to do the A/D conversion at the antenna. First, digitization of the RF signal requires the incoming signal to be sampled, which results in the conversion of the waveform data into a sequence of numbers corresponding to each sample. The higher the frequency, the higher the required rate of sampling to accurately represent the signal.

Additionally, the more information in the signal, the higher the resolution required to capture the information, that is, the more bits that must be represented per sample. Taken together, this means that high bandwidth or high resolution, high frequency RF transmissions require very high sampling rates. The ability to support very high sampling rates, which is especially critical with the use of higher frequency signals (in the GHz range, instead of MHz or KHz), limits the range of what can be digitized. Indeed, it is only recently that sufficiently fast DSPs and wideband A/D chipsets have become available at affordable prices to make it feasible to contemplate A/D conversion of the IF rather than the baseband signal.

Second, it is difficult to design linear amplifiers that can amplify the wideband signal at the antenna without distortion. Linear amplification is needed to keep the signal from being lost in the noise that accompanies the signal received at the antenna. Although new amplifier designs and signal processing techniques can alleviate some of these difficulties, employing these increases the cost of the radio.

The current frontier for software radio research is focused on what is referred to as "cognitive radio". The basic idea is to make radio receivers and transmitters more intelligent (via software, including Artificial Intelligence) and adaptive so that they can respond to changes in their local environment. These may include adapting to changing interference or congestion conditions, or adapting to facilitate interoperability among diverse devices, or adapting to accommodate the requirements of changing applications (e.g. , from wireless email to video to voice).

New Words and Phrases

contemporary	*a.*	当代的
programmable	*a.*	可编程的
bitstream	*n.*	比特流
destine	*v.*	指定,预定
couple	*v.*	联系,耦合
superhet	*n.*	超外差
complementary	*a.*	补充的
prospectively	*adv.*	预期
chipset	*n.*	芯片
diverse	*a.*	变化多的
elegant	*a.*	一流的
octave	*n.*	倍频程
null	*n.*	零点
Polarization	*n.*	极化
scrambling	*n.*	不规则性
preamplification	*n.*	前置放大
exacerbate	*v.*	恶化,使加剧
shielding	*n.*	屏蔽
oversampling	*n.*	过采样

isolation	*n.*	隔离
intermesh	*v.*	互相配合
congestion	*n.*	阻塞
interoperability	*n.*	互操作性
interferer	*n.*	干扰信号
decimation	*n.*	抽选
cell phone		蜂窝电话(指蜂窝移动通信终端或手机)
refrain from		避免
Smart Antenna		智能天线
directional selectivity		方向性
a multi-mode cell phone		多模手机
Artificial Intelligence		人工智能
agile frequency		捷变频

Notes

1. And now the software radio revolution extends these horizons by liberating radio-based services from band, channel bandwidth, and channel coding. 现在,软件无线电革命进一步延伸这些变革,使基于无线电技术的各种服务从频段、信道带宽和信道编码中解放出来。

2. This liberation is accomplished through a combination of techniques that includes multi-band antennas and RF conversion, wideband Analog to Digital conversion and Digital to Analog conversion, and the implementation of IF, baseband, and bitstream processing functions in general-purpose programmable processors. 这种解放是通过结合了多种技术来完成的,包括多频带天线和射频变换、宽带 A/D 和 D/A 转换在通用可编程处理器中完成的中频、基带和比特流处理功能。

3. This was due largely to the difficulties inherent in and limitations in the state of the art in the design of analog signal processing components. 在很大程度上是由于模拟信号处理器件设计中固有的困难和工艺的限制。

4. Software radio alters traditional radio designs in three distinct and complementary ways: it moves analog/digital（A/D）conversion as close to the receiving antenna as possible, substitutes software for hardware processing, and facilitates a transition from specialized to general-purpose hardware. 软件无线电在三个明显的而又相辅相成的方面改变传统的无线电设计,它将模数转换尽可能近地移到接收天线附近,用软件代替硬件处理,使专用到通用硬件的转换更容易。

5. The transition to general-purpose hardware also makes it more likely that there will be open interfaces. 向通用硬件的转换也使得开放接口(指各种通信系统的接口)更加可能。

6. Since channel selection by means of an analog filter bank is not really an approach to a software programmable terminal, we suggest a fixed wide-band analog section with a wide-band channel filter having a bandwidth equal to the digitization bandwidth. 因为利用模拟滤波器组选择信道并不是一种真正的软件可编程终端选择信道的方法,我们建议采用一个带有宽带信道滤波器的固定宽带模拟部件,这个宽带信道滤波器的带宽同数字化的带宽相同。

7. In military applications, for example, a mobile terminal may need to employ VHF/UHF line of sight frequencies, UHF satellite communications, and HF as a backup mode. Switched access to such multiple bands requires octave per band an agile frequency reference in the RF segment. 例如,在军事应用中,移动终端可能需要利用甚高频或超高频的视距频率、超高频卫星通信、以及高频作为一种后备方式。这么多频段的交换需要倍频程的每个频段都参照射频段有捷变频能力。

8. Algorithms that reduce interference through non-spatial techniques can also reduce a large number of interferers with one or with no auxiliary antenna elements. 用一个或不用辅助天线阵元,通过非空间技术减小干扰的算法也能去除大量的干扰信号。

9. Since the tasks of decimation, sample rate adaptation, channel selection and interferer cancellation, basically are filter operations, they can be performed intermeshed using the same filters. 由于采样、

采样率的匹配、信道的选择和干扰对消基本上是滤波工作,它们都能用同样的滤波器互相配合来实现。

10. The question of where one does the A/D conversion determines what radio functions can be moved into software and what types of hardware are required. 在何处完成数模转换的问题决定了向软件加入什么样的功能,以及需要何种类型的硬件。

11. By this definition, a multi-mode cell phone that uses software to control which hardware chain is operational during a call may be construed as a software radio, or perhaps, software defined radio. 根据这种定义,一个用软件来控制、在一个通话期间由硬件链路运行的多模手机就可以认为是一种软件无线电,或者说,软件定义的无线电。

12. At the other extreme, one might choose to reserve the term software radio for only the narrowest of cases A/D conversion at the antenna with all radio functionality implemented in software running on general-purpose hardware. 另一个极端情况是,人们可能仅仅在一种很有限的情况下选择保留软件无线电这个术语——天线端的 A/D 转换、在通用硬件上由软件运行实现所有的无线电功能。

Special Topics in Signal Processing

4.1 THE FAST ALGORITHMS

4.1.1 Introduction

An algorithm, like most other engineering devices, can be described either by an input/output relationship or by a detailed explanation of its internal construction.[1] When one applies the techniques of digital signal processing to a new problem, one is concerned only with the input/output aspects of the algorithm. Given a signal, or a data record of some kind, one is concerned with what should be done to this data, that is, with what the output of the algorithm should be when such and such a data record is the input. Perhaps the output is a filtered version of the input or its Foruier transform. These input/output relationships for an algorithm can be expressed mathematically without prescribing in detail all of the steps by which the calculation is to be performed.

Devising such a good algorithm for an information processing problem, from this input/output point of view, may be a formidable and sophisticated task, but this is not our concern in this book. We will assume that we are given an input/output algorithm described in terms of filters, Fourier transforms, interpolations, decimations, correlations, modulations, histograms, matrix operations, and so forth. All of these can be expressed with mathematical formulas and so can be computed just as written. This will be called the obvious implementation.

One may be content with the obvious implementation; for many years most were content, and even today some are still content. But once people began to compute such things, other people began to look for more efficient ways to compute them. This is the story we aim to tell, the story of fast algorithms. By a fast algorithm, we mean a detailed description of a computational procedure that is not the obvious way to compute the required output from the input. [2] A fast algorithm usually gives up a conceptually clear computation in favor of one that is computationally efficient.

Suppose we need to compute a number A given by

$$A = ac + ad + bc + bd \tag{1}$$

As written, this requires four multiplications and three additions to compute. If we need to compute A many times with different sets of data, we will quickly notice that

$$A = (a + b)(c + d) \tag{2}$$

is an equivalent form that requires only one multiplication and two additions, and so is to be preferred. This simple example is quite obvious but really illustrates most of what we shall talk about. Everything we do can be thought of in terms of the clever insertion of parentheses in a computational problem. But in a big problem the fast algorithms cannot be found by inspection. It will require a considerable amount of theory to find them.

A simple example of a fast algorithm is complex multiplication. The complex product

$$(e + jf) = (a + jb) \cdot (c + jd) \tag{3}$$

can be written in terms of real multiplications and real additions

$$e = (ac - bd) \tag{4}$$

$$f = (ad + bc) \tag{5}$$

We see that these formulas require four real multiplications and two real additions. A more efficient "algorithm" is

$$e = (a - b)d + a(c - d) \tag{6}$$

$$f = (a - b)d + b(c + d) \tag{7}$$

whenever multiplication is harder than addition. This form requires three real multiplications and five real additions. If c and d are constants for a series of complex multiplications, then the terms $c + d$ and $c - d$ are constants also and can be computed off-line. It then requires three real multiplications and three real additions to do one complex multiplication.

We have traded one multiplication for an addition. This can be a worthwhile savings, but only if the signal processor is designed to take advantage of it. Some signal processors have been designed with a prejudice for a complex multiplication that uses four multiplications. Then the advantage of the improved algorithm is wasted.

We can dwell further on this example as a foretaste of things to come.[3] The complex multiplication above can be rewritten as a matrix product

$$\begin{bmatrix} e \\ f \end{bmatrix} = \begin{bmatrix} c & -d \\ d & c \end{bmatrix} \begin{bmatrix} a \\ b \end{bmatrix} \tag{8}$$

where the vector $\begin{bmatrix} a \\ b \end{bmatrix}$ represents the complex number $a + jb$, the matrix $\begin{bmatrix} c & -d \\ d & c \end{bmatrix}$ represents the complex number $c + jd$, and the vector $\begin{bmatrix} e \\ f \end{bmatrix}$ represents the complex number $e + jf$. The matrix-vector product is a way to represent complex multiplication.

The alternative algorithm can be written in matrix form as

$$\begin{bmatrix} e \\ f \end{bmatrix} = \begin{bmatrix} 1 & 0 & 1 \\ 0 & 1 & 1 \end{bmatrix} \begin{bmatrix} (c-d) & 0 & 0 \\ 0 & (c+d) & 0 \\ 0 & 0 & d \end{bmatrix} \begin{bmatrix} 1 & 0 \\ 0 & 1 \\ 1 & -1 \end{bmatrix} \begin{bmatrix} a \\ b \end{bmatrix} \quad (9)$$

The algorithm can be thought of as nothing more than the unusual matrix factorization:

$$\begin{bmatrix} c & -d \\ d & c \end{bmatrix} = \begin{bmatrix} 1 & 0 & 1 \\ 0 & 1 & 1 \end{bmatrix} \begin{bmatrix} (c-d) & 0 & 0 \\ 0 & (c+d) & 0 \\ 0 & 0 & d \end{bmatrix} \begin{bmatrix} 1 & 0 \\ 0 & 1 \\ 1 & -1 \end{bmatrix}$$

$$(10)$$

We can abbreviate the algorithm as

$$\begin{bmatrix} e \\ f \end{bmatrix} = BDA \begin{bmatrix} a \\ b \end{bmatrix} \quad (11)$$

where A is a 3 by 2 matrix that we call a matrix of preadditions; D is a 3 by 3 diagonal matrix that is responsible for all of the general multiplications; and B is a 2 by 3 matrix that we call a matrix of postadditions.

We shall find that many of the best computational procedures for convolution and for the discrete Fourier transform can be put into this factored form of a diagonal matrix in the center on each side of which is a matrix whose elements are $1, 0$, and -1. These fast algorithms will have the structure of a batch of additions followed by a batch of multiplications followed by another batch of additions.

The final example is a fast algorithm for multiplying matrices. Let

$$C = AB$$

where A and B are l by n and n by m matrices, respectively. The standard method for computing the matrix C is

$$c_{ij} = \sum_{k=1}^{n} a_{ik}b_{kj} \qquad \begin{aligned} i &= 1, \cdots, l \\ j &= 1, \cdots, m \end{aligned} \quad (12)$$

which requires nlm multiplications and $(n-1)lm$ additions as it is written. We shall give an algorithm that reduces the number of multiplications by almost a factor of two but increases the number of additions. The total number of operations increases slightly.

We use the identity

$$a_1 b_1 + a_2 b_2 = (a_1 + b_2)(a_2 + b_1) - a_1 a_2 - b_1 b_2$$

on the elements of A and B. Suppose that n is even (otherwise append a column of zeros to A and a row of zeros to B, which does not change the product C). Apply the above identity to pairs of columns of A and pairs of rows of B to write

$$c_{ij} = \sum_{k=1}^{n/2} (a_{i,2k-1} + b_{2k,j})(a_{i,2k} + b_{2k-1,j}) -$$
$$\sum_{k=1}^{n/2} a_{i,2k-1} a_{i,2k} - \sum_{k=1}^{n/2} b_{2k-1,j} b_{2k,j} \qquad (13)$$
$$i = 1, \cdots, l; j = 1, \cdots, n$$

The computational savings results because the second term depends only on i and need not be recomputed for each j and the third term depends only on j and need not be recomputed for each i.[4] The total number of multiplications used to compute matrix C is $\frac{1}{2} nlm + \frac{1}{2} n(l + m)$, and the total number of additions is $\frac{3}{2} nlm + lm + (\frac{1}{2} n - 1)(l + m)$. For large matrices the number of multiplications is about half of the direct method.

This last example may be a good place for a word of caution about numerical accuracy. Although the number of multiplications is reduced, this algorithm is more sensitive to roundoff error unless it is used with care. By proper scaling of intermediate steps, however, one can obtain computational accuracy that is nearly the same as the direct method.[5] Consideration of computational noise is always a practical factor in judging a fast algorithm, although we shall usually ignore it. Sometimes when the number of operations is reduced, the computational noise is reduced because there are fewer sources of noise. In other algorithms, though there are fewer sources of computational noise, the answer may be very sensitive to one or more of them, and so the computational noise in the answer is increased.

4.1.2 Applications of Fast Algorithms

Very large scale integrated circuits[6] called chips are now available. A chip can contain on the order of 100 000 logical gates, and it is not surprising that the theory of algorithms is looked to as a way of efficiently organizing these gates. Sometimes a considerable performance improvement can be realized by choice of algorithm. Of course, a performance improvement can also be realized by increasing the size of the chip or its speed. These latter kinds of improvements are more widely understood.

For example, suppose one devises an algorithm for a Fourier transform that has only one-fifth the computation of another Fourier transform algorithm. By using the new algorithm, one might realize an improvement that can be as real as if one increased the speed or the size of the chip by a factor of five. To realize this improvement, however, the chip designer must reflect the architecture of the algorithm in the architecture of the chip. A naive design can dissipate the advantages by increasing the complexity of indexing, for example, or of input/output flow. An understanding of the fast algorithms will be required to obtain the best system designs in the era of very large scale integrated circuits.

At first glance, it might appear that the two kinds of development— fast circuits and fast algorithms—are in competition. If one can build the chip big enough or fast enough, then it seemingly does not matter if one uses inefficient algorithms.[7] No doubt this view is sound in some cases, but in other cases one can also make exactly the opposite argument. Large digital signal processors often create a need for fast algorithms. This is because one begins to deal with signal processing problems that are much larger than before. Whether completing algorithms for some problem have running times proportional to n^2 or n^3 may be of minor importance when n equals 3 or 4; but when n equals 1 000, it becomes critical.[8]

The fast algorithms we shall develop are concerned with digital signal processing, and the applications of the algorithms are as broad as the application of digital signal processing itself. Now that it is practical to build a sophisticated algorithm for digital signal processing onto a chip, we would like to be able to choose such an algorithm to maximize the performance of the chip. But to do this for a large chip involves a considerable amount of theory. Advanced topics in logic design and computer architecture such as parallelism and pipelining must also be studied before one can determine all aspects of complexity.

We usually measure the performance of an algorithm by the number of multiplications and additions it uses. These measures are about as deep as one can go at the level of the computational algorithm. At a lower level, we would wish to know the area of the chip or the number of gates on it and the time required to complete a computation. Often one judges a circuit by the area-time product. We will make no effort to give performance measures at this level because this is beyond the province of the algorithm designer.

Over the last decade, sonar systems have become almost completely digital. Though they process only a few kilohertz of signal bandwidth, these systems can use tens of millions or even hundreds of millions of multiplications per second and even more additions. Extensive racks of digital equipment are needed for such systems, and yet reasons for even more processing are routinely conceived.

Radar systems also are becoming digital, but many of the front-end functions are still done by conventional microwave or analog circuitry. One needs to notice only that, in principle, radar and sonar are quite similar, but that radar has 1 000 or more times as much bandwidth, to see the enormous potential for more digital signal processing in radar systems.

Seismic processing provides our principal method for exploration deep below the earth's surface. This is an important method of searching for petroleum reserves. Many computers are already busy full time processing the large stacks of data tapes, but there is no end to the computations remaining.

Computerized tomography is now widely used to synthetically form images of internal organs of the human body by using X-ray data from multiple projections. Algorithms are under study that will reduce considerably the X-ray dosage, but the signal processing requirements are far beyond anything that is practical today. Other forms of medical imaging are under study, such as those using ultrasonic data, nuclear magnetic resonance data, or particle decay data, that also use digital signal processing.

Nondestructive testing of manufactured articles such as casting is possible by means of computer-generated internal images based on the response to induced vibrations. [9]

It is also possible in principle to enhance poor-quality photographs. Pictures blurred by camera motion or out-of-focus pictures can be corrected by signal processing. However, to do this digitally takes large amounts of signal processing computations.

Satellite photographs can be processed digitally to merge several images or to enhance features, or to combine information received on different wavelengths, or to create stereoscopic images synthetically. For example, for meteorological research, one can create a moving three-dimensional image of the cloud patterns moving above the earth's surface based on a sequence of satellite photographs from several aspects.

Other applications for the fast algorithms of digital signal processing could be given, but these should suffice to prove the point that a need exists and continues to grow for fast algorithms for digital signal processing.

All of these applications are characterized by computations that are massive but are fairly straightforward and have an orderly structure. In addition, once a hardware module or a software subroutine is designed to do a certain task, it is permanently dedicated to this task. One is willing to make a substantial design effort because the design cost is not what matters; the operational performance is far more important.

4.1.3 Digital Signal Processing

The most important task of digital signal processing is the task of filtering a long sequence of numbers, and the most important device is the digital filter. Normally, the data sequence has an unspecified length and is so long as to appear infinite to the processing. The numbers in the sequence are usually either real numbers or complex numbers, but we shall also deal with other kinds of numbers. A digital filter is a device that produces a new sequence of numbers called the output sequence from the given sequence, now called the input sequence. Filters in common use can be constructed out of those circuit elements called shift-register stages, adders, scalers, and multipliers. A shift-register stage holds a single number, which it displays on its output line. At discrete time instants called clock times, the shift-register stage replaces its content with the number appearing on the input line, discarding its previous content. [10]

The two kinds of filter we shall study that are the most important are those known as finite-impulse-response (FIR) filters and autoregressive filters. A FIR filter is simply a tapped delay line in which the outputs of each stage, multiplied by a fixed constant, are added together. An autoregressive filter is also a tapped delay line, but with the output fed back to the input.

The output of a FIR filter is a linear convolution of the input sequence and the sequence described by the filter tap weights.

Linear convolution is perhaps the most common computational problem found on digital signal processing, and we shall spend a great deal of time studying how to implement it efficiently. We shall spend even more time studying ways to compute a cyclic convolution. This may seem a little strange because a cyclic convolution does not often arise naturally in applications. We study it because there are so many good ways to compute a cyclic convolution. Therefore we will develop fast methods of computing long linear convolutions by patching together many cyclic convolutions.

Given the two sequences called the data sequence

$$d = \{d_i, \quad i = 0, \cdots, N - 1\}$$

and the filter sequence

$$g = \{g_i, \quad i = 0, \cdots, L - 1\}$$

where N is the data blocklength and L is the filter blocklength, the linear convolution is a new sequence called the signal sequence or the output sequence

$$s = \{s_i, \quad i = 0, \cdots, L + N - 2\}$$

given by the equation

$$s_i = \sum_{k=0}^{N-1} g_{i-k} d_k, \quad i = 0, \cdots, L + N - 2 \qquad (14)$$

and $L + N - 1$ is the output blocklength. The convolution is written with the understanding that $g_{i-k} = 0$ if $i - k$ is less than zero. Because each component of d multiplies each component of g, there are NL multiplications in the obvious implementation of the convolution.

There is a very large body of theory dealing with the design of a FIR filter in the sense of choosing the length L and the tap weights g_i. We are not concerned with this aspect of filter design; our concern is with fast algorithms for computing the filter output s from the filter g and the input sequence d.

A concept closely related to the convolution is the correlation, given by

$$r_i = \sum_{k=0}^{N-1} g_{i+k}d_k, \quad i = 0, \cdots, L + N - 2 \tag{15}$$

where $g_{i+k} = 0$ for $i + k \geqslant L$. The correlation can be computed as a convolution simply by reading one of the two sequences backwards. All of the methods for computing a linear convolution are easily changed into methods for computing the correlation.

We can also express the convolution in the notation of polynomials. Let

$$d(x) = \sum_{i=0}^{N-1} d_i x^i \tag{16}$$

$$g(x) = \sum_{i=0}^{L-1} g_i x^i \tag{17}$$

Then

$$s(x) = g(x)d(x) \tag{18}$$

where

$$s(x) = \sum_{i=0}^{L+N-1} s_i x^i \tag{18}$$

This can be seen by examining the coefficients of the product $g(x)d(x)$. Of course, we can also write

$$s(x) = d(x)g(x) \tag{20}$$

which makes clear that d and g play symmetric roles in the convolution. Therefore we can also write the linear convolution in the equivalent form

$$s_i = \sum_{k=0}^{L-1} g_k d_{i-k} \tag{21}$$

Another form of convolution is the cyclic convolution, which is closely related to the linear convolution. Given the two sequences d_i for $i = 0, \cdots, n - 1$ and g_i for $i = 0, \cdots, n - 1$, each of blocklength n, a new sequence s'_i for $i = 0, \cdots, n - 1$ of blocklength n now is given by the cyclic convolution

$$s'_i = \sum_{k=0}^{n-1} g_{((i-k))} d_k \quad i = 0, \cdots, n - 1 \tag{22}$$

where the double parentheses denote modulo n arithmetic on the indices. That is,

$$((n - k)) = n - k \ (\text{mod } n)$$

and

$$0 \leqslant ((n - k)) < n$$

Notice that in the cyclic convolution, for every i, every d_k finds itself multiplied by a meaningful value of $g_{((i-k))}$. This is different from the linear convolution where d_k will often be multiplied by a g_{i-k} whose index is outside the range of definition of g and so is zero.

We can relate the cyclic convolution to the linear convolution as follows. By the definition of the cyclic convolution,

$$s'_i = \sum_{k=0}^{n-1} g_{((i-k))} d_k, \quad i = 0, \cdots, n - 1 \tag{23}$$

We can recognize two kinds of terms in the sum: those with $i - k \geqslant 0$ and those with $i - k < 0$. Those occur when $k \leqslant i$ and $k > i$, respectively. Hence

$$s'_i = \sum_{k=0}^{i} g_{i-k} d_k + \sum_{k=i+1}^{n-1} g_{n+i-k} d_k \tag{24}$$

But now in the first sum, $g_{i-k} = 0$ if $k > i$; and in the second sum, $g_{n+i-k} = 0$ if $k < i$. Hence we can change the limits of the summations as follows:

$$s'_i = \sum_{k=0}^{n-i} g_{i-k} d_k + \sum_{k=0}^{n-1} g_{n+i-k} d_k = s_i + s_{n+i}$$

$$i = 0, \cdots, n - 1 \tag{25}$$

which relates the cyclic convolution to the linear convolution. We say that coefficients of s with index larger than $n-1$ are "folded" back into terms with indices smaller than n.[11]

The linear convolution can be computed as a cyclic convolution if the second term above equals zero. This is so if $g_{n+i-k}d_k$ equals zero for all i and k. To ensure this, one can choose n, the blocklength of the cyclic convolution, so that n is larger than $L+N-1$ (appending zeros to g and d so their blocklength is n). Then one can compute the linear convolution using an algorithm for computing a cyclic convolution and still get the right answer.

The cyclic convolution can also be expressed as a polynomial product. Let

$$d(x) = \sum_{i=0}^{n-1} d_i x^i \qquad (26)$$

$$g(x) = \sum_{i=0}^{n-1} g_i x^i \qquad (27)$$

Then

$$s(x) = g(x)d(x) \qquad (28)$$

The cyclic convolution is computed by folding back the high order coefficients of $s(x)$. This can be expressed as

$$s'(x) = s(x) \pmod{x^n - 1}$$

where by equality modulo $x^n - 1$ we mean that $s'(x)$ is the remainder when $s(x)$ is divided by $x^n - 1$. Hence

$$s'(x) = g(x)d(x) \pmod{x^n - 1}$$

To reduce $g(x)d(x)$ modulo $x^n - 1$, it suffices to replace x^n by 1 or to replace x^{n+i} by x^i wherever a term x^{n+i} with i positive appears. This has the effect of forming the coefficients

$$s'_i = s_i + s_{n+i}, \quad i = 0, \cdots, n-1$$

and so gives the coefficients of the cyclic convolution.

From the two forms

$$s'(x) = d(x)g(x) \pmod{x^n - 1}$$
$$= g(x)d(x) \pmod{x^n - 1}$$

it is clear that the roles of d and g are also symmetric in the cyclic convolution. Therefore we have the two expressions for the cyclic convolution

$$s'_i = \sum_{k=0}^{n-1} g_{((i-k))} d_k = \sum_{k=0}^{n-1} d_{((i-k))} g_k$$
$$i = 0, \cdots, n - 1$$

A more important technique is to use a cyclic convolution to compute a long linear convolution. Fast algorithms for long linear convolutions break the input stream into short sections of perhaps a few hundred samples. One section at a time is processed—often as a cyclic convolution—to produce a section of the output data stream. Techniques for doing this are called *overlap* techniques, referring to the fact that nonoverlapping sections of the input data stream cause overlapping sections of the output data stream, while nonoverlapping sections of the output data stream are caused by overlapping sections of the input data stream.[12]

Another computation that is important in digital signal processing is that of the discrete Fourier transform (hereafter called simply the Fourier transform). Let $v = \{ v_i, i = 0, \cdots, n - 1 \}$ be a vector of complex numbers or of real numbers. The Fourier transform of v is another vector V of length n of complex numbers given by

$$V_k = \sum_{i=0}^{n-1} \omega^{ik} v_i, \quad k = 0, \cdots, n - 1$$

where $\omega = e^{-j2\pi/N}$ and $j = \sqrt{-1}$.

Sometimes we write this as a matrix-vector product

$$V = Tv$$

If V is the Fourier transform of v, then v can be recovered form V by the inverse Fourier transform, which is given by

$$v_i = \frac{1}{n} \sum_{k=0}^{n-1} \omega^{-ik} V_k$$

There is an important link between the Fourier transform and the cyclic convolution. This is known as the convolution theorem and goes as follows. The vector e is given by the cyclic convolution of the vectors f and g:

$$e_i = \sum_{l=0}^{n-1} f_{((i-l))} g_l \quad i = 0, \cdots, n-1$$

if and only if the Fourier transforms satisfy

$$E_k = F_k G_k \quad k = 0, \cdots, n-1$$

There are also two-dimensional Fourier transforms, which are useful for processing two-dimensional arrays of data, and multidimensional Fourier transforms, which are useful for processing multidimensional arrays of data. The two-dimensional Fourier transform is

$$V_{k',k''} = \sum_{i'=0}^{n'-1} \sum_{i''=0}^{n''-1} \omega^{i'k'} \mu^{i''k''} v_{i',i''}, \quad \begin{array}{l} k' = 0, \cdots, n'-1 \\ k'' = 0, \cdots, n''-1 \end{array}$$

where $\omega = e^{-j2\pi/n'}$ and $\mu = e^{-j2\pi/n''}$.

New Words and Phrases

architecture	*n.*	结构
chip	*n.*	芯片
correlation	*n.*	相关
decimation	*n.*	抽选
enormous	*a.*	巨大的
formidable	*a.*	艰难的
histogram	*n.*	直方图
intermediate	*a.*	中间的
interpolation	*n.*	内插
meteorological	*a.*	气象的
modulation	*n.*	调制

notation	*n.*	符号表示法
overlap	*v.*	重叠
parallelism	*n.*	并行化
petroleum	*n.*	石油
pipelining	*n.*	流水线操作
seismic	*a.*	地震的
sophisticate	*v.*	弄复杂
stereoscopic	*a.*	立体的
suffice	*v.*	足够
synthetically	*adv.*	综合地
ultrasonic	*n.*	超声波
factorization	*n.*	因式分解
polynomial	*n.*	多项式
tapped delay line		抽头延时线
autoregressive filter		自回归滤波器
complex multiplication		复乘
computerized tomography		计算机断层成像
cyclic convolution		循环卷积
diagonal matrix		对角阵
dwell on		细想,详述
front-end		前端
linear convolution		线性卷积
matrix postadditions		后加矩阵
matrix preadditions		前加矩阵
nondestructive testing		无损检测
nuclear magnetic resonance		核磁共振
obvious implementation		直接法
off-line		脱机的,离线的
picture blurred		图像模糊
roundoff error		舍入误差

shift-register   移位寄存器

Notes

1. An algorithm, like most other engineering devices, can be described either by an input/output relationship or by a detailed explanation of its internal construction. 像许多其他工程器件一样,一个算法既可以用输入输出关系描述,也可以用内部结构的详细说明来描述。

2. By a fast algorithm, we mean a detailed description of a computational procedure that is not the obvious way to compute the required output from the input. 所谓快速算法,就是计算过程的详细描述,不是根据输入来计算需要输出的直接方法。

3. We can dwell further on this example as a foretaste of thing to come. 我们可详细叙述这个例子来说明下面的问题。

4. The computational savings results because the second term depends only on i and need not be recomputed for each j and the third term depends only on j and need not be computed for each i. 因为第二项仅与 i 有关,不需要对每一个 j 计算;而第三项则仅与 j 有关,不需要对每一个 i 计算,因此节省了计算量。

5. By proper scaling of intermediate steps, however, one can obtain computational accuracy that is nearly same as the direct method. 然而,当在中间的步骤中适当的缩放比例,可得到同直接法相同的计算精度。

6. large scale integrated circuits 大规模集成电路

7. If one can build the chip big enough or fast enough, then it seemingly does not matter if one uses inefficient algorithms. 若有人能设计出容量足够大或速度足够快的芯片,那么人们采用效率低的算法似乎并没有什么关系。

8. Whether completing algorithms for some problem have running times proportional to n^2 or n^3 may be of minor importance when n equals 3 or 4; but when n equals 1000, it becomes critical. 不论解决某个问题的全部算法执行时间正比于 n^2 还是 n^3,当 n 等于 3 或 4 时,并不那么重

要,而当 $n = 1000$ 时,问题就变得很严重了。

9. Nondestructive testing of manufactured articles such as casting is possible by means of computer-generated internal images based on the response to induced vibrations. 机械零件(如铸造零件)的无损检测可以借助由振动响应形成的零件内部的计算机图像来实现。

10. At discrete time instans called clock times, the shift-register stage replaces its content with the number appearing on the input line, discarding its previous content. 在称为时钟时间的离散的瞬间,寄存器用出现在输入线上的数来替换原来的内容,并将原来的内容丢弃。

11. We say that coefficients of s with index large than $n - 1$ are "folded" back into terms with indices smaller than n. 我们说 s 中标号大于 $n - 1$ 的系数都折叠进标号小于 n 的那些项。

12. Techniques for doing this are called overlap techniques, referring to the fact that nonoverlapping sections of the input data stream cause overlapping sections of the output data stream, while nonoverlapping sections of the output data stream are caused by overlapping sections of the input data stream. 这种处理方法称为重叠技术,这是由于输入数据流中的非重叠部分产生输出数据流中的重叠部分,而输出数据流中的非重叠部分是由输入数据流中的重叠部分产生的。

4.2　THE LEAST MEAN SQUARES（LMS）ALGORITHM

Much of this section is concerned with a detailed mathematical analysis of the LMS algorithm. Mathematical analysis is a very important tool, since it allows many properties of the adaptive filter to be determined without expending the time or expense of computer simulation or building actual hardware. Additionally, it is frequently quite difficult, from simulation results, to obtain the same performance insight available through analysis. Indeed, simulation is often used as a method to verify the mathematical analysis.

4.2.1 Effects of Unknown Signal Statistics

The central issue in adaptive signal processing is that there is rarely an a priori knowledge of signal statistics, even for truly stationary environments. In most applications, only an estimate of these signal statistics can be obtained. One approach to the problem of unknown signal statistics is to attempt to implement the method of steepest descent by estimating the gradient from the available data samples. If this approach is used, then a computational method for estimating the gradient must first be determined. One approach is to examine the expression for the true gradient, ∇_w, and formulate an estimated gradient, $\hat{\nabla}_w$. Therefore, one candidate for the form of $\hat{\nabla}_w$ might be

$$\hat{\nabla}_w[\varepsilon(n)] = -2\hat{p}_N + 2\hat{R}_{NN}w_N(n)$$

where the carats signify the quantities estimated from the data. The individual components of $\hat{R}_{NN}$ and $\hat{p}_N$ are estimates of the individual correlation function values. Estimating the individual elements of $\hat{R}_{NN}$ would then produce

$$\hat{\Phi}_x(m) = \frac{1}{K} \sum_{i=0}^{K-m-1} x(n-i)x(n-m-i) \qquad (2)$$

The term $\hat{\Phi}_x(m)$ is an estimate of the true value $\Phi_x(m)$. A similar formulation gives $\hat{\Phi}_{xd}(m)$, the estimate of the true cross-correlation $\Phi_{xd}(m)$:

$$\hat{\Phi}_{xd}(m) = \frac{1}{K} \sum_{i=0}^{K-m-1} d(n-i)x(n-m-i) \qquad (3)$$

Whereas the concept of this approach is straightforward, the computational cost is substantial. A total of $K - m$ multiplications plus $K - m - 1$ additions must be computed simply to obtain each estimate, and this set of computations must be repeated for each $\hat{\Phi}_x(m)$ and $\hat{\Phi}_{xd}(m)$, for $0 \leqslant m \leqslant N$. Furthermore, in many applications such as speech and image coding, the data sequences are often nonstationary, which would require a periodic updating of the computations in (2) and (3) if this approach were used. The computational cost in this case could possibly become prohibitive for real-time applications.

Fortunately, there is a form for the gradient that is much simpler from a computational standpoint.

$$\nabla_w[\varepsilon(n)] = \frac{\partial}{\partial w_N}E\{e^2(n)\} = 2E\left\{e(n)\frac{\partial}{\partial w_N}e(n)\right\}. \quad (4)$$

By expanding $e(n)$ according to its definition

$$e(n) = d(n) - w_N^T(n)x_N(n), \quad (5)$$

it is immediately seen that

$$\frac{\partial}{\partial w_N}e(n) = -x_N(n) \quad (6)$$

Substituting this result into (4) then gives the alternate form for the gradient

$$\nabla_w[\varepsilon(n)] = -2E\{e(n)x_N(n)\}$$

and from $w_N(n+1) = w_N(n) - \mu\nabla_w[\varepsilon(n)]$, an alternate form for the steepest descent weight update becomes

$$w_N(n+1) = w_N(n) + \alpha E\{e(n)x_N(n)\} \quad (7)$$

where again $\alpha = 2\mu$ with no loss of generality. Therefore, this equivalent form for the steepest descent method requires that the cross-correlation of the prediction error with the signal be known. Note that if steepest descent were being applied to predicting $d(n)$ using the signal $x(n)$, then $e(n)$ and $x_N(n)$, as required in (7), would be readily available. Thus, a simple computational estimate for the cross-correlation in (7) is indeed feasible and suggests the following form for the approximation to steepest descent:

$$w_N(n+1) = w_N(n) - \alpha\hat{E}\{e(n)x_N(n)\}, \quad (8)$$

where $\hat{E}\{\cdot\}$ signifies an estimate of the expected value.

To utilize (8) in actual computations, a computational form for $\hat{E}$

$\{e(n)x_N(n)\}$ is now needed. One form is immediately suggested by

$$\hat{E}\{e(n)x_N(n)\} = \frac{1}{K}\sum_{i=0}^{K-1} e(n-i)x_N(n-i) \qquad (9)$$

where K is the number of data samples used in the calculation. Note that (9) produces a vector with components given by

$$\begin{bmatrix} \hat{E}\{e(n)x(n-1)\} \\ \hat{E}\{e(n)x(n-2)\} \\ \vdots \\ \hat{E}\{e(n)x(n-N)\} \end{bmatrix} = \frac{1}{K} \begin{bmatrix} \sum_{i=0}^{K-1} e(n-i)x(n-i-1) \\ \sum_{i=0}^{K-1} e(n-i)x(n-i-2) \\ \vdots \\ \sum_{i=0}^{K-1} e(n-i)x(n-i-N) \end{bmatrix}$$

$$(10)$$

The computation in (9) may be considered as operating over a window of data extending K samples into the past, and therefore incorporates only the most recent data properties. Furthermore, only N of these terms, each requiring K multiplications and $K-1$ additions, need be calculated to estimate the entire gradient vector. Substituting (9) into (8) then gives

$$w_N(n+1) = w_N(n) + \frac{\alpha}{K}\sum_{i=0}^{K-1} e(n-1)x_N(n-i) \qquad (11)$$

Eq. (11) thus provides one method of estimating the gradient and gives an adaptive implementation for updating the $w_N(n)$ coefficients directly from the data. However, the amount of computation involved in (10) is still substantial, and the smoothing effect of the K-sample time window is significant. Therefore, the method of (11) has not found a great deal of application in practical problems. Instead, a very simple approximation to the gradient in (7) may be used, leading to the LMS algorithm that is the topic of the next section.

4.2.2 Derivation of the LMS Algorithm

A very useful algorithm has evolved from simply approximating the expectation in (7) with the instantaneous value of the quantity inside the brackets. That is, let the estimate of the expected value be given simply as

$$\hat{E}\{e(n)x_N(n)\} = e(n)x_N(n) \tag{12}$$

Substitution of (12) into (8) then leads directly to the LMS algorithm:

$$w_N(n + 1) = w_N(n) + \alpha e(n)x_N(n) \tag{13}$$

Due mainly to its simplicity, the LMS algorithm has found wide usage in applications that deal with nonstationary data or time-varying statistics.

The LMS algorithm is sometimes referred to as the noisy gradient or gradient approximation algorithm, since the structure of the method of steepest descent can be preserved by defining the noisy gradient as the gradient of the instantaneous squared error (rather than the gradient of the expected squared error):

$$\hat{\nabla}_w[\varepsilon(n)] = \frac{\partial}{\partial w_N}e^2(n) = -2e(n)x_N(n) \tag{14}$$

It follows from substitution of (14) into (13) that the LMS algorithm may be equivalently written as

$$w_N(n + 1) = w_N(n) - \mu \hat{\nabla}_w[\varepsilon(n)] \tag{15}$$

where $\mu = \alpha/2$.

The popularity of the LMS algorithm stems largely from the simplicity of its computational structure, low storage requirements, and the relative ease with which it may be mathematically analyzed. In this section, the computational and analytical properties of the LMS algorithm will be examined. It will be seen that many of the analytical results for the method of steepest descent will hold for LMS, which should not be surprising since the LMS algorithm has been seen to be an approximation to the method of steepest descent.

Suppose (13) is expanded in terms of each vector component. Then it is easy to derive the scalar update for each weight:

$$w_i(n+1) = w_i(n) + ae(n)x(n-i); \quad 1 \leqslant i \leqslant N \quad (16)$$

Equation (16) explicitly displays one very important difference between LMS and the method of steepest descent. It was found that the statistical property of orthogonality between the prediction error and the filter data must hold for the method of steepest descent to converge. However, in (16), for the LMS algorithm, there is a much more stringent condition for the $w_i^*(n)$ to converge exactly to w_i, namely,

$$e(n)x(n-i) = 0, \quad 1 \leqslant i \leqslant N$$

which is obtained simply by enforcing that $w_i(n+1) = w_i(n)$ in (16). This condition must hold for every time iteration n in order for the $w_N(n)$ produced by LMS to converge to the optimal w_N^*.[1] In general, this condition is quite difficult to achieve in practice since it requires that every product $e(n)x(n-i)$ must be zero, and not just that the expectation of this product vanish. Therefore, an initial impression concerning LMS is that compared to steepest descent, the LMS steady-state solutions might be "suboptimal" in some way.[2] It will soon be seen that at convergence, the instantaneous values of the LMS weights are not exactly equal to the optimal values; however, the expected value or mean of the LMS weight vector $w_N(n)$ will be seen to converge to the optimal w_N as $n \to \infty$, which is the same result derived for the method of steepest descent.

4.2.3　Convergence of the LMS Algorithm

In this section, some of the convergence properties of the LMS algorithm will be examined, which will draw heavily from previous results for the method of steepest descent. An emphasis will be placed upon when the previous results for steepest descent will be directly applicable, and when the stochastic nature of the LMS algorithm requires the development of new analytical results. [3]

This study of convergence of the LMS algorithm will investigate properties of the LMS adaptive prediction filter coefficients as they adapt from a set of initial conditions to a final set of converged coefficients. Begin with (13) for the LMS weight vector update,

$$w_N(n+1) = w_N(n) + ae(n)x_N(n) \qquad (17)$$

and the definition of the LMS prediction error

$$e(n) = d(n) - x_N^T(n)w_N(n) \qquad (18)$$

Substitution of (18) into (17) then gives

$$w_N(n+1) = [I_{NN} - ax_N(n)x_N^T(n)]w_N(n) + ad(n)x_N(n) \qquad (19)$$

Equation (19) may be compared directly to the method of steepest descent,

$$w_N(n+1) = [I_{NN} - aR_{NN}]w_N(n) + ap_N \qquad (20)$$

It is seen that (19) for the LMS algorithm would correspond directly to (20) if the matrix $x_N(n)x_N^T(n)$ were replaced by the R_{NN} matrix, and if the vector $d(n)x_N(n)$ were replaced by the p_N vector. However, from the definitions of R_{NN} and p_N:

$$R_{NN} = E\{x_N(n)x_N^T(n)\} \qquad (21)$$

$$p_N = E\{d(n)x_N(n)\} \qquad (22)$$

It is immediately seen that steepest descent utilizes the expectations of the instantaneous quantities displayed in the LMS algorithm.

This similarity is to be expected, since LMS approximates the method of steepest descent. The primary difference between steepest descent and LMS is that steepest descent is deterministic and requires the exact gradient, whereas LMS is a stochastic recursive algorithm and uses only a noisy approximation of the gradient. [4] In some of the literature,

LMS and its variants are even referred to as stochastic gradient or stochastic approximation methods. The terminology stochastic recursion signifies that the update term, or the driving function of the stochastic difference equation (13) is a member of a stochastic process. This is true since, in LMS, the sequences $x(n)$ and $d(n)$ are members of stochastic processes. However, the method of steepest descent from (2) is deterministic; that is, the parameters R_{NN} and p_N are assumed to be known and constant.

The LMS algorithm, on the other hand, uses only the acquired signals to calculate its recursion for the LMS weight update. If the signals $x(n)$ and $d(n)$ were deterministic, then the LMS algorithm would likewise be deterministic, provided the initial $w_N(0)$ were constant for all trials. However, when $x(n)$ becomes a stochastic signal governed by a probability density, then the situation becomes more complicated since in theory, at least, the specific values of $x(n)$ are never known exactly. A common example of a stochastic signal might be a known sinusoid corrupted by additive, uncorrelated random noise.

One common approach to analyzing stochastic adaptive systems is to partition the problem into the considerations of solving separately for the mean weight behavior and the weight variance characteristics.[5] The LMS predictor weights will have some general probability density function (usually unknown, however) from which the mean (i. e., expected value) and the variance of the weights could theoretically be computed. Unfortunately, the computation of this probability density is exceedingly difficult, if not impossible, and is well beyond the scope of the present text. Engineering analysis is often the science of judicious assumption, and a great deal of insight may be derived by separate considerations of the LMS weight expectation and weight variance. By employing some typically nonrestrictive assumptions concerning the LMS weights and signal data, some very tractable and useful analytical results may be derived. It will be shown that the assumptions used in this approach are valid for a large number of signal processing applications.

4.2.4   The Mean of LMS Weight Vector

To examine the behavior of the mean value of the LMS weight vector, simply take the expectation of both sides of (19):

$$E\{w_N(n+1)\} =$$
$$E\{[I_{NN} - \alpha x_N(n)x_N^T(n)]w_N(n)\} + \alpha E\{d(n)x_N(n)\} =$$
$$E\{w_N(n)\} - \alpha E\{[x_N(n)x_N^T(n)]w_N(n)\} + \alpha E\{d(n)x_N(n)\}$$

$$(23)$$

The second expectation in (23) can be simplified by using the following assumption:

Assumption 1. *The data signal* $x(n)$ *and the LMS weights,* $w_i(n)$, *are uncorrelated with each other.*

In general, the conditions in Assumption 1 are fulfilled by data $x(n)$ and weights $w_i(n)$ that are sufficiently "dissimilar" over the time of observation. One commonly occurring environment in which this assumption holds very well is when the signal changes much more rapidly than the mean value of the weights. [6] For example, a speech waveform might change very rapidly, whereas the LMS weights will attempt to adapt to the statistical model of the speech, which may be fairly constant over the observation time. Usually, this implies the feedback gain parameter, α, of the LMS filter should be fairly small, such that the update term in (13) adds only a small increment to the previous weight value. This discussion is meant to illustrate that whereas a rigorous proof of Assumption 1 would probably be very difficult, a qualitative justification of its viability may often be obtained from consideration of the physical situation. [7] For the wide majority of practical applications, the model of (23) will indeed be valid, and the error introduced by making this assumption is often negligible.

Therefore, incorporating Assumption 1 allows (23) to be written as

$$E\{w_N(n+1)\} = [I_{NN} - \alpha R_{NN}]E\{w_N(n)\} + \alpha p_N \qquad (24)$$

which is exactly (20) with $w_N(n)$ from the steepest descent algorithm replaced by the mean value of the LMS weight vector, $E\{w_N(n)\}$. Therefore, the mean LMS weight vector propagates according to the same recursion as the weight vector obtained by the method of steepest descent. It is necessary to keep in mind that the applicability of (24) is subject to the conditions outlined in Assumption 1. The notation and analysis of this section will be simplified a great deal if the mean LMS weight vector, $\widetilde{w}_N(n)$, is defined as the expectation of the instantaneous weight vector:

$$\widetilde{w}_N(n) = E\{w_N(n)\} \qquad (25)$$

The individual components are therefore give by

$$\widetilde{w}_i(n) = E\{w_i(n)\} \qquad (26)$$

With this notation, (24) simplifies to

$$\widetilde{w}_N(n+1) = [I_{NN} - \alpha R_{NN}]\widetilde{w}_N(n) + \alpha p_N \qquad (27)$$

Note that this result is equivalent to (20) for the method of steepest descent, with the $w_N(n)$ of steepest descent replaced by the mean LMS weight vector $\widetilde{w}_N(n)$.

As an example of the properties of the expected weight vector, consider Fig. 4.1, which illustrates the LMS algorithm used in a linear prediction application. The input signal $x(n)$ was created by a second-order autoregressive (AR) process having poles at $(z_1, z_2) = 0.9e^{\pm j\pi/6}$. It is easy to show that this AR process leads to the following difference

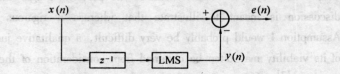

Fig. 4.1   LMS algorithm used as a linear predictor

equation for the second-order system:

$$x(n) = 1.558x(n - 1) - 0.81x(n - 2) + v(n) \qquad (28)$$

where $v(n)$ is a zero mean, uncorrelated stochastic excitation sequence. A two coefficient LMS filter was used to predict $x(n)$ by

$$\hat{x}(n) = \sum_{i=1}^{2} w_i(n)x(n - i + 1) \qquad (29)$$

Since, in this example, there are two AR coefficients in the signal model and there are two coefficients in the LMS filter, then $w_1(n)$ should converge to 1.558 and $w_2(n)$ should converge to -0.81. Fig.4.2 shows the convergence characteristics of the weights for a choice of $\alpha = 0.02$. There is seen to be a great deal of fluctuation in the values

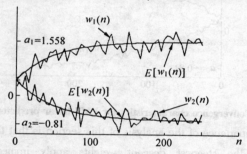

Fig.4.2 Convergence characteristics for LMS linear predictor, $\alpha = 0.02$

of the weights as they converge to a neighborhood around their optimal values a_1 and a_2. This is due to the fact that the "noisy" gradient estimate is used in the LMS algorithm, rather than the true gradient. For comparison, the mean weight trajectories computed from (27) for this choice of α are also shown in Fig.4.3.

Convergence characteristics of the mean LMS weights also shows that the mean weights should take longer to converge if α is decreased. Fig. 4.3 illustrates this phenomenon by showing the convergence results of one trial using $\alpha = 0.004$. Comparing these results with Fig.4.2, it is indeed seen that the LMS weights take longer to converge for the smaller α.

However, there is another property evident in Fig. 4. 2; namely, that decreasing α causes the weight trajectory to be much "smoother," or have less variance about the mean value. This is a fundamental tradeoff in using the LMS algorithm; high α values cause the mean weights to converge more quickly, but also cause the instantaneous weights to fluctuate more. The appropriate α selection will depend upon the degree of accuracy needed and the convergence speed required by the particular application.

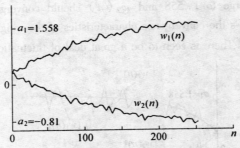

Fig. 4.3   Convergence characteristics for LMS linear predictor, $\alpha = 0.004$

The importance of the analysis of this section is that the convergence results for the steepest descent weights apply immediately to the convergence properties of the mean LMS weights. No new analysis need be done to derive the mean LMS convergence or steady-state weight solutions. However, as illustrated in Fig. 4. 2 and 4. 3, since the instantaneous LMS weights "jitter" about their mean value, this causes an instantaneous error in the LMS weight values, and therefore an excess in the prediction error compared to that suggested by simply using the LMS mean weight equations.[8] The degree of this excess error can be quantified by analysis, which is done by deriving the propagation characteristics for the LMS mean square error (MSE).

4.2.5 LMS Mean Square Error

In Section 4.2.4, solutions were developed for the mean of the LMS weight vector. The actual weights themselves fluctuate about this mean level $\widetilde{w}_N(n)$ since LMS only approximates the true gradient with the instantaneous product. A common method of modeling this weight fluctuation is to assume that the actual LMS weight vector, $w_N(n)$, is the sum of the mean LMS weight vector, $\widetilde{w}_N(n)$, plus a stochastic (i.e., random) noisy component, $z_N(n)$, where

$$w_N(n) = \widetilde{w}_N(n) + z_N(n) \qquad (30)$$

This weight fluctuation affects the performance of the LMS prediction filter since it causes the actual LMS weight to be different from the value that would result from steepest descent. This effectively increases the mean square prediction error obtained using LMS over that obtained using steepest descent. However, it must be emphasized that steepest descent is rarely applicable in practical situations, since the signal statistics are rarely known a priori, and therefore are unavailable for use in steepest descent. Therefore, it is of substantial interest to calculate the mean square error (MSE) propagation characteristic of the LMS algorithm, since this MSE characteristic is often the measure for judging performance of the different adaptive methods.

Consistent with previous development, define the LMS mean square prediction error as

$$\varepsilon(n) = E\{e^2(n)\} = E\{[d(n) - w_N^T(n)x_N(n)]^2\} \quad (31)$$

where the LMS prediction error from (5) has been used. Performing the operations in (31) and using the linearity of the expectation operation then gives

$$\varepsilon(n) = E\{d^2(n)\} - 2E\{w_N^T(n)x_N(n)d(n)\} +$$
$$E\{w_N^T(n)x_N(n)x_N^T(n)w_N(n)\} \qquad (32)$$

Then substituting (30) for the LMS weights into (32) produces

$$\varepsilon(n) = E\{d^2(n)\} - 2E\{\widetilde{w}_N^T(n)x_N(n)d(n)\} +$$
$$E\{\widetilde{w}_N^T(n)x_N(n)x_N^T(n)\widetilde{w}_N(n)\} -$$
$$2E\{z_N^T(n)x_N(n)d(n)\} +$$
$$E\{z_N^T(n)x_N(n)x_N^T(n)\widetilde{w}_N(n)\} +$$
$$E\{\widetilde{w}_N^T(n)x_N(n)x_N^T(n)z_N(n)\} +$$
$$E\{z_N^T(n)x_N(n)x_N^T(n)z_N(n)\} \qquad (33)$$

In general (33) is rather imposing. However, by making use of some previously derived results and the properties of the weight noise model (30), the weight noise expression may be simplified substantially. First, however, consider the first three terms on the right-hand side of (33), which are seen to be entirely a function of the mean LMS weight $\widetilde{w}_N(n)$. Since it is known that the mean LMS weights are equivalent to the weights from steepest descent, the results immediately apply to these terms. From steepest decent, the first three terms on the right-hand side of (33) are seen to be the MSE given by steepest descent at iteration n, then (33) gives

$$\varepsilon(n) = \varepsilon_{\min} + v'^T_N(n)\Lambda_{NN}v'_N(n) -$$
$$2E\{z_N^T(n)x_N(n)d(n)\} +$$
$$E\{z_N^T(n)x_N(n)x_N^T(n)\widetilde{w}_N(n)\} +$$
$$E\{\widetilde{w}_N^T(n)x_N(n)x_N^T(n)z_N(n)\} +$$
$$E\{z_N^T(n)x_N(n)x_N^T(n)z_N(n)\} \qquad (34)$$

The value $\varepsilon_{\min}$ is the minimum MSE achievable by the optimal filter w_N^*, $v'_N(n)$ is the uncoupled difference weight-vector, and Λ_{NN} is the diagonal matrix of eigenvalues of R_{NN}.

It remains to compute the MSE contribution from the last four terms of (34), which is the increase in MSE due to using LMS. To help simplify this problem, the properties of the LMS weight noise model from

(30) may be used. It should be emphasized that the true probability density of the $z_i(n)$ noise terms is, in general, unknown and can really only be approximated according to a model.

A rigorous and exact calculation of a closed form expression for the excess MSE contribution would require a knowledge of the fourth-order joint probability density functions of the LMS weights.[9] However, this approach is extremely involved and is well beyond the scope of this text. To simplify the derivation, use the property that the weight noise $z_N(n)$ is zero mean, uncorrelated with respect to time, and uncorrelated with the data $x_N(n)$. Then the MSE propagation for the LMS algorithm simplifies to

$$\varepsilon(n) = \varepsilon_{min} + v'^T_N(n)\Lambda_{NN}v'_N(n) + \sigma_x^2\mathrm{Tr}[\,E(z_N(n)z_N^T(n)\}\,]$$

$$(39)$$

The matrix $E\{z_N(n)z_N^T(n)\}$ is called the LMS weight covariance matrix, and it specifies the second-order statistics of the LMS weight fluctuations about their mean values. The rigorous computation of the LMS weight covariance matrix is once again a complex problem well beyond the scope of current applications, and is the subject of much present research in adaptive signal processing. For present purposes, an approximation will be used that is equivalent to an assumption that the weight noise $z_N(n)$ is a stationary signal. This basically means that the power of $z_N(n)$ is constant, regardless of whether the LMS algorithm is in the transient converging mode (where n is small) or in the steady-state converged mode ($n \to \infty$). While this assumption is not absolutely true in all cases, its validity is stronger as the feedback gain α becomes smaller. For the wide majority of the applications considered in this book, α is indeed in this required region such that the stationarity of the weight noise is a valid assumption.

New Words and Phrases

bracket	*n.*	括号
carat	*n.*	^(估计的符号)
computational	*a.*	计算的
converge	*v.*	收敛
corrupt	*v.*	掺杂
cross-correlation	*n.*	互相关
derivation	*v.*	推导
deterministic	*a.*	确定性的
dissimilar	*a.*	不同的
evolve	*v.*	引申
excitation	*n.*	激励
gradient	*n.*	梯度
impression	*n.*	印象
investigate	*v.*	研究
issue	*n.*	问题论点
judge	*v.*	判断
judicious	*a.*	明智的
nonstationary	*a.*	非平稳
prohibitive	*a.*	价格过高的,昂贵的
rigorous	*a.*	严格的
standpoint	*n.*	观点
stationary	*n.*	平稳
stem	*v.*	发生于
stochastic	*a.*	随机的
stringent	*a.*	严格的
suboptimal	*a.*	次最佳的
substantial	*a.*	实质的,相当大的
terminology	*n.*	术语

trajectory	*n.*	轨迹
trial	*n.*	试验
variance	*n.*	方差
viability	*n.*	生存能力
simulation	*n.*	仿真
signify	*vt.*	表示
orthogonality	*n.*	正交性
weight	*n.*	加权
vanish	*vi.*	成为零
recursive	*a.*	递归的
tractable	*a.*	易处理的
jitter	*vi.*	抖动
iteration	*n.*	迭代
no loss of generality		不失一般性的
instantaneous value		瞬时值
adaptive filter		自适应滤波器
autoregressive process		自回归过程
correlation function		相关函数
excess error		超调误差
expected value		数学期望
linear prediction		线性预测
priori knowledge		先验知识
steepest descent		最陡下降法

Notes

1. This condition must hold for every time iteration n in order for the $w_N(n)$ produced by LMS to converge to the optimal w_N^*. 为了能使 LMS算法产生的 $w_N(n)$ 收敛到最佳的 w_N^*，这个条件必须在每次迭代时都成立。

2. Therefore, an initial impression concerning LMS is that compared to steepest descent, the LMS steady-state solutions might be

"suboptimal" in some way. 所以，与最陡下降法相比，关于 LMS 算法的最初印象是 LMS 算法的稳态解可能是以某种方式的"次最佳"。

3. An emphasis will be placed upon when the previous results for steepest descent will be directly applicable, and when the stochastic nature of the LMS algorithm requires the development of new analytical results. 应给予足够重视的是，对于最陡下降法，前面的结果要立即应用，而 LMS 算法的随机特性需要推导新的解析结果。

4. The primary difference between steepest descent and LMS is that steepest descent is deterministic and requires the exact gradient, whereas LMS is a stochastic recursive algorithm and uses only a noisy approximation of the gradient. 最陡下降法和 LMS 算法主要的不同之处是最陡下降法是确定的，需要精确的梯度。而 LMS 是随机的递推算法，只能用带有噪声的梯度近似值。

5. One common approach to analyzing stochastic adaptive systems is to partition the problem into the considerations of solving separately for the mean weight behavior and the weight variance characteristics. 分析随机自适应系统一个普通的方法是把问题分成分别解决加权均值特性和加权方差特性来考虑。

6. One commonly occurring environment in which this assumption holds very well is when the signal changes much more rapidly than the mean value of the weights. 这个假设非常充分的一个常见存在的环境是信号变化比加权均值还快。

7. This discussion is meant to illustrate that whereas a rigorous proof of Assumption 1 would probably be vary difficult, a qualitative justification of its viability may often be obtained from consideration of the physical situation. 这个讨论的意思是想说明，尽管对假设 1 严格的证明会很难，但假设的存在通常会从实际情况考虑得到定性的证明。

8. However, as illustrated in Fig.4.2 and 4.3, since the instantaneous LMS weights "jitter" about their mean value, this causes an instantaneous error in the LMS weight, and therefore an excess in the prediction error compared to that suggested by using the LMS mean

weight equations. 然而,正像图 4.2 和图 4.3 表示的那样,由于 LMS 瞬时加权相对均值的抖动,在 LMS 加权引起瞬时误差,因此比 LMS 平均加权式多了额外的预测的误差。

9. A rigorous and exact calculation of a closed form expression for the excess MSE contribution would require a knowledge of the four-order joint probability density functions of the LMS weights. 超调均方误差的闭合表达式严谨、精确的计算需要 LMS 加权的四阶联合概率密度函数的知识。

4.3　PATTERN CLASSIFICATION BY DISTANCE FUNCTIONS

In this section we begin the study of pattern classifiers by considering one of the simplest and most intuitive approaches to the problem: the concept of pattern classification by distance functions. The motivation for using distance functions as a classification tool follows naturally from the fact that the most obvious way of establishing a measure of similarity between pattern vectors, which we also consider as points in Euclidean space, is by determining their proximity.[1] For example, in Fig.4.4 we may intuitively arrive at the conclusion that x belongs to class w_i solely on the basis that it is closer to the patterns of this class.[2]

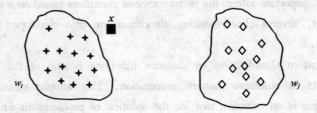

Fig.4.4　Patterns classifiable by proximity concept

The method of pattern classification by distance functions can be expected to yield practical and satisfactory results only when the pattern classes tend to have clustering properties.[3] This can be appreciated by comparing Fig.4.4 and 4.5. In the first figure we see that there would be little difficulty in classifying x into w_i because of its proximity to this class, as mentioned above. In Fig. 4.5, however, although the two pattern populations are perfectly disjoint, one would in general be hard-pressed to arrive at a justification for classifying x into either class based on a measure of the proximity of this pattern to a class.[4]

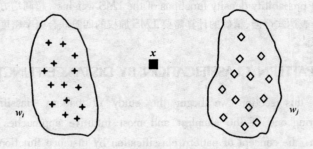

Fig.4.5   Patterns not easily classifiable by proximity concept

The above concepts are generalized and developed in a mathematical framework in the following sections. Since the proximity of an unknown pattern to the patterns of a class will serve as a measure for its classification, the term minimum-distance pattern classification[5] will be used to characterize this particular approach. Since clustering properties play an important role in the performance of classifiers based on a distance concept, several cluster-seeking algorithms are also developed in this section.

Pattern classification by distance functions is one of the earliest concepts in automatic pattern recognition. This simple classification technique is an effective tool for the solution of problems in which the pattern classes exhibit a reasonably limited degree of variability.[6] In this section, the properties and mechanization of minimum-distance classifiers are investigated in detail. We first consider classes which can be characterized by single prototype patterns. The resulting concepts are then extended to the multiprototype case. Finally, the general classification properties of this approach are discussed, and bounds on classification performance are established.

4.3.1 Single Prototypes

In some situations, the patterns of each class tend to cluster tightly about a typical or representative pattern for that class.[7] A typical example is the problem of reading bank checks by machine. The characters in the checks are highly stylized and are usually printed in magnetic ink to facilitate the measurement process. In a situation such as this, the resulting measurement vectors (patterns) of each character class will be almost identical since the same characters in different checks are identical for all practical purpose.[8] Under these conditions, minimum-distance classifiers can constitute a very effective approach to the classification problem.

Consider M pattern classes and assume that these classes are representable by prototype patterns $z_1, z_2, \cdots, z_M$. The Euclidean distance between an arbitrary pattern vector x and the ith prototype is given by

$$D_i = \| x - z_i \| = \sqrt{(x - z_i)'(x - z_i)} \qquad (1)$$

A minimum-distance classifier computes the distance from a pattern x of unknown classification to the prototype of each class, and assigns the pattern to the class to which it is closest. In other words, x is assigned to class w_i if $D_i < D_j$, for all $j \neq i$. Ties are resolved arbitrarily.

Equation (1) may be expressed in a more convenient form. Squaring all terms of this equation yields

$$D_i^2 = \| x - z_i \|^2 = (x - z_i)'(x - z_i) =$$
$$x'x - 2x'z_i + z'z_i = x'x - 2(x'z_i - \frac{1}{2} z'z_i) \qquad (2)$$

Choosing the minimum D_i^2 is equivalent to choosing the minimum D_i since all distances are positive. From Eq. (2), however, we see that since the term $x'x$ is independent of i in all D_i^2, $i = 1, 2, \cdots, M$, choosing the minimum D_i^2 is equivalent to choosing the maximum ($x'z_i - \frac{1}{2}z_i'z_i$). Consequently, we may define the decision functions

$$d_i(x) = x'z_i - \frac{1}{2}z_i'z_i, \quad i = 1, 2, \cdots, M \tag{3}$$

where a pattern x is assigned to class w_i if $d_i(x) > d_j(x)$ for all $j \neq i$.

Observe that $d_i(x)$ is a linear decision function,[9] that is, if z_{ij}, $j = 1, 2, \cdots, n$, are the components of z_i, and we let

$$w_{ij} = z_{ij}, \quad j = 1, 2, \cdots, n$$

$$w_{i, n+1} = -\frac{1}{2}z_i'z_i \tag{4}$$

and

$$x = \begin{bmatrix} x_1 \\ x_2 \\ \vdots \\ x_n \\ 1 \end{bmatrix}$$

then we may express Eq. (3) in the familiar linear form

$$d_i(x) = w_i'x, \quad i = 1, 2, \cdots, M \tag{5}$$

where $w_i = (w_{i1}, w_{i2}, \cdots, w_{i, n+1})'$.

The decision boundary of a two-class example in which each class is characterized by a single prototype is shown in Fig. 4.6. The linear decision surface separating every pair of prototype points z_i and z_j is the hyperplane which is the perpendicular bisector of the line segment joining the two points.[10] We see, therefore, that minimum-distance classifiers are a special case of linear classifiers, in which the decision boundaries are constrained to have this property. Since a minimum-distance classifier categorizes a pattern on the basis of the closest match between the pattern and the respective class prototypes, this approach is also known as correlation or cluster matching.

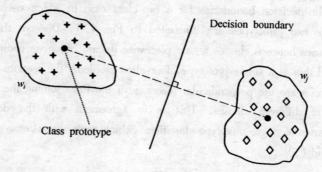

Fig.4.6   **Decision boundary of two classes characterized by single prototypes**

4.3.2   Multiprototypes

Suppose that instead of being representable by a single prototype pattern each class is characterized by several prototypes, that is, each pattern of class w_i tends to cluster about one of the prototypes z_i^1, $z_i^2, \cdots, z_i^{N_i}$, where N_i is the number of prototypes in the ith pattern class. Under these conditions we can design a classifier similar to the one discussed in the preceding section. Let the distance function between an arbitrary pattern x and class w_i be denoted by

$$D_i = \min_l \| x - z_i^l \| , \quad l = 1, 2, \cdots, N_i \quad (6)$$

that is, D_i is the smallest of the distances between x and each of the prototypes of w_i. As before, the distances D_i, $i = 1, 2, \cdots, M$, are computed and the unknown is classified into w_i if $D_i < D_j$ for all $j \neq i$. Ties are resolved arbitrarily.

Following the development in Section 4.3.1 results in the decision functions

$$d_i(x) = \max_l \{ (x' z_i^l) - \frac{1}{2} (z_i^l)' z_i^{l} \} , \quad l = 1, 2, \cdots, N_i \quad (7)$$

where, as before, x is placed in class w_i if $d_i(x) > d_j(x)$, for all $j \neq i$.

The decision boundaries for a two-class case in which each class contains two prototypes are illustrated in Fig. 4. 7. Observe that the boundaries between classes w_i are piecewise linear. Since we could have defined this as a single-prototype, four-class problem, the sections of the boundaries are the perpendicular bisectors of the lines joining the prototypes of different classes. This is in agreement with the decision boundaries of single-prototype classifiers, which are a special case of Eq. (6) and (7).

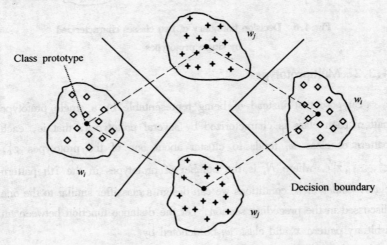

Fig. 4. 7 Piecewise-linear decision boundary of two classes

In the same manner that Eq. (3) was a special case of linear classifiers, Eq. (7) is a special case of a more general form of *piecewise-linear* classifiers. The decision functions of these classifiers are of the following form:

$$d_i(x) = \max_l \{ d_i^l(x) \}, \quad i = 1, 2, \cdots, M; \ l = 1, 2, \cdots, N_i \quad (8)$$

where $d_i^l(x)$ is given by

$$d_i^l(x) = w_{i1}^l x_1 + w_{i2}^l x_2 + \cdots + w_{in}^l x_n + w_{in+1}^l = (w_i^l)'x \quad (9)$$

Unlike the decision functions of Eq. (7), these functions are not constrained to be of the form shown in Fig. 4.7.

One of the basic problems in the design of pattern classifiers is the determination of the decision function parameters. As was previously indicated, general iterative algorithms exist which can be used in the calculation of linear decision fu. ction parameters. Unfortunately, no truly general algorithm is yet known for the piecewise-linear case of Eq. (8) and (9). It is noted, however, that the special case of Eq. (6) or (7) can be easily implemented if the pattern classes are characterized by a reasonably small number of prototypes.

4.3.3   Extension of Minimum-Distance Classification Concepts

Although the ideas of small numbers of prototypes and familiar Euclidean distances are geometrically attractive, they are not limiting factors in the definition of the minimum-distance classification concept. In order to explore further the general properties of this scheme, let us consider a set of sample patterns of known classification $\{s_1, s_2, \cdots, s_N\}$, where it is assumed that each pattern belongs to one of the classes $w_1, w_2, \cdots, w_M$. We may define a nearest neighbor (NN) classification[11] rule which assigns a pattern x of unknown classification to the class of its nearest neighbor, where we say that $s_i \in \{s_1, s_2, \cdots, s_N\}$ is a nearest neighbor to x if

$$D(s_i, x) = \min_l \{D(s_l, x)\}, \quad l = 1, 2, \cdots, N \quad (10)$$

where D is any distance measure definable over the pattern space.

We may call this scheme the 1-NN rule since it employs only the classification of the nearest neighbor to x. There is no reason, however, why we could not define a q-NN rule which consists of determining the q nearest neighbors to x, and using the majority of equal classifications in this group as the classification of x. Comparing Eq. (10) and (6), we see that the 1-NN rule is nothing more than the multiprototype case discussed in the preceding section if we choose D to be a Euclidean distance measure.

An interesting comparison between the 1-NN and the q-NN rules may be derived with the aid of Fig.4.8. Assume that the patterns of both classes shown are equally likely to occur and that the patterns of w_i and w_j are uniformly distributed over the disks R_i and R_j shown. Then, for N samples, the probability that exactly α of these samples belong to class w_i is given by

$$p_i = \frac{1}{2^N} C_\alpha^N \tag{11}$$

where $C_\alpha^N = N!\ /\alpha\,(N-\alpha)!$ is the number of ways in which the N samples can be divided into two classes containing α samples and $N\text{-}\alpha$ samples, respectively, and 2^N gives the total number of ways in which N samples can be divided into two classes. The probability p_j that α of the N samples belong to class w_j is clearly equal to p_i.

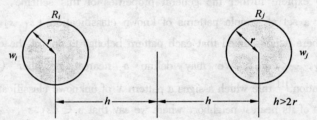

Fig.4.8 Two pattern classes distributed uniformly over identical regions

Suppose that a given unknown pattern x belongs to w_i. Then, the 1-NN rule will commit an error only if the nearest neighbor to x belongs to w_j and, consequently, lies in R_j. But, if x comes from w_i and its nearest neighbor lies in R_j, *all* patterns must lie in R_j, as is evident from the geometry of Fig.4.8. Thus, the probability of error of the 1-NN rule is in this case equal to the probability that all patterns belong to w_j, which is obtained by letting $\alpha = N$ in Eq. (11), that is,

$$p_{e1} = \frac{1}{2^N} \qquad (12)$$

The probability of error of the q-NN rule may be similarly obtained. This rule assigns an unknown pattern to the class of the majority of its q closest neighbors. Since we are considering two classes, the value of q is assumed to be an odd integer, so that a majority will always result.

Suppose that a pattern x comes from w_i and is, therefore, contained in R_i. Then, the q-NN rule will commit a classification error only if there are $(q-1)/2$ or fewer patterns in R_i. Under this condition it will not be possible to arrive at the majority of more than the $(q-1)/2$ nearest neighbors from R_i required for correct classification of x into class w_i. The probability of this happening, which is in fact the probability of error of the q-NN rule, is obtained by summing the probabilities that there are $0, 1, 2, \cdots, (q-1)/2$ samples in R_i. Therefore, the probability of error of the q-NN rule is, from Eq. (11).

$$p_{e_q} = \frac{1}{2^N} \sum_{\alpha=0}^{(q-1)/2} C_\alpha^N \qquad (13)$$

Comparing p_{e_1} and p_{e_q}, we see that, in this case, the 1-NN rule has a strictly lower probability of error than any q-NN rule $(q \neq 1)$.

From this example we may generalize and say that, given M pattern classes, the 1-NN rule is superior to the q-NN rule $(q \neq 1)$ if all the distances between patterns of a class are smaller than any distance between patterns of different classes.

It can also be shown that in the large-sample case $(N \rightarrow \infty)$, and under some mild conditions, the error probability of the 1-NN rule satisfies the following bounds:

$$p_B \leq p_{e_1} \leq p_B \left(2 - \frac{M}{M-1} p_B \right) \qquad (14)$$

where p_B is the Bayes probability of error. The Bayes probability of error is the lowest achievable on an average basis.

We see from expression (14) that the error probability of the 1-NN rule is at most twice the Bayes probability of error. This equation provides the theoretical lower and upper bounds of this classification rule. The drawback in practice is the fact that to achieve the bounds shown above it is necessary to store a large set of samples of known classification. In addition, the distances from each pattern to be classified to all the stored samples must be computed for classification. This represents a serious computational difficulty for large sample sets.

New Words and Phrases

Bayes	*n.*	贝叶斯
boundary	*n.*	边界线
categorize	*v.*	分类
classifier	*n.*	分类器
clustering	*n.*	聚类
commit	*v.*	犯(错误)
facilitate	*v.*	帮助
hyperplane	*n.*	超平面
intuitive	*a.*	直觉的
majority	*n.*	多数
match	*n.v.*	匹配
measurement	*n.*	测量
multiprototype	*n.*	多类
pattern	*n.*	模式
prototype	*n.*	类型
proximity	*n.*	接近
disjoint	*v.*	脱离
uniformly distributed		均匀分布
Euclidean space		欧几里德空间
lower bound		下限

| perpendicular bisector | 垂直平分线 |
| piecewise-linear | 分段线性 |

Notes

1. The motivation for using distance function as a classification tool follows naturally from the fact that the most obvious way of establishing a measure of similarity between pattern vectors, which we also consider as points in Euclidean space, is by determining their proximity. 使用距离函数作为一个分类工具的动机很自然地始于这样一个事实:在模式向量(也可以认为是欧几里得空间的点)之间建立相似性测量最明显的方式是确定它们的接近程度。

2. For example, in Fig. 4.4 we may intuitively arrive at the conclusion that x belongs to class w_i solely on the basis that it is closer to the patterns of this class. 例如在图 4.4 中,我们可凭直觉得到结论:由于 x 比较靠近 w_i 类的模式它只属于 w_i 类。

3. The method of pattern classification by distance function can be expected to yield practical and satisfactory results only when the pattern classes tend to have clustering properties. 只有当模式类型有聚类特性的趋势时,才能期望由距离函数进行的模式分类方法产生实用和满意的结果。

4. In Fig. 4.5, however, although the two pattern populations are perfectly disjoint, one would in general be hard-pressed to arrive at a justification for classifying x into either class based on a measure of the proximity of this pattern to a class. 然而在图 4.5 中,虽然两个模式总体完全分离,但根据测量这个模式与任一类的接近度,一般是很难达成将 x 分为两类中的任一类的正当理由。

5. Minimum-distance pattern classification 最小距离模式分类法

6. This simple classification technique is an effective tool for the solution of problems in which the pattern classes exhibit a reasonably limited degree of variability. 这个简单的分类技术,在模式类别表现出相当有限的可变程度时,是一个解决问题的有效工具。

7. In some situations, the patterns of each class tend to cluster tightly about a typical or representative pattern for that class. 在某些情况下, 每类的模式趋于关于那类模式的一个典型或代表性的模式聚合。

8. In a situation such this, the resulting measurement vectors (patterns) of each character class will be almost identical since the same character in different checks are identical for all practical purpose. 在这种情况下, 每个字符类所得的测量结果的向量(模式)几乎都是相同的, 因为实际上在不同支票上相同的字符是同样的。

9. linear decision function 线性判决函数

10. The linear decision surface separating every pair of prototype points z_i and z_j is the hyperplane which is the perpendicular bisector of the line segment joining the two points. 分开每一对类型点 z_i 和 z_j 线性判决表面的是连接两点线段的垂直平分线的超平面。

11. nearest neighbor classification 最近邻分类

4.4 LEARNING ALGORITHM BY BACK-PROPAGATION

In this section we describe the principles underlying the delta rule, noting especially that it is a gradient descent technique. A section is devoted to demonstrating how the delta rule can be extended from the case wherein there is a fixed target output pattern for each input pattern to the case wherein sets of input patterns are associated with sets of output patterns. The latter part of this section discusses the generalized delta rule an extension to the delta rule, wherein learning proceeds by back-propagation of error signals.

4.4.1 The Delta Rule

From the form of the reinforcement signal, it appears as though the rule functions by making corrections for errors, the corrections being determined by the teacher input $z(t)$. In fact, the rule is typically applied to the case in which pairs of patterns, consisting of an input pattern and a target output pattern, are to be associated. Imagine a situation in which the set of input/output pairs are repeatedly presented. Then the change in weight w_{ji} following pattern p is given by the product of the ith input element and the jth target element.

$$\Delta_p w_{ji} = t_{pj} i_{pi}, \tag{1}$$

where

t_{pj}—desired or target output for jth element of pattern p and

i_{pi}—activation value of the ith element of the input for pattern p.

In vector notation.

$$\Delta_p W = t_p i_p^T \tag{2}$$

(If we assumed that this product rule is the sole criterion in determining the output unit's activation, then the rule is exactly the Hebbian rule.)

We have shown in a similar analysis that if the input vectors are orthonormal, then after the presentation of a series of P patterns, the weight matrix will be given by

$$W = \sum_{p=1}^{P} t_p i_p^T \tag{3}$$

and subsequent presentation of any of the input patterns will result in the retrieval of the unique output.

What is, however, most fascinating about the delta rule is that it is not so much the contents of the specific patterns that matter as it is the pattern of correlations among the patterns. Stone (1986) substantiates this claim by changing the basis of representation from the unit basis to the pattern basis (Fig. 4. 9). In an N-unit system, each pattern is represented by an N-dimensional vector whose elements represent the activations of each of the units (i. e. , each unit is represented by one dimension). Converting to the pattern basis involves transforming the coordinate system so that the patterns line up with the axes. Now each pattern is represented by one dimension.

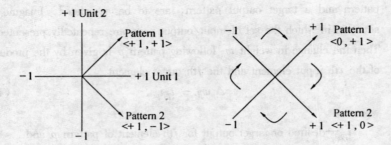

Fig.4.9   Conversion from unit-based coordinates
into pattern-based coordinates

We need two transformation matrices: P_I that transforms the input patterns into a space based on the input patterns and P_T that transforms the output patterns into a space based on the output patterns.

For input vectors,

$$i_i^* = P_I i_i. \qquad (4)$$

For target vectors,

$$t_i^* = P_T t_i. \qquad (5)$$

For output vectors,

$$o_i^* = P_T o_i. \qquad (6)$$

To derive the weight matrix under the new coordinate system, recall that in the old bases $W_i = o$. Therefore, we should now be able to write $W^* i^* = o^*$. Therefore,

$$W^* P_I i = P_T o, \qquad (7)$$

$$P_T^{-1} W^* P_I i = o = W i, \qquad (8)$$

and

$$W^* = P_T W P_I^{-1}. \qquad (9)$$

The rule in the old coordinate system that determined the updated weight matrix when a new (assumed orthonormal) input pattern was presented.

$$W(n) = W(n-1) + \eta \delta(n) i^T(n) \qquad (10)$$

where $W(n)$ = state of the weight matrix after n presentations,

$i(n)$ = input presented on the nth presentation, and

$\delta(n) = t(n) - W(n-1)i(n)$, that is, the difference between the desired and actual output on trial n,

now becomes (when multiplied on the left by P_T and on the right by P_I^{-1})

$$W^*(n) = W^*(n-1) + \eta \delta^*(n)[P_I^{-1}i^*(n)]^T P_I^{-1}$$

where

$$\delta^*(n) = t^*(n) - W^*(n-1)i^*(n)$$

and finally,

$$W^*(n) = W^*(n-1) + \eta \delta^*(n)i^*(n)^T C$$

where

$$C = (P_I^{-1})^T P_I^{-1}.$$

C holds the correlational information among the original input patterns.

The output vectors in the new basis have a very useful interpretation. The jth component of an output vector represents the amount of the jth pattern found in the output. This leads very naturally to the definition of error in such a system.

$$E_p = \sum_j (t_j^* - o_j^*).$$

The proposed learning procedure depends on the presentation of a set of pairs of input and output patterns. Learning (i. e., weight modification) occurs only when the output generated by the network in response to the input does not match the output provided in the pair.[1] The rule used for weight changing following i/o pair p is

$$\Delta_p W_{ji} = \eta (t_{pj} - o_{pj})i_{pi} = \eta \delta_{pj} i_{pi}$$

where

t_{pj} = jth component of the output produced by the net,

o_{pj} = jth component of the actual output pattern, and

$i_{pi} = i$th component of the input pattern.

The delta rule minimizes the squares of the differences between the actual and the desired output values summed over the output units and all pairs of input/output vectors. A cursory outline of the proof is given in this summary. Let

$$E_p = \frac{1}{2} \sum_j (t_{pj} - o_{pj})^2$$

be a measure of the error on input/output pattern p and let $E = \Sigma E_p$ be the overall measure. The proof shows that the delta rule implements a gradient descent in E when the units are linear. This corresponds to performing steepest descent on a surface in weight space whose height at any point in weight space is equal to the error measure. It is shown that

$$-\frac{\partial E_p}{\partial w_{ji}} = \delta_{pj} i_{pi} \propto \Delta_p w_{ji}.$$

Combining this with the observation that

$$\frac{\partial E}{\partial w_{ji}} = \sum_p \frac{\partial E_p}{\partial w_{ji}}$$

Rumelhart (1986) concludes that the net change in w_{ji} after one complete cycle of pattern presentations is proportaional to this derivative, and hence that the delta rule implements a gradient descent in E and thus minimizes the error function.

4.4.2 Extension of the Delta Rule to Statistical Learning

Instead of associating particular pairs of patterns, let us associate pairs of categories of patterns (i. e., the input/output pairs of patterns will be treated as random variables). Thus, when we pick the jth pair, input patterns i_j and target pattern t_j can take on random values. The ensuing analysis, provided by Stone (1986), holds regardless of the underlying distributions of these random variables. We also expect all the input/output pairs to be governed by some probability distribution. None of these distributions should change with time. If we start with the by now familiar form of the delta rule.

$$W(n) = W(n-1) + \eta[t(n) - W(n-1) \cdot i(n)] \cdot i^T(n)$$

and take expected values on both sides, we have

$$E[W(n)] = E[W(n-1)](I - \eta E[i(n) \cdot i^T(n)]) + \eta E[t(n) \cdot i^T(n)]$$

Assuming that each selection of an input/output pair is independent of all previous selections, we can say that

$$E[W(n-1) \cdot i(n)i^T(n)] = E[W(n-1)] \cdot E[i(n) \cdot i^T(n)]$$

If $R_I = E[\ddot{u}^T]$ and $R_{IO} = E[ti^T]$ represent, respectively, the statistical correlations among the input patterns and the statistical correlations between the input and target patterns, we can rewrite our previous result as

$$E[W(n)] = E[W(n-1)](I - \eta R_I) + \eta R_{IO}$$

Now, if we solve this recursive relation with the assumption that we started with an empty weight matrix (i.e., $W(0) = 0$), then we have

$$E[W(n)] = \eta R_{IO} \sum_{j=0}^{j=n} (I - \eta R_I)^j$$

Recall that the pseudo-inverse of a matrix $B^{[2]}$, called B^+, is given by

$$B^+ = \eta B^T \sum_{j=1}^{\infty} (I - \eta BB^T)^j$$

Since R_I has independent rows and columns, we can select a P with independent rows and columns such that $PP^T = R_I$.

In the limit $E[W(n)]$ satisfies the following relation

$$\lim_{n \to \infty} E[W(n)] = E[W_\infty] = R_{IO}(P^T)^{-1}\left[\eta P^T \sum_{j=1}^{\infty} (I - \eta PP^T)^j \right]$$

substitute for the pseudo-inverse of P to get

$$E[W_\infty] = R_{IO}(P^T)^{-1}P^+ = R_{IO}(PP^T)^{-1} =$$

$$R_{IO}R_I^{-1} = R_{IO}R_I^+$$

Now, investigate what happens when the system is presented with an input i. Proceeding on our usual assumption of independence, we have

$$E[\,W_\infty\, i\,] = E[\,W_\infty\,]E[\,i\,]$$

$$E[\,W_\infty\, i\,] = R_{IO}R_I^+E[\,i\,] = E[\,ti^T(ii^T)^+\,]E[\,i\,]$$

$$E[\,W_\infty\, i\,] = E[\,t(i^+\, i)^T(i^+\, i)\,]$$

and

$$E[\,W_\infty\, i\,] = E[\,t\,]$$

which is the required result. Note above that we have used the relation $(AB)^+ = B^+ A^+$, which is true when $A = i$, $B = i^+$, and i is a column vector. Further, $i^+ i = 1$ since i has only one column.

This shows that the average response to inputs is equal to the average of the target patterns. This would imply that the expected response to a particular pattern will be the expected value of the target as long as the i and t patterns are distributed normally with zero means.[3] It is not difficult to convert a set of input vectors into a set of zero mean patterns, nor is the requirement of normal distribution very restrictive when the patterns are of large dimensionality and are themselves the output of a linear system.[4]

4.4.3　The Generalized Delta Rule: Learning by Back-Propagation

For the case that we have discussed (i.e., using a linear activation function in a network with only an input and an output layer), the error surface is very conveniently shaped like a bowl. Consequently, gradient descent is sure to find the single minimum error set of weights. With hidden units, derivative-computation is not obvious and there is the danger of getting stuck at a local minimum on the complicated error surface.[5] Rumelhart (1986) shows that there does indeed exist a way of finding the "elusive" derivatives and that the problem of local minima is irrelevant in a wide variety of learning tasks.[6] We shall have more to say about the necessity of relying on a methodology that will fail in the worst case in the section dealing with the intractability of the network learning problem.

For the purposes of studying simple learning by back-propagation, consider a layered feedforward network with a semilinear activation function. A layered feedforward network is specified by the following characteristics. The bottom and top layers are for input and output, respectively. Every unit receives inputs from layers lower than its own and must send output to layers higher than its own. Given an input vector, the output vector is computed by a forward pass that computes the activity levels of each layer in turn, using the already computed activity levels in the earlier layers. An example of a simple feedforward net is shown in Fig.4.10.

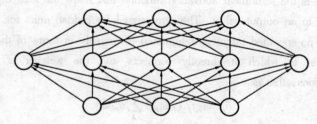

Fig.4.10 Simple feedforward net

A semilinear activation function is one in which the output of a unit is a nondecreasing and differentiable function of the net total output, $\text{net}_{pj} = \sum_i w_{ji} o_{pi}$. That is, for such a function

$$o_{pi} = f_j(\text{net}_{pj}),$$

where f is differentiable and nondecreasing. It is worth emphasizing that it does not make sense to have hidden units with linear activation functions since any combination of linear functions can be combined into a linear function, thus eliminating any justification for having a separate layer. [7]

The proof of the generalized delta rule involves a more elaborate version of the reasoning outlined in the proof of the delta rule. The results that emerge from the proof are:

The generalized rule has the same form as the standard version—that is, the weight on each line should be changed by an amount proportional to the product of an error signal δ, available to the unit receiving input along that line and the output of the unit sending activation along that line

$$\Delta_p w_{ji} = \eta \delta_{pj} o_{pi}$$

There are two other equations that specify the error signal. For output units, the error signal is very similar to the standard delta rule and is given by

$$\delta_{pj} = (t_{pj} - o_{pj}) f_j'(\mathrm{net}_{pj})$$

where f_j is the semilinear activation function that maps the total input to the unit to an output value. The error signal for hidden units for which there is no specified target is determined recursively in terms of those of the units to which it directly connects and the weights of those connections, that is

$$\delta_{pj} = f_j'(\mathrm{net}_{pj}) \sum_k \delta_{pk} w_{kj}$$

The generalized rule is applied in two phases. First, the output value o_{pj} is computed for each unit. This is then compared with the targets (i.e., the output provided as part of the i/o pair) and an error signal δ_{pj} results for each output unit. In the second phase (whose computational complexity is the same as that for the first phase) a backward pass allows the recursive computation for δ as indicated by the equations above.

Note that the linear threshold function, on which the perception is based, is discontinuous—its derivative does not exist and hence it cannot be used for the generalized delta rule. Instead we use the logistic activation function

$$o_{pi} = \frac{1}{1 - \exp\left(-\sum_i w_{ji}o_{pi} - \theta_j\right)}$$

where $\quad \theta_j$ = bias similar in function to a threshold.

Not only is the derivative of this function easy to compute, it has an additional advantage. We can show that the derivative of o_{pj} with respect to total input, net_{pj}, reaches its maximum when $o_{pj} = 0.5$ and its minimum as o_{pj} approaches 0 or 1. [Note that $0 < = o_{pj} < o_{pj} < 1$] Since the weight change is proportional to the derivative, maximum change occurs for those units near their midrange, that is, for those units that are not yet committed to being either on or off. This feature contributes to the system stability.

There is a point to be made regarding some of the terminology that we have been employing. In a strict gradient descent, we would modify a particular weight w_{ji} only after we had determined the true direction of steepest descent. Now, this true direction is determined by the vector sum of directions of descent suggested by the presentation of individual patterns in the ensemble.

$$\frac{\delta E}{\delta w_{ji}} = \sum_P \frac{\delta E_P}{\delta w_{ji}}$$

Since the process described above changes the weight w_{ji} after each presentation of a pattern, rather than after the presentation of a complete cycle of patterns, the resultant descent in weight space is not necessarily the steepest.[8] However, as long as the weight changes at any instant are not too large, the approximation to steepest descent is valid. This can be ensured by using a small learning rate, η. Shown in Fig. 4. 11 is a simple diagram illustrating this point. Here, the pattern ensemble is composed of only two patterns, p_1 and p_2. The process described above causes descent to occur along the directions suggested by the individual patterns rather than along that of stee pest descent.

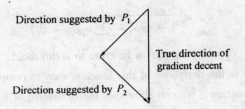

Fig. 4.11　The directions of decent

The magnitude in weight changes is determined in part by the constant of learning, η. We would like this to be as high as possible without inviting oscillatory phenomena during descent along some "unfriendly" surfaces.[9] One way to implement a reduction in such phenomena is to introduce a momentum term that gives some importance to past weight changes on the current weight change being considered:

$$\Delta w_{ji}(n+1) = \eta(\delta_{pj}o_{pi}) + \alpha\Delta w_{ji}(n)$$

where

　　n = presentation number,

　　η = learning rate, and

　　α = constant that determines the effect of past weight changes on the current direction of movement in weight space.

Remember that true gradient descent would require that the learning rate be infinitesimally small (i. e., the movement in weight space after every ensemble presentation be extremely small and in the direction of the gradient vector). Experiments have shown that a faster way to achieve the results brought about by a small-learning rate is to use a large learning rate, η, in conjunction with a large momentum factor, α.[10]

New Words and Phrases

activation	*n.*	激活
coordinate	*n.*	坐标
cursory	*a.*	粗略的

derivative	*n.*	导数
differentiable	*a.*	可微的
elaborate	*a.*	详细描述的
elusive	*a.*	难以捉摸的
emerge	*v.*	显现,形成
fascinating	*a.*	吸引人的
feedforward	*n.*	前馈
generalized	*a.*	广义的
govern	*v.*	控制
gradient	*n.*	梯度
intractability	*n.*	难处理
irrelevant	*a.*	不相关的
layer	*n.*	层
minima	*n.*	极小
modify	*v.*	修正
nondecreasing	*a.*	非减的
orthonormal	*n.*	正交
perceptron	*n.*	感知器
recursive	*a.*	递归的
reinforcement	*n.*	增强
restrictive	*a.*	限制性的
semilinear	*a.*	半线性
stick	*v.*	粘,留住
threshold	*n.*	门限
infinitesimally	*adv.*	无穷小
underlying	*a.*	在下面的,根本的
terminology	*n.*	术语
inviting	*a.*	引人注目的
oscillatory	*a.*	摆动的
momentum	*n.*	动量

derivative	*n.*	导数
back-propagation		反向传播
delta rule		δ准则
hidden unit		隐元
in response to		适应
learning procedure		学习过程
proportional to		成正比

Notes

1. Learning (i. e., weight modification) occurs only when the output generated by the network in response to the input does not match the output provided in the pair. 只有当由网络产生输出,并且对应的输入输出对不匹配时,才发生学习(即权值修正)。

2. Pseudo-inverse of a matrix B 矩阵 B 的伪逆矩阵

3. This would imply that the expected response to a particular pattern will be the expected value of the target as long as the i and t patterns are distributed normally with zero means. 这意味着只要 i 和 t 模式是具有零均值的正态分布,对一个特定模式的期望响应将是目标的数学期望。

4. It is not difficult to convert a set of input vectors into a set of zero mean patterns, nor is the requirement of normal distribution very restrictive when the patterns are of large dimensionality and are themselves the output of a linear system. 当模式的维数比较大,且线性系统的输出是它本身时,将一组输入向量转换为一组零均值模式也并不困难,正态分布的必要条件也没有完全限制。

5. With hidden units, derivative computation is not obvious and there is the danger of getting stuck at a local minimum on the complicated error surface. 加上隐元,引进的计算量并不明显,但是在复杂的误差曲面情况下,却有停留在局部极小值处的危险。

6. Rumelhart (1986) shows that there does indeed exit a way of finding the "elusive" derivatives and that the problem of local minima is irrelevant in a wide variety of learning tasks. Rumelhart 在 1986 年表明

确实存在寻找"难以捕获"导数的方法,并表明局部极小值问题在各种各样的学习任务中是没关系的。

7. It is worth emphasizing that it does not make sense to have hidden units with linear activation functions since any combination of linear functions can be combined into a linear function, thus eliminating any justification for having a separate layer. 值得强调的是具有线性激励函数的隐元一点意义也没有,因为任何线性函数的组合都可以组成线性函数,因此排除了有分离层的任何理由。

8. Since the process described above changes the weight w_{ji} after each presentation of a pattern, rather than after the presentation of a complete cycle of patterns, the resultant descent in weight space is not necessarily the steepest. 因为前面所述的处理在每个模式表述后而不是在一个完整周期模式述后之后改变加权,所以在加权空间下降的结果并不必是最陡的。

9. We would like this to be as high as possible without inviting oscillatory phenomena during descent along some "unfriendly" surface. 在沿着某个"不利"表面下降期间,我们希望它尽可能大而没有引人注目的振动现象。

10. Experiments have shown that a faster way to achieve the results brought about by a small-learning rate is to use a large learning rate, η, in conjunction with a large momentum factor, α. 实验证明,一种由小学习速率导致的快速获得结果的方法,就是使用大的学习速率 η 结合大的动量因子 α。

5

Instruction Manual

5.1 MOBILE PHONE

5.1.1 Assembly Instructions

1. *Inserting SIM card*

Place the Card with golden connectors facing down and the cut corner turned to the left.

Slide the SIM Card into the SIM Card slot. The SIM release button will slide towards the antenna as the SIM Card is pushed in.

Removing SIM Card

- Make sure the battery is removed.
- Slide the SIM release button towards you.
- Pull out the SIM Card.

2. *Attaching battery*

Place the battery on top of the phone and push until you hear a click.

Removing Battery

- Make sure the phone is turned off.
- Press the locking catch on the bottom of the battery.
- Lift the battery up and away from the phone.

3. *Connecting charger to phone*

Have the battery attached to the phone and connect the charger. Use the power plug that fits your mains.

Disconnecting Charger

Lift the plug up and pull it out.

4. *Connecting charger to mains*

Plug the charger into a mains socket. The phone now starts to charge the battery and you can see the battery meter in the display move while charging.

5. *About the charging function*

When you connect external power to the phone, the battery is charged. When the battery is fully charged the charging stops. You cannot overcharge your battery.

When you are charging the battery you can use your phone as normal; however the charging time will be longer.

6. *About the battery and the SIM card*

The Battery

Your phone is supplied with a Nickel Metal Hydride battery.[1] The battery is not charged before shipment, even though there might be enough power to turn the phone on.

The SIM Card

Before you can start using your phone, you need to order a SIM Card from a GSM service Provider. The SIM Card is a computer circuit that keeps track of your phone number, the services that you have ordered from the service provider, and your phone book information.

Your SIM Card is supplied with a security code or PIN (Personal Identity Number)[2] that you need to enter into the phone to gain access to the phone and network.

5.1.2 Turning On the Phone and General Information

1. *Turning on the phone*

(1) Press and hold down the NO key until you hear a click. The display will prompt you to enter the PIN (the security code that follows your SIM Card).

| PIN: |

(2) Enter the PIN and press YES.

The PIN is indicated as * * * * in the display. If you entered the PIN correctly, you will be welcomed by your phone. Then it searches for a network.

When a network is found, the indicator light on top of the phone flashes green once every second and the standby display is shown

| **WORLD** |

2. *Turning off the phone*

Press and hold the NO key until you hear a click and the display is dark.

5.1.3 Making and Receiving Calls

1. *Making a call*

Enter the area code and phone number. The phone number is shown in the display. If the number is longer than 10 digits, the beginning of the number will be shown as arrow

| ←123456789 |

To erase a digit, press CLR. To erase the entire phone number, press and hold down CLR for a couple of seconds.

Press YES to make the call. The display shows **Calling** , followed by **Connecting** and the phone icon is lit.

If the number is busy, you will hear a busy tone and the display shows Busy .

Holding the Phone

Put the earpiece to your ear for optimum speech and reception quality.

2. *Ending a call*

Press NO to end the call.

3. *Making an international call*

(1) Press and hold the zero key until the international + prefix is displayed.

(2) Enter the country code, area code (without any leading zero) and the phone number.

(3) Press YES to make the call.

4. *Making an emergency call*

Enter 112 (The international emergency number) and press YES. The display shows Emergency .

The 112 emergency number can be used in any country with or without a SIM Card, provided a GSM network is within range.

5. *Retry function*

If the call connection fails, the display shows Retry? . Press YES to redial the number, otherwise NO.

6. *Receiving a call*

When you receive a call, the phone rings and the indicator light on the top of the phone blinks green rapidly. The display shows Answer? .

7. *Answering a call*

• Press YES to answer the call.

• When the call is finished, press NO.

8. *Rejecting a call*

Press NO or press a volume key twice when the phone rings. The display now looks like this:

BUSY TONE

If the caller's network supports it, the caller will hear a busy tone.

If you have been unable to answer, or you have rejected a call, the number of the unanswered call will be shown in the display until you press CLR (this depends on your subscription).[3]

9. *Putting a call on hold*

If you are engaged in a call, you can put it on hold by pressing YES. This mutes the microphone so that you can have a private conversion without the person at the other end hearing. To put the call off hold, press YES again.

10. *About calling line identification* (*CLI*)

The Calling Line Identification service shows the caller's phone number when you receive a call (you have to order this service). If the caller's name is stored in your phone book, the name is displayed instead of the number.

Showing Your Phone Number

If you subscribe to normally withhold your number when calling, you can show the number on a particular call.[4]

(1) Enter the number you wish to call.

(2) Press right arrow. The display shows Send Id? .

(3) Press YES to make the call.

Hiding Your Phone Number

If you subscribe to normally show your number when calling, you can hide your number on a particular call.

(1) Enter the number you wish to call.

(2) Press right arrow twice. The display shows Hide Id? .

(3) Press YES to make the call.

11. *Handing two calls*

Your phone can handle two calls simultaneously. This allows you to hold one call and make or receive another, then you can switch between the two calls.

To be able to receive a second call, you must activate the **Call Wait** function.

Receiving a Second Call While a Call Is in Progress

When you receive a second call, you will hear a tone in the earpiece and the display shows ‖ **Call Wait** ‖.

Press YES answer the second call. The current call is put on hold. The display now looks like this:

‖ **1 On Hold** ‖

To reject the second call, press zero followed by YES.

Switching Between Two Calls

Press YES to switch between the two calls.

Ending the Current Call and Return to the Held Call

(1) Press NO to end the current call. The display shows

‖ **Retrieve?** ‖

and you hear two beeps.

(2) Press YES within three seconds to return to the held call.

If you do not press YES within three seconds, the held call is automatically ended.

Making a Second Call while a Call is in Progress

Enter the second phone number and press YES. The first call is put on hold and the display looks like this:

‖ **2 On Hold** ‖

Receiving a Third Call

If you are engaged in one call and have a second one on hold, you may receive a third call. You will hear a tone in the earpiece and ‖ **Call Wait** ‖ is shown in the display.

You can only have one call on hold at a time, so you need to end the first or second call before you answer the call.

You can do one of the following:

- Press zero followed by YES to reject the third call.
- End the first call, retrieve the held call, and answer the incoming call.
- End both calls. The phone rings and the question | **Answer**? | appears in the display. Press YES to answer the call.

5.1.4   Useful Information while Talking

1. *Changing volume while talking*

During a call, you can use the volume keys to increase or decrease the earpiece volume.

2. *Using phone as scratch pad*

(1) Enter a phone number on the keypad while talking. When you end the call, the number remains in the display.

(2) Press YES to make the call in the display.

3. *Sending tone signals*

During a call you can press keys 0 ~ 9, * and # to second DTMF tones. For example, to perform banking by phone or to control an answering machine.

4. *Checking time or cost of calls*

When you start a call (incoming or outgoing), the airtime is counted in minutes and seconds and shown on the display.

If you want the phone to keep track of the cost you need to set that specifically. Also check if your service provider supports that service.

5.1.5   Navigating the Menu System

1. *About the menu system*

You control the functions of your phone by a menu system. There are two sizes of the menu system:

- The reduced

- The extended

The default menu size is the reduced. In this manual package you find a separate leaflet which describes all the original settings of both the reduced and extended menu system.

Hint!

When you go through this manual, have the leaflet with all menus handy at the same time.

Some menus have sub-menus that have individual settings. If the menu has sub-menus, three dots appear after the menu name. See the example below:

Settings...

The Reduced Menus

The reduced menu consists of those functions and settings you probably use most. This menu system can be personalized to fit your specific needs. When you personalize the system, you move menus and sub-menus from the extended menu system to the reduced.

The Extended Menus

The extended menu contains all functions and settings available from the phone.

2. *Moving through the menu system*

Use left and right arrow keys to move through the menus system and to find the different menus.

When you reach the desired menu, press YES to choose the menu. Use the left and right arrow keys until you reach the function or setting you want. Then, in the same way you choose a menu, press YES to select the setting or function.

YES	confirm a setting or selection.
NO	reject a setting or a function.
CLR	return to the standby display.
←	scroll to the left in the menu system.

→   scroll to the right the menu system.

Glossary

These terms will be used throughout the manual.

Scroll: Pressing the left or right arrow key to move between the menus.

Select: Scrolling to a menu and then press YES.

Enter: Keying in letters or numbers from the keypad.

3. *Selecting the extended menus*

- Press CLR to clear the display.
- Press the left arrow key four times until you reach the **Menu Size** menu.
- Press YES.

You are now in the **Menu Size** menu where you can switch to the Extended menu mode.

- Press YES at the Extend prompt.

5.1.6 Diverting Calls

1. *About diverting calls*

When supported by your service provider, you can use the **Divert menu** to divert (forward) your calls to another number, for example your voice mail or home phone.

Note!

If your SIM card and your service provider support two lines, you need to set each line separately. Here we assume you have one line.

The divert service lets you divert:

- Al calls: regardless of if your telephone is turned on or off.
- Unanswered calls: if you do not answer within 30 seconds, if your phone is busy, turned off or out of reach of a network.

You can divert calls both from the reduced and extended menu. In the reduced menu you only divert all calls to one phone number; while in the extend menu you define how you want your divert, i. e. which number and which type of calls. [5]

As a reminder, the display will inform you about any activated call divert each time you turn on the phone. [6]

2. *Diverting from reduced menu*
- Select the **Divert** menu.
- You are prompted to enter a number (if you have not previously entered a number). Or you can press the left arrow key to enter a name.
- Enter the desired number (or name) at the prompt and press YES.
- There may be a short delay before the network responds and your display will read:

PLEASE WAIT

Followed by a divert message and phone number.

3. *Diverting from extended menu*
- Select the **DivertLine** menu.
- Select a divert option.
- Choose **Activate** and press YES.

You may now do one of the following:

(1) Enter a number at the prompt where you want your calls to be diverted, including the area code, and press YES.

(2) Press the left arrow key to enter a name from your phone book and press YES.

(3) Use the phone number that is suggested and press YES.

You will only get a number suggested if you have activated the divert function before.

There may be a short delay before the network responds to your divert option, and your display will prompt you when the divert is active (on or off).

4. *Viewing states of call divert*

- Select the **DivertLine** menu.
- Select the divert option you wish to view and choose **GetStatus.**

There may be a short delay before the network responds, and your display will prompt you which divert is active (on or off).

5. *Canceling call divert*

- Select the **DivertLine** menu.
- Select the divert option you wish to cancel and choose **Cancel.**

There may be a short delay before the network responds, but you will be prompted that your divert is cancelled.

5.1.7　Barring Calls—Restricting Calls

1. *About barring calls*

The call barring service lets you control which kind of calls can be made to or from your phone. This feature is convenient if you lend your phone to somebody else. This feature is GSM service dependent.

Barring Options

Your phone supports the following barring options (but your subscription might not support all):

- All outgoing calls—you cannot make any calls.
- All outgoing international calls—you cannot make any international calls.
- All outgoing international calls except to your home country—you cannot make any international calls except to the SIM Card home country.
- All incoming calls—you will not receive any calls.
- All incoming calls when you are abroad—you will not receive any calls when abroad.

Note!

To activate any of the barring functions, you need a password that comes with your subscription.

2. *Activating call bars for any call type*

- Select either **Incoming** or **Outgoing** call bars from the Barring menu.
- Select the barring option you want.
- Select **Activate**.
- Enter your password (provided with your subscription) and press YES.

There may be a short delay before the network responds and your display will prompt you which call bars have been activated.

Press CLR to stop the responses from the network.

3. *Canceling all call bars*
- Select the **Cancel All** option in the **Barring** menu.
- Enter your password at the prompt and press YES.

There may be short delay before the network responds and your display will prompt you which call bars have been cancelled.

Press CLR to stop the responses from the network.

5.1.8 Sending and Receiving Text Messages

1. *About text messages*

The Short Message Service (SMS) function allows you to send and receive text messages that contain up to 160 characters. Text messages can be received when the phone is in standby mode, when you are engaged in a call, or when incoming calls are diverted to another phone number. Also, if you have had your phone turned of for a while the network will keep track of the message and send it to your phone as soon as it is turned on.

After a message is received, it is left in the phone's memory, which works similar to a computer's working memory. The message remains in the phone's memory until you read it. You can even turn off the phone and the message will remain intact. If you, on the other hand, change SIM Card, you will lose the unread message. This is because messages should be personal.

Note!

You need to set the service center number before you can send any messages. If you only want to receive messages, you do not need to do anything.

2. *Checking subscription*

Call your service provider to see which services your subscription supports, or check the service provider's manual.

3. *Setting service center address*

• Check the service center address (number) for your service provider.

• Select **Options** in the **Send** menu.

• Select **ServCent.**

• Enter the service center address with the international prefix and press YES.

4. *Sending SMS*

• Select **New** in the **Send** menu.

• Enter your message and press YES. You can also enter a phone number.

• Enter the phone number, or press the left arrow key to enter a name you want to send to and press YES.

If your message does not go through, it will be sent back to you.

Setting Duration of Message

• Select **Options** in the **Send** menu.

• Select **ValidPer.**

• Select how long you want the message to be repeated.

The service center repeats the message for the set duration or until the receiver can receive it.

5. *About other message types*

You can send SMS from your phone to the service center and the service center can change the message into the following types (if supported):

E-mail

The E-mail address cannot contain more than 20 characters.

Telex

FAX

Both group 3 and 4.

X400

Voice

Changing Message Type

- Select **Options** in the **Send** menu.
- Select **MsgType**.
- Select the message type you want.

6. *Receiving a message*

When you receive a message the display looks like this:

READ?

At the same time you will hear a beep as loud as the ring signal and the green light on top of the phone will flash.

Reading an Incoming Message

(1) Press YES when you have received a message. The display will show you the date of the incoming SMS, you can see the time by pressing *.

(2) Press YES. The display will show you from which phone number the message is sent, or the name if stored in your phone book. The display could now look like this: Jenny→

The arrow shows you that you can start scrolling through the message with the right arrow key.

(3) Press the right arrow key to read the message.

When you have read a message, you can do one of the following:

- Call a phone number in the message by pressing YES.

• Erase the message by pressing YES at the erase prompt.

• Store the message by pressing NO at the erase prompt (you may get a reply prompt if the sender has required a reply). Press YES at the Store prompt and the message is stored on the SIM Card.

Erasing a Message

Press CLR any time during the message and answer YES on the question prompt.

7. *Reading an old message*

• Select the **Read** menu.

• Scroll to the message you want to read and press YES.

• Read through the message by pressing the right arrow key.

5.1.9　Receiving Area Information

While the SMS function is a personal service with message directed to you, the Area Information is a broadcast type message that is sent to all subscribers at the same time.[7] You can set your phone to receive only those types of messages you want to listen to, e. g.: the local weather forecast or the local traffic report. Each message is identified by a 3-digit code. Check with your service provider for which message types are available in your network.

New Words and Phrases

assembly	*n.*	装配
bar	*v.*	禁止
click	*n.*	滴答声
divert	*v.*	转移
earpiece	*n.*	听筒
emergency	*n.*	紧急
GSM	*abbr.*	全球移动通信系统
incoming	*a.*	打进的(电话)
intact	*a.*	完整无缺的

leaflet	*n*.	传单
mains	*n*.	电源
menu	*n*.	菜单
navigate	*v*.	操纵
outgoing	*a*.	打出的
overcharge	*n*.*v*.	过度充电
prompt	*n*.*v*.	提示
scratch	*a*.	打草稿用的
SIM	*abbr*.	用户标识模块
slide	*v*.	滑动
standby	*n*.	备用
subscriber	*n*.	用户
withhold	*v*.	保留
go through		被通过
mobile phone		移动电话
sub-menu		子菜单
subscribe to		预订

Notes

1. Nickel Metal Hydride battery 镍氢电池
2. Personal Identity Number（PIN）个人身份号码
3. If you have been unable to answer, or you have rejected a call, the number of the unanswered call will be shown in the display until you press CLS (this depends on your subscription). 如果你不能接电话,或者拒绝接一个电话,未接电话的号码便显示出来,直到按 CLS 键为止(这取决于你是否同意)。
4. If you subscribe to normally withhold your number when calling, you can show the number on a particular call. 如果你通常是预设打电话时保留你的电话号码,你也可以在一次个别的电话中发出你的电话号码。
5. In the reduced menu you only divert all calls to one phone number; while in the extend menu you define how you want your divert, i.e.

which number and which type of calls.在简化菜单中,你只能将所有电话转移到一个电话号码上,而在扩充菜单上,你可以定义你的转向,即哪类电话到哪个电话号码。

6. As a reminder, the display will inform you about any activated call divert each time you turn on the phone. 提示一下,每当你打开电话,显示的内容将告诉你所有转移过的电话。

7. While the SMS function is a personal service with messages directed to you, the Area Information is a broadcast type message that is sent to all subscribers at the same time. 短信息服务功能是带有直接给你信息的个人服务,而区域信息是一种广播形式的信息,同时送给所有用户。

5.2　SPECIFICATIONS FOR SOME ELECTRICAL APPLIANCE

5.2.1　Recorder

1. *Power supply*

Battery Power Operation

• Open the battery compartment lid by pushing the knobs in the direction of arrow.

• Install 5 "D" size (UM – 1) flashlight batteries carefully. [1]

• Close the battery compartment lid.

External DC Power Operation

• Connect the plug of a 7.5V external battery into the external DC socket.

• When a plug is connected into the external DC socket, the internal batteries are automatically disconnected.

AC Power Operation

• Before operating the unit for the first time in a new area, it is absolutely necessary to make sure that the setting of the voltage select plug (located on the back of the unit) corresponds as closely as possible to you local voltage. [2] To adjust the voltage, take off the cover of the voltage select plug, then pull out the plug and replug it into the socket which corresponds with your local voltage.

• Connect one end of power cord to the AC input socket and the other end to an AC outlet.

Note:

The batteries are automatically disconnected when AC power cord is plugged into the AC input socket.

2. *Radio operation*

Reception of Radio Program

• Set the radio switch to the radio position. Set the desired radio band with the band select switch.

• Tune in a desired station by turning the tuning knob. For SW reception, return in the station accurately with the fine tuning knob.

• For FM or SW reception pull out the aerial and determine the direction, length and angle to give the best reception.

• For MW reception, the aerial inside of the unit is somewhat directional, reception from distant station may sometimes be improved by rotating the unit.

• Adjust the volume and tone controls for your desired sound.

• If you desire to listen to the radio program privately, plug in an optional earphone into the earphone socket.

• To turn off the radio, set the radio switch to the tape position.

To Listen to a Radio Program while Going to Sleep

If you desire to listen to a radio program in bed, the auto-stop mechanism system of this unit works as a sleep timer. The radio operating time is determined by the cassette to be used.

• Press the stop/eject button and insert a selected cassette into its compartment and close the lid.

• Set the radio switch to the radio position and tune in a desired station.

- Press the play button. Or if you wish to record the radio program, press the record and play buttons simultaneously.
- Set the radio switch to the timer position.
- When the tape is wound completely, the play button or record and play buttons will be released and the radio power is shut off automatically.
- To listen to a radio program continuously, set the radio switch to the radio position.

3. *Compact cassette*

Open the cassette compartment lid by pressing the stop/eject button. Insert the cassette with the full reel to the right (visible through the window) and tape slot at the top.[3] The cassette fits into the unit only in the correct position. Push the cassette compartment lid at the top to put the cassette in place. Now the unit is ready to operate. To use the second track, press the stop/eject button and remove the cassette. Turn the cassette over and reinsert it.

4. *Recording*
- Recording through the built-in microphone
- Recording from an External Microphone
- Recording of telephone conversation
- Recording from the built-in radio
- Recording from an External sound source

5. *Playback*
- Press the stop/eject button and insert the recorded cassette into its compartment, then close the lid.
- Press the play button.
- Adjust the volume and tone controls for your desired sound.
- To stop the playback at any position on a tape, press the stop/eject button. When the tape is wound completely, the play button will be automatically released.

6. *Erasing*

To erase the recorded tape without a new recording, set the radio switch to the tape position. Plug an optional erase plug to the MIC socket and let the unit operate in the record mode.

7. *Maintenance*

To ensure continued high performance from your unit, periodically clean the heads and pinch roller whenever dust or reddish-brown oxide has accumulated. Failure to clean these parts will result in inferior sound quality, distortion of recordings, deterioration of high frequency reproduction, and inconsistent tape speed.

- Press the stop/eject button and open the cassette compartment lid.
- Press the play button.
- Moisten a cotton applicator with cleaner or alcohol and apply to the face of both heads, rubbing gently until all traces of dirt or oxide are removed. Also clean the surface of the pinch roller and the capstan. [4]
- Dry, clean and polish the face of the heads with a piece of cloth.

8. *Specifications*

Recording system	DC bias, double track
Erasing system	DC erase
Rewind & fast forward time	Rewind: 1'30" (C-60)
	Fast forward: 3'48"(C-60)
Signal to noise ratio	40 dB
Frequency range	MW: 530 ~ 1 605 kHz
	SW1: 2.3 ~ 7.0 MHz
	SW2: 7.0 ~ 22 MHz
	FM: 87.5 ~ 108 MHz
Terminal impedance	EXT. MIC: 4 kΩ
	Earphone: 8 Ω
Output power	2.5 W maximum

Power source   DC: 7.5 V "D" cell (UM – 1) × 5

                                    AC: 120/200/240 V, 50/60 Hz

5.2.2   Cassette Tape Deck Amplifier

General

Power requirements

   European models   AC 220 V, 50/60 Hz

   U.K. and Australian models   AC 240 V, 50/60 Hz

   Other models   AC 110/120 ~ 127/220/240 V

                                    (Switchable)[5], 50/60 Hz

Power consumption   480 W

Dimensions   360 (W) × 270 (H) × 330 (D)

                                    mm[6]

Weight (without package)   10 kg

Amplifier Section

Continuous power output

Music power (both channel driven)   90 W + 90 W(1 kHz, T.H.D.[7]

                                    1% 8 Ω)

Peak music power   500 W

Graphic equalizer frequency band   100 Hz, 300 Hz, 1 kHz, 3.3 kHz,

                                    10 kHz, ± 7 dB

Hum and noise   72 dB

Total Harmonic Distortion (40 Hz   No more than 0.2%

   to 20 000 Hz, 30 W, 8 Ω)

Tape Deck Section

System   4-track, 2-channel stereo[8]

Heads   Recording/playback head × 1

                                    Playback head × 1

                                    Erasing head × 1

Motor   DC servo 2-speed motor × 1

Wow and flutter[9]	No more than 0.09%
Fast winding time	Approximately 95 seconds
	(C-60 tape)

Frequency response:

  – 20 dB recording:

Normal tape	35 Hz to 14 000 Hz ± 6 dB
CrO$_2$	35 Hz to 15 000 Hz ± 6 dB
Metal tape	35 Hz to 16 000 Hz ± 6 dB
S/N[10]	
Dolby NR[11] OFF	56 dB

Noise reduction effect

Dolby B type NR ON	More than 10 dB (at 5 kHz)

Accessories

Operating instructions	1
Remote control unit[12]	1
Dry cell batteries	2

5.2.3 FM/AM Tuner

General

Power requirements

European models	AC 220 V, 50/60 Hz
U.K. and Australian models	AC 240 V, 50/60 Hz
Other models	AC 110/120 ~ 127/220/240 V
	(Switchable), 50/60 Hz
Dimensions	360(W) × 60(H) × 330(D) mm
Weight (without package)	3 kg

FM Tune Section

Frequency range	87.5 ~ 108 MHz
Sensitivity	Mono 0.9 μV/75 Ω
	Stereo 50 μV/75 Ω

Signal-to-noise ratio	Mono 66 dB
	Stereo 60 dB
Distortion	Stereo: 0.5% (1 kHz)
Antenna input	300 Ω balanced
	75 Ω unbalanced[13]

MW (AM) Tune Section

Frequency range	
When 10 kHz step	530 ~ 1 700 kHz
When 9 kHz step	531 ~ 1 602 kHz[14]
Sensitivity(Loop antenna)	350 μV/m
Antenna	Loop antenna
Output level (AM 30% MOD)[15]	150 mV

Accessories

FM T-type antenna	1
AM loop antenna	1

5.2.4 Multi-play Compact Disc[16] Player

General

Power requirements	
European models	AC 220 V, 50/60 Hz
U.K. and Australian models	AC 240 V, 50/60 Hz
Other models	AC 110/120 ~ 127/220/240 V
	(Switchable), 50/60 Hz
Power consumption	
European & U.K. models	11 W
Other models	11 W
Operating temperature	+5℃ ~ +35℃
Dimensions	360(W) × 85(H) × 330(D) mm
Weight (without package)	5 kg

Audio Section

Frequency response	4Hz ~ 20 kHz ± 1 dB
Signal-to-noise ratio	98 dB or more
Channel separation	95 dB or more
Output voltage	2.0 V ± 0.5 V
Wow and flutter	less than ± 0.001% (W. peak)
Channels	2-channel (stereo)

Output Terminal

Audio line output[17]

Functions

Number of discs to be stored   maximum 6

Search function
   Disc selection
   Manual search
   Track search

Programming
   Maximum 32 steps
   Pause
   Direct programming
   Program clear

Repeat functions
   All discs repeat
   Program repeat
   1 disc repeat (with program)
   Track repeat (with program)

Random play[18]

Accessories

Operating instructions	1
Six-compact-disc magazine[19]	1
Control cord	1
Output cable	1

New Words and Phrases

aerial	*n.*	天线
applicator	*n.*	涂药器
balanced	*a.*	平衡的,匹配的
capstan	*n.*	绞盘
cassette	*n.*	盒式磁带
deterioration	*n.*	劣化,退化
earphone	*n.*	耳机
eject	*v.*	弹出
EXT	*abbr.*	外部
FM	*abbr.*	调频
head	*n.*	磁头
hum	*n.*	交流声
inconsistent	*a.*	不协调的
inferior	*a.*	劣等的
lid	*n.*	盖子
magazine	*n.*	(工具)箱,(软盘)盒
MIC	*abbr.*	麦克风
microphone	*n.*	麦克风
MOD	*abbr.*	调制
mono	*a.*	单(声道)
MW	*abbr.*	中波
outlet	*n.*	出口
playback	*n.*	录音重放,播放
plug	*n.*	插头
reel	*n.*	(磁带的)盘
reproduction	*n.*	再现
sensitivity	*n.*	灵敏度
servo	*n.*	伺服

specification	*n.*	规格,指标
stereo	*n.*	立体声
SW	*abbr.*	短波
switchable	*a.*	可变换的
wind	*v.*	缠,绕
built-in		内置
channel separation		通道隔离度
DC bias		直流偏磁
DC erase		直流消磁
graphic equalizer		图形均衡器
harmonic distortion		谐波失真
loop antenna		环天线
pinch roller		夹送滚轮
power cord		电源线
Power supply		供电
shut off		关掉
tune in		收听

Notes

1. Install 5 "D" size (UM - 1) flashlight batteries carefully. 其中 D 型电池即为我们用于手电筒的 1 号电池,而在日本称为 UM - 1 型。

2. Before operating the unit for the first time in a new area, it is absolutely necessary to make sure that the setting of the voltage select plug (located on the back of the unit) corresponds as closely as possible to you local voltage. 在新的地点首次使用本机时,务必确认本机的电压选择插头(在本机后面)的设置符合最接近于当地的电压。

3. Insert the cassette with the full reel to the right (visible through the window) and tape slot at the top. 插入在右边绕满带盘的磁带(可通过窗口看见),录音带缝隙应在上面。

4. Moisten a cotton applicator with cleaner or alcohol and apply to the face of both heads, rubbing gently until all traces of dirt or oxide are

removed. 将一块棉团用清洁剂或酒精弄湿,用它轻擦两个磁头的表面,
直到清除所有的污迹或氧化物为止。

5. AC 110/120 ~ 127/220/240 V (Switchable),从交流 110/120 V 到
127/220/240 V 可切换。

6. Dimensions　360(W) × 270(H) × 330(D) mm,这句话中的 W,H,D
分别代表宽、高、长(深)。

7. T.H.D.总谐波失真,是 Total Harmonic Distortion 的缩写。

8. 4-track, 2-channel stereo 四磁道、两通道立体声。

9. Wow and flutter,速度不均匀性

10. S/N 信噪比,是 Signal-to-noise ratio 的缩写,有时也写成 SNR 或
Signal to noise ratio。

11. Dolby NR,杜比降噪,NR 是 Noise Reductiond 的缩写。

12. Remote control unit 遥控器。

13. Antenna input,300 Ω balanced,75 Ω unbalanced,天线可以是 300 欧
同轴线(匹配),也可以是不匹配的 75 欧扁平馈线。

14. When 10 kHz step,530 ~ 1 700 kHz,When 9 kHz step,531 ~ 1 602
kHz,由于有 10 kHz 和 9 kHz 两种调谐步长,因此频率范围也有所不同。

15. Output level (AM 30% MOD),在 30% 幅度调制时的输出电平。

16. Compact disc 就是常说的 CD 盘片。

17. Audio line output 音频线路输出。

18. Random play 随机播放,即不按 CD 盘片上音乐的顺序播放。

19. Six-compact-disc magazine,可装 6 张 CD 盘片的盒。

5.3　SKYsystem FAMILY

Providing up to 20 GFLOPS in a single VME chassis, the new
SKYsystem comes out of the box ready to run your application
instantly. [1] SKYsystem arrives pre-configured with the most commonly
used workstation tools to enable you to begin development within ONE
hour. Guaranteed.

SKY accelerates your design and deployment schedule by providing a ready to run system solution. SKYsystem includes the Solaris operating system, the easy-to-use SKYvec Software Development Environment running on a SPARC-based VME slot # 1 processor, up to 16 SKYbolt application accelerators, an Sbus-based frame buffer, SCSI mass storage devices, a monitor, a keyboard and a mouse.[2]

SKY's systems experts, in partnership with your design team, will help evaluate your requirements and configure your system to precisely meet the performance requirements of your application. From medical imaging to radar/sonar to seismic data processing, SKYsystem provides the fastest path to a complete solution.

5.3.1 SKYsystem Family Overview

The SKYsytem's standards-based modular design and supporting software accelerate time to solution, time to market and, ultimately, your time to success, SKY's development and target systems are fully integrated, tested and ready to use.[3] Optimum development and runtime performance are achieved through a variety of industry-standard SPARC-based slot # 1 controllers.[4] Maximum application performance is derived from the optimum combination of processors, I/O and memory on configurable SKYblot application accelerators.

High-performance application software can be developed quickly and easily by using the unique SKYvec Software Development Environment. SKYvec includes automatic vectorizing and parallelizing compilers[5], the Standard math and Vector Libraries, and our advanced debugging environment.

The modular SKYsystem architecture, shown below, can be custom configured to precisely meet your application needs. Sixteen SKYbolt application accelerators provide up to 20 GFLOPS of compute power. You can select the slot # 1 and mass storage capabilities that fit you programming requirements.

5.3.2   SKYbolt Family Overview

At the heart of system's superior performance is the SKYbolt family of application accelerators. The SKYbolt family includes motherboards in 6U and 9U form factors. The 6U motherboard can be configured with a single daughtercard, the 9U with up to four daughtercards. An i960 System Processor located on the mothercard manages all I/O tasks, freeing the i860s on the daughtercards for their role as compute processors.[6]

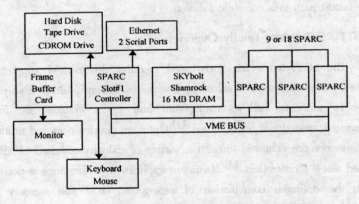

Fig.5.1   SKYsystem 6U Block Diagram

Daughtercards are available in two basic configurations. The uni-processor daughtercard has a single i860 processor and up to 8 MB of SRAM or 18MB DRAM. The Shamrock daughtercard is configured with four i860 processors and either 16 or 64 MB of DRAM. SKYcrossbar, a digital crossbar switch, connects the four processors to the four memory banks.

Shamrock processors, the SKYcrossbar and memory are implemented with a Uniform memory Access architecture, giving each processor a linear address range for all four banks of memory and equal access to each bank. This advanced design gives the shamrock the highest density, the greatest programming flexibility and the highest performance available in a single slot today.

5.3.3   Shamrock Daughtercard

The Shamrock Daughtercard contains four i860 processors and 16 or 64 MB of memory. The memory is divided into four banks that can either be shared among all four processors or distributed one bank per processor. A high-speed digital crossbar connects each memory each processor and each memory bank for an aggregate processor to memory bandwidth of 640 MB/sec per Shamrock daughtercard.

The Shamrock implements SKY's exclusive Parallel Compute Cluster Architecture, allowing all four processors to work in parallel on the same problem.[7] In this programming model, the data is automatically striped across the four memory banks. Each processor may access its portion of the data without contention from the other processors. Performance is maintained during processor-to-processor synchronization by using hardware-based barrier Synchronization Registers, instead of costly shared memory accesses, for memory-based semaphores.[8] All four processors work to run a single program together efficiently, with nearly linear speedup.

5.3.4   System Processor

The SKYbolt architecture includes a System Processor to offload system-level functions from the compute processors. The System Processor reduces the workload of the compute processors and executes system commands faster because the System Processor is optimized to service asynchronous requests for data management, I/O and control functions.

The heart of the System Processor (SP) is an i960CA superscalar processor chip from INTEL. The SP also includes 256 KB zero-wait-state SRAM used for List I/O processing and 512K Flash RAM for non-volatile

storage of user-configurable boot code. The System Processor:
- Handles all communication and control
- Fields all interrupts
- Only informs an i860 when there is a task for that i860
- Manages all external resources, including remote data acquisition
- Provides the bulk of the operating stem, freeing the i860s to run more efficiently with a small kernel
- Schedules the SKYmpx real-time executive
- Coordinates the i860s in a multi-processor environment
- Controls synchronization, polling and setup, freeing the i860s for compute processing

5.3.5 Standard Slot # 1 Controller

The SKYsystem comes standard with a SPARC-based VMEbus slot # 1 controller that is SPARCstation-2 compatible and includes Sun's Solaris operating system and SKY's SKYvec Development Tools installed and ready to use. This controller has all the features of a SPARCstation-2 with the addition of a Weitek clock doubler processor and a VMEbus interface. The FORCE CPU-2CE series will run all programs that run on the Sun SPARCstation-2. The FORCE CPU-2CE/16-80 is a single slot, embedded, VMEbased host that is ideally suited for numerically intensive application development.

5.3.6 High Performance Slot # 1 Controller

The SKYsystem can optionally be configured with a Themis VMEbus slot # 1 controller that is based on the SPARCstation 10 architecture and processor. The Sun Solaris operating system and the SKYvec Development Tools are installed and ready to use. This controller has many of the same features as a SPARCstation 10, with the addition of a VMEbus interface capable of Block Transfers (BLTs).

The Themis CPU-10HS will run most programs that run on the Sun SPARCstation 10. The CPU-10HS is a single slot, embedded, VME-based host that provides the highest SPARC performance available today in a single 6U VME slot. It is ideally suited for numerically intensive split applications that also require high performance host interaction.

5.3.7 Sun Solaris Operating System

Solaris provides an advanced development and run-time environment for the embedded SPARC-based slot # 1 controller. Solaris is comprised of SunOS, ONC networking environments. Open Windows, OPEN LOOK and DeskSet. SunOS is the highest quality and most widely supported enriched UNIX implementation available today.

ONC is the industry standard for heterogeneous networking. Open Windows is the network-extensible graphical application development platform. OPEN LOOK is an intuitive graphical user interface, and DeskSet is a suite of personal and work group productivity applications.

By carefully merging the functionality of UNIX System V, Berkeley BSD and Xenix, SunOS offers the optimum balance of UNIX capability and performance. The Solaris operating system conforms to the POSIX, X/Open, XPG, SVID and FIPS standards.

5.3.8 SKYvec Development Environment

The SKYvec Software Development Environment speeds application porting and development for the SKYsystem. Built on open systems principles, SKYvec includes compilers, libraries, development tools, a real-time executive, and host computer support. Each component is designed to provide a familiar and congenial development environment for the users of UNIX-based workstations.

The SKYvec compilers and tools automatically optimize, strip-mine, vectorize and parallelize most applications. Automatic strip-mining breaks the application's data set into smaller groups, which minimizes cache thrashing and takes maximum advantage of the i860's cache. Automatic vectorizing of the application code takes advantage of the i860's deeply pipelined architecture to increase performance of the original scalar code by up to 6x. [9] Automatic parallelization analyzes program loops and splits them among different processors. The compiler inserts all synchronization code required to manage the · Parallel Compute Cluster, providing transparent access to up to 4x the processing power.

SKYvec's exclusive automatic strip-mining, auto vectorizing, and auto parallelizing tools, compilers and advanced libraries are the only tools available today from any vendor that automatically optimize code for a single or four processor i860 architecture.

The SKYvec standard math Library contains over 600 vector functions for real, double, and complex data types. The library includes functions for image and signal processing, such as FIR filters and convolutions. Certain routines such as the FFT include a parallel version that is hand-coded to maximize performance of the parallel Compute Cluster. [10] All routines utilize an industry standard calling interface for source-code compatibility with applications that use QTC or FPS library calls. Combined with the auto-vectorizing compiler, the Standard math Library makes fast vector operations easy to use.

The SKYmpx Run-time Executive achieves optimum performance while transparently providing maximum flexibility with minimum overhead. The interrupt-driven monitor on the System Processor provides predictably fast response to urgent events. Real-time events are queried according to priority to guarantee the deadlines of critical tasks. Full support for multitasking and interprocessor communication makes the SKYsystem easy to program.

New Words and Phrases

accelerator   *n*.   加速器

acquisition	*n.*	获取
boot	*v.*	导入
bulk	*n.*	大量
chassis	*n.*	底板
contention	*n.*	争用，争议
distribute	*v.*	分配，散布
DRAM	*n.*	动态存储器
embedded	*a.*	嵌入的
heterogeneous	*a.*	不同种类的
interrupt	*n. v.*	中断
intuitive	*a.*	直观的
kernel	*n.*	内核
merge	*v.*	合并
modular	*a.*	模块的
offload	*v.*	卸载
overview	*n.*	评论，概述
share	*n. v.*	供享
SRAM	*n.*	静态存储器
synchronization	*n.*	同步
flash RAM		快速存储器
mass storage		大容量存储
non-volatile storage		固定存储器
runtime performance		运行性能
system-level		系统级
zero-wait-state		零等待

Notes

1. Providing up to 20 GFLOPS in a single VME chassis, the new
   SKYsystem comes out of the box ready to run your application
   instantly. 一个 VME 底板能提供高达 20 GFLOPS 的计算能力，

SKYsystem 开箱即可立即执行应用程序。VME 由 Motorola 公司于 1981 年推出的第一代 32 位标准总线，GFLOPS 每秒 109 次浮点运算。

2. SKYsystem includes the Solaris operating system, the easy-to-use SKYvec Software Development Environment running on a SPARC-based VME slot # 1 processor, up to 16 SKYbolt application accelerators, an Sbus-based frame buffer, SCSI mass storage devices, a monitor, a keyboard and a mouse. SKYsystem 包括 Solaris 操作系统、易于应用的基于 SPARC 1 号 VME 插槽处理器的 SKYvec 软件开发环境、最多 16 个 SKYbolt 应用程序加速器、基于 S 总线的帧缓存、带有 SCSI 接口的大容量储存装置、一个监视器以及键盘和鼠标。Solaris operating system 是 SUN 公司开发的一种网络操作系统，SPARC 是 SUN 公司的一种工作站系统，SCSI 则是一种小型计算机接口。

3. SKY's development and target systems are fully integrated, tested and ready to use. SKY 的开发和目标系统经过充分地集成、测试，并马上即可应用。

4. Optimum development and runtime performance are achieved through a variety of industry-standard SPARC-based slot # 1 controllers. 最佳开发环境和运行性能是通过满足多种工业标准的基于 SPARC 工作站的 1 号插槽控制器来达到的。

5. vectorizing and parallelizing compilers 矢量化和并行处理的编译器。

6. An i960 System Processor located on the mothercard manages all I/O tasks, freeing the i860s on the daughtercards for their role as compute processor. 安装于母板上的 i960 系统处理器完成处理所有的 I/O 任务，免除子卡上 i860 的 I/O 任务，使其作为专门计算用的处理器。

7. The Shamrock implements SKY's exclusive Parallel Compute Cluster Architecture, allowing all four processors to work in parallel on the same problem. Shamrock 实现 SKY 独有的并行计算结构，允许所有四个处理器并行的完成同一任务。

8. Performance is maintained during processor-to-processor synchronization by using hardware-based Barrier Synchronization

Registers, instead of costly shared memory accesses, for memory-based semaphores. 在处理器之间同步时,系统的高性能是靠硬件同步屏蔽寄存器来达到的,而不是用代价很高的访问共享内存的做法。

9. Automatic vectorizing of the application code takes advantage of the i860's deeply pipelined architecture to increase performance of the original scalar code by up to 6x. 应用程序的自动矢量化充分利用了 i860 处理器的管道结构,使原始标量代码效率提高六倍。

10. Certain routines such as the FFT include a parallel version that is hand-coded to maximize performance of the parallel Compute Cluster. 像 FFT 这样的子程序都含有并行化的版本,并经手工代码优化以充分发挥并行计算的性能。

5.4 ADSP-2106x

5.4.1 Overview

The ADSP-2106x SHARC Super Harvard Architecture Computer is a high-performance 32-bit digital signal processor for speech, sound, graphics, and imaging applications. The SHARC builds on the ADSP-21000 Family DSP core to form a complete system-on-a-chip, adding a dual-ported on-chip SRAM and integrated I/O peripherals supported by a dedicated I/O bus. With its on-chip instruction cache, the processor can execute every instruction in a single cycle. Four independent buses for dual data, instructions, and I/O, plus crossbar switch memory connections, comprise the Super Harvard Architecture of the ADSP-2106x. The ADSP-2106x SHARC represents a new standard of integration for digital signal processors, combining a high-performance floating-point DSP core with integrated, on-chip features including a host processor interface, DMA controller, serial ports, and link port and shared bus connectivity for glueless DSP multiprocessing.

Architectural features of the ADSP-2106x:

- 32-Bit IEEE Floating-Point Computation Units Multiplier, ALU, and Shifter
  - Data Register File
  - Data Address Generators
  - Program Sequencer with Instruction Cache
  - Interval Timer
  - Dual-Ported SRAM
  - External Port for Interfacing to Off-Chip Memory & Peripherals
  - Host Port & Multiprocessor Interface
  - DMA Controller
  - Serial Ports
  - Link Ports
  - JTAG Test Access Port

Three on-chip buses of the ADSP-2106x are the PM bus (program memory), DM bus (data memory), and I/O bus. The PM bus is used to access either instructions or data. During a single cycle the processor can access two data operands, one over the PM bus and one over the DM bus, an instruction (from the cache), and perform a DMA transfer.[1]

The ADSP-2106x's external port provides the processor's interface to external memory, memory-mapped I/O, a host processor, and additional multiprocessing ADSP-2106xs. The external port performs internal and external bus arbitration as well as supplying control signals, global memory and I/O devices.

5.4.2 ADSP-21000 Family Features

The ADSP-2106x SHARC processors belong to the ADSP-21000 Family of floating-point digital signal processors (DSPs). The ADSP-21000 Family architecture further addresses the five central requirements for DSPs established in the ADSP-2100 Family of 16-bit fixed-point DSPs:

- Fast, flexible arithmetic computation units
- Unconstrained data flow to and from the computation units
- Extended precision and dynamic range in the computation units
- Dual address generators
- Efficient program sequencing

Fast, Flexible Arithmetic

The ADSP-21000 Family processors execute all instructions in a single cycle. They provide both fast cycle times and a complete set of arithmetic operations including Min, Max, Clip, Shift, and Rotate, in addition to the traditional multiplication, addition, subtraction, and combined multiplication/addition. The processors are IEEE floating-point compatible and allow either interrupt on arithmetic exception or latched status exception handling.

Unconstrained Data Flow

The ADSP-2106x has an enhanced Harvard architecture combined with a 10-port data register file. In every cycle:

- Two operands can be read or written to or from the register file
- Two operands can be supplied to the ALU
- Two operands can be supplied to the multiplier
- Two results can be received from the ALU and multiplier

The processor's 48-bit orthogonal instruction word supports fully parallel data transfer and arithmetic operations in the same instruction.

40-Bit Extended Precision

The ADSP-21000 Family processors handle 32-bit IEEE floating-point format, 32-bit integer and fractional formats, and extended-precision 40-bit IEEE floating-point format. The processors carry extended precision throughout their computation units, limiting intermediate data truncation errors.[2] When working with data on-chip, the extended-precision 32-bit mantissa can be transferred to and from all computation units. The 40-bit data bus may be extended off-chip if desired. The fixed-point formats have an 80-bit accumulator for true 32-bit fixed-point computations.

Dual Address Generators

The ADSP-21000 Family processors have two data address generators (DAGs) that provide immediate or indirect (pre- and post-modify) addressing. [3]

Efficient Program Sequencing

In addition to zero-overhead loops, the ADSP-21000 Family processors support single-cycle setup and exit for loops. [4] Loops are both nestable (six levels in hardware) and interruptible. The processors support both delayed and non-delayed branches.

The ADSP-21000 Family processors include several enhancements that simplify system development. The enhancements occur in three key areas:

- Architectural features supporting high-level languages and operating systems
- IEEE 1149.1 JTAG serial scan path and on-chip emulation features
- Support of IEEE floating-point formats

High Level Languages

The ADSP-21000 Family architecture has several features that directly support high-level language compilers and operating systems:

- General purpose data and address register files
- 32-bit native data types
- Large address space
- Pre- and post-modify addressing
- Unconstrained circular data buffer placement[5]
- On-chip program, loop, and interrupt stacks

Additionally, the ADSP-21000 Family architecture is designed specifically to support ANSI-standard Numerical C extensions—the first compiled language to support vector data types and operators for numeric and signal processing.

Serial Scan and Emulation Features

The ADSP-21000 Family processors support the IEEE standard P1149.1 Joint Test Action Group (JTAG) standard for system test. This standard defines a method for serially scanning the I/O status of each component in a system. The JTAG serial port is also used by the ADSP-2106x EZ-ICE to gain access to the processor's on-chip emulation features.

IEEE Formats

The ADSP-21000 Family processors support IEEE floating-point data formats. This means that algorithms developed on IEEE-compatible processors and workstations are portable across processors without concern for possible instability introduced by biased rounding or inconsistent error handling.

The number of bits of precision of A/D converters has continued to increase, and the trend is for both precision and sampling rates to increase.

Compression and decompression algorithms have traditionally operated on signals of known bandwidth. These algorithms were developed to behave regularly, to keep costs down and implementations easy. Increasingly, however, the trend in algorithm development is not to constrain the regularity and dynamic range of intermediate results. Adaptive filtering and imaging are two applications requiring wide dynamic range.

Radar, sonar and even commercial applications like speech recognition require wide dynamic range in order to discern selected signals from noisy environments.

The extent to which this is true depends on the floating-point processor's architecture. Consistency with IEEE workstation simulations and the elimination of scaling are two clear ease-of-use advantages. High-level language programmability, large address spaces, and wide dynamic range allow system development time to be spent on algorithms and signal processing concerns rather than assembly language coding, code paging, and error handling.

5.4.3   ADSP-2106x Architecture

The following sections summarize the features of the ADSP-2106x SHARC architecture.

1. *Core Processor*

The core processor of the ADSP-2106x consists of three computation units, a program sequencer, two data address generators, timer, instruction cache, and data register file.[6]

Computation Units

The ADSP-2106x core processor contains three independent computation units: an ALU, a multiplier with a fixed-point accumulator, and a shifter. For meeting a wide variety of processing needs, the computation units process data in three formats: 32-bit fixed-point, 32-bit floating-point and 40-bit floating-point. The floating-point operations are single-precision IEEE-compatible. The 32-bit floating-point format is the standard IEEE format, whereas the 40-bit IEEE extended-precision format has eight additional LSBs of mantissa for greater accuracy.

The ALU performs a standard set of arithmetic and logic operations in both fixed-point and floating-point formats. The multiplier performs floating-point and fixed-point multiplication as well as fixed-point multiply/add and multiply/subtract operations. The shifter performs logical and arithmetic shifts, bit manipulation, field deposit and extraction and exponent derivation operations on 32-bit operands.[7]

The computation units perform single-cycle operations; there is no computation pipeline. The units are connected in parallel rather than serially. The output of any unit may be the input of any unit on the next cycle. In a multifunction computation, the ALU and multiplier perform independent, simultaneous operations.

Data Register File

A general-purpose data register file is used for transferring data between the computation units and the data buses, and for storing intermediate results. The register file has two sets (primary and alternate) of sixteen registers each, for fast context switching. All of the registers are 40 bits wide. The register file, combined with the core processor's Harvard architecture, allows unconstrained data flow between computation units and internal memory.

Program Sequencer & Data Address Generators

Two dedicated address generators and a program sequencer supply addresses for memory accesses. Together the sequencer and data address generators allow computational operations to execute with maximum efficiency since the computation units can be devoted exclusively to processing data.[8] With its instruction cache, the ADSP-2106x can simultaneously fetch an instruction (from the cache) and access two data operands (from memory). The data address generators implement circular data buffers in hardware.

The program sequencer supplies instruction addresses to program memory. It controls loop iterations and evaluates conditional instructions. With an internal loop counter and loop stack, the ADSP-2106x executes looped code with zero overhead. No explicit jump instructions are required to loop or to decrement and test the counter.

The ADSP-2106x achieves its fast execution rate by means of pipelined fetch, decode and execute cycles. If external memories are used, they are allowed more time to complete an access than if there were no decode cycle.

The data address generators (DAGs) provide memory addresses

when data is transferred between memory and registers. Dual data address generators enable the processor to output simultaneous addresses for two operand reads or writes. DAG1 supplies 32-bit addresses to data memory. DAG2 supplies 24-bit addresses to program memory for program memory data accesses.

Each DAG keeps track of up to eight address pointers, eight modifiers and eight length values. A pointer used for indirect addressing can be modified by a value in a specified register, either before (pre-modify) or after (post-modify) the access. Each DAG register has an alternate register that can be activated for fast context switching.

Circular buffers allow efficient implementation of delay lines and other data structures required in digital signal processing, and are commonly used in digital filters and Fourier transforms. The DAGs automatically handle address pointer wraparound, reducing overhead, increasing performance, and simplifying implementation.

Instruction Cache

The program sequencer includes a 32-word instruction cache that enables three bus operation for fetching an instruction and two data values. The cache is selective—only instructions whose fetches conflict with program memory data accesses are cached. This allows full-speed execution of core, looped operations such as digital filter multiply-accumulates and FFT butterfly processing.

Interrupts

The ADSP-2106x has four external hardware interrupts: three general-purpose interrupts and a special interrupt for reset. The processor also has internally generated interrupts for the timer, DMA controller operations, circular buffer overflow, stack overflows, arithmetic exceptions, multiprocessor vector interrupts, and user-defined software interrupts. For the general-purpose external interrupts and the internal timer interrupt, the ADSP-2106x automatically stacks the arithmetic status and mode registers in parallel with the interrupt servicing, allowing four nesting levels of very fast service for these interrupts.

Timer

The programmable interval timer provides periodic interrupt generation. When enabled, the timer decrements a 32-bit count register every cycle. When this count register reaches zero, the ADSP-2106x generates an interrupt and asserts its TIMEXP output. The count register is automatically reloaded from a 32-bit period register and the count resumes immediately.

Core Processor Buses

The processor core has four buses: Program Memory Address, Data Memory Address, Program Memory Data, and Data Memory Data. On the ADSP-2106x processors, data memory stores data operands while program memory is used to store both instructions and data (filter coefficients, for example)—this allows dual data fetches, when the instruction is supplied by the cache.

The PM Address bus and DM Address bus are used to transfer the addresses for instructions and data. The PM Data bus and DM Data bus are used to transfer the data or instructions stored in each type of memory. The PM Address bus is 24 bits wide allowing access of up to 16M words of mixed instructions and data. The PM Data bus is 48 bits wide to accommodate the 48-bit instruction width. Fixed-point and single-precision floating-point data is aligned to the upper 32 bits of the PM Data bus.

The DM Address bus is 32 bits wide allowing direct access of up to 4G words of data. The DM Data bus is 40 bits wide. Fixed-point and single-precision floating-point data is aligned to the upper 32 bits of the DM Data bus. The DM Data bus provides a path for the contents of any register in the processor to be transferred to any other register or to any data memory location in a single cycle. The data memory address comes from one of two sources: an absolute value specified in the instruction code (direct addressing) or the output of a data address generator (indirect addressing).

Internal Data Transfers

Nearly every register in the core processor of the ADSP-2106x is classified as a universal register. Instructions are provided for transferring data between any two universal registers or between a universal register and memory. This includes control registers and status registers, as well as the data registers in the register file.

The PX bus connect registers permit data to be passed between the 48-bit PM Data bus and the 40-bit DM Data bus or between the 40-bit register file and the PM Data bus. These registers contain hardware to handle the 8-bit width difference.

Context Switching

Many of the processor's registers have alternate registers that can be activated during interrupt servicing to facilitate a fast context switch. The data registers in the register file, the DAG registers, and the multiplier result register all have alternates. Registers active at reset are called primary registers, while the others are called alternate (or secondary) registers. Control bits in a mode control register determine which set of registers is active at any particular time.

Instruction Set

The ADSP-21000 Family instruction set provides a wide variety of programming capabilities. Multifunction instructions enable computations in parallel with data transfers, as well as simultaneous multiplier and ALU operations. The addressing power of the ADSP-2106x gives you flexibility in moving data both internally and externally. Every instruction can be executed in a single processor cycle.

2. *Dual-Ported Internal Memory*

The ADSP-21060 contains 4 Mbits of on-chip SRAM, organized as two blocks of 2 Mbits each, which can be configured for different combinations of code and data storage. The ADSP-21062 includes a 2 Mbits SRAM, organized as two 1 Bit blocks. Each memory block is dual-ported for single-cycle, independent accesses by the core processor and I/O processor or DMA controller.[9] The dual-ported memory and separate on-chip buses allow two data transfers from the core and one from I/O, all in a single cycle.

On the ADSP-21060, the memory can be configured as a maximum of 128K words of 32-bit data, 256K words of 16-bit data, 80K words of 48-bit instructions (and 40-bit data), or combinations of different word sizes up to 4 Mbits.[10] On the ADSP-21062, the memory can be configured as a maximum of 64K words of 32-bit data, 128K words of 16-bit data, 40K words of 48-bit instructions (and 40-bit data), or combinations of different word sizes up to 2 megabits. All of the memory can be accessed as 16-bit, 32-bit, or 48-bit words.

A 16-bit floating-point storage format is supported which effectively doubles the amount of data that may be stored on chip. Conversion between the 32-bit floating-point and 16-bit floating-point formats is done in a single instruction.

While each memory block can store combinations of code and data, accesses are most efficient when one block stores data, using the DM bus for transfers, and the other block stores instructions and data, using the PM bus for transfers. Using the DM bus and PM bus in this way, with one dedicated to each memory block, assures single-cycle execution with two data transfers. In this case, the instruction must be available in the cache. Single-cycle execution is also maintained when one of the data operands is transferred to or from off-chip, via the ADSP-2106x's external port.

3. *External Memory & Peripherals Interface*

The ADSP-2106x's external port provides the processor's interface to off-chip memory and peripherals. The 4-gigaword off-chip address space is included in the ADSP-2106x's unified address space. The separate on-chip buses—for PM addresses, PM data, DM addresses, DM data, I/O addresses, and I/O data—are multiplexed at the external port to create an external system bus with a single 32-bit address bus and a single 48-bit data bus. External SRAM can be 16, 32, or 48 bits wide; the ADSP-2106x's on-chip DMA controller automatically packs external data into the appropriate word width, either 48-bit instructions or 32-bit data.

Addressing of external memory devices is facilitated by on-chip decoding of high-order address lines to generate memory bank select signals. Separate control lines are also generated for simplified addressing of page-mode DRAM. The ADSP-2106x provides programmable memory wait states and external memory acknowledge controls to allow interfacing to DRAM and peripherals with variable access, hold, and disable time requirements.

4. *Host Processor Interface*

The ADSP-2106x's host interface allows easy connection to standard microprocessor buses, both 16-bit and 32-bit, with little additional hardware required. Asynchronous transfers at speeds up to the full clock rate of the ADSP-2106x are supported. The host interface is accessed through the ADSP-2106x's external port and is memory-mapped into the unified address space. Four channels of DMA are available for the host interface; code and data transfers are accomplished with low software overhead. The host can directly read and write the internal memory of the ADSP-2106x, and can access the DMA channel setup and mailbox registers. Vector interrupt support is provided for efficient execution of host commands.

5. *Multiprocessing*

The ADSP-2106x offers powerful features tailored to multiprocessing

DSP systems. The unified address space allows direct interprocessor accesses of each ADSP-2106x's internal memory. Distributed bus arbitration logic is included on-chip for simple, glueless connection of systems containing up to six ADSP-2106xs and a host processor.

Master processor changeover incurs only one cycle of overhead. Bus arbitration is selectable as either fixed or rotating priority. Processor bus lock allows indivisible read-modify-write sequences for semaphores.

A vector interrupt capability is provided for interprocessor commands. Maximum throughput for interprocessor data transfer is 240 Mbytes/sec over the link ports or external port. Broadcast writes allow simultaneous transmission of data to all ADSP-2106xs and can be used to implement reflective semaphores.

6. *I/O Processor*

The ADSP-2106x's I/O Processor (IOP) includes two serial ports, six 4-bit link ports, and a DMA controller.

Serial Ports

The ADSP-2106x features two synchronous serial ports that provide an inexpensive interface to a wide variety of digital and mixed-signal peripheral devices. The serial ports can operate at the full clock rate of the processor, providing each with a maximum data rate of 40 Mbits/s.

Independent transmit and receive functions provide greater flexibility for serial communications. Serial port data can be automatically transferred to and from on-chip memory via DMA. Each of the serial ports offers a TDM multichannel mode. They offer selectable synchronization and transmit modes as well as optional m-law or A-law companding. Serial port clocks and frame syncs can be internally or externally generated.

Link Ports

The ADSP-2106x features six 4-bit link ports that provide additional I/O capabilities. The link ports can be clocked twice per cycle, allowing each to transfer 8 bits per cycle. Link port I/O is especially useful for point-to-point interprocessor communication in multiprocessing systems.

The link ports can operate independently and simultaneously, with a maximum data throughput of 240 Mbytes/s. Link port data is packed into 32-bit or 48-bit words, and can be directly read by the core processor or DMA-transferred to on-chip memory. Each link port has its own double-buffered input and output registers.

Clock/acknowledge handshaking controls link port transfers.[11] Transfers are programmable as either transmit or receive.

DMA Controller

The ADSP-2106x's on-chip DMA controller allows zero-overhead data transfers without processor intervention. The DMA controller operates independently and invisibly to the processor core, allowing DMA operations to occur while the core is simultaneously executing its program. Both code and data can be downloaded to the ADSP-2106x using DMA transfers.

DMA transfers can occur between the ADSP-2106x's internal memory and external memory, external peripherals, or a host processor. DMA transfers can also occur between the ADSP-2106x's internal memory and its serial ports or link ports. DMA transfers between external memory and external peripheral devices are another option. External bus packing to 16, 32, or 48-bit words is automatically performed during DMA transfers.

Ten channels of DMA are available on the ADSP-2106x—two via the link ports, four via the serial ports, and four via the processor's external port (for host processor, other ADSP-2106xs, memory or I/O transfers). Four additional link port DMA channels are shared with serial port 1 and the external port. Asynchronous off-chip peripherals can control two DMA channels using DMA Request/Grant lines. Other DMA features include interrupt generation upon completion of DMA transfers and DMA chaining for automatic linked DMA transfers.

Booting

The internal memory of the ADSP-2106x can be booted at system power-up from an 8-bit EPROM, a host processor, or through one of the link ports. Selection of the boot source is controlled by the BMS, EBOOT, and LBOOT pins. Both 32-bit and 16-bit host processors can be used for booting.

5.4.4   Development Tools

The ADSP-2106x is supported with a complete set of software and hardware development tools, including an EZ-LAB Development Board, EZ-ICE In-Circuit Emulator, and development software.

The ADSP-21000 Development Software provides tools for programming and debugging applications in both assembly language and C. The EZ-ICE emulator allows system integration and hardware/software debugging.

The ADSP-21000 Family Development Software includes G21K, an ANSI C Compiler based on the industry-standard C Compiler of the Free Software Foundation. Numerical C provides extensions to the C language for array selection, vector math operations, complex data types, circular pointers, and variably dimensioned arrays. Other components of the ADSP-21000 Family Development Software include a C Runtime Library with custom DSP functions, CBUG C Source-Level Debugger, Assembler, Assembly Library/Librarian, Linker, and Simulator.

The ADSP-2106x EZ-ICE Emulator uses the IEEE 1149.1 JTAG test access port of the ADSP-2106x processor to monitor and control the target board processor during emulation. The EZ-ICE provides full-speed emulation, allowing inspection and modification of memory, registers, and processor stacks. Non-intrusive in-circuit emulation is assured by the use of the processor's JTAG interface—the emulator does not affect target system loading or timing.

5.4.5　Mesh Multiprocessing

　　Mesh multiprocessing is a parallel processing system architecture that offers high throughput, system flexibility, and software simplicity. The ADSP-2106x SHARC processor includes features which specifically support this system architecture. Mesh multiprocessing systems are suited to a wide variety of applications including wide-area airborne radar systems, interactive medical imaging, virtual reality, high-speed engineering simulations, neural networks, and solutions of large systems of linear equations.

New Words and Phrases

accommodate	*a.*	使适应
accumulator	*n.*	累加器
arbitration	*n.*	仲裁
buffer	*n.*	缓冲器
cache	*n.*	高速缓存
changeover	*n.*	转变
commercial	*a.*	商业的
companding	*n.*	压缩扩展
consistency	*n.*	结合
decode	*v.*	译码
decompression	*n.*	解压缩
decrement	*n.*	消耗
dedicated	*a.*	专门的
distributed	*a.*	分布式的
DMA	*abbr.*	直接存储器存取
enhancement	*n.*	增强
fractional	*a.*	小数的
glueless	*a.*	非粘接
inconsistent	*a.*	不一致的
interactive	*a.*	交互式

interrupt	*n. v.*	中断
interruptible	*a.*	可中断的
LSB	*abbr.*	最低有效位
mantissa	*n.*	尾数
nestable	*a.*	可嵌套的
operand	*n.*	操作数
overflow	*n. v.*	溢出
overhead	*n.*	开销
peripheral	*n.*	外设
programmable	*a.*	可编程
shifter	*n.*	移位器
stack	*n.*	堆栈
throughput	*n.*	吞吐量
truncation	*n.*	截断
address pointer		地址指针
bit manipulation		位操作
clock/acknowledge		时钟/应答
development tool		开发工具
direct addressing		直接寻址
double-buffered		双缓冲
dual-ported		双端口
FFT butterfly processing		FFT 蝶形处理
fixed-point		定点
floating-point		浮点
high-level languages		高级语言
I/O bus		输入输出总线
indirect addressing		间接寻址
interprocessor accesses		处理器间存取
non-intrusive		非插入
on-chip		片上

request/grant	请求/允许
speech recognition	语音识别
tailor to	使适合
universal registers	通用寄存器
virtual reality	虚拟现实

Notes

1. During a single cycle the processor can access two data operands, one over the PM bus and one over the DM bus, an instruction (from the cache), and perform a DMA transfer. 在单个周期内,处理器可以通过程序存储器(PM)总线和数据存储器(DM)总线读取两个操作数,从高速缓存中读取一条指令,并完成 DMA 传输。

2. The processors carry extended precision throughout their computation units, limiting intermediate data truncation errors. 处理器在所有计算单元里都能达到扩展的精度,并能限制中间结果的截尾误差。

3. The ADSP-21000 Family processors have two data address generators (DAGs) that provide immediate or indirect (pre- and post-modify) addressing. ADSP-21000 系列处理器有两个数据地址产生器,可以提供立即寻址和间接寻址。这里 pre- and post-modify 是指寻址前或寻址后修正地址指针。

4. In addition to zero-overhead loops, the ADSP-21000 Family processors support single-cycle setup and exit for loops. 除了无开销循环外,ADSP-21000 系列处理器支持单周期内进入或退出循环的功能。

5. Unconstrained circular data buffer placement 无约束循环缓存器规划

6. The core processor of the ADSP-2106x consists of three computation units, a program sequencer, two data address generators, timer, instruction cache, and data register file. ADSP-2106x 核心处理器包括三个计算单元、一个程序队列、两个数据地址产生器、定时器、指令高速缓存器和数据寄存器文件。

7. The shifter performs logical and arithmetic shifts, bit manipulation, field deposit and extraction and exponent derivation operations on 32-bit operands. 移位器完成逻辑移位和算术移位、位操作、32 位内字段存

取以及浮点数的指数部分提取。

8. Together the sequencer and data address generators allow computational operations to execute with maximum efficiency since the computation units can be devoted exclusively to processing data. 由于计算单元专门用于处理数据,它们与程序队列和两个数据地址产生器结合起来,使得计算操作以最大效率进行。

9. Each memory block is dual-ported for single-cycle, independent accesses by the core processor and I/O processor or DMA controller. 每个存储器块都是单周期双端口工作,与核心处理器和 I/O 处理器以及 DMA 的存取是独立的。

10. On the ADSP-21060, the memory can be configured as a maximum of 128K words of 32-bit data, 256K words of 16-bit data, 80K words of 48-bit instructions (and 40-bit data), or combinations of different word sizes up to 4 Mbits. 对于 ADSP-21060,存储器最大可以配置成 128K 32 位字长存储器、256K 16 位字长数据存储器、80K 48 位字长指令或 40 位数据存储器、或不同字长直至 4 Mbits 的存储器。

11. Clock/acknowledge handshaking controls link port transfers. 时钟/应答握手信号控制链接口的传输。

5.5 TMS320C5x

This user's guide discusses the TMS320C5x generation of fixed-point digital signal processors (DSPs) in the TMS320 family. The C5x DSP provides improved performance over earlier C1x and C2x generations while maintaining upward compatibility of source code between the devices.[1] The C5x central processing unit (CPU) is based on the C25 CPU and incorporates additional architectural enhancements that allow the device to run twice as fast as C2x devices. Future expansion and enhancements are expected to heighten the performance and range of applications of the C5x DSPs.

5.5.1 TMS320 Family Overview

The TMS320 family consists of two types of single-chip DSPs: 16-bit fixed-point and 32-bit floating-point. These DSPs possess the operational flexibility of high-speed controllers and the numerical capability of array processors.

Combining these two qualities, the TMS320 processors are inexpensive alter-natives to custom-fabricated VLSI and multichip bit-slice processors. The following characteristics make this family the ideal choice for a wide range of processing applications:

- Very flexible instruction set
- Inherent operational flexibility
- High-speed performance
- Innovative, parallel architectural design
- Cost-effectiveness

In 1982, Texas Instruments introduced the TMS32010, the first fixed-point DSP in the TMS320 family. Before the end of the year, the Electronic Products magazine awarded the TMS32010 the title product of the Year. The TMS32010 became the model for future TMS320 generations.

Today, the TMS320 family consists of eight generations: the C1x, C2x, C2xx, C5x, and C54x are fixed-point, the C3x and C4x are floating-point, and the C8x is a multiprocessor. Source code is upward compatible from one fixed-point generation to the next fixed-point generation (except for the C54x), and from one floating-point generation to the next floating-point generation. Upward compatibility preserves the software generation of your investment, thereby providing a convenient and cost-efficient means to a higher-performance, more versatile DSP system.

Each generation of TMS320 devices has a CPU and a variety of on-chip memory and peripheral configurations for developing spin-off devices. These spin-off devices satisfy a wide range of needs in the worldwide electronics market. When memory and peripherals are integrated into one processor, the overall system cost is greatly reduced, and circuit board space is saved.

The TMS320 family of DSPs offers better, more adaptable approaches to traditional signal processing problems, such as filtering, and error coding. Furthermore, the TMS320 family supports complex applications that often require multiple operations to be performed simultaneously. Fig.5.2 shows many of the typical applications of the TMS320 family.

Consumer	Pattern recognition	Sonar processing
Digital radios/TVs	Image enhancement	**Telecommunications**
Educational toys	Image compression/	1200- to 19200-
Music synthesizers	transmission	bps modems
Power tools	Robot vision	Adaptive equalizers
Control	Workstations	ADPCM transcoders
Disk drive control	**Instrumentation**	Channel multiplexing
Engine control	Function generation	Data encryption
Laser printer control	Pattern matching	Digital PBXs
Motor control	Phase-locked loops	Digital speech
Robotics control	Seismic processing	interpolation (DSI)
Servo control	Spectrum analysis	Echo cancellation
General Purpose	Transient analysis	Fax
Adaptive filtering	**Medical**	Line repeaters
Convolution	Diagnostic equipment	Spread spectrum
Correlation	Fetal monitoring	communications
Digital filtering	Hearing aids	Video conferencing
Fast Fourier transforms	Patient monitoring	Personal
Hilbert transforms	Ultrasound equipment	communications
Waveform generation	**Military**	systems
Windowing	Missile guidance	**Voice/Speech**
Graphics/Imaging	Navigation	Speech enhancement
3-D rotation	Radar processing	Speech recognition
Animation/digital map	Radio frequency modems	Speech synthesis
Homomorphic processing	Secure communications	Speaker verification
		Voice mail

Fig.5.2   Typical Applications for the TMS320 Family

The C5x generation consists of the C50, C51, C52, C53, C53S, C56, C57, and C57S DSPs, which are fabricated by CMOS integrated-circuit technology. Their architectural design is based on the C25. The operational flexibility and speed of the C5x are the result of combining an advanced Harvard architecture (which has separate buses for program memory and data memory), a CPU with application-specific hardware logic, on-chip peripherals, on-chip memory, and a highly specialized instruction set.[2] The C5x is designed to execute up to 50 million instructions per second (MIPS).[3] Spin-off devices that combine the C5x CPU with customized on-chip memory and peripheral configurations may be developed for special applications in the worldwide electronics market.

The C5x devices offer these advantages:

• Enhanced TMS320 architectural design for increased performance and versatility

• Modular architectural design for fast development of spin-off devices

• Advanced integrated-circuit processing technology for increased performance and low power consumption

• Source code compatibility with C1x, C2x, and C2xx DSPs for fast and easy performance upgrades

• Enhanced instruction set for faster algorithms and for optimized high-level language operation

• Reduced power consumption and increased radiation hardness because of new static design techniques

Table 1 lists the major characteristics of the C5x DSPs. The table shows the capacity of on-chip RAM and ROM, number of serial and parallel input/output (I/O) ports, power supply requirements, and execution time of one machine cycle. Use Table 5.1 for guidance in choosing the best C5x DSP for your application.

Key features of the C5x DSPs are listed below. Where a feature is exclusive to a particular device, the device's name is enclosed within parentheses and noted after that feature.

• Compatibility: Source-code compatible with C1x, C2x, and C2xx devices

• Speed: 20-/25-/35-/50-ns single-cycle fixed-point instruction execution time (50/40/28.6/20 MIPS)

Power

• 3.3-V and 5-V static CMOS technology with two power-down modes

Table 5.1 Characteristics of the C5x DSPs

TMS 320 Device	ID	On-Chip Memory (16-bit words)			I/O Ports		Power Supply (V)	Cycle Time (ns)
		DARAM	SARAM	ROM	Serial	Parallel		
C50	PQ	1056	9K	2K	2	64K	5	50/35/25
LC50	PQ	1056	9K	2K	2	64K	3.3	50/40/25
C51	PQ	1056	1K	8K	2	64K	5	50/35/25/20
LC51	PQ	1056	1K	8K	2	64K	3.3	50/40/25
LC52	PJ	1056	—	4K	1	64K	3.3	50/35/25/20
C52	PJ	1056	—	4K	1	64K	5	50/35/25/20
C53	PQ	1056	3K	16K	2	64K	5	50/35/25
LC53	PQ	1056	3K	16K	2	64K	3.3	50/45/25
C56	PZ	1056	6K	32K	2	64K	3.3	50/35/25
LC57	PBK	1056	6K	32K	2	64K	3.3	50/35/25

• Power consumption control with IDLE1 and IDLE2 instructions for power-down modes

Memory

• 224K-word × 16-bit maximum addressable external memory space × 64K-word program, 64K-word data, 64K-word I/O, and 32K-word global memory)[4]

- 1056-word × 16-bit dual-access on-chip data RAM
- 9K-word × 16-bit single-access on-chip program/data RAM (C50)
- 2K-word × 16-bit single-access on-chip boot ROM (C50, C57S)
- 1K-word × 16-bit single-access on-chip program/data RAM (C51)
- 8K-word × 16-bit single-access on-chip program ROM (C51)
- 4K-word × 16-bit single-access on-chip program ROM (C52)
- 3K-word × 16-bit single-access on-chip program/data RAM (C53)
- 16K-word × 16-bit single-access on-chip program ROM (C53)
- 6K-word × 16-bit single-access on-chip program/data RAM (LC56, LC57)
- 32K-word × 16-bit single-access on-chip program ROM (LC56, LC57)

Central Processing Unit (CPU)

Central arithmetic logic unit (CALU) consisting of the following:

- 32-bit arithmetic logic unit (ALU), 32-bit accumulator (ACC), and 32-bit accumulator buffer (ACCB)
- 16-bit × 16-bit parallel multiplier with a 32-bit product capability
- 0 to 16-bit left and right data shifters and a 64-bit incremental data shifter[5]
- 16-bit parallel logic unit (PLU)
- Dedicated auxiliary register arithmetic unit (ARAU) for indirect addressing
- Eight auxiliary registers

Program Control

- 8-level hardware stack
- 4-deep pipelined operation for delayed branch, call, and return instructions

- Eleven shadow registers for storing strategic CPU-controlled registers during an interrupt service routine (ISR)
- Extended hold operation for concurrent external direct memory access (DMA) of external memory or on-chip RAM
- Two indirectly addressed circular buffers for circular addressing

Instruction Set

- Single-cycle multiply/accumulate instructions
- Single-instruction repeat and block repeat operations
- Block memory move instructions for better program and data management
- Memory-mapped register load and store instructions
- Conditional branch and call instructions
- Delayed execution of branch and call instructions
- Fast return from interrupt instructions
- Index-addressing mode
- Bit-reversed index-addressing mode for radix-2 fast-Fourier transforms (FFTs)[6]

On-chip Peripherals

- 64K parallel I/O ports (16 I/O ports are memory-mapped)
- Sixteen software-programmable wait-state generators for program, data, and I/O memory spaces
- Interval timer with period, control, and counter registers for software stop, start, and reset
- Phase-locked loop (PLL) clock generator with internal oscillator or external clock source
- Multiple PLL clocking option (x1, x2, x3, x4, x5, x9, depending on the device)
- Full-duplex synchronous serial port interface for direct communication between the C5x and another serial device[7]
- Time-division multiplexed (TDM) serial port (C50, C51, C53)

- Buffered serial port (BSP) (LC56, LC57)
- 8-bit parallel host port interface (HPI) (C57)

5.5.2　Architectural Overview

This section provides an overview of the architectural structure of the C5x, which consists of the buses, on-chip memory, central processing unit (CPU), and on-chip peripherals. The C5x uses an advanced, modified Harvard-type architecture based on the C25 architecture and maximizes processing power with separate buses for program memory and data memory. The instruction set supports data transfers between the two memory spaces.

All C5x DSPs have the same CPU structure; however, they have different on-chip memory configurations and on-chip peripherals.

1. *Bus Structure*

Separate program and data buses allow simultaneous access to program instructions and data, providing a high degree of parallelism. For example, while data is multiplied, a previous product can be loaded into, added to, or subtracted from the accumulator and, at the same time, a new address can be generated. [8] Such parallelism supports a powerful set of arithmetic, logic, and bit-manipulation operations that can all be performed in a single machine cycle. In addition, the C5x includes the control mechanisms to manage interrupts, repeated operations, and function calling.

The C5x architecture is built around four major buses:

- Program bus (PB)
- Program address bus (PAB)
- Data read bus (DB)
- Data read address bus (DAB)

The PAB provides addresses to program memory space for both reads and writes. The PB also carries the instruction code and immediate operands from program memory space to the CPU. The DB interconnects various elements of the CPU to data memory space. The program and data buses can work together to transfer data from on-chip data memory and internal or external program memory to the multiplier for single-cycle multiply/accumulate operations.

2. *Central Processing Unit* (CPU)

The C5x CPU consists of these elements:

- Central arithmetic logic unit (CALU)
- Parallel logic unit (PLU)
- Auxiliary register arithmetic unit (ARAU)
- Memory-mapped registers
- Program controller

The C5x CPU maintains source-code compatibility with the c1x and c2x generations while achieving high performance and greater versatility. Improvements include a 32-bit accumulator buffer, additional scaling capabilities, and a host of new instructions. The instruction set exploits the additional hardware features and is flexible in a wide range of applications. Data management has been improved through the use of new block move instructions and memory-mapped register instructions.

Central Arithmetic Logic Unit (CALU)

The CPU uses the CALU to perform 2s-complement arithmetic. The CALU consists of these elements:

- 16-bit × 16-bit multiplier
- 32-bit arithmetic logic unit (ALU)
- 32-bit accumulator (ACC)
- 32-bit accumulator buffer (ACCB)
- Additional shifters at the outputs of both the accumulator and the product register (PREG)

Parallel Logic Unit (PLU)

The CPU includes an independent PLU, which operates separately from, but in parallel with, the ALU. The PLU performs Boolean operations or the bit manipulations required of high-speed controllers. The PLU can set, clear, test, or toggle bits in a status register, control register, or any data memory location.

The PLU provides a direct logic operation path to data memory values without affecting the contents of the ACC or PREG. Results of a PLU function are written back to the original data memory location.

Auxiliary Register Arithmetic Unit (ARAU)

The CPU includes an unsigned 16-bit arithmetic logic unit that calculates indirect addresses by using inputs from the auxiliary registers (ARs), index register (INDX), and auxiliary register compare register (ARCR). The ARAU can auto-index the current AR while the data memory location is being addressed and can index either by × 1 or by the contents of the INDX.[9] As a result, accessing data does not require the CALU for address manipulation; therefore, the CALU is free for other operations in parallel.

Memory-Mapped Registers

The C5x has 96 registers mapped into page 0 of the data memory space. All C5x DSPs have 28 CPU registers and 16 input/output (I/O) port registers but have different numbers of peripheral and reserved registers. Since the memory-mapped registers are a component of the data memory space, they can be written to and read from in the same way as any other data memory location. The memory-mapped registers are used for indirect data address pointers, temporary storage, CPU status and control, or integer arithmetic processing through the ARAU.

Program Controller

The program controller contains logic circuitry that decodes the operational instructions, manages the CPU pipeline, stores the status of CPU operations, and decodes the conditional operations. Parallelism of architecture lets the C5x perform three concurrent memory operations in any given machine cycle: fetch an instruction, read an operand, and write an operand. The program controller consists of these elements:

- Program counter
- Status and control registers
- Hardware stack
- Address generation logic
- Instruction register

3. *On-Chip Memory*

The C5x architecture contains a considerable amount of on-chip memory to aid in system performance and integration:

- Program read-only memory (ROM)
- Data/program dual-access RAM (DARAM)
- Data/program single-access RAM (SARAM)

The C5x has a total address range of 224K words × 16 bits. The memory space is divided into four individually selectable memory segments: 64K-word program memory space, 64K-word local data memory space, 64K-word input/output ports, and 32K-word global data memory space.

Program ROM

All C5x DSPs carry a 16-bit on-chip maskable programmable ROM (see Table 1 for sizes). The C50 and C57S DSPs have boot loader code resident in the on-chip ROM, all other C5x DSPs offer the boot loader code as an option. This memory is used for booting program code from slower external ROM or EPROM to fast on-chip or external RAM. Once the custom program has been booted into RAM, the boot ROM space can be removed from program memory space by setting the MP/MC bit in the processor mode status register (PMST). The on-chip ROM is selected at reset by driving the MP/MC pin low. If the on-chip ROM is not selected, the C5x devices start execution from off-chip memory.

The on-chip ROM may be configured with or without boot loader code. However, the on-chip ROM is intended for your specific program. Once the program is in its final form, you can submit the ROM code to Texas Instruments for implementation into your device.

Data/Program Dual-Access RAM

All C5x DSPs carry a 1056-word × 16-bit on-chip dual-access RAM (DARAM). The DARAM is divided into three individually selectable memory blocks: 512-word data or program DARAM block B0, 512-word data DARAM block B1, and 32-word data DARAM block B2. The DARAM is primarily intended to store data values but, when needed, can be used to store programs as well. DARAM blocks B1 and B2 are always configured as data memory; however, DARAM On-Chip Memory block B0 can be configured by software as data or program memory. The DARAM can be configured in one of two ways:

- All 1056 words × 16 bits configured as data memory
- 544 words × 16 bits configured as data memory and 512 words × 16 bits configured as program memory DARAM improves the operational speed of the C5x CPU. The CPU operates with a 4-deep pipeline. In this pipeline, the CPU reads data on the third stage and writes data on the fourth stage. Hence, for a given instruction sequence, the second instruction could be reading data at the same time the first instruction is writing data. The dual data buses (DB and DAB) allow the CPU to read from and write to DARAM in the same machine cycle.

Data/Program Single-Access RAM

All C5x DSPs except the C52 carry a 16-bit on-chip single-access RAM (SA-RAM) of various sizes (see Table 1). Code can be booted from an off-chip ROM and then executed at full speed, once it is loaded into the on-chip SA-RAM.

The SARAM can be configured by software in one of three ways:

- All SARAM configured as data memory
- All SARAM configured as program memory

• SARAM configured as both data memory and program memory

The SARAM is divided into 1K- and/or 2K-word blocks contiguous in address memory space. All C5x CPUs support parallel accesses to these SARAM blocks. However, one SARAM block can be accessed only once per machine cycle. In other words, the CPU can read from or write to one SARAM block while accessing another SARAM block. When the CPU requests multiple accesses, the SARAM schedules the accesses by providing a not-ready condition to the CPU and executing the multiple accesses one cycle at a time.

SARAM supports more flexible address mapping than DARAM because SARAM can be mapped to both program and data memory space simultaneously. [10] However, because of simultaneous program and data mapping, an instruction fetch and data fetch that could be performed in one machine cycle with DARAM may take two machine cycles with SARAM. [11]

On-Chip Memory Protection

The C5x DSPs have a maskable option that protects the contents of on-chip memories. When the related bit is set, no externally originating instruction can access the on-chip memory spaces.

4. *On-Chip Peripherals*

All C5x DSPs have the same CPU structure; however, they have different on-chip peripherals connected to their CPUs. The C5x DSP on-chip peripherals available are:

• Clock generator
• Hardware timer
• Software-programmable wait-state generators
• Parallel I/O ports
• Host port interface (HPI)
• Serial port
• Buffered serial port (BSP)

- Time-division multiplexed (TDM) serial port
- User-maskable interrupts

Clock Generator

The clock generator consists of an internal oscillator and a phase-locked loop (PLL) circuit. The clock generator can be driven internally by a crystal resonator circuit or driven externally by a clock source. The PLL circuit can generate an internal CPU clock by multiplying the clock source by a specific factor, so you can use a clock source with a lower frequency than that of the CPU.

Hardware Timer

A 16-bit hardware timer with a 4-bit prescaler is available. This programmable timer clocks at a rate that is between 1/2 and 1/32 of the machine cycle rate (CLKOUT1), depending upon the timer's divide-down ratio. The timer can be stopped, restarted, reset, or disabled by specific status bits.

Software-Programmable Wait-State Generators[12]

Software-programmable wait-state logic is incorporated in C5x DSPs allowing wait-state generation without any external hardware for interfacing with slower off-chip memory and I/O devices. This feature consists of multiple wait-state generating circuits. Each circuit is user-programmable to operate in different wait states for off-chip memory accesses.

Parallel I/O Ports

A total of 64K I/O ports are available, sixteen of these ports are memory-mapped in data memory space. Each of the I/O ports can be addressed by the IN or the OUT instruction. The memory-mapped I/O ports can be accessed with any instruction that reads from or writes to data memory. The IS signal indicates a read or write operation through an I/O port. The C5x can easily interface with external I/O devices through the I/O ports while requiring minimal off-chip address decoding circuits.

Host Port Interface (HPI)

The HPI available on the C57S and LC57 is an 8-bit parallel I/O port that provides an interface to a host processor. Information is exchanged between the DSP and the host processor through on-chip memory that is accessible to both the host processor and the C57.

Serial Port

Three different kinds of serial ports are available: a general-purpose serial port, a time-division multiplexed (TDM) serial port, and a buffered serial port (BSP). Each C5x contains at least one general-purpose, high-speed synchronous, full-duplexed serial port interface that provides direct communication with serial devices such as serial analog-to-digital (A/D) converters, and other serial systems. The serial port is capable of operating at up to one-fourth the machine cycle rate (CLKOUT1). The serial port transmitter and receiver are double-buffered and individually controlled by maskable external interrupt signals. Data is framed either as bytes or as words.

Buffered Serial Port (BSP)

The BSP available on the C56 and C57 devices is a full-duplexed, double-buffered serial port and an autobuffering unit (ABU). The BSP provides flexibility on the data stream length. The ABU supports high-speed data transfer and reduces interrupt latencies.

TDM Serial Port

The TDM serial port available on the C50, C51, and C53 devices is a full-duplexed serial port that can be configured by software either for synchronous operations or for time-division multiplexed operations. The TDM serial port is commonly used in multiprocessor applications.

User-Maskable Interrupts

Four external interrupt lines and five internal interrupts, a timer interrupt and four serial port interrupts, are user maskable. When an interrupt service routine (ISR) is executed, the contents of the program counter are saved on an 8-level hardware stack, and the contents of eleven specific CPU registers are automatically saved (shadowed) on a 1-level-deep stack.

New Words and Phrases

ADPCM	*abbr*.	自适应音频脉冲编码
animation	*n*.	动画
Boolean	*n*.	布尔值
diagnostic	*a*.	诊断
enclose	*v*.	装入
equalizer	*n*.	均衡器
fabricate	*v*.	制作
fax	*n*.*v*.	传真
generation	*n*.	一代
homomorphic	*a*.	同态的
incorporate	*v*.	合并
incremental	*a*.	增加的
inherent	*a*.	固有的
innovative	*a*.	创新的
instrumentation	*n*.	使用仪器
investment	*n*.	投资
latency	*n*.	反应时间
maskable	*a*.	可屏蔽的
modem	*n*.	调制解调器
multiplexing	*n*.	多路技术
navigation	*n*.	导航
oscillator	*n*.	振荡器
parallelism	*n*.	并行化
parentheses	*n*.	圆括号
prescaler	*n*.	预定值
repeaters	*n*.	中继器

resident	*a.*	常驻的
servo	*n.*	伺服系统
shadow	*v.*	屏蔽
strategic	*a.*	关键的
synthesizer	*n.*	电子合成器
transcode	*n.*	代码转换器
transient	*a.*	瞬态的
upgrades	*n.v.*	升级
versatile	*a.*	通用的
versatility	*n.*	多功能性
3-D rotation		三维旋转
bit-reversed		位反转
data encryption		数据加密
echo cancellation		回波对消
full-duplex		全双工
Hilbert transform		希尔伯特变换
memory-mapped register		存储器映射寄存器
missile guidance		制导
pattern recognition		模式识别
personal communications		个人通信
phase-locked loop		锁相环
robot vision		机器人视觉
speaker verification		话音确认
speech synthesis		语音合成
spin-off		派生的
spread spectrum communications		扩频通信
upward compatible		向上兼容的
video conferencing		电视会议
voice mail		语音邮件

Notes

1. The C5x DSP provides improved performance over earlier C1x and C2x generations while maintaining upward compatibility of source code between the devices. C5x 数字信号处理芯片提供了比早期 C1x 和 C2x 改善了许多的功能,但在器件之间维持源码向上兼容。

2. The operational flexibility and speed of the C5x are the result of combining an advanced Harvard architecture (which has separate buses for program memory and data memory), a CPU with application-specific hardware logic, on-chip peripherals, on-chip memory, and a highly specialized instruction set. C5x 操作上的灵活性和速度是因为结合了先进的哈佛结构(具有分开的程序存储总线和数据存储总线)、专有硬件逻辑的 CPU、片上存储器以及高度专用的指令集。

3. The C5x is designed to execute up to 50 million instructions per second (MIPS). C5x 被设计成能执行高达每秒 50 兆条指令。注意 MIPS 和 MFLOPS 的区别,后者是指每秒多少兆次(百万次)浮点运算。

4. 224K-word × 16-bit maximum addressable external memory space (64K-word program, 64K-word data, 64K-word I/O, and 32K-word global memory). 最大 16 位 224K 字可寻址外部寄存器空间(64K 字程序存储器、64K 字数据存储器、64K 字 I/O 地址和 64K 字全局存储器)。

5. 0 to 16-bit left and right data shifters and a 64-bit incremental data shifter. 0 到 16 位向左和向右移位器和 64 位增序移位器。

6. Bit-reversed index-addressing mode for radix-2 fast-Fourier transforms (FFTs). 位反转变址寻址模式用于基 2FFT(即完成我们通常所说的 FFT 中的到序功能)。

7. Full-duplex synchronous serial port interface for direct communication between the C5x and another serial device. 全双工同步串行接口用于 C5x 与其他串行设备间的直接通信。

8. For example, while data is multiplied, a previous product can be loaded into, added to, or subtracted from the accumulator and, at the same time, a new address can be generated. 例如,当做乘法时,以前的

乘积可以装入,与累加器相加或相减,并同时产生新的地址。

9. The ARAU can auto-index the current AR while the data memory location is being addressed and can index either by 1 or by the contents of the INDX. 当对数据存储器的位置寻址时,辅助寄存器算术单元(ARAU)可以对当前的辅助寄存器(AR)自动变址,并且可以乘1或乘以变址寄存器(INDX)中的内容。

10. SARAM supports more flexible address mapping than DARAM because SARAM can be mapped to both program and data memory space simultaneously. 单口存取的随机存储器(SARAM)支持比双口存取的随机存储器(DARAM)还灵活的地址映射,因为SARAM可以同时映射到程序存储空间和数据存储空间。

11. However, because of simultaneous program and data mapping, an instruction fetch and data fetch that could be performed in one machine cycle with DARAM may take two machine cycles with SARAM. 然而,由于程序存储器和数据存储器的映射,在DARAM中取指令和取数用一个机器周期,而在SARAM中却需要两个机器周期。

12. Software-Programmable Wait-State Generators 软件可编程等待周期产生器

Appendix A 内容提要

第一章 数字电路和模拟电路

电子线路包括模拟电路和数字电路,本章分别叙述了数字电路设计和模拟接收机的基本知识。

1.1 数字电路

数字电路通常分为两大类。一类是确定功能的集成块,另一类是可编程器件,如 PROM、EPROM 等。数字电路的设计和模拟电路有很大区别,更像小规模的系统设计,但很多电路既包含模拟部分又包括数字部分。

大规模集成电路是由大量的逻辑门组成的,因此数字电路的基础就是逻辑门电路。逻辑门电路包括与门、或门、非门、与非门、或非门等,一般用真值表来表示逻辑运算。

数字电路分为 TTL,MOS 及 ECL 电路。TTL 电路有很多系列,不同系列在功耗及速度之间折衷。MOS 电路为中速器件,工作电压 3 ~ 15 V。ECL 电路功耗较大,低电平为 – 1.8 V,高电平为 – 0.9 V。

数字电路一般集成了多个逻辑门,并集成了不同的功能,如函数产生器、触发器、计数器、移位寄存器、解码器、比较器、单稳态等等。

1.2 接收机

接收机是无线电系统中的一个重要设备,从小小的收音机,到卫星转发器,尽管复杂程度不同,但接收机的组成和功能是相似的。接收机的用途就是选择来自不同发射机的有用频段,除去载波,放大信号,滤除噪声,最后获得所需的信息。

超外差接收机主要功能是选频、放大和滤波,它主要由射频放大器、混频器、本地振荡器、中频放大器等部分组成。

在设计和使用接收机时,还需要了解如调谐范围、灵敏度、接收机带宽、寄生信号及接收机的一些典型参数。

射频放大器接收天线的弱信号,将它有选择地放大。一般情况下,天线接收的信号电平比较弱,且带宽比较宽。因此射频放大器除了要有足够的放大倍数,还需要有较好的噪声性能、频率选择性及很好的线性度。

混频器的任务则是根据输入的射频信号和本地振荡器提供的本振信号产生所需的中频输出。混频器应尽量使用高电平本振,并在混频器前端设置低噪声滤波器。滤波器必须能滤除镜像频率及任何一组可以互相混频可能产生中频输出的频率。

中频放大器设置在混频器和检波器之间,中频放大器需要有较高的增益,滤除所有不需要的带外噪声且保持带内信号不失真。

第二章 信号处理和数据处理

信号处理和数据处理是电子系统、通信系统必不可少的技术。本章着重讲述了数字信号处理的基本思想、图像处理中最基础的图像增强技术、电子系统和通信系统经常用到的数据库及专业系统的软件包。

2.1 数字信号和离散时间系统

根据信号的时间和幅度是否连续,信号分为模拟信号和数字信号,模拟信号的时间和幅度都是连续的,而数字信号的时间和幅度都是离散的。此外还有时间连续、幅度离散和时间离散、幅度连续的情况。在理论分析时一般不考虑数字信号的字长效应,往往都用离散时间信号来分析,离散时间信号也称为序列。处理离散时间信号的系统是离散时间系统,离散时间系统也是数字系统不考虑字长效应的一种情况。

同模拟信号一样,序列也有频域表达式即频谱。在离散域,具有不同性质的序列其频谱计算方法也不同。周期序列的频谱由离散傅立叶级数(DFS)来计算。一般序列的频谱利用离散时间傅立叶变换(DTFT)来计算。另外,有限长序列还可以看成是周期序列的一个周期,这样有限长序列频谱的计算可以用离散傅立叶变换(DFT)。由于离散傅立叶变换有很多快速算法,如FFT算法,它在数字信号处理中应用非常广泛。

z变换是广义的傅立叶变换,它可以把很多信号表示成幅度不同的复指数的线性组合。使z变换定义式成立的那些z值的集合就是z变换的收敛域。z变换的收敛域有很多有用的性质。

与离散信号一样,离散线性系统的频率响应也可以表示成幅度不同的复指数的线性组合。线性系统还有时变和时不变系统之分,线性时不变系统是数字信号处理中常见的系统。

线性时不变系统一般用常系数差分方程来描述。常系数差分方程所定义的系统还可以用对应的系统流图来表示。有限冲激响应系统流图一般用直接型表示,而无限冲激响应的系统流图包括直接型1和直接型2。

2.2　数字滤波器

数字滤波器分为有限冲激响应滤波器和无限冲激响应滤波器。数字滤波器的频域指标包括通带截止频率、阻带截止频率、通带波纹和阻带波纹。滤波器设计就是寻求最接近给定参数允许范围的滤波器频率响应。

无限冲激响应滤波器的设计方法有冲激不变法、双线性法以及计算机辅助设计方法。冲激不变法是将模拟滤波器映射到数字滤波器的一种设计方法,这种映射并不是简单的代数映射,它存在频率混迭问题。双线性法也是一种映射方法,实现了S平面到Z平面的一一映射关系,这种映射是简单的代数关系,因此不存在频率混迭问题。在无法给出滤波器的解析表达式时,一般用计算机辅助设计方法,这时可以通过数值方法来进行优化设计。

数字滤波器在数字信号处理领域中有着重要的应用,因为在数字信号处理时,很多功能都是由数字滤波器来完成的。信号处理中最普遍的问题之一是从被噪声污染的信号中提取有用信号,例如,一个原始信号包括有用信号和典型的背景噪声信号,通过数字滤波器能够滤除噪声分量,从里面提取出有用信号分量。

滤除噪声和无失真的提取出有用信号是两个不同方面的要求。如果信号和噪声的频带有交迭,在这种情况下,我们必须在两个要求之间折衷。根据实际应用,我们可能需要设计滤波器来去除尽可能多的噪声,允许有用信号有一定的失真。或者我们可能要尽可能不失真的保留有用信号,允许在输出端有一定的噪声。

在实际应用中,FIR 和 IIR 滤波器有着不同的应用场合。在需要线性相位的情况下,一般使用 FIR 滤波器。在限制计算量并希望滤波器有较好的幅度特性时,一般使用 IIR 滤波器。本节最后分别给出 IIR 滤波器和 FIR 滤波器应用的例子,并就计算量、瞬态效应、噪声抑制比给出二者的比较。

2.3 图像增强

图像增强是应用客观准则恢复一个已知失真的图像,改进图像质量,使图像满足某种应用。

图像增强分为空间域和频域处理。空间域处理主要是对图像像素进行处理,灰度变换是图像增强的主要技术之一。灰度变换主要是对不同灰度进行拉伸或压缩,使得动态范围有所变化。

分段线性变换尤其是三段线性变换常用于对比度增强。三段线性变换需要两个断点和三个斜率,当某段斜率小于 1 时,对应的灰度进行压缩,当斜率大于 1 时,对应的灰度进行拉伸。如果图像信息是由三个部分混合而成,而每部分都具有高斯分布,那么在各个分布之间可以用最大似然门限确定断点。一般情况下断点和斜率通常用观察灰度直方图的方法来合理地选择。

对数变换用于压缩高亮度值的灰度,拉伸低亮度值的灰度。对数变换特别适合对低对比度图像进行变换,以提高对比度。

一般来讲,进行指数变换图像的细节要比原始图像差,因此指数变换不是一个理想的图像增强变换。

对于很多图像来讲,灰度分布的理想情况应该是具有均匀分布的直方图,这样可以增强低对比度图像的信息。虽然与连续随机变量不同,不能证明离散变换可以产生均匀分布的离散值。但如果把图像的灰度作为随机变量,总可以通过某个变换将图像的直方图表示的灰度拉得很宽。这就是直方图均衡。

2.4 数据库

数据库可以方便、高效处理和管理大量数据,因此数据库在很多领域都有相当广泛的应用。在数据库出现之前,用户只能自己管理、更新自己负责的数据。

数据库包括大量记录,每个纪录又包括很多字段,字段可以是数字,也可以是字符。数据库操作包括检索、修改和维护。

检索就是在众多记录中查询用户所需的一个或多个满足查询条件的记录,检索并不修改这些纪录,而是从数据库中备份、显示或打印这些纪录。

修改是对数据库的更新。这种操作只修改或更新一个或多个纪录的一个或几个字段,而不增加或减少文件的记录。

维护就是从文件中增加或删除纪录,因为数据库的记录总会随时间而变化。如人事档案管理数据库,会因为新员工的加入和老员工的退休和辞职需要增加和删除纪录。

按时间分,数据库操作又分为实时处理和批处理。批处理是将许多存取文件的需求存起来,并在同一个时间成批处理。如银行系统使用的数据库,平时的检索操作就是实时的,而每天的备份工作就利用批处理。

数据库应用程序包括查询、修改,维护及生成报表。应用程序是由程序员写的,然后编译成可运行的应用程序。

数据库管理系统是一个用户程序。在使用数据库管理系统时用户只需输入他的需求进行查询,并不需要写程序。

另一个数据库的应用是关系数据库。

2.5 SKYvec 软件包

SKYvec 软件包是为 SKYsystem 设计的一个先进的软件开发环境。SKYvec 包括编译器、数学库、开发工具、运行程序和支持主机工作的一些程序。它们提供高度的源码透明度,允许与 SKY 产品直接进行输入输出操作。

SKYvec 软件部分包括汇编、C 和 FORTRAN 语言编译器、标准数学库和向量库、可以使四处理器作为一个处理器编程的并行计算工具包、执行多任务的可执行文件,此外还包括连接、调试等实用程序。

SKYvec 可编程模式包括多处理器独立编程、多处理器作为一个处理器的并行编程。标准数学库和向量库编程采用的是经过优化和向量化的库函数,标准数学库包括几百个单精度和双精度子程序。此外还包括 FIR 滤波器和 FFT 等常用程序。

开发支撑工具包括目标管理工具、源码级和高级调试程序以及仿真器。

第三章 通信

现代通信给很多技术领域的发展提供了机会和平台。本章简述了语音通信和 PCM 通信的基本原理、先进的全球定位系统及正在快速发展的软件无线电技术。

3.1 语音通信

在典型语音通信系统中,发送端包括一个输入传感器也就是话筒,它把空气中的声音振动波形转换为电信号。在接收端,扩音器把接收到的电信号变换回声音。传输信道是电信号在发送端和接收端中间的传输介质。

当信号通过电信系统传输时会遭到衰减,产生损耗。尽管衰减能被以后的放大补偿,但实际上放大器本身会引入一些随机噪声。描述信道中的噪声和信号大小的量叫信噪比(S/N 或 SNR),就是信号功率与噪声功率之比。当信号进入传输信道时,它已经包括大量的污染噪声,传输过程中信号和噪声都将衰减,并加入新的噪声,因此在信道的输出端信噪比可能比输入端要小。

另一个需要考虑的因素是信源的动态范围,它定义为在输入终端最大和最小输入信号之比。此外还有电信系统的工作带宽。如果一个信号通过系统,为了避免失真,必须保证系统的带宽应该不小于信号的带宽。但如果系统的带宽过大,就会接收不必要的噪声,致使信噪比下降。显然我们希望噪声和干扰越小越好。因此,在大噪声的电信系统中,要保证信道、发送端和接收端的频率特性与信号一致。

通信系统包括有线通信和无线通信。有线通信的介质包括双绞线、同轴线、波导及光纤。双绞线广泛应用于电话通信中,双绞线的缠绕方式降低了串话,但当频率较高时衰减太大。同轴线的带宽大于双绞线,由于有一个屏蔽层,信道最高频率可达 61.6 MHz,而一般话音的频带是 300~3 400 Hz,海底同轴电缆一般可传输几千路电话。调制技术是频分复用的关键技术,把不同电话信号调制到不同的频率上,才能使它们同时在一个信道中传输。波导可用来传输较高频率的无线电波,传输信号容量最大的是光纤。

无线通信是指发射机和接收机之间都是无线电传输。无线电波被分为极低频、甚低频、中频、高频、甚高频、超高频、极高频等,各种频率的电磁波有不同的传输特性。

3.2 PCM 与数字传输

时分多路复用是人们一直追求的目标,但模拟通信无法做到。PCM 编码使得时分多路复用成为可能,不仅使信道利用得更充分,数字传输也降低了传输附加的噪声。

任何一个实际通信系统都是在通信质量和成本之间折衷的产物,而 PCM 正是很好的对通信质量和成本进行了折衷。

PCM 传输包括采样、量化、压扩、编码。

首先根据采样定理,对话音信号进行采样,由于话音频带不宽,语音信号频谱位于 300～3 400 Hz,因此一般采样频率定为 8 kHz 标准可以保证话音通信的质量。

为了用有限个数字表示采样脉冲,需要对采样后的脉冲进行量化。一般来说,量化的层次越多,话音质量越好,但需要传输的信息也越多。量化会产生量化噪声,量化噪声根据舍入方式和编码方式不同,一般是在一个量化间隔内均匀分布。由于量化噪声依赖于信号的存在,它有别于持续存在的背景噪声。

话音音量范围大概是 25 dB,如果考虑不同说话人,再加上系统衰减,那么所要处理的范围就是 60 dB,这将需要很多量化电平。为了在传输质量和传输效率之间有一个折衷,一般需要对量化的话音信号进行压缩与扩展。也就是说,在发送端对采样的信号进行非均匀量化,在收信端对信号进行反向的扩展。这样可以在尽可能小的传输率的情况下获得较高的传输质量。

编码就是将量化的幅度用二进制数字来表示。理论上,任何一种可逆的二进制编码都可以用作 PCM 编码,常见的二进制码有自然二进制码、折叠二进制码和格雷二进制码。PCM 通信中使用折叠码。

PCM 中继系统的两个主要参数是编码位数及采样率。编码有 7 位也有 8 位,采样率一般是 8kHz。

编码也分为信源编码和信道编码,前面的编码指信源编码。信道编码有很多形式,最简单的是二进制单极性非归零码,单极性非归零码有直流不利于传输且不能直接提取同步信号。双极性归零码是一种三电平编码,收发之间不需要特别定时,得到了比较广泛的应用。交替极性码无直流成分,可提取同步信号,据有很多优点。

3.3　全球定位系统

全球定位系统（GPS）是设立在太空的无线电定位系统,它可以获得目标的时间和三维空间的地理位置和运动速度的信息。

全球定位系统由三个部分组成:空间站,控制台和用户端。空间站组成全球定位系统的空间部分。在距离地球 20 200 公里的高空分布着 24 颗人造卫星,每时每刻在地球任何位置上至少可以看到六颗卫星。这个卫星星座可以不断地收集目标位置和时间等数据。控制台由主控制台、五个监视追踪站、和三个地面的天线组成。用户端由全球定位系统的众多独立用户组成，他们使用接收机可以精确地计算他们的地理位置、运动速度和时间。

全球定位系统提供二种不同精度的服务：标准的定位服务（SPS）和精确的定位服务（PPS）。PPS 用于美国军事方面，而 SPS 由大众广泛使用。

差分全球定位系统 DGPS 是除去全球定位系统中接收机的误差使输出更准确的一种定位方法。DGPS 只是在普通的全球定位系统基础上增加了从地面站点发射的校正信号。因为一些共同的误差是由像时钟偏离、轨道的偏离、多路径衰落、内部噪声等因素引起的。

除了 GPS 系统外，还有其他的无线电导航系统。如俄国的 GLONASS 系统由 24 颗人造卫星组成，在高度为 19 100 公里轨道上运行。

GPS 在民用方面有着广泛的应用。使用 GPS 可以进行准确定时，目前由 GPS 所获得的时间准确度是几十亿分之一秒。地理数据系统 GIS 结合了 GPS、通信、计算机网络，使数字地球成为可能。

利用记录的 GPS 位置数据，可以监视公路通行、改善公路运行安全、减轻交通阻塞。把 GPS 接收器和无线的发射器装在野生动物上，由 GPS 得到的数据传送到控制站，用来追踪动物并研究它们的生活习性。GPS 技术可以用来处理紧急的情况，依靠 GPS 的汽车防盗系统能准确地定位被盗汽车的位置。

3.4 软件无线电

以现代通信理论为基础，以数字信号处理为核心，以微电子技术为支撑的软件无线电在近些年取得了引人注目的进展。

软件无线电突破了传统的无线电台以功能单一、可扩展性差的硬件为核心的设计局限性，强调以开放性的硬件为通用平台，尽可能地用可升级、可重配置的应用软件来实现各种无线电功能的设计新思路。这样，用户在同一硬件平台上可以通过选购不同的应用软件来满足不同时期、不同使用环境的功能需求。不仅可以节省大量硬件投资，而且可以大大缩短新产品的开发研制周期。

软件无线电作为一种实现无线通信的新概念和体制，它的核心是：将宽带 A/D 和 D/A 变换器尽可能地靠近天线，软件无线电把硬件作为无线通信的基本平台，对于无线通信功能尽可能用软件来实现。这样，无线通信系统具有很好的通用性、灵活性，使系统互联和升级变得非常方便。

与传统的通信体制相比,软件无线电有以下几个特点:

1.软件无线电将 A/D 变换尽量向射频端靠拢,而将中频以后全部进行数字化处理,使通信功能可由软件来控制;系统的更新换代变成了软件版本的生级,开发周期与费用大为降低。

2.它采用模块化设计,不同的模块实现不同的功能,同类模块通用性好,通过更换或升级某种模块就可实现新的通信功能。

3.不同通信系统都基于相同标准的硬件平台,只要加载相应的软件就可完成不同体制、不同系统之间的互联。

4.由于软件无线电至少在中频以后进行数字化处理,通过软件就可很方便地完成宽带天线监控、系统频带调整、信道监测与自适应选择、信号波形在线编程、调制解调方式控制及信源编码与加密处理。

第四章　信号处理专题

现代信号处理技术给现代通信、消费电子、医疗仪器、自动化等领域提供了新型实用的技术,本章只是给出了众多新算法、新技术中的几个话题。

4.1　快速算法

在数字信号处理中,一种算法既可以用来描述系统的输入输出关系,也可以描述系统的内部结构。算法分为直接法和间接法,一般我们所熟悉的算法是直接法,直接法非常直观地描述系统的功能。而间接法往往是一种快速算法,间接法通常舍弃算法的概念明确,而追求计算的效率。

高速芯片和快速算法是数字信号处理领域的两个发展方向。若有人能设计出容量足够大、速度足够快的芯片,那么采用低效率算法似乎也无关紧要了。在某些方面可以这样认为,而在另一些情况下,却不是这样。因为大型信号处理器通常需要采用快速算法,当 n 等于 3 或 4 时,执行时间正比于 n^2 似乎不那么重要。而当 $n = 1000$ 时,问题就变得很严重了。

本节从简单的复数乘法入手,说明一次复数乘法可以用 4 次乘法完成,也可以用 3 次乘法完成,那么对于数字信号处理中大量的运算,也可以找到节省运算量的途径。然后讨论了数字信号处理中涉及的主要运算,包括线性卷积、循环卷积、相关、长序列分段卷积、离散傅立叶变换、多维离散傅立叶变换等等。本节还讨论了这些运算之间的联系,如线性卷积和循环卷积、循环卷积和离散傅立叶变换等。

4.2 LMS 算法

自适应滤波器不同于传统滤波器,在设计传统滤波器时,必须知道有用信号及噪声或干扰的频谱,滤波器的通带和阻带是根据信号及噪声所占据的频带设计的。而在有用信号及噪声先验知识未知的情况下,无法设计具有确定通带和阻带的滤波器,此时利用自适应滤波器就可以解决这个问题。

LMS 算法是自适应滤波器的最基本算法。LMS 算法之所以受欢迎主要是因为其简单的计算结构,低存储要求,以及相对简单的数学分析。

由于在一般的应用中很多先验知识是未知的,因此本节首先推导了最陡梯度法,然后给出了基于未知先验知识的 LMS 算法的数学推导和特性的分析,还明确地给出 LMS 算法和最陡下降法的区别。

LMS 和最陡下降法的最主要区别是,最陡下降法是确定性的,并且需要梯度的精确值,而 LMS 是随机的递推算法,只能用带有噪声的梯度近似值。LMS 算法也称为噪声梯度法,这是因为它不像最陡梯度法利用统计均方误差求梯度,而是利用瞬时均方误差求梯度。本节还证明了最陡下降法的许多分析结果对 LMS 同样成立,因为 LMS 本身就是最陡下降法的近似。

收敛是 LMS 算法的主要问题,研究 LMS 收敛域需要研究 LMS 自适应预测滤波器的系数特性,因此本节还检验了 LMS 算法的一些收敛域特性,从 LMS 权向量均值开始讨论步长对收敛速度的影响,最后讨论了 LMS 算法的均方误差。

4.3 最小距离分类

在自动模式识别中,基于距离函数的模式识别是最早的模式识别方法之一。用距离函数进行模式分类是自动模式识别的基本概念,本节详述了最小距离模式分类的基本原理及最小距离模式分类法的性质。

首先给出单类模式的情况,模式分类器计算出未知模式到每一类的距离,然后根据这个最小距离对该模式确定它的归属。在二维特征空间里,决策边界为一直线,即线性决策函数。在三维特征空间里,决策边界为一平面。在多维特征空间里,决策边界则为超平面。多类模式是单类模式的推广,在两类问题中,多类模式的决策边界一般为分段线性函数。

本节还将最小距离分类的观念拓展到最近邻分类,并给出最近邻分类的判决规则。最后讨论了最近邻模式分类的特点,给出了 1 – NN 规则的分类错误概率,并推广到 q – NN 规则的错误概率。

4.4　反向传播算法

神经网络是现代信号处理的一个重要方法,反向传播学习算法实现了包含隐层的多层神经网络的目的。

本节首先论述 δ 准则的基本原理。Widrow 的 LMS 算法可用于单个神经元的自适应学习,δ 准则可使实际输出与理想输出的均方差最小。这个最小的过程实际上是加权空间曲面的最陡下降过程。

本节还讨论了广义 δ 准则,即通过反向传播进行学习。反向传播神经网络除了有输入层、输出层节点,还有隐层节点。对于输入信号,先向前传播到隐层节点,经作用函数后再传播到输出节点。如果在输出层不能得到期望的输出,则转向反向传播,将误差信号沿着原来的通路返回。通过修正各层神经元的加权值,使误差信号功率最小。

第五章　说明书和手册

说明书和使用手册几乎在所有电子仪器、电子设备中都可以见到。认真阅读说明书、正确理解使用方法是安全有效运用仪器和设备的前提。本章给出几个小到手机大到专用信号处理系统的使用手册,期望读者对仪器设备的电气指标、芯片组件的性能有一个初步的了解。

5.1　移动电话

近些年来,移动电话终端的数量大有超过固定电话的趋势,尽管不同厂家生产的手机不同,但主要的功能基本上是相似的。

本节给出了手机的安装、开机、关机的方法,拨打电话、接听电话、发送短信的操作步骤及显示的信息。

5.2　电子设备指标

对于电子工程师,电子设备的指标不论在设计阶段还是使用阶段都是非常重要的。

本节给出了常用的录音机及音响的使用操作说明,并给出了电源、放大部分、盒带部分、收音部分、CD 部分的各种电气指标。

5.3　SKYsystem 系列

SKYsystem 是运行在 Solaris 操作系统、包括软件开发环境在内的数字信号处理系统。它有基于 VME 总线插槽的处理器,带有 SCSI 接口,最多可扩充到 16 个 SKYbolt 板,最大可达到 20GFLOPS 的运算能力。

5.4　ADSP-2106x

ADSP-2106x SHARC 是具有 Harvard 计算结构的 32 位数字信号处理器,在语音、图像处理方面有广泛应用。ADSP-2106x SHARC 具有高性能的浮点运算能力,使用 32 位 IEEE 浮点格式、32 位整数及 40 位扩展精度 IEEE 浮点格式。

5.5　TMS320C5x

TMS320 系列数字信号处理器有两大类,16 位定点和 32 位浮点运算能力。此系列中的 TMS320C5x 则是具有先进的哈佛结构的定点数字信号处理器,具有灵活的指令集、分开的程序存储总线和数据存储总线。C5x 能执行高达每秒 50 兆条指令。最大 16 位 224K 字可寻址外部寄存器空间,包括 64K 字程序存储器、64K 字数据存储器以及 64K 字 I/O 地址和 64K 字全局存储器。

Appendix B 数学公式与运算

1. Real numbers

2/3	two-thirds
1/10000	one ten-thousandth
$2\dfrac{3}{5}$	two and three-fifths
$3 + 8 = 11$	Three plus eight is eleven.
$9 - 7 = 2$	Nine minus seven is two.
$6 \times 5 = 30$	Six times five equals thirty. (or Multiply six by five is thirty.)
$8 \div 4 = 2$	Eight divided by four equals two.
$x + y$	x plus y
$x - y$	x minus y
$x \pm y$	x plus or minus y
xy	x multiplied by y
x/y	x over y
$(x - y)(x + y)$	x minus y, x plus y
$x = y$	x equals y (or x is equal to y)

$x \equiv y$	x is identically equal to y
$x \neq y$	x is not equal to y
$x \approx y$	x is approximately equal to y (or x approximately equals y)
$x > y$	x is greater than y
$x \geq y$	x is greater than or equal to y
$x \gg y$	x is much greater than y
$x < y$	x is less than y
$x \leq y$	x is less than or equal to y
$x \ll y$	x is much less than y
$p < x < q$	p is less than x is less than q
$p \ll x \ll q$	p is less than or equal to x is less than or equal to q
$|x|$	modulus x
x^2	x squared (or x to the second power)
x^3	x cubed (or x to the third power)
x^{-4}	x to the minus fourth
x^n	x to the nth
x^{-n}	x to the minus nth
$(x + y)^2$	x plus y all squared
$(x/y)^2$	x over y all squared
$\sqrt{x}$	the square root of x
$\sqrt[3]{x}$	the cube root of x
$\sqrt[n]{x}$	nth root of x
$x!$	factorial x
$\dot{x}$	dot x
$\ddot{x}$	two dots x
$\hat{x}$	hat x
$\bar{x}$	bar x

x_i	x_i (or x sub i)
$\displaystyle\sum_{i=1}^{n} x_i$	the sum from i equals one to n x_i (or the sum as i runs from 1 to n of the x_i)

2. Functions

$\displaystyle\lim_{x\to 0} x$	the limit as x approaches zero
$\log_{10} x$	log x to the base 10 (common logarithm)
$\ln y$	log y to the base e (natural log logarithm)
$f(x)$	fx (or f of x, the function f of x)
$f'(x)$ or $\dfrac{\mathrm{d}}{\mathrm{d}x}f(x)$	the first derivative of f with respect to x
$f''(x)$ or $\dfrac{\mathrm{d}^2}{\mathrm{d}x^2}f(x)$	or the second derivative of f with respect to x
$f^{(n)}(x)$ or $\dfrac{\mathrm{d}^n}{\mathrm{d}x^n}f(x)$	or the nth derivative of f with respect to x
$\dfrac{\partial}{\partial x}f(x,y)$	the partial derivative of f with respect to x
$\dfrac{\partial^2}{\partial x^2}f(x,y)$	the second partial derivative of f with respect to x
$\displaystyle\int_0^\infty$	the integral from zero to infinity

3. Linear algebra and Sets

$\| x \|$	the norm (or modulus) of x
$\overrightarrow{OA}$	vector OA
$\overline{OA}$	the length of the segment OA
A^{T}	A transpose (or the transpose of A)
A^{-1}	A inverse (or the inverse of A)
$x \in A$	x belongs to A (or x is a member of A)
$x \notin A$	x does not belong to A (or x is not a member of A)
$A \subset B$	A is contained in B (or A is a subset of B)

$A \supset B$	A contains B (or B is a subset of A)
$A \cup B$	A cap B (or A meet B)
$A \cap B$	A cup B (or A join B)
$A \setminus B$	A minus B (or the difference between A and B)
$A \times B$	A cross B (or the cartesian product of A and B)

Appendix C 希腊字母表

大写	小写	国际音标	大写	小写	国际音标
A	α	['ælfəː]	N	ν	[njuː]
B	β	['biːtə]	Ξ	ξ	[ksai]
Γ	γ	['gæmə]	O	o	[əu'maikən]
Δ	δ	['deltə]	Π	π	[pai]
E	ε	[ep'sailən]	P	ρ	[rəu]
Z	ζ	['ziːtə]	Σ	σ	['sigmə]
H	η	['iːtə]	T	τ	[tau]
Θ	θ	['θiːtə]	Φ	φ	[fai]
I	ι	[ai'əutə]	X	χ	[kai]
K	κ	[kæpə]	Υ	υ	[juːp'saliən]
Λ	λ	['læmdə]	Ψ	ψ	[psai]
M	μ	[miu]	Ω	ω	['əumigə]